Praise for Kara Isaac

Then There Was You

"Brilliantly funny, unceasingly romantic, and emotionally charged. Then There Was You is sublime." (Rel Mollet, Relz Reviewz)

"From the sassy banter, the laugh-out-loud humor, and the breath-stealing romance to the sincere emotion and poignant spiritual insight... *Then There Was You* belongs on every romcom fan's must-read list!" (Carrie Schmidt, Reading Is My Superpower)

Close To You

"A terrific set up...Isaac showcases a strong romantic sensibility and clever plotting." (Publishers Weekly)

"Kara Isaac is a fresh new voice in the world of inspirational contemporary romance . . . and I can't even decide what I love most about her debut novel. The setting, the romance, the wit, I love it all! I especially loved the undercurrent of hope and redeemed dreams. (Melissa Tagg, author of From the Start and Like Never Before)

"Kara Isaac is a fresh new voice in inspirational contemporary romance! *Close to You* is well crafted, funny, unique, and endearing. A delight!" (Becky Wade, author of A Love Like Ours)

"The perfect combination of sweet and sass, *Close To You* is a charming debut that had me laughing and left me smiling. Well done Ms. Isaac!" (Katie Ganshert, award winning author of The Art of Losing Yourself)

Can't Help Falling

"Filled with grace, beauty, and love… Any book that can make a reader laugh, cry, and get goosebumps of amazement all in the same story is one for the keeper shelf." (*RT (Romantic Times, Top Pick!)*

"Enchanting . . . One need not be a Narnia fan to settle in and enjoy Isaac's story, which romance readers will easily fall in love with." (*Publishers Weekly*)

"*Can't Help Falling* is a rich and redemptive tale of tangled regret, bittersweet coincidence, and the courage it takes to embrace a second chance." (Nicole Deese, author of the Love in Lenox series and The Promise of Rayne)

Books by Kara Isaac

Close To You
Can't Help Falling

Then There Was You
All Made Up

One Thing I Know
Start With Me

Start With Me

KARA ISAAC

Start With Me

The characters and events in this book are fictional, and any resemblance to actual characters or events is coincidental.

Trade paperback ISBN 978-0-473-52534-7
eBook ISBN 978-0-473-52536-1

Bellbird Press

Cover design: © Evelyne Labelle / Carpe Librum Book Design
Formatting: BB eBooks

Raise A Hallelujah Lyrics © 2019 Bethel Music

For Melly

I raise a hallelujah
My weapon is a Melody
I raise a hallelujah
Heaven comes to fight for me

Psalm 118:1-17

CHAPTER ONE

"OF COURSE, THIS LATEST ALLEGATION has been a huge shock to all of us."

Lacey O'Connor glanced up from her phone as Mitchell Tremain, Head of People and Culture, uttered the bald-faced lie without so much as a twitch.

He wore a blue Ralph Lauren dress shirt with his tie loosened and the sleeves pushed up to his elbows. An image carefully constructed to say *professional but accessible, management but still in there getting his hands dirty*. Why he bothered in a room full of PR and advertising professionals, she had no idea.

Around the crowded boardroom, people shuffled their feet and looked at their shoes. Lacey returned to tapping out her message to her cousin. Just because she was stuck in here while Mitchell worked his way through the next steps in *The Dummies Guide to Handling a Corporate Scandal* didn't mean she couldn't be productive at the same time.

Next, there'd be the spiel about employee wellbeing and doors being open.

"I hope you all know that Langham & Co is first and foremost about our people." Mitchell hit the next step right on cue. "If you have anything at all that you need to talk about, my door is always open."

Unless it was after three on a Friday. Mitchell's tee-off time was four sharp. Not even the scandal that had kept on giving for six weeks had managed to divert Mitchell away from his standing date at the New York Country Club.

Lacey let the side of her mouth lift. She guessed the guy deserved his respite wherever he could find it. Trying to maintain the facade that Langham & Co was something other than a cesspit of inappropriate behavior had to be exhausting. Her small and perfectly formed team the only exception.

Book publicity may well be seen as the prudish great-aunt in the world of advertising and PR. Still, not a single person in her team had been fired in the recent company clean-out. Another bow in her quiver for promotion. One that was already watertight but should come borne on a silver platter. After all, if there ever was a time for the Executive to add another XY chromosome around their table brimming with middle-aged white men, the time was now.

"I'll hand it over to Guy for the final agenda item, the Chair's Update."

Mitchell took his seat as the CEO stood from his end of the table and moved toward the front of the room. Distressed designer jeans and white shirt completed by a carefully curated five o'clock shadow.

There were two good things Lacey could say about Guy McRoberts. The first was that the man kept his hands to himself. Which, until recent weeks, had been a character trait in short supply in Langham & Co. Second, he knew she was by far the best candidate for the next President of PR and Publicity. Had all but promised the job was hers.

She had even done him the favor of drafting the press release announcing her appointment. One that was long on experience and nonexistent on pedigree and family connections.

There was no silver spoon in her mouth. No mother called Bitsy. No father with numerals after his name subsidizing her "little book job." No antebellum mansion in the South. No youthful summers at Martha's, sailing and eating clam chowder.

Just her. And her 150 *New York Times* Best Sellers.

Lacey hit send on her message to Emelia and put her phone on her lap. The Chair's message had gotten terser as the weeks had gone by, as the headlines continued and the body count had grown.

Guy cleared his throat and winced as he looked at the piece of paper in his hands. Lacey straightened in her chair. This promised to be interesting.

A knock at the door and Guy's assistant, Sandra, stuck her head through the gap. "Um, Guy. You're needed right away."

Guy looked up from the sheet of paper. "Can it wait a couple of minutes, Sandra? We're just about to wrap up here."

Sandra shook her head, eighties spiral perm bouncing. "No. It really can't."

"Sorry, guys, I'll be back as soon as I can." Guy looked resigned as he headed for the door, no doubt braced for more bad news on the other side.

"Who do you think it is this time?" Jeremy from accounts sat a little straighter in his chair.

"No idea." Lacey's phone buzzed in her lap, and she reached for it. No point worrying about whatever Guy was dealing with. They'd know when they left the room and found another empty desk. Lacey certainly had a few wishes for whose desk she hoped would be vacant.

The door opened, and a woman walked into the room, Guy shuffling behind her.

Lacey's phone clattered to the floor, but she didn't even look to see where it had gone. Her eyes were glued to the tall figure at the front of the room.

Meredith Langham. Their owner. The Chair. Her red hair

with its famous asymmetrical cut swung across the shoulders of a navy Versace trench coat. In Lacey's entire decade at Langham & Co., Meredith hadn't appeared in person once. Not for funerals. Not to hand out bonuses. Not even to put in a token appearance at the Christmas drinks.

Never.

Meredith Langham was not a *Lean In* kind of woman. She was a kick the ladder down behind you one. Meredith Langham was one of the reasons it was ten times harder for a woman to get into the executive suite than a man.

There was an audible sucking in of breath and jerking of heads as the rest of the room realized who was taking Guy's place at the head of the table.

Guy stood diagonally behind the Chair, hands clasped behind him and body ramrod like he was on a parade ground at West Point.

Going by his buggy eyes, he either knew what was coming and was in shock, or else he had no idea what was coming and was bracing himself along with the rest of them.

Lacey's mind raced through the possibilities as the woman took her time surveying the room as if she was memorizing every face. Was she going to fire Guy? In front of everyone? Would he be the next person added to the body count?

As far as Lacey knew, Guy had never harassed anyone. And she had no intel of him trying to cover anything up either. He'd only been in the job for a year. A year many women in the company had spent trying to determine if he was friend or foe. The consensus had been leaning toward friend, but that wouldn't mean anything if Ms. Langham was out for blood.

Sell the company? Langham & Co. had been started by her father. According to urban lore, Meredith had bested her three brothers for the role of Chair through a coup that was bloodless in name only. And nothing suggested she was the type of woman who would sell when Langham's stock prices had hit a record low.

"I apologize for not giving more notice of my appearance." The woman's English accent sliced through the charged room. "Please make sure that you note it for the minutes." She nodded to Sheryl, whose hands had frozen midair above her laptop keyboard.

There were no minutes at these meetings, and Sheryl was a graphic designer who probably didn't know how to open a Word document. Hopefully, Meredith wouldn't ask to see the minutes afterward.

"First." Meredith raised a long bejeweled finger. "Obviously, you're all now aware that there is no longer any tolerance for people who can't keep their hands or their misogyny to themselves. But it's become apparent to me over the last few weeks that stance is not going to be sufficient if I want to salvage anything out of this organizational dumpster fire. So, starting now, there is a strict no fraternization policy. If you are currently fraternizing, you have three options. One. End it. Two. One of you is no longer here in thirty days. Three. Get married. If you don't, both of you will be clearing your desks."

Lacey's gaze flicked across the table to Sam and Mei, who shifted subtly away from each other. Further up the table, an associate's gaze tangled with his boss's before they quickly looked away.

The place contained more fraternization than a frat house. And going by the glimmer in Meredith's green eyes, she knew it.

"Second. As some of you may know, you have a sister company in the UK called Wyndham House. Unfortunately, while some of you can't keep your hands to yourselves, some of your compatriots over the pond have been busy greasing the wrong palms. The result is I currently have two misbehaving children, not just one."

Lacey had known Wyndham House was part of the Langham Holdings stable, but the two companies had nothing to do with each other.

"So, I've decided to merge you."

Guy jumped behind her. A startled hop like a baby rabbit. So he didn't know. Lacey forced air into her lungs. A merger might not impact her. People did mergers in name only all the time. A bit of rebranding. A bit of PR gloss. Like a new coat of paint. But nothing changed underneath.

"The Boards and executive teams will be combined." The Chair checked her watch, perhaps checking to see if she was breaking her previous record for destroying an empire.

Combined. The word rang in Lacey's ears. Combined meant fewer seats at the table. Combined meant there wouldn't be enough senior positions for the people who were already in them, let alone space for a newcomer. Combined meant the promotion she had worked her guts out for, that she had *earned,* was no closer than it had been five years ago. Lacey bit the inside of her cheek to stop herself from physically reacting.

"I will be making other decisions about restructuring in due course. You are, of course, free to provide input." She said input like she'd just bitten into a sour lime. So that would be a definite no.

"Don't you think this is a bit drastic, Meredith?" Halfway up the table, a young associate whose skull was clearly a lot larger than the brain it contained leaned back in his chair. Next to him, his manager turned a shade of white similar to the color that Lacey had once considered painting her ceiling.

The woman turned her gaze on the clueless man-boy like a praying mantis zeroing in on her soon-to-be dinner. "I'm sorry.

You are?"

His chest puffed up. "Zen Holden. Sports advertising. You may have seen—"

"Your cleared desk. Yes, that's exactly what I expect to see when I leave this room." She snapped the words out. "Are there any other questions?"

The room was as silent as everyone held their breath as if hoping this was some kind of mass hallucination.

"I didn't think so. Further information will be forthcoming. In the meantime, carry on." The woman swept out of the room, carrying Lacey's future with her.

VICTOR CARLISLE HAD BEEN RESPONSIBLE for—and gotten away with—a lot of havoc in his life. The irony that the one time he had nothing to do with anything might be his undoing was not lost on him.

"Can you accept how far-fetched it sounds that you had absolutely no idea this was happening?"

Across the table, the bobby leaned back in her chair, seemingly indifferent to the fact that they had covered and re-covered the same ground for over an hour.

"We've covered this, Sergeant." Ann-Maree, one of the company's lawyers, tapped a staccato on her legal pad with her pen.

"No, I told you. I thought Garrett had great networks. I had no idea he had members of Parliament on the take." It had been a month since his boss had been caught in a cash-for-access sting. He'd boasted to a journalist posing as the chief executive of a Russian pharmaceutical company that he could get her access and influence right up to Downing Street if the price was right.

Their conversation could have been passed off as the bragging of a stupid man trying to impress a beautiful woman until a phone tap caught him negotiating with two MPs about the price for their votes on an upcoming trade bill.

The policewoman flipped a page in her notebook and scratched something with her pen.

This was Victor's second interview in two weeks. The police pretty much had a permanent presence in the building now, interviewing and re-interviewing everyone in an attempt to uncover some kind of company-wide conspiracy.

It didn't help that most people perceived lobbyists as lifeforms just one step up from amoeba.

"Let's talk about your previous involvement with the law." The bobby looked down at her pad. "Public drunkenness, assault, in charge of a vehicle with excess alcohol, careless driving causing damage to public property."

Victor didn't so much as blink. He'd known this would come up and already prepared his response. "None of those are dishonesty offences. And, as I'm sure you also have there, I completed all the requirements of my conditional discharge two years ago. I haven't had so much as a parking ticket since."

She looked at him, stone-faced. He couldn't blame her. The old Victor probably would have been up to his neck in Garrett's shenanigans.

He took a deep breath. Clearly, he was going to have to give her more. "Yes, there was a period in my life where I was not exactly a model citizen. But that's not now. It hasn't been for years." Rehab. Twelve steps. Therapy. All the meetings. He'd done it all. And just when he thought he was finally starting to make some headway with his family, this happened.

Victor's throat tightened as the policewoman regarded him with narrowed eyes. He was good at his job. For once, he had gotten somewhere not because of his connections or ability to schmooze and charm, but because he had worked his butt off to prove himself. He had done nothing wrong. Surely God wouldn't let it all get ripped away from him now.

"Sergeant, we've been more than generous with our time. If you don't have anything more, this meeting is over." Ann-Maree stood. "Let me show you out."

The bobby reluctantly rose. "I'll be back if I have more questions."

"You know where to find me."

As the two women left his office, his phone buzzed. Peter.

He swiped and put the phone up to his ear. "Hi. Is Mum okay?" His brother rarely called unless there was a parentally associated reason. The two people who still bound them together.

"She's fine." Fine was relative since their mother's multiple sclerosis continued advancing, but he'd take it.

"Okay. Great." Victor paused, waiting for Peter to get to the reason for his call, but his brother didn't take the hint. "How can I help?"

There was a pause. "I just wanted to see how things were with you. With everything happening at Wyndham House."

He could imagine his brother's knowing expression if it came out that Victor was under suspicion of aiding and abetting corruption. Once the family screwup, always the family screwup.

"Fine. Well, obviously not fine. The company is in turmoil."

"But you still have a job?"

"Don't worry, Peter. I'm not coming back to Oxford to cramp your style." The sarcastic quip was out before he'd even thought it.

This was how it was for them. They couldn't even manage a simple phone conversation without decades of enmity rising to the surface. Most of which was his own fault. But in the four years he'd been doing his best to travel the straight and narrow, it felt like all he'd gotten from his brother was an expectation of inevitable failure.

Meanwhile, Emelia—who had almost as much of a tainted past as he did—practically walked on water as far as Peter was concerned. Victor tried to force back the swell of resentment.

"Speaking of Oxford, are you coming home anytime soon? Emelia says Mum mentioned today you hadn't been back recently."

Home. The estate had never felt like home. Instead, it was a millstone hanging around his father's neck and one that would hang around his after Dad died. Which was just what he deserved.

"I'll check my schedule and let Mum know." Victor was juggling Garrett's job and his own, and doing his best to hold onto the clients they still had. Which meant late nights and weekends showing up at functions all over the city and playing whatever cards he had to.

He was exhausted, but not a single client had left since he'd started his campaign. Hopefully, that would give him pole position for a promotion once this all blew over.

There was a sharp knock on his door. It flew open, and Sean barreled into the room. The team assistant never came in without being invited, let alone with his headset askew and his tie flung over his shoulder. "Peter, I have to go. I'll text you later."

Victor rose from behind his desk. "What is it? What's happened."

"Meredith just sent out an all-company email. She's merging Wyndham House with one of her American companies. It's every man for himself."

CHAPTER TWO

"**L**ACEY, YOU KNOW GETTING OBSESSED isn't going to help anything, right?" Anna's mouth puckered at the sight of yet another internet news clip detailing the Wyndham House debacle on Lacey's laptop screen.

"I'm not obsessed. I'm detail-oriented." Lacey scrolled down the screen, scanning the article, pretending not to see her two best friends exchanging looks across the kitchen.

"What's obsessed?" Libby piped up from across the table, face smeared with chocolate frosting.

"Obsessed is what your Auntie Lacey gets when something gets between her and something she wants." Rachel swiped a cloth off the kitchen counter and handed it to the little girl. "Time to clean up that face, kiddo."

Libby swiped the cloth across her mouth, spreading the chocolate even further afield. "What are you obsessed with, Auntie Lacey?"

Lacey rolled her shoulders. They seemed to be permanently hunched to her ears ever since Meredith's announcement. "Just work stuff, kiddo. It's not important."

Libby studied her across the table, her green eyes serious. "It's important if it's important to you." The kid was almost four but possessed the insights of an old soul. Not surprising, given what she and Anna had been through.

Lacey had gotten on the plane to Denver without telling

Anna or Rachel she was coming. She hadn't done that before. Not ever. But with her roommate away, her condo had been too quiet, too empty, and the voices in her head telling her that she'd worked her guts out for too many years for nothing had gotten too loud.

She had second-guessed herself the whole four-and-a-half-hour flight. Anna and Rachel both had their own big things going on. And this attempt at reestablishing their tripartite friendship after years of separation was still new.

But when the Uber had turned into Anna's street, she'd been standing on her front porch like she'd been expecting Lacey all along.

"You're the best publicist in the business, Lacey. You have nothing to worry about. Any other firm would snap you up in an instant. Or you could freelance. Plenty of people are making great money working for themselves these days." Rachel lowered herself into the chair beside Lacey and swiped another donut from the plate in the center of the table. The woman had the metabolism of a racehorse.

Lacey pushed her own untouched donut away. "I know they do. But I want to stay. Be part of the next iteration." She'd never told Rachel or Anna how bad some things had been. How for her first five years at Langham she didn't even change the photocopier paper without enlisting someone to watch her back. How a group of like-minded women shared a Google doc of all the men to avoid being alone with.

"Time to brush your teeth, sweet pea." Anna appeared back in the kitchen before Rachel could prod any more. "Say goodnight to Auntie Lacey and Auntie Rachel."

Libby slid off her chair and pattered around to Rachel. "Night Auntie 'Achel." Her little arms reached around Rachel's waist, and her chocolatey cheek pressed frosting into Rachel's dark blonde hair.

"Night, sweet girl." Rachel grabbed the cloth off the table and rubbed it on Libby's cheek. "I love you."

"Love you too."

They interacted with ease, and Lacey felt a flicker of regret. She was mostly a stranger to Libby, their relationship stunted by distance and occasional visits. She braced herself for Libby to skip right past her, a goodnight flung over her shoulder.

"I'll—" She reached out to gather up the plates and mugs scattering the table as if that would shield her from the coming rejection. Anna's kitchen walls were still Pepto-Bismol pink from when the apocalypse had hit. Maybe they could fix that while she was here. Slapping paint across a few surfaces might help her work out her angst.

"Auntie Lacey." Libby stopped beside her chair, her green eyes questioning. Her pink pajama bottoms sagged a little and were slightly too long, so small flannel ponies gathered around her feet. "Will you do my bedtime goodnights. Please."

Lacey looked at her for a second. She didn't do kids. Kids scared her. They were unpredictable and had a penchant for telling the unfiltered truth. Libby was the only kid she even knew apart from the hooligans who played soccer in the hallway outside her condo, but they didn't count. "Honey, I would love to, but I think that's a special job for your mommy." The last thing she wanted was to overstep the bounds. Anna and Libby probably had some special goodnight routine and everything.

"Ha!" Anna laughed as she gathered the mugs. "You can't escape that easy. It's all yours." She gave her a wink. "Just remember. You're the boss."

Libby's small hand grasped hers, and she led Lacey up the stairs. Large polka dotted letters spelling L I B B Y across one of the doors provided an excellent clue as to which one was her bedroom.

"Okay, kiddo." Lacey tried to insert a breezy tone into her voice as she pushed open the door to reveal a bedroom the same shade of pink as the kitchen. "Here we go."

"I haven't done my teeth yet."

"Right. Okay."

Libby gave her a look. "Do you even know how to put a kid to bed?"

"Not really. No."

"Thank you for being honest." Lacey had to bite back a smile as Libby's parroting of something that Anna obviously said regularly was pitch perfect. "I can do it. You wait here." Libby disappeared through another door, and the sound of toothbrushes rustling and water being turned on followed.

A few seconds later, Libby appeared back in the doorway. "Finished." That had to be the world's fastest toothbrushing, but Lacey wasn't going to argue.

"What comes next?" Might as well let Libby tell her how this was done.

Libby skipped into her bedroom. Lacey followed and found herself in a room filled with more pink and purple than she'd known could exist in a few square feet. Toys and clothes were strewn across the floor, books were stacked in piles, and the pink wall was decorated with pictures and photos.

"Now we say goodnight to Daddy." Libby picked up a picture of her with Anna and Cam from her nightstand and gave it a kiss, rosy lips smooshing against the glass covering her father's face. "Night, Daddy. We miss you."

Lacey sucked in a breath as the rawness of the moment almost sent her to her knees.

Libby held the photo out to her. "Your turn."

Lacey crouched down, her heels wobbling on the carpet.

Three grinning faces. It had been over six months, and it was still hard to believe one of them was gone. "Night, Cam." She whispered the words. "She's doing okay."

"And a kiss." Cam's copper hair and green eyes lived on in the little girl shaking the photo at her.

Kissing a photo of her best friend's dead husband felt wrong. Even at the behest of a bereaved four-year-old. So Lacey pressed her fingers to her lips then placed them on Cam's cheek.

Libby climbed onto her bed, and sat with the photo on her lap, her little legs dangling over the side of the mattress. "Auntie Lacey?"

"Yes, Libby?"

Old soul eyes peered at her. "Do you think mommy will be happy one day again?"

Lacey felt the tears sting the back of her eyes. "I know you make her very happy."

"But she's still sad sometimes. Because Daddy is gone." Libby's bottom lip wobbled.

Lacey blinked rapidly. Forced herself to hold it together. "I know, sweet girl. Your mom loved your dad a lot. But you know what? She's going to be okay because she has you. And you're like a piece of your dad still here with her."

"Do you think he remembers me? Up in heaven?"

Lacey had never cried about Cam's death. At the time she'd been focused on Anna. But now tears trailed down her cheek. "Libby-Belle." Her voice wobbled, and it took everything she could to pull herself together. "Your dad loved you and your mom more than anything else in the whole wide world. He would never ever forget you. Not ever. I promise."

That much was true. Lacey had her own private doubts about the whole heaven thing, but if there was one thing she did know, it was that Cam had lived and breathed his family. The chances of any other man meeting the standard he had set were slim.

"Now you tuck me in, and we say prayers." Libby carefully put the photo back on the bedside table, then shoved her feet under the covers and snuggled into her pillow.

Prayers. Lacey didn't do praying, apart from the frantic ones she'd uttered to a God she didn't engage with begging for Cam's life. She'd certainly not said a prayer in the presence of another person for well over a decade.

Libby saved her by shutting her eyes. "Dear Jesus. Thank you for Auntie Lacey coming to visit. Thank you for Mommy and Auntie 'Achel and Gramma and Poppa and Grandy and Nan. And when you see Daddy, can you please tell him that we miss him, but we hope he's having fun. Dear Jesus. Amen."

Libby cranked open an eye and directed her gaze at Lacey. "Now your turn."

Her turn? Anna hadn't mentioned prayer in the job requirements. And she knew Lacey didn't do praying. Or religion in general. "That was a beautiful prayer, baby girl. I'm sure I can't do any better.

Knowing eyes flew open and looked at Lacey as if she'd said she didn't like sparkles and rainbows. "You're *not* going to pray for me?"

Ooookay, clearly that wasn't an acceptable option. Lacey cleared her throat, her knees sinking into the carpet. "Jesus." If he was listening, he'd just have to roll with her ham-fisted attempt. "Thank you for Libby. Please help her to have a good sleep." What did people even pray with kids? She had no clue. "And thank you for her beautiful room and all her books and toys. And especially for her amazing mom. Amen."

"Amen." Libby opened her eyes and smiled at her.

"Goodnight, sweet girl. See you in the morning." Lacey got to her feet and looked around. "Do you have a night light or anything?"

"No, you just leave the door a little bit open and the light on outside." Libby had closed her eyes again, tucking her pillow between her head and shoulder.

"Love you, Auntie Lacey." The sleepy words came as Lacey flicked off the light, and her breath caught. When was the last time anyone had said they loved her?

DRIVING FROM LONDON TO OXFORD was soul-destroying on a Friday night, but Victor had figured he had might as well sit in traffic. He had nothing better to do.

The rest of the office had retreated to their local pub to speculate about Meredith's plans for the company. Ordinarily, Victor would have joined them. The first rule of being an alcoholic working in London was the acceptance that you would always be surrounded by alcohol the same way Bodiam Castle was surrounded by a moat.

But between yesterday's grilling by the sergeant and the news that his job might be under threat, he didn't trust himself not to give in to the pull of a glass of good whisky. On the rocks.

Sitting in Friday night traffic for two hours with no access to liquor was the perfect solution. He'd made it past the gridlock that was the M40 and A40, and finally managed to get some speed as he covered the last twenty minutes to his parent's home.

The scenery outside his window changed from a concrete jungle into the hedgerows and pastoral settings most people associated with the English countryside. Most people would probably also find the fields and greenery relaxing, but Victor's fuse felt like it shortened a little more with every passing mile.

He was sober. He had a job. He led a functional—some might even say contributing—life. Yet returning home always felt like the return trip of the prodigal son.

Except, in his case, it was the younger brother who had stayed and never put a foot wrong. The brother who—if life was fair—would be heir to the Downley estate.

But there was one thing the archaic rules surrounding nobility had never been—fair.

His phone beeped from its hands-free attachment to the dashboard, and a message popped up on his screen from the team's assistant saying he was busy researching Langham & Co.

By the time he got back into the office on Sunday, Sean will have probably assembled a dossier on their newly discovered American half-sister. It was like discovering you had a sibling no one had told you about. No doubt the feeling across the Atlantic was mutual. The arranged marriage nobody wanted.

His phone trilled, signaling an incoming call. Mark Holden. The conversation he had been chasing—dreading—since this whole debacle started. The account he'd been chasing for months. The one he'd work for free if that was what was required.

"Evening, Mark." Victor slowed the car down and pulled onto the side of the road. His voice was steady, not belying how much rode on the next few minutes.

"Victor! Sorry, it's taken me a while to get back to you." The government relations manager of Enrite Pharmaceuticals sounded in a good mood.

"No problem at all. Sorry if there's some background noise. I'm in the car." As if on cue, a lorry roared past his window.

"Off for a romantic rendezvous, huh. Who's this week's lady?" Victor closed his eyes at the innuendo in Mark's voice, thankful he didn't have anyone sitting in the passenger seat. He'd long left his playboy lifestyle behind, but—London society being what it was—his past would probably shadow him into his dotage.

"No one. Just heading home to see the parents."

"Right. Well, I won't keep you." Mark cleared his throat, and Victor sensed the shadow of bad news approaching.

News he couldn't accept. Even though he knew there was no logical reason why Enrite would attach their business to the scandal-plagued Wyndham brand.

"I have some good news and some bad news."

Victor's hopes lifted. "Go on."

"For obvious reasons, the executive team are reluctant to give Wyndham House the account."

"It was one bad egg. We've had the coppers crawling all over us ever since this broke, and they haven't found any evidence that anyone else was involved, let alone there being some kind of company-wide practice." Darn Garrett for tarring them all with his brush.

"I know. But you know as well as I do that perception is more important than reality in this business. And it's not just that. We've heard the news about Meredith merging Wyndham House which brings in another aspect of instability. Why would we give you the account when you might not even be there once Meredith is through?"

Both excellent points.

"I'll be honest. None of that is sounding like good news."

"It's not. The good news is that we've had a delay of a couple of months on analyzing some of the data from a couple of trials. So I've managed to convince the exec to hold off on appointing our external advisor."

"Okay."

"You're still in the running, but bluntly, you're an outside chance. Most of them are leaning toward McMillan, but you've got a couple of things in your favor."

He'd take whatever he could get.

"The CFO went to Oxford and is a big Boat Race fan, so you have a fan there. Also, I'm pretty sure one of the others has a soft spot for Meredith and wouldn't be averse to sending a bit of business her way. But that's only two out of five."

Victor waited a second as another lorry roared past, rattling the car. "I'll take whatever I can get."

"Rumor around town has it that Meredith is going to move quickly on the merger and restructuring. When the dust is settled, you not only need to be left standing, but you need to be in senior management. That's the only thing that will give you a real shot."

Victor stifled a groan of defeat. *Senior management?* It would have been better if Mark had put him out of his misery now. There was no way he was going to make that happen. The people currently in those roles had ten years plus of experience. He was going to assume the same across the ocean. He had three. And he'd only been heading his own accounts for one. In what world was he going to somehow crack the upper organizational echelons in a restructure pitted against all the highly qualified and experienced people already competing for fewer chairs at the table?

Mark seemed to read his mind. "Do you know what the CFO said at the meeting when I named you as the account lead for Wyndham? He said that you walked into the blue boat with no rowing history, beating elite-level men who had been rowing for years. Even I know that's unheard of."

To his eternal shame, he'd only trialed to get a rise out of Peter. He'd been as surprised as anyone when he turned out to be freakishly good.

His brother had never forgiven him. And Victor could hardly blame him. What kind of man took up a sport just to rub his brother's face in everything he'd lost?

Mark's voice came out of the phone. "Don't get me wrong. I don't even know if it's possible. But Meredith is nothing if not unpredictable, and she's obviously intending to give things a good shake-up. And if she does decide to go unconventional, you could be in with an outside chance."

Something shifted inside at Mark's words. He was right. Meredith smashing these two companies together gave Victor his best chance. All bets were off. A clean-out at the top and some fresh blood might be exactly what the new company needed.

He had to try. Because if he somehow made it and landed the Enrite account, the prodigal son might finally be able to return home with something of value.

CHAPTER THREE

L OVE YOU, AUNTIE LACEY. LIBBY'S declaration echoed in Lacey's head as she made her way down the stairs. Her mind tripped back years as she tried to uncover the last time she'd heard the words.

Blake—the last guy she'd dated and who was long gone—had called her many things. Great. Sexy. Intimidating. A workaholic. It had been the last one that had been the deal-breaker. But they'd never said they loved each other. Not even close.

She'd liked Blake enough to date him for three months. Then he'd had gotten a bit too whiny about how much she traveled and the hours she worked, and she'd called it quits during a fractious FaceTime conversation from a hotel somewhere in the Midwest.

The only thought she'd given him since was the following morning when she'd realized it would have been handy if she'd held off a couple of weeks and broken up with him after the company Christmas party.

Hardly the kind of heartbreak anyone writes books about.

She had dated plenty of men. Hadn't said I love you to a single one since she was seventeen.

Emelia was probably the last person to say she loved her. In a rushed end-of-a-conversation kind of way. Or Anna, who ended every other text with one of those heart blowing emojis. But that didn't count. Anna loved everyone. Down to and including the UPS guy.

But as the last thing someone said as they were drifting off to sleep?

Not ever.

Her feet hit the bottom of the stairs, and she kicked off her heels near a pile of Anna and Libby's shoes. She only had one more night here. No point wasting it on unnecessary melancholy.

Tomorrow night she would be back in New York. She'd spend it with more research on Meredith and Wyndham, looking for anything else that might give her an edge in whatever was coming.

The kitchen was empty. Rachel and Anna's low voices drifted out from the lounge. "Can I make a coffee?"

"There's a pod in the machine waiting for you and the milk in the cup is hot," Anna called out, ever the consummate hostess.

Lacey hit the button on the Nespresso machine, savoring the familiar whirring sound and the brown crema dripping into the mug Anna had placed underneath the spout. She wrapped her hands around the warm pottery and carried it into the bookshelf-lined lounge where Rachel and Anna sprawled on opposite couches.

"Here." Anna curled up her legs to make room for Lacey on her couch.

"Thanks." Lacey propped her feet up on the coffee table and took a sip of her coffee before settling it on her knees.

Rachel placed her phone on the cushion beside her with a dreamy smile. No doubt Lucas was at the other end of whatever little electronic love note had just been sent.

"Do you want to do something in the morning while Anna's at church?" Her flight wasn't until four, so they'd have time for lunch after Anna was liberated. Lacey might not understand the appeal of church, but she had to admit she'd never seen anyone support someone the way Anna's church had after Cam died.

Right after she'd arrived the night before one of the vicars—or whatever they were called—had dropped off a meal and collected her teenage son who had been mowing Anna's lawn with the familiarity of someone who had done it many times before.

"Um," Rachel's gaze flicked to Anna. "I usually go to church too. But I don't have to. We could totally do something." The last two sentences were dropped hastily on the end as Rachel realized the current plan would leave Lacey alone for the morning. But Lacey was more stuck on her first sentence.

Was there something in the water at the moment? First Anna, then Emelia, now maybe Rachel had gone and caught religion. Was this what falling in love did for people? They suddenly needed some deeper purpose in life? Needed to connect with some higher power?

Her coffee sloshed in her cup, and she lifted it to her lips to buy herself a few seconds. Lucas wasn't the type of man who needed some kind of crutch. But then neither was Cam. Or Peter.

"No, let's do something. I'll ask Mom if she can take Libby. She loves Sunday school. And then we can go out for brunch. Mom will be thrilled to have her to herself." Anna picked up her phone.

"But won't they notice you're not there?"

Anna laughed. "They don't take attendance, Lace. It's not parole." She tapped into her phone, and it pinged a few seconds later. "There. All sorted."

Lacey couldn't even gather the energy to protest, even though she felt bad that Anna was missing something important to her so she wouldn't be alone.

A contemplative silence settled over them, a testament to how much they had all changed since they'd been roommates and had filled every silent space with conversation and laughter. Trying to rebuild their friendship after ten years apart meant they were still navigating how their older selves fitted together now.

"You need a haircut." Lacey blurted out the first thing that came to her mind as Anna shook her brown hair loose from its ponytail, it tumbling down her shoulders. Lacey could see the split ends even from the other end of the couch. Anna also needed to see a good colorist. The mousy brown did nothing to play up her petite features and big eyes.

"I know." Anna fingered the tips of her hair, a look of resignation on her face.

"Do you need me to watch Libby? I can do it next week sometime." Rachel tipped back her mug to get the last drop of whatever was in it then set it on the coffee table.

"No, it's fine. I'm thinking we might just keep it long." Anna shrugged. "New look and all that."

There was a difference between a new look and a Raggedy Anne look. "What's going on?" Lacey tapped Anna's foot with hers. A foot that needed some maintenance as desperately as her hair did.

Anna looked away, but not before Lacey caught some rapid blinking. "Anna?"

"What is it?" Rachel leaned forward, elbows propped on her jean-clad knees as she exchanged a glance with Lacey. Life-shattering grief—as Lacey had learned in the last six months—was nothing if not unpredictable. The things she'd thought would bring Anna to her knees—like Libby starting Pre-K—Anna had endured as solid as the Wall of China. Another day, she'd called Lacey from a grocery store aisle, sobbing because the label on Cam's favorite peanut butter had changed.

Anna pulled her hair onto the top of her head and twisted it around before letting it fall back down. "I can't afford a haircut." She looked down at her knees. The next words were muffled against her chest. "Cam's life insurance is almost gone. We're running out of money."

"How much do you need?" This one was on her. Rachel didn't have spare cash. All hers went to the cost of her father's care. Lacey had some. That and her condo were her safety net. Her nest egg. Her guarantee that she would never end up back where she came from.

"It's fine. Honestly. If worst came to worst, I can always sell the house and move back in with Mom and Dad."

Lacey would buy the house herself before she would let that happen. There was no way Libby was being forced to leave her princess bedroom or Anna the home where she'd made a life with Cam. Plus, Anna would be a far superior tenant to the two she already had.

Anna offered up a wry smile. "Joking. It'll be fine. I'm just procrastinating about having to grow up and get a job. That's all."

A job. Lacey hadn't even thought about that. Anna hadn't worked since Libby was born. But of course, she'd have to get a job at some point. Neither her parents or Cam's were destitute, but Lacey doubted they had the means to support Anna and Libby long term—not that Anna would ever rely on their help.

"Well then, tomorrow morning we'll go shopping for some clothes and get you a haircut. My treat. Don't even think about arguing."

Anna opened her mouth just as Lacey's phone buzzed, and an email appeared on her screen. Meredith. Lacey grabbed the phone and swiped it open.

"What is it?"

Lacey scanned the email, sucking air in until her lips stuck to her teeth. "We're being summoned. On Monday. Apparently, Meredith's version of the corporate Hunger Games is about to commence."

VICTOR REREAD THE EMAIL ON his phone. For the fourth time. Of all the ways this merger might go, he hadn't picked Meredith flying a third of Wyndham to the US for some kind of team bonding with the Langham people.

He scanned the names of the people who were staying behind to man the ship. He couldn't, for the life of him, work out whether they were the ones guaranteed a place in the new regime or already tagged for departure.

As one of the people going, he at least had some kind of chance at still having a job at the end of all this.

Victor opened the first attachment and reviewed his flight. London Heathrow to JFK. The second attachment was a hotel reservation that a quick Google search revealed to be not too shabby at all.

What are you up to, Meredith?

The company owner was half-urban legend, half-human, with both her business decisions and personality seemingly curated to constantly keep people off balance.

The world's ugliest calico cat leaped on to the dining room table and gave him the stink eye. "You'll need to pick a number, buddy," Victor muttered.

"I doubt he hates you as much as he hates me." His brother's fiancée walked into the room. "Isn't that right, Reep?" The cat arched his back and hissed at Emelia as she passed. Victor couldn't stop the side of his mouth from lifting.

"See." Emelia opened the pantry, grabbed a biscuit tin, and opened the lid. She pulled out a ginger snap and offered the tin to Victor. "Want one?" Her question was tentative.

"Sure." Victor grabbed a couple from the tin. Ginger wasn't

really his thing, but if this was some kind of olive branch, he wasn't going to turn it down. He could count on one hand the number of times he and Emelia had been alone together in the years since Peter and Emelia had been dating.

Peter usually limpeted himself to Emelia's side whenever Victor was around, even though she was a lot tougher than her slight build and nondescript appearance would have anyone suspect at first glance.

Victor shoved the biscuit in his mouth for lack of anything better to do and waited for Emelia to leave him to his solitude. He couldn't blame her for the reticence. They both reminded each other of pasts they would rather forget.

Once his parents died, they would probably become the type of family whose only contact was cursory annual Christmas updates.

There was a scrape of wood against tile as Emelia pulled out a chair and sat down at the table with a glass of water and the rest of her snack. Victor looked over his shoulder, expecting to see Peter coming through the doorway. Nothing. Weird.

"So what are you going to do about him when you get married?" He nodded toward Reepicheep, whose hair now stood on end as he bristled at both of them.

Emelia rolled her eyes. "I keep hoping he'll find a magical doorway to cat heaven, but I'm pretty sure he's going to live to a hundred just to spite me."

"Probably."

She glanced sideways at him. "You don't want him, do you? He'd make an excellent guard cat."

Victor burst out laughing. There weren't many things he wanted less in life than his brother's antisocial some-might-say-possessed pet. "Not on your nelly."

Emelia bit her remaining ginger snap in half and stared at the cat glumly. "Then hopefully, your parents will agree to keep him. They've been asking what we want as a wedding present. Maybe it will work if I tell them their chances of grandchildren will be greatly enhanced without a scary spawn feline in residence."

"How are the wedding plans going?" Victor clung to the most neutral thing he could find in her sentence. The wedding was just over a month away, but he knew nothing about it beyond what was on his invitation.

Emelia threw the last of her biscuit in her mouth. "I'm still working the elopement angle. Turns out getting married to even minor nobility is a massive pain in the behind." Her glance darted his way. "No offense."

"None taken."

"I even tried to lose Harry and Meghan's invitation, but the wedding planner noticed it was missing."

"Why?" He had to admit, her admission made him like her even more. Most American women would be falling over themselves at the possibility of coming within a mile of the Duke and Duchess.

Emelia groaned. "Because my stepmother is a royal-obsessed social-climbing harridan who wouldn't know British etiquette if it bit her on her surgically-enhanced bust."

"I'm sure she's not that bad."

Emelia pitched an eyebrow. "She named my half-siblings Charles, George, Katherine-Elizabeth, William, and Charlotte."

Note to self. Avoid Emelia's stepmother at said wedding. "Don't worry. Sadly for your stepmother, the best she might be able to hope for is a random earl or an accidental viscount."

"From your lips to God's ears." Emelia reached for another biscuit.

"There's probably not much that makes that journey." Peter. Finally. He stomped into the room, pulled out a chair, and slumped into it.

"I was wondering where you were. Emelia and I have been unchaperoned for a whole four minutes." Victor grimaced as the sarcastic quip leapt straight out of his mouth.

Peter opened his mouth, then slapped it shut again as Emelia gave him a look that could ice over the Thames.

Victor's respect for her ratcheted up another notch. She was probably the last woman in the world he would have chosen for his brother, but he could admit that she was more than his match. She also wasn't a rowing groupie, which was good for Peter's ego.

Victor had given up on ever meeting someone. He'd played the field too widely, hurt too many women, for that. He still occasionally woke up in a cold sweat at the possibility he might one day check his phone and find himself plastered over social media tagged to an accusation about a night that he probably didn't remember.

Emelia got up and closed the door. "You two can save your squabbling for later. We have some things we need to talk about first."

"I didn't realize I'd been summoned to a next generation family meeting." At least Emelia was here to mediate. Except the last time she'd tried to mediate between them had resulted in a brawl that ended up with him in rehab and Peter not speaking to him for a year. The memory hung in the air like an unwelcome ghost.

She ignored him. Smart woman. "What do you want to do first, Peter?"

His brother was tapping into his phone.

"PETER!" Emelia snapped the word, and his brother snapped his head up. "Sorry. Just had to reply to coach."

"Give me that." Emelia held out her hand. Peter just looked at her. "For the love, Peter Carlisle. You spend fifty hours a week with your coach. When you're not with him, you're on all the stupid training apps. Are you going to whip that thing out at the altar to check your glycemic index?"

Victor smirked. His brother saw and shot him a glare, then dropped his phone face down on the tabletop.

"Sorry, Em."

Emelia muttered something under her breath about the World Champs and being a widow before she'd even been married. "Okay, Victor. Peter has something he would like to ask you."

This should be good. Going by his brother's sagging posture and shuttered expression, it could be anything. And there probably wasn't anything that Victor wouldn't give him, up to and including his hereditary title, if that didn't require his death.

"Peter." Emelia titled her head at her fiancé and raised her eyebrows.

Peter furrowed his brows and mumbled something under his breath, but Victor couldn't make out hide nor hair of what it was.

Instead, he tipped himself back on the rear legs of his chair and waited. He wasn't getting in the middle of whatever this was. Not for all the acreage on the estate.

"Louder, so he can hear you, darling," Emelia said sweetly, appearing not to notice that her fiancé had about five inches and a good thirty kilos of rowing-hardened muscle on her.

Peter huffed out his breath. "Fine. Do you want to be my best man?"

There was a crash, and Victor found himself flat on his back on the kitchen tiles, staring up at the roof, air shoved out of his lungs.

Peter loomed above him, hand out. Victor clasped it, and his brother hauled him to his feet, then picked up his chair behind him and set it back on the ground with a bang.

Victor stayed on his feet, his gaze running over his brother's tousled red hair, ginger half-beard, and unsmiling expression. "You don't want me to be your best man. Why haven't you asked one of the guys from the team?"

Elite rowing teams were tighter than brothers. That was the legend and the truth. Well, unless you were him and managed to ruin even those hard-forged bonds, but that was a different story for a different day.

And, not that he was a wedding planner or anything, but he was pretty sure the bridal party was supposed to be picked long before now.

"Because you're family." That was Emelia. "And when your parents are gone, you're what's left of the Carlisles. For better or worse."

Victor instinctively raised his hand to the jagged scar that zagged down his cheek, a move that wasn't lost on his brother.

Emelia sighed. "Sit down. Both of you."

Victor and Peter both pulled out their chairs and sat down, eyeing each other like boxers banished to opposing corners.

"I don't have any brothers or sisters, and I'm old enough to be the mother of my half-siblings. All I have is my cousin. And I'm not saying you have to be each other's people—we all know that's not going to happen anytime soon. But I do think you will both regret it if you don't try to find some common ground. Plus ..." Emelia paused before she threw in the killer blow. "You know it would mean everything to your mom."

Peter's shoulders dropped. "She's right." His admission came out gruffly. "We need to try to do better. At least for her sake."

It was hardly a warm invitation, but it was probably the best he was going to get.

Peter lifted his head and pinned Victor with his green-eyed gaze. "Just don't stuff it up."

A not-so-subtle reminder that somehow he always did.

CHAPTER FOUR

VICTOR DIDN'T KNOW WHAT MEREDITH'S plan was, but he doubted most of Wyndham had been flown to New York for a swanky cocktail party.

The fourteenth-floor office of Langham & Co. overlooked the glittering lights of the Big Apple. Victor had stayed away from the US the last few years. But it could be worse. At least they weren't in LA.

He'd chatted to a few colleagues, introduced himself to a few of the Americans. Nobody was hostile, but no one went out of their way to be friendly either. Not that he could blame them. The staff of the two companies wanted to be merged together about as much as South Korea wanted to be merged with her northern neighbor.

Grabbing his crystal tumbler of ginger beer, he took a stroll around the office, trying to stifle a yawn but not succeeding. It was after two in the morning in London, and he had the bedtime habits of an old man these days.

Most of the offices were dark, but one had a light on.

Lacey O'Connor – Publicity Director read the nameplate next to the door. His memory connected the name with a photo of an aloof-looking blonde from the dossier Sean had assembled of Langham staffers. Victor guessed she was around his age, but this was New York—where some women shaved ten years off their faces as often as they shaved their legs—so she could well be older. But there had been something about the set in her jaw and the steel in her eyes that pinged his competitive radar. She also had a huge advantage over him—according to the website, she had been with Langham for over ten years.

He pushed open the ajar door. The room was lined with books and large posters of international bestsellers, including an autographed cover of the first book of a new dystopian series touted as the next Harry Potter.

He looked over his shoulder at the empty corridor then stepped into the office. Lacey O'Connor was no doubt busy doing what he should be doing. Working the room, sizing up the competition, and, if she was smart, playing the blonde card with his colleagues to make herself appear less of a threat.

He approached the framed poster-sized cover and read the salutation scrawled across it. *Lacey, best publicist in the business. Bar none. Bring on the next one! Hugo.*

A shelf running below the poster was cluttered with framed pictures of the blonde with people he assumed to be clients. Actresses. A former First Lady. A couple of sports stars. All smiling. Some holding framed copies of what looked like a bestseller list.

How was he supposed to compete with that kind of resume? Victor sunk down onto the small love seat in the office and did a quick scan of his inbox. The only new email was a reminder from HR that his annual ergonomic workstation assessment was overdue. A quick swipe, and it was gone.

He leaned his head against the back of the couch, closing his gritty eyes against the glare of the ceiling light.

What's your secret plan, Meredith? Addicts needed routine. That had been drilled into him in rehab, where every day had been the same. Except Sunday. Visiting day. Even Sundays had followed their own rigid pattern. Routine allowed your brain to anticipate and to plan. Routine had helped keep him on the wagon for the last three years. A wagon he needed to stay on if he was to have any chance of helping his mother.

He should find a meeting. He hadn't been to one in four days. Or go back to his hotel. He'd left instructions to clear out the minibar. Hopefully, they'd done it.

Voices burst down the hallway, followed by a round of laughter. Laughter that was tainted just enough to reveal that its bearers had all had a glass too many.

It was an all-too-familiar sensation. The warmth of the whisky sliding down his throat. The buzz of feeling smarter, wittier, better looking than he actually was. His arm around an attractive woman, her leaning into him, face tilted up in invitation.

An invitation he would always regret accepting.

LACEY'S FINGERS TAPPED ACROSS HER phone's screen as her feet walked the familiar path to her office. If she had to be here, she had might as well close out some business on the West Coast.

From further up the hallway came the sound of forced laughter and conversation. Good luck to them. She was going to wage this war on results, not on pouring herself into a cocktail dress and drinking with the interlopers.

Her office door was wide open. Huh. She'd have sworn she hadn't left it that way. If some nosey Brit had—Lacey blinked. Then blinked again. There was a man slumped on her couch. And not just any man.

It couldn't be. She had to be hallucinating. There was no way that Victor Carlisle could be on her couch, in her office.

Except he was. Because while there were plenty of blond, tall, muscular men in the world, there were only one with that particular jagged scar lancing his cheek.

She'd only done one cursory round at the cocktail party. But she knew one thing. Victor Carlisle had not been in that room.

Victor's breath rose and fell evenly, his phone pressed against his chest. Her fingers curled around her own phone, its edges digging into her palm.

Of course, she'd known it was only a matter of time before their paths would cross again. Short of a huge familial falling-out, he would be at Peter and Emelia's wedding. But that was still a month away.

She studied him from across the small space, unwilling to go any closer. Victor Carlisle was the kind of man who sucked you into his orbit if you got too close. There was a trail of destruction behind him to prove it. One that had already ended up with one person dead, and had almost derailed her cousin's chance at happiness.

She leaned forward, sniffing the air for booze. Emelia had reported he'd completed rehab years ago, but Lacey's experience was that the only thing most people graduated rehab with was a whole new bag of tricks on how to hide their addiction.

Her phone buzzed in her hands as laughter echoed down the hallway. Victor's eyes fluttered as if about to open. If she was going to keep her advantage, it had to be now.

"Do you often go creeping around other peoples' offices, Mr. Carlisle?" Her question cracked the room like a whip, and his blue eyes flew open.

After she'd gotten home from Colorado, she'd spent the rest of the night researching Wyndham House. There wasn't so much as a mention of him on their website, which had to mean he was a junior staffer. Unlike her, whose web page bio, complete with testimonials, generated substantial new business for Langham in an ever-tightening market. So, all things being equal, he was no competition.

She huffed out a breath as he lurched to his feet. Except he was. Because he was a man. A very attractive man. A very attractive man who had been an elite athlete. A very attractive man who had been an elite athlete and would one day inherit a place in the British aristocracy. It was like one of those children's stack-a-block games. Except the grown-up version ended up with Victor on the top of the pyramid of privilege.

"Sorry about that."

Lacey held her place in the doorway as Victor stood and tugged the bottom of his jacket.

"It's late in London." He looked sheepish but sober, with no swaying to his posture, no slur to his words. His gaze was clear, the red rims around his eyes attributable to jet lag and fatigue.

His suit was expertly cut, emphasizing the length and breadth of a man in excellent physical shape. The gray stripe in his tie matched the gray in his eyes. She would bet a hundred bucks there was a saleswoman's phone number on the back of the receipt from wherever he'd bought it.

He came around his desk and held out his hand. Even with her in heels, he still had almost a head on her. "Victor Carlisle, from Wyndham House."

Lacey forced herself to meet his clear gaze. All that it held was restrained curiosity. Not so much as a glimmer of recognition.

Unless he was an actor of Bradley Cooper caliber, Victor Carlisle didn't remember her. He had no idea who she was. She squashed the flicker of hurt that tried to ignite. "I know who you are." Her words came out snooty as his large hand encompassed her much smaller one.

"I'm impressed." He slipped his phone into his pocket with an easy smile. "Unlike you, Ms. O'Connor, I'm a very small cog in the Wyndham wheel."

Lacey's hand dropped to her side. *We met six years ago. You're my cousin's fiancé's brother.* The words were on the tip of her tongue, but she held them back. Emelia would have mentioned her, but if Victor hadn't made the connection between his soon-to-be sister-in-law's cousin and the Lacey standing in front of him, she wasn't going to offer it up for free.

As for their other connection … Well, not even Emelia knew about that. A fact she was profoundly grateful for with all the water under that particular bridge.

"And what kind of cog are you, Mr. Carlisle?" Might as well get as much information out of him as she could before he realized who she was. Try and work out how much of a threat he could pose.

"Please, call me Victor. I'm an associate in Government Relations."

In other words, a lobbyist. "Of course you are." She hadn't meant to say it out loud. But it was under her breath, so maybe he hadn't—

His smile faltered. "Do you have a problem with that?"

"I guess that depends on exactly what your clients are trying to convince the government to do."

Victor jabbed a thumb over his shoulder. "Given that one of your photos is with the President of the American Gun Owner's Association, I'm not sure you're entitled to an opinion on that."

"You really don't want to debate the Second Amendment with me, Mr. Carlisle." The President of AGOA had been a loathsome creep of a man, whose book she had only worked on under protest. It was also the only book she'd ever worked on that she'd held her breath and hoped wouldn't make a single bestseller list, but there was no way she was sharing that information with this trumped-up piece of privilege.

"I'm sorry. I didn't mean to offend you." Victor held both his hands up in surrender. "Can we call it a truce?"

The last time she had met Victor Carlisle, he had walked into a party a stranger, and he walked out of it with a piece of her self-respect. A truce was the absolute last thing she was signing up for.

IT HAD TAKEN VICTOR ALL of two minutes to put his foot in his mouth. Hardly an auspicious start to leaving this merger in a better position than he entered it.

Why had he been stupid enough to mention guns? Americans and their guns were like the British and football. Only a foolish person said anything definitive about either until you knew well and good what side the other person supported.

Lacey's phone buzzed in her hands, and she glanced down at it. "We need to get back to the conference room. Meredith is about to speak."

She hadn't answered his question about the truce, but if that was an olive branch, he'd take it. Victor bet more than a few people had been professionally buried by underestimating Lacey O'Connor. He wasn't going to be one of them.

Lacey turned and swept back up the hall without saying another word. Victor followed her, keeping a careful distance. The last thing he needed was her thinking he was a creep on top of whatever she thought about his unwelcome visit to her office.

As she walked back into the conference room, he realized that what he'd assumed to be a long black skirt was in fact a pair of trousers. Interesting. Every other woman in the room was wearing a cocktail dress. Very professional, classy cocktail dresses, but dresses just the same. What statement was she trying to make?

A New Zealand Prime Minister had once caused great furor by wearing trousers when she met the Queen. The random fact flickered into his mind. If Lacey met the Queen, would she be the kind of woman to wear trousers?

Victor watched as an entirely different person took the place of the fiery, feisty woman he had just sparred with, as if entering the conference room was crossing a portal into another world. Within seconds, she was chatting to a group of colleagues, champagne glass in hand, spinning a tale that ended with them all in laughter.

"So, who is she?" One of the PR associates for Wyndham, leaned against the wall next to Victor, glass of Scotch in hand.

"Who?"

"The blonde you walked into the room with." Simon looked down into his glass and clinked the large boulder of ice around it. "Trust you to leave the room for ten minutes and return with a goddess, Carlisle."

Goddess? He'd wasted so much of his life on the party circuit with models and B-list actresses that the phrase had ceased to have any meaning. He'd also discovered that most beautiful women hid a well of insecurity so deep the Atlantic Ocean couldn't fill it.

"Oh, I see how it is."

"How what is?" Victor had completely lost track of what Simon was saying.

"You're not going to tell me who she is. That must have been some ten minutes." The stupid kid actually looked pleased with himself at the moronic innuendo.

"Shut up, Simon." Victor glanced to where Lacey was placing her still half-full champagne glass on a tray. The movement meant that the man with dark hair who had placed his hand on her arm had to remove it. Interesting. "She's Lacey O'Connor, the director of publicity. She could well end up being your next boss." When the waiter moved on, Lacey took another half step back, placing even more distance between her and the arm lingerer. Ex-boyfriend? Wannabe boyfriend? Current boyfriend in a lovers' quarrel?

"She should be so lucky." Simon tipped his glass in Lacey's direction before knocking back the rest of the amber liquid.

Victor restrained an eye roll. Simon was yet another iGen with an inflated view of his own appearance and attributes. The truth was, Simon was a six both in looks and competence. Maybe a seven on a good day. But he thought he was a nine. Courtesy of being indoctrinated by a mother who thought her son was the most special snowflake who ever did sparkle.

Ignoring Simon, Victor let his gaze crisscross the room, assessing his competition. About ten people had already had too much to drink—voices too loud, laughter too pitched, posture starting to droop. He couldn't imagine any of them being senior management contenders.

Another ten weren't competition for the opposite reason. Faces pinched with stress, gazes darting everywhere, hands strangling glasses, the process taking its toll before it had even started. They would be the first to crack under pressure.

He may not have as much experience as most of the people in this room. He may not have a fancy resume filled with big accounts. But he was good under pressure. The more, the better.

His best chance at progressing would be if Meredith threw something at them that was so crazy, so out of the box, that everything everyone else thought would count for them no longer mattered.

Speaking of whom, the woman herself strode into the room and the buzz of conversation silenced so abruptly it was like the room had been a movie soundtrack that someone had hit pause on.

Meredith wore a bright red suit, the same kind of red as Santa's. Except her pinched face was not bringing tidings of joy and good news for all men.

"Good evening. I'm sure you are all eager to hear the next stage in the process. Hopefully, none of you were stupid enough to think it would be one of those standard interview processes which would probably end up with me having one company just as rubbish as the current two."

How to win friends and influence people, Meredith style.

"I'll tell you what the next stage of the process is shortly but first some names." She reeled off ten names, including Simon's, whose chest swelled. "If I have called your name, you are not required in the merged company. Jennifer has the details of your severance package at the door. If you're from Wyndham, she will also provide you with your amended travel itinerary. If you're from Langham, there will be a box containing your belongings at reception."

Wow. Meredith was not messing around.

Stunned silence soaked the room as people tried to absorb what had just happened.

"We'll reconvene in two minutes." She stepped back from the podium, clearly expecting the people she had just fired to remove themselves from the room.

"Simon." Victor tapped him on the shoulder. The man looked like he had just turned into stone. "Did you hear her?"

Simon's glass shook. "Did she *fire* me?"

Victor winced. "I think she fired ten of you."

"She can't do that. Can she?"

Victor shrugged. "They're her companies. She can do whatever she likes." Even if it wasn't technically legal, the woman had deep enough pockets to pay her way out of any problems.

"But … but … I had a PowerPoint prepared and everything. I was going to go for Senior Associate."

Senior Associate? The kid was even more deluded than Victor had thought. "Hopefully it can be of some use while you're job hunting."

"I'm going to take her to the Employment Tribunal. This can't be legal."

The woman had lawyers and HR people from two companies advising her, not to mention the plenty of money for outside counsel if she didn't want to use any of those. Whether it was legal was irrelevant. "Who knows? Maybe this will be the best thing that ever happened to you."

Simon gave him the kind of bug-eyed look of someone who had had a lot of life handed to him too easily. Victor perversely envied him. Maybe if something had slapped him sidewise when he was younger, it would have knocked some of the entitled arrogance out of him, and he would have made a better fist at being a decent human being.

"This must be some kind of joke, right? A test." Simon knocked back the last of his drink. "That's what it is. She wants to see which of us is going to prove our mettle. Stand our ground. Prove we're in this."

Victor looked at the white faces of the employees leaving the room. Three others were from Wyndham. He didn't know where Meredith's intelligence had come from, but it was flawless. None of them would be missed. At least not for their work ethic or professional abilities—he'd miss the baking that Jack's wife sent in with her husband every Friday. "I don't think this is a joke."

Simon squared his shoulders. "You would say that."

In the shuffle of the room, Lacey had ended up about eight feet away from him. Based on the tilt of her head and attempted neutral set of her face, Victor suspected she was eavesdropping.

A dark-haired young woman cut through the crowd and handed a piece of paper to Meredith, who glanced at it. "Simon Cramer. If you haven't collected your severance from Jennifer within the next thirty seconds, it's off the table and you will receive your minimum legal entitlements and be escorted from the premises by security. I'd get moving if I were you."

At that Simon dropped his glass and rushed to the door mowing through the people in his path like a prop for the English rugby team.

Victor watched as Lacey struggled to suppress a smile. He shuffled a couple of feet closer to her. "You can just say it."

"Say what?" Lacey arched an eyebrow at him.

"Good riddance."

"That wasn't what I was thinking." She turned her head away from him. "I was thinking that if all of your colleagues are like him, this is going to be easier than I thought." The words came to him in a murmur, so subtle he couldn't be sure if she said them or he'd imagined them.

"Right. That was the easy cull." Meredith's face had moved from pinched to satisfied. "Now we need to get the New Yorkers off their home ground and even the playing field. If you are with Langham, you have tonight to make any arrangements you need to for the next week. Your next stop is Minnesota. You will be given an envelope with further details on your way out."

At that, Lacey's face leeched white.

Victor had heard of Minnesota but why he had no idea. Which had to mean that it was some flyover state with a large ratio of land to people.

As Meredith exited the room, everyone reached for their phones like it was a programmed response. Victor did a quick Google search. Border state with Canada. Less than six million people. Lots of lakes and wide-open space.

The city girl being lobbed into the country. So much for being easier than she thought.

CHAPTER FIVE

SMALL HARBOR. MINNESOTA. LACEY HADN'T planned on setting foot in the place for a couple of years yet. Wikipedia generously called it a city with its entire three thousand inhabitants. If you Googled Small Harbor, the "related searches" were concubines and cash crops. Make of that what you will.

She flicked on the car's blinker and turned into the familiar neighborhood. Ramshackle houses and overgrown lawns. Her shiny rental car would already be making its way down the grapevine.

In the glove compartment sat the papers with her actual destination. Her platinum Delta status had made it easy with a seat at the front, and she'd made sure to gap it from the plane and get lost in the crowd.

The last thing she needed was any of her colleagues—current or future or soon-to-be-past—on this little jaunt into her history. Or even knowing she had gone somewhere other than the assigned hotel.

She had a carefully created image to maintain. Small Harbor did not feature in it. Slowing her car, she pulled up outside the house and turned into the driveway. When she'd bought the property five years ago, it had a nicely kept lawn, a fresh coat of paint, and a picket fence around the front. Now the grass grew long, the fence had posts missing, and the paint looked dull and dirty.

All things she'd sent money to maintain. Money that had clearly gone elsewhere. As she'd known it would.

Pushing open her door, she placed a Jimmy Choo heel down on the cracked cement. *In and out, Lacey.* She was going to have to be fast; otherwise, the odds were decent she'd come out to find the car stripped.

At least the group had been split across two flights. If all went well, she'd get back to Duluth at the same time as the second group, and no one would notice her little detour.

Lacey knocked on the door and waited a few seconds. The muffled sound of the shopping channel came from inside, so Mom was home. TV. The soundtrack of her mother's life.

Then there was the familiar shuffle, and the door opened, her father's large build filling the doorway. Arms folded across his chest, familiar silver ring glinting on his finger. He'd been a promising footballer in his day. Two state championships. Decades later, he still got free drinks because of it.

"What?" He barked out the words before even looking at who was on the doorstep. His face filled with confusion as he looked at her. "Lacey?"

"Hey, Dad."

Her father tipped his chin over his shoulder. "Doreen! Lacey's here!"

"What are you talking about, you old fool?" Her mother's voice screeched back. "You're going blind. Put your glasses on."

His father gestured for Lacey to come in. She slipped past him and walked down the hallway. Wallpaper peeled off the walls. Tattered scraps sat where they fell.

You knew this would happen. She tried to keep the grimace off her face as she trod over cat hair-covered carpet that hadn't seen a vacuum in months. She had promised she would act as if it was their own, as long as they paid the rent so the mortgage and utility payments were covered. If it fell down around their ears, she'd done all she could.

"It's me, Mom." She stuck her head into the den, raising her voice above the blare of the TV. The only clear path in the room was from her mother's recliner to the television. Every other square foot of the floor, every surface, was covered with the result of her mother's addiction. Cooking appliances on top of exercise machines, clothing, makeup, even a water blaster. Some stacks looked like they defied gravity. Most were unopened, their appeal already diminished in the whole twenty-four hours it took them to arrive.

Her mother only glanced away from the screen for a second. Her grey hair was scraped back in a braid that looked like it hadn't met shampoo in weeks. Her floral dress was threadbare, feet holding tattered slippers. The lines and crevices in her face made her appear much older than her sixty years. "Look at this umbrella. It can withstand winds up to fifty miles an hour! And the first fifty callers get a mini kids version for free." On the screen, some made-for-TV host stood in a wind tunnel demonstrating said umbrella.

No nice-to-see-you. No attempt to get up from her chair and give Lacey a hug. No asking what had brought her back for the first time in years.

"You already have plenty of umbrellas, Mom." From her vantage point in the doorway, she could see at least three, one of which looked identical to the one on the screen.

A wave of defeat swept over her. She'd tried. When her mother's TV shopping habit had first gotten out of control, she'd used her leave to come back, clear the place out on eBay, and pay off the credit card debt. She'd even managed to get the bank to refuse to issue more cards.

But it hadn't lasted. Eventually, she'd had to accept that no one could fix someone else's addiction. Which was why the house was in her name. When the debt collectors came calling, at least they couldn't touch that.

"What brings you here?" Her father's voice rumbled behind her, and Lacey turned to see him scrutinizing her from the door. At least he looked like he'd seen a shower recently. His clothes were rumpled but clean.

Her parents were good people. They'd done their best. But they'd been dealt a tough hand in life. Always scrimping and saving to make ends meet. Sometimes managing, other times her dad losing the little they had to some pyramid scheme. When she'd left, she'd sworn she was leaving it all behind. No one ever mentioned that poverty seeps into your veins in a way that even years of never going without can't obliterate.

"I need a gun."

The ghost of a smile threatened his face. "That's my girl." He ambled down the hallway toward the spare room where he kept his gun safe. She followed. He'd added a ponytail since she last saw him, the crime against style trailing down his neck like a grey slug. "What do you need?" Pulling a ring of keys from his pocket, he opened the large metal vault, revealing a vast array of weapons.

"Good grief, Dad. Are you planning on arming a militia?"

An avid hunter, he'd had a healthy collection when she left home, but this was next level. Rifles, semiautomatics, handguns, and magazines of ammunition all gleamed in the low light. One shelf contained boxes and boxes of bullets and cartridges.

She bit her lip as she counted at least thirty weapons. She had grown up hunting, her pink child-sized rifle a natural extension of her arm during the season. For large swathes of her childhood, the ability to hunt was the only reason her family didn't starve.

But thirty? That was a whole lot of guns for one man.

She ground her teeth together to stop herself from saying

anything. They'd already had this caustic debate more times than she could count in the years after she'd left for university and discovered a different world to the one she'd grown up in. Her father saw her views as yet another way that she had betrayed her roots and joined the ranks of the liberal elite.

"A handgun." She didn't say it until she trusted herself to talk. "One I can conceal." The more she thought about it, the more convinced she was that there was only one reason Meredith would have flown twenty-something of them to Duluth for a week of "team bonding." She wasn't going into it unarmed.

"You still got your permit?" Her father picked up one of his rifles and pointed it at the wall in a practiced maneuver.

"Yup." She'd had a permit to carry in Minnesota since she'd been legally allowed one. She kept renewing it. There was something oddly comforting about the fact that if she ever returned home, she could at least pack a pistol—which was more than anyone could do in New York short of being in law enforcement or a celebrity.

"Here." Her dad reached into the safe. "I got this one for your mom, but she won't mind if you borrow it. It's a G19."

Lacey took the Glock and held it in her palm. It was light and compact, fitting her hand well. She used to be a crack shot, but she hadn't fired a gun in years. And she wasn't going to have time to find a range. Muscle memory would have to suffice if she needed it. Hopefully, she wouldn't. She slid the clip out and checked that it was empty, then checked the chamber.

Her father pulled a small case out from under the bed. "How many bullets you want? A couple of hundred? More?"

"Just one box." She placed the Glock into the cushioned case, then added the box of bullets her father handed her. Zipping the case shut, she lifted it off the spare bed.

"Here's the holster I got with it." Her father flipped a leg holster up from under the bed. "I have others if you want."

"This will be fine." A leg holster was the best way to conceal it. All going well, she'd never have a reason to use it, and her colleagues would never know it was there. "I'll bring it back before I leave. Won't be more than a week."

"That'll be fine." His father rubbed the scruff on his cheek. "Is everything okay?"

"Why don't you tell me, Dad?" Lacey looked pointedly at the overflow of boxes stacked along the wall. "What happened to the money I sent for house maintenance?"

"We'll get to it, baby. I promise." They both knew they wouldn't. Not as long as her mother sat in the den with a credit card in one hand and her phone in the other.

But they'd always been good at playing pretend.

CHAPTER SIX

YOU HAD TO FEEL A little sorry for the British contingent. They'd been expecting an all-expenses-paid week in New York at some swish hotel.

As soon as she'd walked into the cocktail party, Lacey had known that Meredith was lulling people into a false sense of security. A sleight of hand, switching a week in the city that never sleeps for ... well, they'd find out soon enough. But their anonymous two-star hotel somewhere in Duluth was only a staging ground.

Lacey scanned the buffet set up in the bland hotel conference room and helped herself to some fruit. She'd made good time with her side trip, even with the stop she made after her parents' place. She'd arrived a few minutes before the taxis had appeared with the people who'd been on the second flight.

She studied the room for a second, determined to keep her gaze away from Victor, who was in a huddle with his colleagues.

The Brits and the Yanks clustered in their separate groups, each occasionally glancing warily at the other. Both sets tainted in different ways.

At least her side already had a leg up on the British set, who would still be jet-lagged. Not that she had a side. There was just her, as far as she was concerned. She'd look out for Jen if she could. Otherwise, she'd only form alliances if she needed them.

A *tap tap tap* sounded as someone tested the podium mic.

"Everyone, take a seat. We're about to get started." Everyone dutifully filed into the row of chairs in the center of the room. Lacey slipped into one at the end of a row next to Jen.

"Have you checked out the imports?" The curly haired woman murmured. "Some of them look mighty fine. Who was the blond you were talking to last night? He would give Adonis a run for his money."

Lacey arched an eyebrow at her. "Just a lobbyist." She didn't even have to try to infuse her voice with disdain. "Anyway, I'm pretty sure Meredith's no-fraternization rule applies to them as much as it does to anyone from our side."

Jen pouted, her black curls bouncing. "But we're not technically colleagues yet."

"You're HR. Aren't you supposed to be the light of Langham for everyone else to be guided by?"

Jen rolled her eyes at the line her useless boss had recently used in a company-wide memo. Soon to be ex-boss if this exercise was what Lacey anticipated. Chase wouldn't last ten minutes in real America.

Meredith walked into the room and there was instant silence as if someone hit mute on the world. Another woman appeared behind her, carrying a clipboard. Meredith strode to the podium and gripped the lectern.

"Good afternoon, everyone. I trust your flights were sufficient. I'm not one for small talk, so let's cut to the chase. You have all been identified as having potential for senior roles in the merged company." At that a murmur swept through the room.

Lacey leaned back in her seat, giving Meredith her full attention.

"However, given what has brought us to this point, it is clear to me that standard appointment processes are not going to work to get me the types of people I want leading the new company. If you thought you were going to be able to schmooze and network your way into a new job, you might as well leave now. Backslapping and the old boys' club isn't going to work either. I don't care how many accounts you've landed, best sellers you've had, or advertising dollars you've pulled in. Some of your previous colleagues made me a lot of money but had the moral code of cretins and, quite frankly, the profit margin has not been worth the media I've had to deal with. It certainly hasn't covered the stock market's response."

That had to be directed at Langham staff. Wyndham was entirely privately held.

"The fact you are in this room means you are competent. But it doesn't tell me a thing about your character. That's what this next stage is about. And it starts now."

The door opened, and a line of hotel staff marched in carrying large olive green backpacks. Placing them against the wall, they left the room and returned with more.

The thrill of vindication swept through Lacey at the sight of the packs. She was right. She'd known exactly why they were here.

Going by the looks of confusion covering most of the faces in the room, she was a step ahead of most.

"Each rucksack is labeled with a name. You have fifteen minutes to find yours, get changed, collect any personal items you may need, and be on the bus. If you are not on the bus, you will be returning to New York or the UK tonight."

There was a burst of sound as people sprinted for the side of the room. Lacey pulled her shoes off, carrying them. She was not missing this bus for anything.

Her bag was the third one she checked, and she lugged it back up to her room in record time. Stripping her clothes off, she grabbed the fatigues out of the rucksack and put them on. She didn't know who had sized everyone, but they had gotten hers perfect.

She opened her suitcase, giving thanks that she'd put everything she might need into one corner. Granola bars, candy bars, insect repellant, matches, sunscreen, dry shampoo, blister packs, hiking socks, deodorant, toothbrush, toothpaste, battery pack, and a baseball cap. All got shoved into her rucksack.

Pulling her pants leg up, she strapped the holster around her calf. She opened the locked gun box and slid the handgun into the holster. The Glock was already loaded. No point carrying an empty gun around. The gun box went in the rucksack. Hopefully, there wouldn't be a search.

She stood, letting her pants leg drop. There was a slight bulge but nothing that would make anyone think she was packing a piece.

Her phone went in her front pocket. It would be next to useless within an hour if they were going up north, but at least she'd have it. Search and rescue could ping her if she fell down a ravine or something. She'd have to let Emelia and the girls know she was going to be offline for a few days. She couldn't remember the last time she'd been uncontactable for longer than the length of a flight.

She'd need to send some emails on the bus ... Focus! Four minutes left.

Lacey grabbed the brand new pair of hiking boots, shoved her feet into them, and laced them with the knot her father had taught her. No time for untied laces when hunting.

Everything else was thrown back into her suitcase. Presumably, someone would come and claim it and store it or send it wherever it needed to go. Shouldering her pack, she pulled open her door and walked into the hall. Only to get knocked down by a blur of khaki.

Before she could even catch her breath, let alone try to get back up, two hands had grasped her straps and hauled her back onto her feet.

"You okay?" Victor's concerned and harassed face swam above her.

"Fine. Let's go." She jogged down the hall before he could even reply.

She didn't know how Victor—heir to the Viscount of Downley and well-known womanizer—had survived the first cull, but she did know that the man who loved the high life wouldn't last a night in the Minnesota wilderness.

All going well, she'd be rid of him by this time tomorrow.

Victor: Hey, just so you know, I'm in the US for the next week or so for work and might be off the grid for some of it. I've let Mum know, but you know how she worries if she can't get hold of us.

Peter: Got it. Where are you going?

Victor: Some kind of corporate boot camp, I think. Is there anything you need me to do for the wedding? Mum took my measurements for the suit when I was home.

Peter: Don't think so. Last I saw, Emelia and Mum had the spreadsheet all under control. I'm at training camp this week.

Victor: Do you want me to organize you a bachelor's party?

Peter: Nah. Not really my thing. Training schedule doesn't allow for it anyway. I'll have a beer with the guys or something.

Peter: You don't need to worry about a speech

either. I'll ask one of the guys to do it.

Victor: Got it. Hope the training camp goes well.

Peter: Thanks. Good luck at boot camp.

Lacey: So I'm going to be off the grid for a week or so. Is there anything you need from your maid of honor before I'm out of reach?

Emelia: Ha ha, very funny.

Lacey: ???

Emelia: Lace, you consume internet data like the rest of us consume air. Your cell provider would think you were dead if you went more than a few hours without contact.

Lacey: I'm serious. This merger thing is next level. I'm in Minnesota. I'm pretty sure Meredith is sending us off into the BWCA.

Emelia: Sending you where now?

Lacey: Boundary Waters Canoe Area. It's a wilderness area on the border with Canada.

Emelia: You're going camping???

Lacey: Camping. Canoeing. Hiking. If I'm right. Which I'm pretty sure I am. We're almost at Ely. The only thing anyone goes to Ely for is this.

Emelia: Once a Minnesota girl, always a Minnesota girl. I'm sure it will all come back to you.

Lacey: I borrowed a gun from Dad. A nice little Glock.

Emelia: Of course you did. Because Lacey O'Connor in the wilderness without her phone and armed isn't terrifying at all.

Lacey: I'm not going to be waving it around like a crazy woman. It's for emergencies.

Emelia: Seriously. When was the last time you were without your phone for more than a few hours? I have clear memories of you being wheeled into surgery to get your appendix out and them having to physically wrest it from your hands.

Lacey: That was because my stupid appendix chose the week of a book release to explode. Thank goodness I don't have one for another few weeks. How's the magic wedding spreadsheet?

Emelia: It's now a spreadsheet and a Gantt chart ☺

Lacey: You are a strange, strange woman.

Emelia: I have to have something to entertain me while Peter's training. He's away all week at a camp this week. I can't wait until the World Champs are over.

Lacey: Okay. I've gotta go and clear some final things. Wish me luck!

Emelia: You don't need luck. I pity your poor competitors. They'll need all the help they can get.

CHAPTER SEVEN

PETER DIDN'T WANT A BACHELOR party or for him to give a speech. Best man in name only. He should be grateful he was the best man at all, but that hadn't dulled the twinge when his brother's text made it clear he wanted Victor to have nothing to do with anything that actually mattered.

Victor rubbed his hands over his face. Could he blame him after everything? If he'd been Peter, he wouldn't want Victor giving a speech at his wedding. But Peter was the better man of the two of them. So he'd thought he might have a chance.

At least he knew now before he wasted his time trying to write something that wasn't wanted or needed.

God, I don't know how to fix things with my brother. Could you give us a hand at all?

His attempt at prayer was stilted. He'd first turned his mind to spiritual things in rehab. The twelve steps gave you no choice. Made it an entire step even.

He'd wrestled and refused to participate and tried to barter with the counsellor to let him skip it. But at the end of the day, he couldn't get around the fact that living life only for himself had turned him into someone he didn't like and hurt everyone he loved.

So here he was, with his awkward prayers and occasional church attendance, trying to figure out what his mother and Peter and Emelia had that seemed to give them a sense of purpose that had remained elusive to him his whole life.

Victor shifted in his seat. His knees were wedged up against the seat in front, his attempt to keep his body in the allocated space. Next to him, Lacey tapped furiously on her phone. He'd been stunned when she dropped into the seat next to his on the bus until he realized it was one of the few left, and two of them were next to people who took up one and a half seats.

She'd promptly proceeded to ignore him for the next hour and a half as she conducted warfare via text and email.

At least that had reminded him to tell his family he was disappearing for a week. Check his emails. Reply to the whole five that needed responses.

It felt like another life ago that he had been working fourteen-hour days, barely able to keep up with the accounts he was juggling. Once the scandal broke, the work had disappeared faster than figgy pudding at Christmas. Now he sat here, twiddling his thumbs while the woman next to him burned through work like it was kindling and she was kerosene. *Thanks for nothing, Garrett.*

He glanced down at her screen. The text seemed to go on and on. "Why don't you just call them?"

Nothing.

"O'Connor?" Lacey seemed too informal, and Ms. O'Connor too stilted. So, since they were all sitting here in army fatigues headed off to boot camp, he figured he had might as go with that.

She glanced up from her phone. "Sorry, what?"

"Why don't you just call them? Surely that would be easier than those novels you're writing."

Her eyes narrowed. "If by easier, you mean quicker, then sure. But if by easier, you mean ensuring that there is no confusion about what needs to be done while I'm away then, no. Now, I really need to get this done." Her attention went back to her screen like they'd never spoken.

He watched the scenery roll by outside. He had no idea where they were or where they were going. He'd Googled Duluth, trying to find out if there was some kind of military-themed corporate boot camp nearby and came up dry. After the stunt last night, he wouldn't put it past Meredith to have paid someone to create one just for them.

"What about voice to text?" Even as the words came out of his mouth, he knew they were a mistake.

Lacey's face jerked up. "Oh, I don't know. Could it be that I'm dealing with commercially sensitive information and I have no idea who half the people on this bus are?"

"Sorry." Even to his own ears, he sounded petulant and condescending.

Her eyes narrowed. "Seriously? Is this what you do to the women at Wyndham? Keep interrupting them when they're trying to get work done? Is it unimaginable that someone could be in your presence and not be falling over themselves to talk to you? Or can you just not help yourself from mansplaining to them how to do their jobs?"

Ouch. "Are you calling me a sexist?"

Lacey huffed out a breath, blue eyes narrowing like he was trying her last atom of patience. "I'm just saying. If a man was sitting beside you, trying to work, would you be interrupting him like you're interrupting me?"

Victor realized that the low level of conversation on the bus had died. Everyone was eavesdropping on their argument. One he had stupidly started and had no way of winning. But the competitor in him refused to concede.

"That depends. Are you my boss?"

"I could be." She snapped out the very words he had said to Simon last night, and blaring alarms sounded in Victor's head.

He'd never considered they might apply to him. He hadn't

considered anything except his mission. But Lacey was right. She was more senior than him. He could come out of this merger with her as his boss. In fact, the odds of that happening were better than his ridiculous hope that he might be able to pull something out of the bag and leapfrog his way into senior management.

She could be his boss. If a miracle didn't happen, he'd still need a job. He was good at his job. He liked his job. He needed to keep his job. It was the only thing he had that gave him any credibility in his family's eyes. He had to try and save this, and he had to do it now.

His mind tumbled over explanations and excuses. Lacey had gone back to her messages, ignoring him, which was exactly what he deserved.

Would he have interrupted her if it had been a guy next to him? Would he have jumped in with unwanted and unneeded advice?

It wasn't a question he particularly wanted to dwell on. At the front of the bus, a woman was scribbling on a clipboard. He could imagine what she was writing. Victor Carlisle. Sexist. Chauvinist. Uncomfortable with strong women. Wouldn't be able to handle having a female boss. Cull.

None of which was true. At least, he hoped it wasn't. Something else to add to the list of things to talk to his sponsor about. "I'm sorry. You were right. I shouldn't have interrupted you, and I certainly shouldn't have tried to tell you how to do your job. I apologize."

Lacey's fingers paused for a second, then resumed tapping. Another message whooshed off into cyberspace. Then she placed her phone on her khaki-clad leg. "So, why did you?"

She turned her head and looked at him straight on, and he was hit by the full force of her light blue eyes. He had one chance to tell her the truth. No excuses. No spinning a story.

He shrugged, his borderline-too-small shirt tightening across his shoulders. "I guess I was jealous."

She blinked. "Why?"

"A few weeks ago, that would have been me. But since the corruption thing …" He leaned his head against the window. "Well, it would be fair to say we don't have many clients at the moment. And the stuff we do have is low-level. You obviously have a lot of people counting on you, people who value what you do. I guess I wished that was me."

Her icy gaze melted around the edges. Not much. But enough to give him some hope that if he did ever end up as an underling to Lacey O'Connor, her inaugural duty wouldn't be to fire his sorry butt. "Okay."

But until that happened, she was his competitor. And he wouldn't be leaving anything off the field as he attempted to survive this thing at least as her equal.

KEEP YOUR FRIENDS CLOSE AND your enemies closer. That had been what Lacey had been thinking as she had landed herself in the seat next to Victor.

Besides, the only other remaining seats held even less appeal. Two were half seats, two were next to people who would talk to her the whole way, and one was next to a Wyndham guy she'd seen openly eyeing her up the night before. At least she knew what Victor Carlisle brought to the table. And that she would never be fooled by him again.

And better she sit here than one of her female colleagues, someone he would flirt with and charm.

She sent messages to Rachel and Anna, then scrolled through her inbox. Nothing remained that Janna couldn't deal with. Her gaze lifted to the man next to her. After his apology, he'd turned and spent the last fifteen minutes peering out the window without saying a word.

He had actually apologized. She had to give him that. Most of the men she worked with would have blustered and made excuses or told her she was overreacting.

Victor shifted slightly next to her. She did have to feel a bit sorry for the guy. He was wedged into his seat tighter than a Kardashian in a playsuit. His knees were jammed against the seat in front, his quads folded up toward his chest. And his shoulder was pushed against the window. The bus was clearly not designed for someone either his height or girth.

She looked down at the small gap between their seats. Not a single part of him encroached on her space. That had to be taking deliberate effort.

Maybe he…she shook her head at the thought trying to encroach. No, whether he had changed or not was irrelevant. He was the competition. Everyone was the competition.

Tapping her screen, she drafted a quick email to her assistant with the remaining tasks that she'd need to be on top of in Lacey's absence. At least Janna would have a peaceful week. The only people left in the office were assistants, junior staff, and interns.

Her phone buzzed with a text from Rachel.

I was just researching the BWCA. Group sizes are limited to nine, and there are restricted entries, so you could all be split up. What if you have to choose your own teams? Do you know who you would want to be with?

Lacey opened her browser and did a quick search. Rachel was right. No more than nine people in a group. And each entry point had daily restricted numbers on a first-in, first-served basis.

Permits for the most popular entry points were booked out months in advance. May was still off-season but only just.

Turning her head she did a quick count of the bus. Twenty-four people excluding the driver and some woman up the front with a clipboard that she didn't know. Four teams of six or three teams of eight, assuming each team had a guide. Not even Meredith would send a bunch of corporate softies into the Minnesota wilderness without professional supervision.

Assuming this had been pulled together in the last few weeks, the odds were that they would be split up to different entry points. They weren't in New York now. No corporate schtick could usurp US Forest Service regulations.

Lacey sat back on her seat. If she was Meredith, what would she do to keep people constantly off-kilter? She scanned the people across the aisle from her. Most were on their phones. A few were chatting to the person next to them. The rest were gazing out the window or into space. All of them looked like people who assumed that once they got off this bus, they would be told exactly what to do.

If she was in control, she would make people pick their teams. With a time limit of thirty seconds. And all teams would have to be a mix of Langham and Wyndham. That would send people into mass confusion and panic.

Jen. The HR director had grown up in the Bronx. She looked like a beauty pageant contestant, but steel ran through her. That was how she'd made it as the only black woman in a senior position in the firm.

Lacey pulled out her phone and opened up a message to Jen.

If we have to pick our own teams when we get off this bus, then we need to be together.

Blue dots appeared. Then, Got it. Do you know something?

No, just a hunch. Who's next to you?

Some guy from Wyndham.

Would you want to be with him in the wilderness for a week?

That would be a negative. Who's next to you?

Lacey glanced up. Victor hadn't moved from his position staring out the window. Her mouth lifted slightly as she typed out. Adonis. Then quickly added. Just FYI, he has a reputation as a womanizer.

Who cares? Jen's response came back quickly. If we're going to be in the wilderness for a week, we need someone who is strong and can carry stuff. He has to be a better possibility than any of the men on our side.

Lacey went through all the Langham men on the bus. Some golfers. A couple of cross-fitters. The rest wouldn't last a game of Little League. All had an inflated sense of their own abilities. As fun as it would be to watch them all crumble under pressure in any other circumstance, they wouldn't bring a thing to a team.

Victor had been a pain, but it had been an hour and a half before he'd started with his mansplaining. It would have taken most of her male colleagues from Langham all of five minutes. And he'd apologized. Give me a second. Let me do some digging.

"Do you still row?" She asked the question quietly. He didn't move, so she gave him a little poke in the shoulder.

Victor turned his head. "Sorry, am I in your space?" He tried to shift over even more, but he had nowhere to go short of out of the window.

"No." She kept her voice down. "Do you still row?"

His brow crinkled. "How did you know I row?"

Because Emelia told me. "Research." If she told him about their connection, he would immediately put up the front of the person he wanted her to report back to Emelia.

"Occasionally. As I'm sure your research also told you, my brother is the real rower."

"But you rowed for Oxford in the Boat Race. On the winning team." If it wasn't for her cousin, she wouldn't have any clue what that meant or how impressive it was. Jen was right. She may have underestimated Victor. Being any kind of elite-level athlete took grit and determination. Even if his motivation was to be a jerk to his brother.

"That was years ago."

Interesting. Every other man she had ever met still dined out on any and all of their athletic achievements. Even when they were decades old.

The five miles to Ely sign flashed past them out the window. If she was right about where they were going, then she had less than ten minutes until they got there.

"I think we might be going into the Minnesota wilderness." Her words were so quiet, Victor leaned in to hear what she was saying. His blue eyes had grey flecks in them. "If I'm right, we'll be split up because there's a maximum of nine people in a group."

"How do you know this?"

"I've spent some time here." She said it nonchalantly, like her family had a summer cottage or something. The truth was that in the first eighteen years of her life, the only time she had left the state was for her aunt's funeral. "We're five miles from Ely. The only reason anyone goes to Ely is to access the National Forest or Boundary Waters."

Victor looked down at his pants. "And here I was, thinking we were going to some military-themed boot camp."

"We might be. I could be wrong."

Victor turned more toward her, wedging his back against the window. "But you don't think you are."

"No." If Meredith had wanted to send them to a boot camp, there were plenty of places closer to New York that would provide the same kind of experience.

"So if I'm Meredith and I'm sending people into the wilderness, and I want to keep them unbalanced …" His words trailed off as he thought for a few seconds, then he looked at her with something that seemed to hint at respect. "You think she might make us chose our own teams. Of course." He continued talking, almost as if to himself. "That would be complete chaos."

"You row, so you should be able to pick up handling a canoe. And you're strong, so you can carry stuff."

One side of Victor's mouth lifted. "So basically you want me for my body."

"Entirely." Lacey refused to let her gaze go anywhere south of his chin.

He blinked. For a second, she thought he might have recognized her, but the look was gone as quickly as it came. "Okay, I'm in."

Lacey tapped on her phone and messaged Jen to stay close when they got off the bus.

"What else would you do if you were Meredith?" Victor kept his voice low.

He was probably pumping her for information in case they did get separated, which was a smart move on his part. But it wouldn't do him any good. Whatever she said wouldn't give him an edge. Not over her, anyway. "Good try, Mr. Carlisle, but you've gotten all you're getting from me."

"Mr. Carlisle sounds like I'm your teacher. Please call me Victor."

"Fine, Victor."

"And?" He looked at her.

"And what?"

"This is the part where you say 'And you can call me Lacey.'"

The way he said *Lacey* in his British accent stirred memories she had successfully deleted from her mental hard drive until yesterday. "O'Connor is just fine."

He grinned. "Okay, then. O'Connor it is."

She was not making nice with Victor Carlisle. She was not. She was just making a strategic alliance. That was all.

Re-opening Rachel's message, she replied with thanks for the heads up.

For a second, she thought about telling Rachel more. Except she didn't know about Victor. Nobody knew about Victor. They had no idea why finding herself sitting next to him on a bus, let alone potentially about to spend a week in the wilderness with him, was even a thing.

A thing from the past. That was all.

Even if he had reformed, there were a million other reasons why he had to stay there.

CHAPTER EIGHT

*Y*OU HAVE ALL BEEN IDENTIFIED *as having potential for roles at senior levels in the merged company.* Victor focused on Meredith's proclamation as he dug his paddle into the water, enjoying the feel of resistance for a second before it cut cleanly through, propelling his shared canoe forward.

Lacey had been half right. As the bus had pulled to a stop, clipboard lady had informed them that whoever they were sitting with was their first team member. As soon as they got off the bus, they'd been ordered to form a team with two other pairs. Lacey had moved at warp-speed to grab a colleague called Jen and her partner. The other two had simply been the pair closest to them. They'd ended up with three from Langham, three from Wyndham. If this turned Survivor-style, at least it was an even pairing.

In the front seat, Richard plunged his paddle into the water, determination in his movements. Victor had to give it to him. For a man who openly admitted that he considered a three-star hotel to be roughing it, he hadn't uttered so much as a word of complaint during the three-hour paddle.

"We are going to need to portage soon. Not for long. Just twenty minutes or so. Then another short paddle and it will be time to set up camp for the night." Kelvin, their guide, issued the instruction from the back of the three-man canoe a few meters across the water. "Follow us to the exit spot."

Victor glanced left. Lacey and Louisa lagged about ten meters behind them. Even from across the water, Victor could see the sweat beading down Louisa's beet-red face. Thank goodness they weren't doing this in the heat of summer. The woman would be melting down like a nuclear disaster.

He felt for her. Louisa had a whip-sharp legal mind. But this was far from the right context for her to shine.

Kelvin, Cassie, and Jen beached their canoe gently into the edge of the lake. Kelvin jumped off the back with a splash while Cassie and Jen exited the front.

A few seconds later, theirs nudged up beside the first canoe. Victor jumped out after Richard, the water lapping at his ankles. Wet feet didn't bother him. He had spent an entire English spring and winter drenched when he was rowing. Once you'd spent six hours rowing in sleet and hail, a few days in wet socks and boots was a mere annoyance.

Victor pulled their canoe a bit further up the shore so that there was no chance of it floating away, then unloaded their backpacks from inside.

Lacey and Louisa's canoe scraped against the rocks just as he finished. Louisa, then Lacey, jumped up off the front. Lacey grabbed the canoe to pull it up next to Victor's.

Victor itched to offer to help, but he'd learned his lesson on that front.

Kelvin checked his watch. "Right, take a few minutes break. Then we'll portage."

"I can do ours by myself and Richard can carry the other two-man one." Victor was a head taller than anyone else in the group. It made sense for him to portage one canoe by himself. That would leave two women to carry the three-person canoe. Then the other two would only have to carry their packs for however long this hike was going to take.

Kelvin didn't respond.

"Kelvin?"

"I'm not the team captain. Decisions like that are her job." The man nodded toward Lacey.

In all the hustle, Victor had forgotten that Lacey had pulled the *Captain* bandana out of a bag Kelvin had passed around. "Is that okay, O'Connor?"

Lacey looked up from where she was pulling a pack out of her canoe. "Sorry, what was that?"

"I was just saying that Richard and I can portage the two-man canoes." He left it there. Heaven forbid he be accused of mansplaining again.

Lacey scanned the group. Louisa had taken a seat on a large rock and was moping her brow with her bandana, while the rest of them were standing or in the process of extracting their water bottles from their packs.

"Okay. Jen and I can do the three-man. Cassie and Louisa can have a break."

"I can portage." Louisa offered up her feeble protest from the ground.

"I know. But we need someone without a canoe on their head to navigate."

"Can I answer the call of nature first, Captain?" There was an edge of sarcasm in the way Cassie said *Captain*, but if Lacey noticed it, she gave no sign.

"Sure. Louisa, can you go with her?" The two headed off into the surrounding bush. Victor couldn't stop his gaze from following them. He was sure Kelvin wouldn't let them go wandering off if it was dangerous, but if someone got hurt out there, help was hours away, if not longer.

"I'm going to practice getting this canoe on my head. You in?" Jen shoved her water bottle back in her pack and turned to Lacey.

"Sure."

"Are you going to give us any instructions or just leave us to it?" Jen directed the question to Kelvin, who didn't even look up from his granola bar.

"My instructions are you have to work all this sort of stuff out by yourselves."

Victor didn't say anything. A canoe couldn't be that different from a scull, but he wasn't offering any advice unless he was asked for it.

"I think I know how. Let's do the two-man first. That'll be easier to start." Lacey walked to the side of the canoe she'd shared with Louisa. This should be interesting.

The two women stood beside the boat. Jen in the back, Lacey in the front. "Okay, so. Tip it on its side. Bend at the knees. Reach across with your right arm and grab the brace in the middle. Then as you stand, left hand goes across to the other side of the canoe and grabs the edge. Right hand comes off the brace and to the other side of the canoe. Then lift and flip."

They got about halfway through the lift before everything unraveled, and the canoe slipped from Jen's grasp. It was only Lacey grabbing the brace that stopped the canoe from hitting the ground.

"Okay, it might be easier if I do it myself and you watch."

"I can't wait to see this." Richard muttered from beside Victor. "She thinks because she's the captain that she's got some kind of wilderness superpowers?"

Lacey put the canoe back on the ground, then completed the whole maneuver by herself, spinning the canoe up and onto her head like a pro. Victor's hand itched to high five her as Richard's jaw sagged in disbelief.

"Who are you and what did you do with Lacey O'Connor?" Jen had her hands on her hips.

Lacey flipped the canoe back to the ground with ease. "I did a little canoeing when I was younger."

She said the words nonchalantly, and Victor had a vision of a vacation cottage on a lake and a pigtailed Lacey fishing with her dad.

"Show me again."

"Probably just a fluke." Richard was still not willing to let it go.

"Or maybe not." Victor countered as Lacey lifted the canoe and did it all again.

"Guess what!" Everyone turned as Cassie came sprinting out of the woods. Including Lacey. There was a blur of yellow as the canoe swung with her, then end smashed into Victor's nose.

"Ooooompf." He stumbled back, bringing his hand to his face as blood spurted. Beside him, Richard ducked as the tip of the canoe swooshed over his head before coming to an abrupt stop.

Lacey had it off her head and on the ground a few seconds later, then grabbed the first aid kit.

"Tip your head back." Her face wasn't far away from his as he leaned forward, his hand catching the blood dripping from his nose. Victor shook his head.

"Don't be so stubborn. Tip it back."

"O'Connor." Flip, it hurt. It had been long enough since he'd been last punched that he'd forgotten what a solid smack to the nose was like.

"What?"

"You may know canoes, but you don't know first aid. You tip your head forward. If I tip it back, the blood could run down my throat, and I could choke." He lifted his eyebrows at her. "Or is that what you're going for?"

She flushed, and he tried to smother a smile at seeing the

imperturbable Lacey O'Connor flustered.

"Well, since you clearly know more than I do, I assume you're okay to sort yourself out while I see what has Cassie so worked up." She handed him the first aid kit. "Kelvin said there should be something in here you can use to stem the bleeding."

"Got it. Just give me a couple of minutes."

Lacey stood. "Oh, and Carlisle."

"Yes, O'Connor?"

She smiled angelically at him. "Maybe don't stand so close next time."

The woman had nerve. He had to give her that.

LACEY HAD BEEN AWESOME LIFTING that canoe. She'd seen it in Richard's expression as he struggled to compute the person he'd assumed she was with the person in front of him.

There had been a second when she'd worried she was going to make a fool of herself, but it all came back to her as soon as she gripped the side, even though it had been over a decade. It had been easier than she remembered. The sleek Kevlar hull was a huge upgrade compared to her father's battered wooden canoe.

Then she'd gone and smacked Victor in the face and given him terrible first aid advice. Whatever upper hand she had gained, she'd lost in five seconds.

Whatever had excited Cassie didn't seem to be a thing any more, as the woman perched on her pack typing furiously into her phone.

Her phone?

"There's coverage here." Cassie held her phone aloft. "Only one bar, but you can get messages."

She was checking her phone while answering the call of nature? The mind boggled.

"Photos." Cassie said defensively, as if she read Lacey's mind. "I had it in my pocket because if I'm spending a week in Nevernever Land, I'm at least going to get some awesome photos out of it. And Brewsters have been talking about us pitching some kind of back-to-nature campaign. Thought I could kill two birds with one stone."

"Okay." There was no rule that said people couldn't have their phones, as far as she knew.

"Lacey." Kelvin appeared beside her. "We need to get moving. We don't want to risk still being on the next lake after dusk."

"Five minutes, everyone. Then we need to get going." Lacey called out so everyone could hear her.

Beside her, Jen tapped her phone off. "I can't get anything. Must be a different provider."

"Me neither." Louisa's face echoed disappointment. "I was hoping to send a message to my kids. I've never been away this long before."

Cassie looked to Louisa, to her phone, and back again. "Do you want to use mine?"

"Really?" Louisa's face lit up. "That would be great, thank you. I'll be fast."

"No rush." Cassie shrugged as she stood up and picked up her rucksack.

Just the thought of turning on her phone and seeing what was there was exhausting. Everyone who mattered wasn't expecting to hear from her for days yet. And she'd be stressed and distracted the second she saw the demands from clients.

But Cassie had a point about taking photos. Since Lacey had no plans to ever return, she should at least take some photos. Lakes and trees and sunsets would be exactly the kind of thing Anna would want to see when Lacey got out of here.

"Um, Lace." Jen had settled her pack on her back and was

looking at something over Lacey's shoulder. "Do you see what I see?"

Lacey turned around and scanned the area. Kelvin and Richard both had their rucksacks on. Victor was bent over his, tightening a strap on the top. Small waves lapped against the shore, the sun sitting at an angle that said it was about three o'clock. The trees stood sentry around them, and there wasn't another man-made object or group to be seen.

"What am I looking at?" Jen's expression wasn't one of concern, so she clearly hadn't seen anything she thought was dangerous.

"Just give it a second. Wait for Victor to stand up."

"Is this a trick? You want him to catch me staring at him when he looks up? The man has an ego the size of Everest. You know what he'll think."

Jen rolled her eyes. "Fine. You look away, and I'll let you know when to look back."

Lacey turned back to Louisa and Cassie. Cassie was slipping her phone back into her pocket. Louisa struggled to lift her pack. "Do you want some help?"

"That would be great."

Lacey lifted and held the bag while Louisa slipped her arms through. "Tighten your straps a bit more. It will give your back better support."

Louisa tugged on the straps until the bag rested flush against her back. "Like that?"

"Does it feel better?" Lacey lifted hers and shrugged it on, checking the straps.

"Yes, thanks."

"Now. Look now." Jen said the words loud enough that Cassie and Louisa both looked at her. Lacey casually glanced over her shoulder. Victor was standing, the first aid kit in one hand and water bottle in the other.

He seemed to have stopped bleeding, and a wad of gauze was stuck up his nose.

"Oh my gosh." Cassie half laughed, half gasped. "Is that—"

"Shh." Jen held her finger to her lips. "Lacey hasn't seen it yet."

Hadn't seen what? She looked again. This time she gave up on the attempt at subtle and turned around as Louisa let out a guffaw.

She was the last person to get it. She was never the last person to get anything! This time she started from the top of Victor's head and traveled down. Fine, fine, fine, fine, OH!

No, there was no way. She squinted. Next to her, Jen was silent laughing so hard her shoulders bounced, and tears streamed down her cheeks.

It wasn't gauze. It was a tampon. Victor Carlisle had a tampon shoved up his nose. The strings trailed from the bottom like the tails of a kite, traveling past his lips.

"Oh my gosh." She swung back into the women and they huddled like snails.

Louisa held her belly like a woman in labor. "I can't breathe." She gasped out the words.

"Do you think he knows what it is?"

"Of course not. No man would shove a tampon up his nose if he knew what it was." Cassie managed to get the words out between snorts of laughter.

There must have been some in the first aid kit. Of all the things he could have chosen.

"He has to be thirty-something. How can you reach thirty and not know what a tampon looks like?" Lacey hissed out the words, hoping the men would assume they were having some kind of women-only moment and stay away.

"It's more than possible." Jen wiped some tears off her cheek but more kept coming. "If he doesn't have any sisters and hasn't dated women who have enlightened him."

"Seriously?"

Cassie nodded. "I dated a guy once who had no idea what they were. I came home one night to find him throwing them around my apartment like they were some kind of mini-missile for my cat to chase. He was thirty-two."

A laugh burst from Lacey's chest at the image.

"Who's going to tell him?"

Everyone immediately put their thumbs to their heads like they were twelve and back at summer camp.

"You saw it first." Lacey looked at Jen.

"Nah uh. You're the one who smacked him in the nose, and you're team captain."

"You're the HR director."

Jen snorted. "Good try."

"Louisa, you have kids, right? You must have awkward conversations all the time. What's one more?"

The older woman grinned at her. "Which is exactly why I'm exempt from this one."

Lacey was not telling Victor Carlisle he had a sanitary product up his nose. No way, no how. Because if they were right and he had no idea, she would then have to explain to him what it was.

Lacey would rather teach sex ed to thirty ninth graders than have that conversation. "We could not tell him."

The other three looked at her. "What? How long can he keep it there? An hour? He'll have his head under a canoe for most of that time."

Cassie shook her head. "You can't let him carry a canoe for who knows how long with that thing hanging out of his nose."

"It is not my fault if he has reached however old he is without enlightening himself as to some specific facts of life. Why should it be my job to tell him?"

Jen pulled her dark curls back in her hands, then let them fall loose again. "Let's vote. Hands up, who votes Lacey has to tell Victor." Three hands shot up in the air.

Traitors.

VICTOR HAD BEEN SENT OVER by Kelvin to break up the women, who were huddled together like a high school clique.

His nose throbbed like his heart had just taken up residence and was pumping all the blood to his body via his sinuses. At least he'd managed to stop the worst of the bleeding.

A cauldron of low words and fierce whispers emanated from the pack. "Hands up, who votes Lacey has to tell Victor." Jen's voice carried over to him.

Huh? What did this have to do with him?

Three hands shot up, while Lacey's remained folded. He could tell by the way her elbows stuck out like wings.

"Tell Victor what?" Might as well announce his presence before someone looked up and thought he was eavesdropping.

Three heads came up. Jen and Louisa fanned out to stand beside Cassie as Lacey slowly turned around, rocks crunching underneath her hiking boots.

She cast a defiant look at her smirking compatriots. "Nothing. It's fine. We should get going."

"O'Connor." He drew out the last syllable of her name. Whatever it was, she had might as well get it out. They were going to all be here a few days yet.

"What?" She snapped.

"I'm pretty sure you were outvoted. Which means you have to tell me."

"No one said this was a democracy."

"Don't make me start guessing. Because my first guess is that you are hopelessly and madly in love with me."

At that, Jen laughed out loud.

"You think I'm terribly irresistible and want to ask to share my tent tonight." Victor waggled his eyebrows at her, knowing entire ice ages would pass before that would be it.

Lacey crossed her arms. "Don't be ridiculous."

He took a step closer because it would unsettle her. And because his curiosity was now killing him. "Should I keep guessing, or are you going to tell me?"

She stayed her ground. "You're going to be sorry."

"I'll take my chances."

"Fine." She cocked her chin. "You have a tampon up your nose. Happy?"

He had a what up his nose? His finger touched the circular cotton wad he'd found in the first aid kit. It had wedged in his left nostril perfectly. "This?"

"Yes."

The three musketeers behind her were laughing so hard that two of them were doubled over. Must be an American thing.

"You're going to have to fill me in on the joke, O'Connor."

"It's not a nosebleed stopper. It's a women's sanitary product."

Something flashed back to him from Year 8 health class when a mortified teacher had taught them human reproduction.

"I have a sanitary product up my nose." If he stopped and thought about this in any detail, he would be as embarrassed as Lacey. But watching her squirm was worth any and all embarrassment.

"Yes."

He stepped forward. "It makes an excellent nosebleed stopper. Think of the cross-marketing opportunities."

"I'd rather not."

"Are you embarrassed by the miracle of the human body, O'Connor?" He pulled out another random fact from health class. "Did you know, you had all your eggs before you were even born?"

She looked him straight in the eye. "You seriously want to talk about my eggs, Carlisle?"

Um, nope. No, he didn't. He had fallen into a trap entirely of his own making.

Lacey stepped forward with a hint of a smile on her lips and for a second—a foolish self-indulgent second—he allowed his gaze to linger on them. Then she reached up and yanked the cotton bud out of his nose.

"Ouch!"

She looked at his face for a second. "It's stopped bleeding. You're good. Let's go."

And another round to Lacey.

Losing was not a feeling Victor was familiar with. And it wasn't one he planned on getting used to.

CHAPTER NINE

IT HAD BEEN THE LONGEST day possible, short of crossing the international date line. Starting with a three a.m. wake-up call and a red-eye flight and ending with canoeing. They had canoed and portaged and canoed some more. Now, the last peg had finally gone in the last tent, and camp setup was completed under the glow of flashlight, the sun long since having turned in. The one-hour time difference between New York and here felt like about ten.

Everything about Lacey was tired. Even her *eggs* were tired.

Lacey hadn't given her eggs a thought in the last decade, except for when tech companies offered to pay for their employees to freeze theirs and a fierce debate had erupted between her colleagues as to whether comped egg freezing was the hallmark of a great employer or patriarchy gone mad.

Then Victor Carlisle had to go and make a comment about her eggs—one she knew from the glint in his eye had been purely to fluster her—and she had proceeded to spend the next hour wandering through the wilderness with a canoe on her head and contemplating how weird it was that all the mini-half-hers existed before she was even born.

Cassie and Jen had almost finished dinner. Prepreparered food that appeared out of vacuum-packed bags. Thank goodness. She probably would have cried if Kelvin had pulled out a bag of vegetables and told them to start chopping. The Minnesota girl might still exist deep down inside, but the Minnesota girl's fitness did not.

Richard appeared beside her. He was some kind of crisis PR manager from Wyndham, the kind of guy who would act all appalled at sexual harassment but be the first to laugh at a smutty joke.

"Kelvin said I had to give this to you." He handed her an envelope with "Team Challenge" typed across the front. Lacey groaned.

Just when she'd thought the day couldn't get any longer.

"Everyone get your food and gather round. We have a team challenge." There was a collective groan, but within a few minutes, everyone had plates of food and were sitting in a circle around the smoldering fire.

Lacey held up the envelope with one hand while scooping up the bland stew with her fork. "Who wants to read it?"

"I will." Louisa reached out from beside her and Lacey passed the envelope over.

Ripping open the end of the rectangle, Louisa fished out a piece of paper. "Getting to know each other." She flipped the paper over. "There are three questions below. Each team member has to choose one question to ask another team member. Questions can only be asked twice, and every person has to answer a question. Points awarded for openness and vulnerability."

Louisa looked up as almost everyone shifted uncomfortably. "The topics are biggest regret, first love, scariest moment. Should I start?"

Shrugs and mumbles of assent around the circle.

Louisa looked around the group. "Jen, scariest moment."

Jen poked her dinner with a fork for a second, then placed her plate down on the ground. "When I was twelve years old, my dad got pulled over on a traffic stop. They said later that our car matched the description of a stolen vehicle, even though the plates were completely different. The truth was they were suspicious of a black man driving a nice car. He pulled over and placed his hands on the steering wheel. He told me to watch. That if anything happened, I needed to be able to tell people that he had his hands in view the entire time."

Lacey's gut dropped like a rock thrown into a pond.

Jen shifted her legs, pulling them into her body. No one said a word. Even the wildlife around them seemed to have frozen. "The next thing I know, there's a cop pointing a gun in the window. I'm screaming. They're asking for his license and registration, but when he moves his hand to get them the cop starts yelling and waving his gun and telling my dad to keep his hands where he can see them. I thought they were going to shoot him on the spot. That's the scariest moment of my life."

No one said a word. Or even breathed.

"What happened?" Louisa asked the question everyone was thinking.

"They got my dad out of the car, had him spread-eagled over the hood. Made me get the registration out of the glove compartment and his license out of his wallet. After they'd checked them, they just got in their car and drove away. No apology. No explanation. Nothing."

Jen picked up her plate. "My dad sold his car and bought an older generic model. He's Head of Pediatrics at Boston General, and he still refuses to own a car less than ten years old."

Jen won. Jen won, and Lacey didn't want to play this stupid game any more.

Nobody spoke until Jen looked up from her plate. "I think that makes it my turn."

Louisa passed the piece of paper to Jen who didn't even

glance at it. "Lacey, first love?"

Any answer she could give to any question felt trite after what they'd just heard. Across the fire Jen gave her a nod, as if knowing what she was thinking.

She'd end up at the bottom of the scoring, but that was fine. She'd get her points another way. "I don't have one." It was true. She'd only been seventeen. Who even knew what love was at seventeen? The most that could be said was that she'd mistaken deep like for love. When she was seventeen. Not now. Now she would crawl over broken glass to have never met Damon or his two-faced parents.

Right, who to ask next. "Okay—"

"You've never been in love?" Cassie asked, incredulous. Like Lacey had said she didn't believe in oxygen. Or martinis. Or the US Constitution.

"High school? College? There must have been someone. How old are you?"

"Thirty-two."

"You can't go thirty-two years and not have fallen in love at least once. Even if it was unrequited." Louisa stuck her oar in.

Lacey sighed. "There was a guy in high school. But I wasn't in love with him. I probably could have been if it had lasted longer, but it didn't."

"What happened?"

Lacey picked up her fork and dug it into an attempt at mashed potato. "His parents didn't like me."

"Why not?"

Fine. If she was in this, she had might as well get some points for it. She reached for the easiest answer. "He was the only son of the local pastor. My parents are happy heathens who worship at the altar of football. It would be fair to say they didn't think we were a good match."

She'd gone to their church and joined the youth group and even begun to think all the things Damon's dad preached from the pulpit might be true. Worse, she'd let herself dream that maybe she had a future in their family.

Never mind that they were only seventeen. Never mind that she'd already determined to get out of Small Harbor as soon as she graduated. Never mind that she had a 3.8 GPA and would graduate valedictorian. She'd been ready to trade all of that in because for the first time in her life she'd felt like she belonged somewhere.

Then Damon's cousin had gone and gotten her sister pregnant.

Her friends thought she didn't believe in God. The truth was she'd found out a long time ago that God didn't believe in her. And, quite frankly, she had enough of that in her life without Him weighing in.

"His loss." The defensive words came from Cassie, but when she looked up, it was Victor studying her. As if knowing there was more to the story than she had admitted to. But wasn't there always?

She squirmed under his gaze as if she needed to escape her own skin.

"Victor, biggest regret."

It was unfair her asking that, given she knew a whole lot about him while he had no clue who she was. But she wanted to know what he would say in a group of people he thought knew hardly anything about him. What would he admit to?

"It's a pretty long list."

At that, everyone's gaze zoomed in on him.

Victor rubbed his hand through his hair, the light of the fire making his scar appear even more ominous. "Um, but just one. Okay, right. Five years ago, I was based in LA. My cousin lived there too. We were out together one night. Her fiancé had just broken up with her, and she was upset. She wanted me to get her some coke. I refused, but she got some from someone else. So I cut a line for her. I made it the smallest I could. Well, I tried, but truth is I wasn't exactly sober either. And then I got a cab and took her home. I offered to stay, but she said she was fine. So I left. A few hours later, she was dead."

His gaze flickered up, caught hers for a second, then darted away. No one said a word.

"The coroner recorded it as an open verdict because he couldn't decide if it was a suicide, or an accidental overdose because she was too wasted to form the required intent."

It was a story Lacey knew, yet didn't. She knew her cousin's side of the story. The one that had almost ruined Emelia. She knew the story that cast Victor as the feckless, selfish addict who cared about no one other than himself.

"So my greatest regret is that if I had insisted on sleeping on Anita's couch that night, she might still be alive."

CHAPTER TEN

THE SUN WAS CRESTING OVER the horizon when Lacey crawled out of her tent in the morning, Jen still softly snoring on the bedroll beside hers.

Everyone had gone to bed tired and subdued, the questions adding a mental weight onto the physical exhaustion.

Her tent mate had fallen into a coma-like sleep as soon as she'd hit the sleeping mat, giving in to the exhaustion of a brutal twenty-hour day. But Lacey had stared into the darkness for a couple of hours, her brain struggling with the dissonance between the Victor she knew about secondhand and the man who had sat opposite the fire from her, his face weathered with grief and regret.

Part of her wished he knew who she was. Then she could believe it had been a story spun for her consumption, an attempt at manipulating her into believing he was a better person than he really was. But he didn't, and it wasn't. She knew what real regret was. Was so intimate with its haunting grip that it was easy to see it mirrored in someone else.

Pushing herself to her feet, she surveyed the campsite. No one else was up yet. And the group had at least two loud snorers, going by the sounds coming from two different tents.

The rustle of the breeze through the trees and occasional birdcall were the only other sounds. Back home, Wednesday was trash collection day. Birds were nice enough, but part of her missed the comforting familiarity of the machinery and cussing that accompanied the collection.

Her skin felt tight, and her eyes gritty. She needed a shower. She couldn't see herself—and she was glad—but as she'd braided her hair, she'd felt its usual smoothness replaced with kinks. Testimony to the hair appointment she'd had to miss thanks to the cocktail party. It would probably be a halo of fuzz around her head by the end of the trip.

"C'mon, you're the captain. Do something useful." She muttered the direction under her breath. Might as well get the coffee started. No doubt at least half the group would need coffee before they would be able to face whatever this day held for them. Lacey lowered the bag containing the cooking equipment from the tree branch it was slung over, her arms complaining with every tug, and extracted the small camping stove and coffee pot.

What was the whole point of this thing? She felt aimless without a goal. Without a target. Get a book on the NYT Best Seller list. Move fifty thousand copies in the first week. Land author interviews on *Good Morning America*. Figure out the right twist to get a social media post to go viral. All those things were straightforward and measurable. She knew when she had achieved them, and she knew when she failed.

Canoeing through the wilderness with a ragtag bunch of colleagues for who knew how long with no known scoring system measuring her performance? That was a form of torture.

She placed the coffee pot on a smooth stump and had just filled it with filtered water when there was the sound of another tent zipper opening. She glanced up to see Victor's head poke through the flap, followed by the rest of his body.

Standing, he stretched, his frame dwarfing the two-person tent he was sharing with Richard. He must have slept curled up or with his head and feet pressed against opposite ends of the shelter.

"Morning." Lacey stood and tried to sound casual. She felt oddly exposed after the conversation the previous night. Not that she had shared anything *that* personal. Not compared to him. But still. She had a strict rule about keeping her personal and business lives as separate as the east was from the west. The only other time she'd broken it was when she'd agreed to work for Rachel and her Aunt Donna on their books.

"Morning." Victor brushed a hand through his hair. "Looks like it's going to be a nice one."

He was right. The air was crisp but hinted at warmth to come. The breeze stirred through the trees, promising some relief when they were out on the lake. The stillness was almost deafening. Her body was primed for noise after years of cars, sirens, and the buzz of people stacked on top of and beside each other in all directions.

Even worse, far from looking out of his comfort zone, Victor looked completely at ease in his surroundings as he shoved his feet into his boots and laced them up, his T-shirt stretching across his shoulders as he bent over.

Stop it, Lacey! "How'd you sleep?"

"Not bad. Even if Richard snores like he's in hibernation."

As if to underscore his point, a loud rumble came from the tent behind him and Lacey stifled a laugh. "Do you camp a lot?"

Victor shrugged. "Not since I was a teenager. But there were training camps when I was rowing. After sharing a dorm with five men, sharing a tent with one isn't really a hardship. You?"

"A bit when I was younger." An understatement if ever there was one. Great chunks of her childhood memories involved "adventuring" as her father called it. It was only in her twenties that she'd realized it had been one of her parents' ways of trying to save on the electric bill. And that her tendency to leave every light on in her condo was her sign of defiance.

"That looked like a deep thought."

Lacey jumped. Victor was suddenly a whole lot closer to her than he had been a few seconds ago. "Not at all, unfortunately."

Victor squinted at her like he didn't believe her but left it alone. "What do you need me to do? Should we get started on breakfast?"

"Um, sure." Lacey stepped back, her movement stopped by a log behind her. "Do you know where the meal plan is? There's a certain order we need to eat the food in." Lacey peered into the bag holding the cooking equipment, looking for the folder that Kelvin had referred to the night before. Reaching in, she extracted it and held it out to Victor. "It should be in here."

Victor's fingers grazed hers as he took it, and an unwanted and inconvenient spark traveled up her arm.

He looked at her a couple of seconds longer than necessary, and Lacey's breath stalled in her lungs. He couldn't recognize her now. What if he did? She could brush it off, saying she hadn't said anything because she knew it would be awkward, but there was no doubt the rest of the trip would then be exactly that.

"Right." She forced the breezy words out. "You sort the food, and I'll sort the coffee."

She broke their gaze. Where had she been in the process before Victor had thrown her equilibrium?

She picked up the coffee pot just to have something to do with her hands. As she did, movement in the undergrowth caught her eye, and her spine stiffened. Most of the predators in the wilderness were nocturnal and would be tucked up in bed by now. A bear would be making more noise.

As she watched, a raccoon weaved then stumbled out of a bush. "Uh, oh."

"What's that?" Victor turned around, his gaze lighting on the rodent.

Lacey didn't say anything.

"Aww. Hey, little fella. Good morning to you."

Good morning to you? What had he been smoking in his tent?

"Should we give him something to eat?"

Lacey only half-listened to Victor's prattling. Her gaze focused on where the raccoon righted himself, only to make it a few more steps before taking another stumble.

"We probably have some leftovers from last night. What if we put them in a bowl for him? Or do raccoons prefer dry food? Cereal? Biscuits?"

She tuned back into Victor just as he reached for the rope that strung up the bag containing their food. "Victor," she kept her voice steady. "Do not touch that rope."

"Why not?"

The stupid man was in shorts. If he went near the raccoon and it bit him on the leg, he'd have to be medevaced.

"I need you to come and step behind me. The coon probably has rabies."

"What makes you think that?"

Victor, because he was an idiot, didn't take so much as a step toward her.

"Raccoons are nocturnal. If you see one during the day, there's a good chance it has rabies. If you see one out in the day and it is weaving and stumbling like a drunkard, then it almost definitely has rabies."

Reaching down, Lacey picked up a rock the size of her fist and hefted it in the direction of the coon. "Shoo! Go away!" The animal blinked but made no attempt to retreat. Instead, it took another couple of steps in her direction.

Victor threw another rock. It landed near the raccoon. "Scat!

Off you go!" Again, it blinked but stayed its ground.

Shoot. She was going to have to use her gun. She was going to have to use her gun, and the Brit would freak. But the coon was only a few feet away from Louisa and Cassie's tent. If one of them came out and gave it a fright, it might go for them.

Victor was off to her right. There was no chance she would accidentally shoot him. She was an excellent shot. But she couldn't take any chances that he would do something that could put himself in danger either.

"Victor." She kept her voice low and clear. "In three seconds I'm going to shoot the raccoon. I need you behind me when I do." Crouching down, she lifted up her pant leg and pulled her Glock out of its holster, clasping both hands around the grip. She stood, keeping the gun facing toward the ground.

Victor dropped an astounded expletive just as Jen's head popped out of their tent. Excellent. "What's all the—"

"Get back in the tent, Jen. I need to shoot this coon."

Jen's head went back in the tent, and the zipper went down without another question.

"Is that real?" Victor asked the question in the kind of annoying tone men used when they thought they were entitled to an immediate answer.

"No, I came into the wilderness with a pretend gun." Seriously. How much stupid did she have to deal with before the sun had even gotten above the trees? "For the last time, you need to get behind me." Lacey racked the slide, and the rasping sound seemed to make her point because the man suddenly found his legs.

Lacey scanned her surroundings. There was nothing in her direct line of fire other than the raccoon and trees. If she missed the coon—which she wouldn't—the trajectory of the bullet would send it into the ground.

She could feel Victor behind her, his gaze boring into the back of her body. But at least he'd stopped asking questions.

Deep breath, loosen shoulders, sight the target. Out of her peripheral vision, Lacey saw the zipper on Cassie and Louisa's tent start traveling up. The raccoon took another step, and Lacey lined up the shot and pulled the trigger. A sharp crack sounded, and the coon dropped to the ground just as a tousled head appeared out of the tent.

Cassie took one look at Lacey with her still-pointed weapon and started screaming.

LACEY HAD PULLED OUT A handgun and shot that raccoon as coolly as if she was doing something as innocuous as tying her boot.

Five minutes later, Victor's heart still thundered in his chest as if she'd aimed the gun at him.

The raccoon—deader than a dead thing—was still splayed out on the ground. A small pool of blood seeped from underneath. If it wasn't for that, it could have been mistaken for being asleep.

The gunshot and Cassie's hysteria had gotten everyone out of their tents faster than if Meredith herself had appeared to do roll call. Including Kelvin, who thundered out of his tent in a pair of long johns like a buffalo was chasing him.

"Permit." Kelvin barked the word at Lacey. She dug into her pocket, extracted a card, and handed it to him. Kelvin studied it with an expression that was half relief, half exasperation. "What were you thinking, bringing a gun into the BWCA without notifying me?"

"You didn't ask, and nothing on the paperwork said there was a notification requirement." Lacey was as calm as anyone Victor had ever seen.

"You could have killed someone."

At that Lacey flared. "There was no chance of that. I am an excellent shot. I cleared my surroundings, I took aim, and I made my shot."

"Coon hunting ended on March 31."

"I wasn't hunting."

"And you let off a firearm within 150 yards of a campsite."

"I had a reasonable belief the raccoon posed a danger. We tried other ways to scare him off, but they were not sufficient. He was showing all the risk signs of rabies. I had no choice."

"We? Who's we?"

Lacey jerked her head toward Victor. "Victor was helping me fix breakfast."

Victor, who had thought the raccoon was cute and wanted to feed it. He had never felt stupider. And by the scathing way Lacey had looked at him, he wasn't the only one.

"Is that true? Did you try other methods?"

Was it true? His brain seemed to have frozen on the moment he turned around and saw Lacey wielding a handgun like he'd somehow found himself in a Bond movie.

"Um, yes. I think so."

Now Kelvin narrowed in on him. "You think so?"

Victor forced his brain past the blond-wielding-a-deadly-weapon moment. "Yes. We both threw rocks near it to try and scare it away."

"And what did it do?"

Victor shrugged. "Just stumbled around."

Kelvin turned his attention back to Lacey. "You should have come and gotten me."

"I didn't know if you were in your tent, and I was worried about the target's proximity to Louisa and Cassie's tent."

The target's proximity. She said it like the pile of fur hadn't been a living thing only ten minutes ago. Yes, it was just a raccoon, but still.

Lacey had had a gun holstered against her leg the entire time they spent together the last couple of days. His brain was entirely incapable of knowing how to process that revelation.

If the whole book publicity thing didn't work out, she'd have an excellent career in the CIA.

"Did you bring a gun across state lines illegally?" Kelvin suddenly seemed to become aware that he was still in his long johns—ones that left very little to the imagination if Victor did say so himself.

Lacey gave Kelvin an even more scathing look than she'd given Victor. "I flew here. That's literally impossible without getting arrested."

Kelvin sighed and seemed to give up. "Okay, well go and dispose of the body. We need to break camp and get moving."

Lacey stood, grabbed the spade they'd used to dig their latrines and used it to scoop up the carcass in one smooth move.

"Jen, want to come with me to get rid of this thing?"

Jen wrinkled her nose and held up her mug. "Not on your life and certainly not before I've finished my coffee."

Victor looked around and realized that while Lacey had been getting scolded, the others had wandered off to fix breakfast.

"I'll come." He'd been about to feed the thing. He might as well help bury it.

"Fine. Let's go so I can have some coffee before it's all gone." Holding the shovel in front of her, Lacey dove into the nearest woods, her confident steps weaving through trees and over logs.

"How far do we have to go?"

"Not far. A wolf or coyote will find it tonight. You just don't want it to be too close to the campsite."

"So um," Victor cleared his throat. "What kind of gun is that?"

"It's a Glock. A G19 semiautomatic handgun, if you'd like to be exact." Lacey hopped up onto a log and down the other side. Now Victor looked, he could see a slight change in one pant leg where it crested over the holster. But someone would have to be looking for it to even suspect.

"Do you always carry a gun?" Lacey O'Connor did not fit the mental image he'd had in his head of someone who walked around with a loaded weapon. But given what had just happened, it looked like he was going to have to redraw that image.

The side of her mouth lifted. "Not all the time."

Great. So he only had to worry about it some of the time. But presumably all of the time during this particular part of Meredith's little sorting of the wheat from the chaff.

"Can I hold it?" He immediately regretted that question as she and her dead raccoon swung around and stared at him.

"No, you can't hold it. It's not a toy. It's a lethal weapon, and we are in the middle of nowhere, not on a supervised gun range."

"So why do you have it?"

Lacey sucked in a breath. "Because I have a permit from the great state of Minnesota that says that I can. And you should be grateful I do and that I was up. If it wasn't for me, you would have fed breakfast to a rabies-riddled rodent. And if it had bitten you, you'd have required a medical airlift to get you to a hospital." She stopped. "This should be far enough." Flipping her shovel, she dumped the animal on the ground.

"I'm surprised you didn't let it bite me then."

"Why would I do that?" Lacey tucked the shovel back under her arm.

"C'mon. It never crossed your mind to let me fall victim to my own stupidity? It would have meant one less person to compete with."

Lacey turned and started walking back the way they had come in. Everything looked the same to him. Trees, bushes, dirt, but she strode on confidently, seeing some path he didn't. "It might have occurred to me if you were an actual threat. But you aren't. What are you going for? Middle management?"

"Senior management." He immediately regretted his admission—something he seemed to be having a streak of today. He shouldn't have said anything. Should have let her think he was going for a more junior position.

Lacey laughed as if he had said something hilarious. His pride prickled. *Don't say anything. Just let her believe whatever she wants.*

It wasn't the first time he had been underestimated, and it certainly wouldn't be the last. It would make success that much sweeter and defeat ... Well, if he failed, at least she wouldn't know he had ever tried.

CHAPTER ELEVEN

IF LACEY HAD THOUGHT SHE was in pain after the first day of canoeing, by the end of the second day, she was pretty sure even her eyelashes were yelling at her.

She wasn't the only one. As the day progressed, everyone had gotten shorter with each other. By the end of dinner, most people had disintegrated into grunts and wincing movements. The minute dinner had been cleaned up, and the sun had disappeared over the horizon, people disappeared into their tents like rabbits into a warren.

"So," Jen whispered from across the small distance between their bed mats. "How's it going, Team Captain?"

"Everything hurts." Lacey muffled a groan.

"The rest of us mortals have been feeling it since the first hour. Glad you could finally join us." There was the sound of the bed shifting, and Lacey turned her head to make out the profile of Jen's head propped up on her elbow. "So ..."

"So ..." Lacey was too tired to play games. If Jen had a question, she was going to have to come out and ask it.

"I'd always tagged you as a Connecticut girl. But as I thought about it today, I realized you've never told me where you grew up. I'm not even close, am I?"

Lacey had never lied about where she'd come from. People had assumed, and she'd let them. "I grew up here. In a town a couple of hours from Duluth."

"Is your family still here?"

"Yes."

"You never talk about them. Your family, I mean."

"It's complicated." Lacey knew all about Jen's family, even though she'd never met any of them. Jen had the type of family who talked every day and went on holidays together. It was about as far from Lacey's family as she could imagine.

"What about Victor? Is he complicated too?"

Lacey rolled over at the sudden change in topic. She'd taken out the braid for the night and regretted it as her hair flopped in her face. "Not even close."

"He watches you, you know."

"I'm sure he does. I'm the competition." Thank goodness it was dark, and Jen couldn't see the flush Lacey felt chasing up her neck.

"Uh-huh." It was impressive how much skepticism the woman managed to fit into two syllables.

"Besides, he's my cousin's fiancé's brother."

There. That silenced her for a second.

"So you already knew each other?"

"No." Why had she said anything? Now she was going to have to tell Jen the rest. Otherwise, she'd put her foot in her mouth with Victor. "He doesn't know who I am. I mean, I'm pretty sure he knows Emelia has a cousin called Lacey, but he doesn't know I'm that Lacey."

"And you don't think you should've mentioned that?"

"Victor and his brother don't have a great relationship. I guess I didn't want him to feel weird. Like I might be reporting back on him."

"Hmm." The sound was a drowsy one. "Well, you're going to have to tell him soon. Otherwise, it's going to be super weird when he finds out."

Jen was right. "Maybe I'll tell him at the end of this trip."

Silence from the other side of the tent. When Lacey looked over, Jen's head was buried in her pillow, her curls sticking up in the shadows like a halo.

Lacey rolled onto her back and stared at the low ceiling of the tent. Even though her body was weary, her brain was still buzzing.

She and Victor had barely spoken to each other since breakfast. Coincidence, or was he avoiding her? She didn't really care. Hopefully, he now believed her to be some kind of gun-slinging redneck and would keep his distance for the rest of the trip.

It may make her a horrible person, but she didn't like Victor not being the person she'd had in her head for over five years. A version that had been reinforced by her cousin's tales of his fecklessness, run-ins with the law and propensity to swing first and ask questions later. Not to mention Anita's death.

She tossed over again, unable to find a comfortable spot. Beside her, Jen's breathing had deepened. She thought she'd done an okay job today as captain—if she ignored the coon incident, because who knew if that would add or take away her score. But she still had ground to make up. Everyone had their eye on the prize. Everyone had shared more than her the previous night. So, if Meredith was going for some kind of vulnerable leader schtick, she was even further behind.

Beside her, Jen let out a little snuffle and rolled toward Lacey, making the small tent seem smaller still. Half an hour of deep breathing exercises later, sleep was no closer than it had been when she'd first laid down.

Lacey pulled her hoodie over her head, slipped her feet into flip flops, grabbed her gun, and crawled out of the tent. There were more dangerous things roaming around at night than the day.

The May air nipped around her. She reached back into the tent and dragged out her sleeping bag, unzipped it and wrapped it around her body, holding it in place with one hand.

They'd set up camp a short distance from the water, and she wandered down to where the lake lapped the edges and the moonlight streamed down, glimmering off the surface. It was lighter out here than in the tent as the stars held vigil in the sky.

Someone else was there. Standing at the water's edge. Of course, he was.

Lacey turned to retreat back to her tent, but her sleeping bag scraping across the ground was like a thunderclap across the still night. Victor turned toward her.

"You shouldn't be out here alone at night. It's not safe." Her reprimand carried across the distance between them.

Victor grinned at her. "Then I guess it's good that my personal bodyguard is back on duty."

Against her will Lacey found herself approaching the lakeshore. "What are you doing?"

Victor leaned down and picked up a couple of rocks off the ground. "I used to be really good at skipping rocks when I was a kid. I'm trying to get my mojo back."

Quite frankly, Lacey could do without thinking about Victor Carlisle and his mojo. Especially with the moonlight making him look like he existed on the other side of an Instagram filter.

Victor turned back to the river and spun the rock in his hand across the surface. It skipped once, twice, before sinking. Not bad. But she was better.

"Prove it."

"Prove what?"

Victor shook his head at her. "You've got that look on your face. You can beat me. Prove it."

It unsettled her that he could read her so easily. "I haven't tried to skip a rock in years." She couldn't even remember when. Probably the summer she had left.

"So you're conceding? I get to claim rock skipping?"

"I never said that." Without fully realizing what she was doing, Lacey dropped her adapted cloak and leaned down, palming the slimmest, smoothest pebbles she could find.

Looking up, she saw a glimmer of victory cross Victor's face, one he smoothly erased as soon as he saw her looking at him.

She pulled the magazine from her gun, stashed it in her pocket, and handed the gun to Victor. "Hold this."

Turning her attention to the lake, she eyed up the distance between her and the water, then crouched down and sent her pebble sailing across the air. It skipped once ... then sank.

Once! She hadn't skipped a rock once since she was a toddler. She could do three blindfolded with a boulder.

Palming her second pebble, she gave it a rub and a kiss and sent it flying. Once ... twice ... then under the water. A growl of frustration purred in the back of her throat.

"Not your best night, O'Connor?" Beside her, Victor let a pebble fly, and it skipped four times. Four!

She crouched down to pick up more pebbles, as did Victor. The grip of her gun peered out from where he'd tucked it into the waistband of his shorts.

Which was fine. She had the mag tucked safely in her pocket. Her body stiffened as it registered something before her brain did.

The chamber. She hadn't cleared the chamber before she'd given Victor the gun. And the gun would have automatically put one in there after she'd shot the raccoon.

"Victor." The odds of the gun going off accidentally were pretty much nil, but Victor didn't know it might be loaded. Given the casual way he had it stuffed down the back of his shorts, he'd probably be equally casual about getting it out again.

If he decided to pretend he was in some action movie and wrapped his finger around the trigger with the light pull ... her stomach bottomed out just thinking about it.

"What's up, O'Connor?"

"Don't move. I'm getting my gun."

His eyes widened, and his gaze darted around, trying to find the threat, not knowing it was in his pants. Lacey covered the distance, trying to ignore the heat emanating off his body as she reached around his body and grabbed the gun by its grip, careful to avoid the trigger.

Sliding it free from his waistband, she quickly cleared the chamber and tucked the bullet into her pocket.

"What the heck, O'Connor?"

Victor murmured the words, and she suddenly realized how close they were still standing. Their gazes locked, and his breath wafted across her lips.

Lacey forced herself to take a step back. "Sorry. I ... may have forgotten to clear the chamber."

Victor blinked. "Are you telling me I had a loaded gun down the back of my shorts?" His accent became even more pronounced as he said the words, his scar twitching.

"Yeah. Kind of." Lacey held the gun firm in her hand, berating herself for her thoughtlessness. Her father had raised her to be meticulous about gun safety. All it had taken was one hot British guy on a moonlit night, and she was giving a loaded gun to someone who had no idea how to handle it. What was wrong with her?

Victor squinted at her. "Did you do it on purpose? So you had a handy reason to distract me when you got trounced at stone skipping?"

"Don't be ridiculous." She slid the gun into her hoodie pocket, making sure the magazine was aligned with the barrel. "And I was not getting trounced. I was just warming up. I told you it's been a few years."

Victor smirked down at her. "You go right ahead and tell yourself that."

VICTOR TRIED NOT TO GRIN as Lacey's shoulders got closer to her ears and her scowl deeper as stone after stone sunk on the second or third skip. She'd forgotten the number one rule of skipping. Relax.

Meanwhile, he rubbed salt into her wound with his cheerful whistling as he managed consecutive fours and the occasional five.

Lacey O'Connor was used to being good at everything she did. That much had become clear as she refused to concede. Victor had lost track of time, but he was pretty sure they had to have been out here for at least an hour. The shore beneath their feet was dotted with grainy patches, as all the suitable skipping stones were now in the lake.

"Feel free to let me know when you'd like some tips," Victor called as his latest rock skipped past Lacey's sinking stone.

Her response was basically a snarl, her blond waves buffeting on the breeze. This was not the polished Lacey O'Connor of their first meeting in the New York office. This was the stripped-back version, and he had the sense that not many people got to meet her.

At least the gun wasn't loaded.

Any more.

He still couldn't believe he'd shoved a loaded Glock down the back of his pants without even thinking about it. Almost worse was the way all his senses had stood to attention for the few seconds Lacey had brushed against him as she'd taken back possession.

He hadn't dated anyone since he'd gotten out of rehab. Hadn't wanted to. Hadn't been interested. Now was the worst possible time for that interest to flare back up again. Lacey was American. Lacey was his competition. Anything with Lacey would get one—or both—of them fired. Not to mention Lacey thought he was a stupid Neanderthal.

Lacey, of course, had been all business. For all he knew, she was in a relationship.

Even if she wasn't, she was too good for him. Any woman was too good for him but especially her.

Peter was going to be marrying the love of his life soon. At least he and Emelia might be able to provide his parents with some longed-for grandchildren. Hopefully, sooner rather than later.

And Victor? Well, he would be the fun bachelor uncle. If Peter ever trusted him enough for even that role.

Lacey muttered something under her breath as her next stone sunk, then bent down and scooped up another handful.

Victor dropped to the ground and sat on Lacey's sleeping bag, rubbing his hands along his arms. He hadn't planned to be out here half the night when he'd given up on tossing and turning and come down to the lake. At this rate, he'd be sleeping here before she'd give in. "You just let me know whenever you're ready to concede," he called as she sent another stone rocketing into the water. He didn't watch. She'd be lucky if it skipped once.

She whipped around, holding her hair back with her hand. "Fine. Tell me what I'm doing wrong."

"You need to relax."

"I am relaxed!" Lacey's hands clenched by her sides as she whisper-shouted the words.

Victor couldn't stop himself from laughing. The woman was wound tight as one of the clockwork trains he'd had as a kid.

"Take a deep breath, loosen your shoulders, think happy thoughts." He'd thought about rowing. About how it felt to be flying across the water when everything was in sync.

Lacey shook out her arms, took a deep breath, and let her stone fly. One, two, almost three. Probably the best she'd done all night. Not that she'd admit it.

She turned, trudged back to where he was sitting, and lay on the ground. Her hair fanned out around her head like a fallen angel as she stared up at him. "This is not me conceding. This is me taking a break."

Seriously? What was it going to take? The sun creeping back over the horizon? Not that he was complaining about being on a lakeshore in the middle of nowhere with a beautiful woman, but it had to be almost one in the morning. If today was anything like yesterday, some sleep would probably be a good idea. "O'Connor, you're a terrible loser. You know that, right?"

She bit her lip. "It may have been mentioned once or twice in my life." She wrinkled her nose at him. "I prefer to think of it as strong-minded."

Victor had kissed a lot of women in his life. Many he couldn't even remember. But he had never wanted to kiss anyone quite like he wanted to kiss this strong-minded fierce woman with halo hair.

"Victor." There was something in the way she said his name that made him think the attraction wasn't entirely one-sided.

Victor cleared his throat and shifted sideways. "Nothing wrong with being strong-minded." His back hurt from a day of canoeing and portaging, and he envied how comfortable Lacey looked lying on the ground. But joining her would be a bad idea. The worst idea.

He had spent too much of his life acting on base instinct and already carried too many regrets. The last thing he needed was to add more.

As if reading his thoughts, Lacey pushed herself up. She pulled the gun and magazine out of her pocket, placed them on the ground beside her, and pulled her knees into her chest, wrapping her arms around them.

"Are you really going for a senior role?" Lacey tucked some hair behind her ears but didn't look at him.

And maybe he was wrong. Maybe Lacey didn't feel a darn thing except the need to scope out her competition.

He had might as well tell her the truth. Part of it, anyway. At least that way she wouldn't think he was some entitled tosspot with an over-inflated sense of his own abilities. "I know it sounds delusional. And it probably is. But I want to land a new client—a pharmaceutical company with a promising new multiple sclerosis drug. They're obviously reluctant with everything that's happened at Wyndham." He omitted anything about his mother. Lacey already knew more about the night Anita died than he'd told his own family.

He should probably resent that she'd been holding things back when she'd answered her question. But rehab had forced him to do enough hard work on himself to be able to recognize the difference between people holding back because they thought it gave them power over others, and those holding back to protect themselves. Even in the darkness he could pick up the pain behind Lacey's eyes which put her firmly in the latter camp.

"And what do they have to do with being senior management?"

He started, realizing he'd gotten caught in his thoughts and lost track of what he was saying. "The last thing they need is to be tainted by scandal when they're trying to get a new drug through the regulatory hoops. But the CFO is Oxford alumni, so they've said they'll let me have a shot at pitching for the business if I come through the merger as senior management. What about you?" He tacked the question on before Lacey could ask any more.

Lacey shrugged. "I've been at Langham for ten years. I've built the book publicity team up from nothing to one of the best in the business. I've earned it." She didn't need to say any more. He'd seen her office. Seen the evidence that made her case.

The unspoken hung between them. She deserved it. He didn't. But there were seven seats at the executive table. Even with her in one, that still left six.

Lacey wasn't his competition. Everyone else was.

CHAPTER TWELVE

"SO ..." JEN DROPPED DOWN to her haunches with a smirk. "Where were you last night?"

Lacey looked up from tying one of the tents into a canoe and blew a kinked strand of hair out of her face. Three days without her straightening conditioner and her usual sleek locks were well on the way to crazy-frizz town. Just getting it into a braid when she'd woken up had been a battle akin to wrestling a small hairy animal. "I couldn't sleep, so I went out to stretch my legs."

The stones under Jen's feet crunched as she wrapped a bandana around her dark curls. "That must have been some stretch. I was awake for over an hour."

"Sorry. I didn't mean to worry you." Jen had been snoring like a baby rhino when Lacey finally crawled back into the tent, so she obviously hadn't been that worried.

Jen snorted. "Firstly, after that raccoon execution yesterday, I think you're the last person any of us will worry about out here. Secondly ..." She arched an eyebrow and lowered her voice. "I may have stuck my head out of the tent and seen that you weren't alone."

As she spoke, Lacey's gaze flickered across the campsite to where Victor was packing down the final tent.

She didn't want to like Victor. It was all sorts of inconvenient, not to mention unwise. Not as foolish as the time she had begrudgingly said yes to allowing a trainee to do her bikini wax, but still unwise.

At least her undesirable softening toward Victor was only damaging her ego and self-respect. The wax had had her sitting on a bag of peas every night for a week.

"I say go for it. It's not fraternization until the companies merge." Jen gave her a wink as she stood.

Meredith wouldn't care about technicalities. And no man, let alone that one, was worth putting her career on the line for. "We should get into the canoes. We have a few hours on the water today."

Lacey stood and scanned the campsite. Victor was tying the last tent into one of the other canoes. Apart from a few backpacks waiting to be loaded, the campsite was clear. *You leave nature like you were never here.* Her father had drilled the mantra into her growing up.

She bent and picked up a smooth stone from the beach, rubbed her thumb across it, and idly flicked it at the surface of the lake. It skipped. One. Two. Three. Four times! She gave a little squawk of triumph, only to realize Victor had his back turned and hadn't seen her moment of redemption.

"Everything secure?" Kelvin came to stand beside her, his grey beard bristly like a toilet brush. "We're going to hit some bumpy water today."

"I need to check Victor's canoe, then we're good." Lacey covered the distance to the third canoe and checked the ties holding the gear in, tugging on them for good measure.

"I can be trusted to tie some knots, O'Connor." She couldn't tell from Victor's tone if he was teasing her or offended, and didn't want to look into his face to see.

"Just doing my job. You alright to paddle with Louisa in the three-man?" Victor and Louisa, Richard and Jen, her and Cassie. She tried to always team a strong canoeist with a weaker one.

Kelvin sat in the back of the three-man and only chipped in to help if they hit rough water. Must be the easiest gig he'd ever had.

"Right as rain."

"Actually, we need to swap Victor and Cassie." Lacey hadn't even noticed that Kelvin had followed her over to Victor's canoe. "I'd rather have Cassie in the canoe with me."

Cassie was by far and away the weakest canoeist, but Lacey bristled at the insinuation that she couldn't manage the canoe with her in it. "I don't—"

"I know you're captain, but there are some things that guides retain the decision rights on, as per the rules. Canoe allocation for days with rough water is one of them."

"Fine." She'd been going for airy, but the single syllable came out sounding like she'd been asked to clean the camp commode.

Kelvin put his fingers in his mouth and let loose a piercing whistle. Everyone looked up. "Everyone, we're going to be hitting some rapids early today. Canoe allocation is Richard and Jen, Victor and Lacey, Louisa and Cassie with me. Remember what I told you. We'll be taking the first set of rapids from the left. My boat will be the first one down. Follow our lead. And whatever you do, don't stop paddling."

At Kelvin's nod, people shrugged into their life jackets and dragged their canoes into the water until the stern was the only thing left on land. She would have to be in the front. Weight distribution during rapids mattered. Victor had to be at the back, no matter how much she hated the idea of him having control.

One of the many reasons why she'd rowed with everyone except him the last few days. Lacey clambered over the gear and settled herself into the bow of their canoe as she grabbed her oar.

Behind her, Victor pushed the boat off, then jumped in and settled himself in the stern.

The bottom of the canoe scraped across the bottom of the

lake as the canoe rocked and his weight settled. Grabbing her paddle, she pushed it against the lake's floor, and they glided across the smooth surface of the water.

"Do you want to paddle left or right?" She knew the answer. He'd paddled on the left-hand side the entire trip. She'd somehow catalogued the information without even knowing she had.

Looking over her shoulder, her gaze caught Victor's. "You're the boss, O'Connor. I'll row on whatever side you tell me to."

"Left will be fine." As tempting as it was to make him row right, this wasn't the day for testing his ambidextrous abilities.

"Left it is." He gave her a wink. The breeze skittering across the water ruffled his hair, and the morning sun glinted off his muscular arms like he was starring in some great outdoors commercial. Even the scar running down the side of his face made him look even more like he belonged here. Just like the night before, as he'd skipped the rocks with unconscious ease.

Lacey turned around, her hand tightening around the wooden oar as she tried to get a grip on her unprofessional thoughts.

"O'Connor." Victor's voice was tinged with amusement, but she resisted the urge to turn back around as the canoe cut smoothly through the water.

"Yes?"

"While I'm flattered by your obvious confidence in my abilities, are you planning on sticking your oar in the water any time soon?"

Lacey's head jerked up to see the other two canoes already ahead of them.

Their canoe, meanwhile, was turning toward the right-hand shore, the result of Victor paddling on the left and Lacey not paddling at all.

"Sorry!" She dug her oar into the water and leveraged all her weight into it, sending the canoe moving ahead and turning back on course. One more deep row and they were straight again.

Lacey dug her oar in, their canoe picking up speed and closing the gap on the other two. *Get a grip, O'Connor. You're supposed to be the captain!*

Within a couple of minutes, they were back with the others, their pace slowing slightly to remain with them and not get ahead. Across the water, she could see Jen and Richard talking. Cassie and Louisa did the same. It made the silence in her canoe feel all the more obvious.

She could feel her shoulders tensing, creeping up toward her ears, just at the knowledge that Victor was less than a body length away. Staring at her back. Watching her every move.

Lacey cleared her throat, searching for something to say. "So what are your plans for after this?"

Stupid question. Like he was going to tell her anything. She was the competition.

There was silence from the back of the boat for so long that she relaxed, thinking he hadn't heard her.

"You hinting I might be back on the job market, O'Connor?"

Lacey pushed her oar into the water and gave it a good shove. Just keep the rhythm. "That's up to Meredith. Nothing to do with me." Her words sounded cold. "I meant besides work. Anything waiting for you back home?"

Crap. Now she sounded like she was fishing for information about his personal life.

"My brother's getting married soon. That's about it."

The perfect opportunity to reveal their connection dangled in front of her. She had might as well get it over with and done with. Probably wasn't going to be any better moment than when they were in a canoe. If she kept her head straight, she wouldn't even have to look at him for a few hours.

"You got any siblings, O'Connor?" Victor diverted the conversation before she could get the words out.

"Just one. A sister."

"Older or younger?"

"Older. By two years." Though on the rare occasions the two of them saw each other, it looked more like ten. Betsy wore every single one of her hard years like a war veteran.

"Is she in New York too?"

"No, she's still in our hometown." Lacey's words came out more clipped than she'd intended. The edge in her voice saying more than she wanted to. "Sorry. Our family ... it's complicated."

"Families usually are."

Lacey chanced a glance over her shoulder, but Victor wasn't looking at her. His gaze was set somewhere over the treetops, his expression weighed down like gravity had gotten a lot stronger.

She turned her attention forward and dug her paddle back into the water. The sound of rushing water carried across the lake's surface, an early sign that the first set of rapids were close.

As they paddled, the sound got louder, drowning out any possibility of conversation. Then, as they rounded a corner, the rapids appeared about a hundred feet away. A decent run of choppy turbulent water poured over the rocks, foam frothing around the glistening obstacles.

Kelvin held up his hand, and they changed to backward strokes to keep themselves steady in the water. Kelvin's canoe would go first, so the rest of them could see the path.

Lacey studied the rolling water, picking out the line she thought Kelvin would take. She was gratified to see his canoe travel through exactly as she'd picked, the craft bouncing over the turbulence before being evicted into the calm patch at the end.

Next up were Richard and Jen. There was a shriek from Jen

as their canoe moved sideways and got a bit closer to a large rock than was comfortable before also being spat out the other side.

Lacey checked the straps on her life jacket. Tightened one. The last thing she wanted if pitched into rough waters was for her lifejacket to go shooting off over her head because it wasn't snug enough.

"You all good?" Victor had to yell the words to be heard.

"Yup, let's go." Lacey dug her oar into the water, trusting Victor would do the same behind her. The canoe skimmed across the surface, one, two, three, four strokes then the bow plunged into the roller coaster.

Fingers tightening around her oar, Lacey dug into the churn, focused on the line that they needed to hold for safe passage. The boat bounced, but the line held, Victor's powerful strokes matching hers to keep them on course.

There was a yell, and the boat swung out from beneath her, the front veering off course. From the weight, she knew Victor was still in the canoe, but there was no time to look back and see what had happened.

"You okay?" She yelled, but the words were whipped away by the roar of the water. There was no power coming from the back. Either Victor had lost his oar, or something had happened that meant he could no longer paddle. Both left her as the only thing getting them through.

Gritting her teeth, she swapped sides and dug her oar into the left, just managing to push them away from a large rock. Her arms burned as she paddled for two people, changing sides, trying to ensure she left enough space for the back to swing in a larger arc than the front.

White water sprayed across her, the cold causing her breath to be whisked out of her lungs. She shook her head, trying clear water from her eyes. Thank goodness the fat braid she'd tied her hair into was holding.

They plunged into the next set of rolling water, Victor's weight in the back lifting the front and she braced her legs and torso to stop herself being flung out of the canoe.

Paddle, paddle, paddle. There was no time to think of anything else as she made split-second decisions about what side to paddle on to try and keep them upright as water slammed against both sides of their vessel and rocks loomed on both sides.

Another spray of water rolled over her body. Vibrations echoed up her arm as she dug her oar in, only for it to hit a rock hiding under the surface.

She could see the anxious faces of the rest of the team, waiting on the smooth water. Jen leaned forward, mouth open, words lost.

They were almost there. She pushed her oar in, and the canoe bounced through the last two sets of rough water, spitting them out onto the calm.

They'd made it.

Her body sagged with relief. Then suddenly the canoe was tipping, the water drowning out the words that came out of her mouth. She'd made the rookiest error of all.

She'd gotten to the calm water and stopped paddling.

VICTOR BRACED HIMSELF AS THE canoe rolled, but nothing could have prepared him for the way the air was ripped out of his lungs by a full-body plunge into the icy mountain waters. Getting his legs wet was one thing. Complete immersion was another.

He kicked, his heavy hiking boots fighting against the current. His life jacket would bring him to the surface, but he wanted to be clear of the canoe when it did.

It was nothing less than he deserved. As they'd entered the

rapids, he'd lost his focus for a split second as he tugged his life jacket down. That was all it took for the churning water to whip his oar out of his hands like it was a piece of kindling.

His head broke through the water, and he sucked in a breath. A couple of meters away, Lacey was also clear, her hands gripping the inside seams of her life jacket.

Lacey had been a superhero as she'd navigated the canoe through the rapids single-handed, with all the downside of his weight and none of his help.

And they'd almost made it. The front of the canoe had made it into the clear water. Their undoing was the undertow lurking under the calm surface, catching the back of the canoe, sweeping it around and tipping them over.

He could already see the self-recrimination written all over Lacey's furious face as she paddled in the water a couple of meters away.

"It's not your fault, O'Connor. It's mine."

"We need to get the canoe to shore so we can flip it." Her refusal to even address the question, let alone look him in the eye, told him everything he needed to know.

"You guys okay?" Kelvin's call echoed across the water. Lacey acknowledged him with a wave of her hand.

"I'll get the front; you get the back." She started swimming with strong, sure strokes toward the prow without waiting for his response.

Victor breaststroked his way to the stern, thankful for the life jacket that conserved some of the energy he would have otherwise used to stay afloat. Gripping the end of the canoe, he kicked and pushed it through the water toward the shore. In front of him, Lacey's hand slipped once before she managed to get a grip on the side.

His legs burned as he tried to move through the water in

heavy boots. At least the screaming muscles distracted him from his monumental stuff up.

In his peripheral vision, he saw the other two canoes silently pass them, heading for the riverside.

Lacey would take this badly. Doubly so as captain. By the time the two of them flipped the canoe, sorted out the gear, and changed, they'd lose at least an hour out of the day. If not more.

He kicked harder, gritting his teeth to try and stop them chattering. The team knew it wasn't her fault. They all would've had a bird's eye view of him losing his oar and her superhuman efforts to get them out of the rapids intact.

It was a borderline miracle that she had. If they'd gone over in the rapids, it would have been so much worse. They had life jackets but no helmets. If they'd gone into the water and one of them had hit their head … his mind retreated from even imagining the possibilities.

Just get the canoe to shore. Get the canoe to shore. The self-flagellation could commence once Lacey was safe and dry. His feet finally found purchase on the ground, and he pushed the canoe with more power, sloshing forward, his body slowly exiting the lake. Ahead of him, Lacey dragged the front of the canoe, the water lapping her body from chest to waist to thighs. Her face was bleached white, her body shaking from the adrenaline rush, the cold, or both.

He'd been distracted watching her. He could at least have the guts to admit it to himself. Now the entire team was going to have to pay the price.

Without a word, Lacey pulled the canoe the last few feet to land, the rocks and sand scraping against the bottom of the boat. She didn't even look at him. Victor pushed it up the landing spot, ensuring it was far enough up that there was no chance of it floating back into the water.

Water sloshed off Lacey as she shook her hands and feet to help restore circulation.

"We need to get the gear out." She still wouldn't look at him, instead bending to salvage the gear from the waterlogged bottom. But her hands shook too much to untie the knots.

"This is my fault, O'Connor. It's all on me. I got distracted and lost my oar." Speaking of which, where was it? He scanned the water but couldn't see it anywhere. They had to find it. There were more rapids today, and there was no way Kelvin would let them go through with only one oar in play.

"Something's missing." Lacey's words brought his attention back to where she'd discarded her life jacket and stood surveying the equipment.

She was right. There was a gap. His gaze scanned the surrounds. Both of their packs were there, along with a waterproof bag of what looked like cooking equipment or food.

Oh, no. A rock settled in his stomach.

"The tent."

They both saw it and said the words at the same time. For a second Lacey's face crumpled, before she quickly rearranged it into stoic.

It didn't make sense. Lacey had tied the tent into this canoe. He'd seen her doing it. She'd even come over to check that he'd tied his in properly.

Victor's head jerked up, and he scanned the water. They had to get the tent back. It was in a waterproof cover, so it should be okay. As long as it hadn't gone floating off down the river, never to be seen again.

It wasn't heavy. The poles and the cover were deliberately designed to be lightweight, both to save on the energy needed to carry them, but also for events such as this.

"Here." Kelvin's canoe had nudged into shore. He leaned

forward and threw Victor a couple of ragged towels. He draped one around Lacey's shoulders, and she tucked it into her sides without even acknowledging him, her eyes still scanning the lake.

The smaller towel wouldn't even travel from shoulder to shoulder on him, so he shrugged out of his life jacket and used it to briskly rub his arms and legs, the rough surface adding some sensation to the numbing cold.

C'mon, c'mon. His gaze traveled to the opposite bank then back again. Then away from the rapids and down where the lake widened back out again. In all the chaos, it was possible it had bobbed past the two canoes still in the water and they hadn't seen it.

Nothing.

He tracked back. Moved his head to the left. To the last set of rapids. Holding his hand up over his eyes, he squinted against the morning sun, checking all of the shadows in case they weren't.

His pulse thrummed as he took the moving water as a grid. After a few seconds, his gaze landed on what looked like a shadow, but something about it felt off.

A scraping against the shore indicated both the other canoes were back on land. "Kelvin, do you have the binoculars?" Victor asked the question without taking his eyes off the shadow.

"Sure. What are you looking at?" A couple of seconds later the weight was placed in his palm.

"Just give me a sec." Victor raised the lenses to his eyes and bit back a moan.

It was the sack containing the tent, the top just showing above the surface of the water. In what had to be ridiculous odds, when the canoe had flipped the tent must have sunk just far enough to catch the undertow pulling back toward the rapids.

Now it was caught in the vortex of water swirling around the rock and nothing, short of about three months with no rain, would free it without intervention.

"What can you see?"

Beside him, Lacey dropped her now-soaked towel on the ground and had her hand out for the binoculars.

Victor handed them over. "Look at the rock in the last set, close to the middle."

Lacey twisted the lenses as she held them up to her eyes. A couple of seconds later she swore softly under her breath.

"What happened out there, guys?" Kelvin crunched over the sand and gravel, stopping a few feet from them, hands shoved in the pockets of his shorts. From the shrewd look in his eyes, Victor would bet the estate Kelvin knew exactly what had happened and was still unfolding.

Lacey opened her mouth, but Victor cut her off. "It was my fault. A hundred percent. I got distracted for a second and lost my oar. Lacey showed incredible skill getting us out of the rapids without tipping."

"Except we did." Lacey made the statement without inflection or accusation. "We've also lost the tent because it wasn't tied down properly. But I can get it back."

She what? Victor's gaze darted back to where the tent was still pinned against the rock. Then he looked up the river, trying to calculate what possible run anyone could do that would both get through the rapids safely while getting close enough to the rock to somehow dislodge the tent.

There was no way. Not when the smallest canoe they had was a double hull traveling canoe. None designed for agility in white water. He was just a rower, not a canoeist or kayaker, but it was as plain as the nose on Lacey's face that what she was suggesting was, at best, extremely risky.

"Where is it?"

Lacey handed the binoculars to Kelvin and pointed. "Over by

that rock."

Kelvin took his time studying the water, long enough that Victor began to think he was seriously considering it.

"This is my fault. I lost the oar. If it wasn't for that, none of this would have happened. I'll take whatever the penalty or punishment is."

"I got your oar. I spotted it when it got washed out of the rapids." Cassie stepped forward, holding the oar aloft like a trophy. What did she want? A medal?

"Kelvin?" A twinge of desperation threaded its way through Lacey's question as the guide lowered the binoculars.

He shook his head. "Not a chance, Lacey. Getting that tent dislodged from where it is would be a risky move for the most experienced canoeist."

"But you just saw me. Saw what I can do."

Kelvin turned and put both hands on her shoulders. "Being brilliant when it is forced upon you is one thing. Choosing to place yourself in harm's way is another thing entirely. I'm sorry. But I'm classifying the tent as lost. And because the weather can change on a dime this time of year, the rules are that if a shelter is lost then, two people are to be immediately disqualified and extracted."

A couple of people gasped. Everyone else just stood in stunned silence.

Lacey absorbed Kelvin's words for a second. Her shoulders dropped, and her whole body seemed to shrink a little. "Can I at least choose who I pass my captainship into?"

"You don't have to pass it onto anyone. As captain, you choose who has to leave."

"Well, I have to be one of them." There went his chance of making management. Though that had always been more fantasy than reality. But he'd lost his oar. This was his fault. You break it, you fix it. That wasn't an official step, but it was something his sponsor had drilled into him.

"No way. You're physically the strongest of us here." Richard spoke up. "I think it should be the weakest two members of the team." He didn't even try and hide his look toward Cassie and Louisa. "We need to retain the strongest players to get us to the end. Otherwise, we don't have a chance. You and Lacey are two of them."

Thank goodness someone else had said it. Lacey deserved to be here more than anyone. There was limited justice in the world, and at least some of it should be spent on her staying until the end.

"He's right." Louisa tugged on the bottom of her T-shirt. "I'm not under any illusions that I bring anything to this. You guys would be far better off without me. Let's face it, the fact I've made it this far is only because of the rest of you. So I volunteer as tribute." She offered a glimmer of a smile. "I've always wanted to say that."

"It's settled," Victor said. "Louisa and I will go. The rest of you will continue. We'll see you at the finish line, kicking the other teams' butts." He had no idea what he was talking about. Knowing Meredith, there was probably some gladiatorial contest at the end, not a hand-holding across the finish line. Regardless, all that mattered was that a painless resolution had been reached that kept Lacey in play. "I'll get our bags."

They'd have to abandon one of the canoes, but that wasn't his problem. No doubt Meredith and her fat bank balance had made arrangements for situations like this. There were probably a group of ninja guides plowing through the wilderness rescuing equipment that had been lost, destroyed, or abandoned.

He turned to go and grab his and Louisa's packs. Hopefully, the extraction point wouldn't be too far away. His wet socks squelching against his sodden boots were a recipe for blisters the size of saucers.

"No." Lacey's voice came from behind him. Strong but certain. "No. I'm the captain, so I decide. Right?" She looked at Kelvin, and he nodded.

"I'm the captain. I made a bigger mistake. I didn't tie the tent down properly. If I had, we wouldn't be in this situation." She reached up to her head and tugged off her bandana. "I'm out. Jen's the new captain."

Jen shook her head, her mouth opening as if she was going to say something. One look at Lacey's face and she took the bandana with a silent nod.

Victor shifted so he stood next to Lacey. "Just for the record, if you don't choose me I'll quit."

Lacey looked up at him. "Richard's right. You're the strongest. They need you."

"O'Connor, either you take me out, or I take myself out." If she was wearing this, so was he. It was as simple as that. He would find another way to prove himself.

Lacey bit her bottom lip as she pondered his words. Her wet T-shirt clung to her like a swimsuit, highlighting every curve. He pushed back against the inappropriate longing that rumbled up his chest.

He had met hundreds, if not thousands, of women. But none of them had gotten under this skin like Lacey's combination of fierceness and vulnerability.

"Okay." Lacey faced the group. "Victor and I were the ones in the canoe, so we're the ones who have to go." Her voice caught for a second. "Good luck, everyone. I know you're going to make us proud."

CHAPTER THIRTEEN

LACEY HAD REPLAYED YESTERDAY'S SCENE over and over like Libby replayed her favorite My Little Pony episode.

She could see it so clearly in her mind. Her crouching down and tying the tent into the bottom of the canoe. She could even picture her fingers tying the first knot.

Then Jen had come and teased her about her evening escapades and the only conclusion, the *only* possibility, was that she had gotten so distracted thinking about her time with Victor that she had forgotten to finish tying down the tent.

Worse, she had then gone over and checked Victor's tent but never gone back and checked hers.

And now she was out. Out because she had been distracted by the one person, the *one*, she'd known she should stay away from the moment she had laid eyes on him.

Sixty seconds of distraction because Victor Carlisle had smiled at her in the moonlight and the very thing she'd worked for for ten years, that was so close she could see *Lacey O'Connor* engraved on the place plaque around the executive table, was probably gone.

Her fury at herself had propelled every step of the three-hour hike to take to the nearest extraction point. It had robbed her of sleep in the cabin back at the base in Ely. It taunted her every second of every minute.

Not only had she been so distracted that she'd ruined hers

and Victor's chances, but the team were now also a day behind, thanks to Kelvin having to escort her and Victor on the hike to the extraction spot, then hike back to the team.

Better to have been disqualified because Victor had shot himself in the behind with the forgotten bullet in her chamber. The gun! "Crap!" She slammed her foot on the brake of the rental car.

"Argh!" In the passenger seat, Victor flung his arm up in front of his face, his whole body bracing for impact.

The car came to a screeching halt in the middle of the road. Her seatbelt snapped against her torso and held her body back from slamming into the steering wheel.

Victor wasn't so lucky. His knees—knees that were already situated in tight confines—smacked into the glove compartment. He lowered his arm and rubbed his knees, a grimace running across his face. "Did we hit something?" He looked over his shoulder, searching for whatever had caused her to react like she'd had her license days, not years.

"No. Sorry." Lacey sucked in a shaky breath and pulled over to the side of the road, the car's hood nosing into the long grass. Thank goodness they hadn't seen a car in miles. If there had been someone behind them, she probably would have caused the worst pileup the county had seen in decades.

She checked her rearview mirror. Nothing, except for the black tread her sudden stop had left on the asphalt.

"Did you miss hitting something?"

"I forgot something." She resisted the urge to bang her head against something. How could she have forgotten about the gun?

Victor tilted his head at her, the scar on his cheek twitching as he suppressed whatever expression was fighting him. "You forgot to off me in the wilderness, so you thought you'd take a shot here, where you have no witnesses?"

Her lips twitched. "Tempting, but no."

KARA ISAAC

"Okay. Do we have a minute? I'm going to stretch my legs." Without waiting for an answer, he opened the door, stopping to rub both knees before stepping into the long grass. He strolled up the verge, lifting his arms up and stretching them toward the blue sky. Lacey averted her eyes as his T-shirt rode up, exposing the beginning of a toned torso.

That was exactly what had gotten her in this position in the first place.

She opened her door and stepped onto the road, her bare feet tentative on the cool asphalt. "You should get back in."

Victor was idly swishing grass with his feet a little ways away from the front of the car. He had flipper-sized feet. Bare feet, since both of them had decided to forego their still-damp hiking boots for the car ride.

"I should. But I'm trying to decide what is preferable. Letting you keep driving, or me taking over and hopefully remembering what side of the road to stay on."

"As fair as that decision is, it's going to be taken out of your hands if there's a snake in that grass. And if you get bit, I am not going to be the person holding your hand and crying by your bed."

"Ouch." But he at least pulled his foot out of the grass and walked toward the road. Approaching her, he leaned against the hood of the car. "What about sucking the poison out of the wound?"

"Can you just get back into the car? We need to make a short detour."

At that interest sparked in his expression. "Where are we going?"

"Nowhere interesting." They needed to get going. It was going to be tight to divert to Small Harbor and still make it to Duluth in time to get the last flight out.

"I disagree. I think it must be incredibly interesting for it to slow your return to the Big Apple." He studied her face in a way that made her feel far too seen.

"I'm getting in the car now. Either get in or get out of my way." Lacey jerked open her door and thumped into the driver's seat, turning the motor back on.

Victor eyed her through the windshield for a second before shifting off the bonnet and sauntering around the vehicle as if he had all the time in the world.

Finally, he was back in his seat, his seatbelt very deliberately snapped and checked. "You've decided city life isn't for you and you're going to chuck it all in to do up an old B&B."

"What?" Lacey put on her blinker and pulled back onto the road.

"I'm going to guess what this mysterious detour is until you tell me."

"Not even close."

"You have an ex-boyfriend whose wife died in a tragic accident, leaving him and his three-year-old twins, and you're returning home to comfort him in his grief."

"Don't be ridiculous."

"Your grandmother left you a surprise inheritance, and you're giving into your secret passion to open up a small-town ice cream parlor."

Lacey kept her eyes on the road.

"In case I haven't told you, I'm not dating at the moment, and I'm not great with tools."

Lacey's eyes snapped from the road to his serious face.

He shrugged. "Your plans for your new B&B might include a hot handyman with a sexy accent for the city girl to fall in love with."

A smile fought to land on the corner of her mouth. She

forced her focus on the rural road. "You're safe. I promise."

"Funny. That's not the first word that comes to mind when I think of you." Against her better judgement, Lacey glanced to the right and found Victor looking at her intently. She jerked her gaze away.

She wasn't stupid enough to deny an attraction. But she was smart enough to know that behind her attraction sat the desire to prove herself to a man who didn't even remember rejecting her.

Eyes on the prize, Lacey. And the prize was not sitting next to her. "Far be it for me to ruin your Hallmark fantasies, but there is no B&B, ice cream parlor, widowed ex, or inheritance. I just need to take the gun back." Because that would be the cherry on the top of the sundae that was this insane week—showing up at the airport with a firearm that, in her fury, she'd forgotten was in her possession.

What could only be described as a chuckle rumbled out of Victor's chest. Lacey refused to look at him. "*That* was the reason for impaling me on my seat belt back there, O'Connor? You forgot about your handgun?" More laughter emanated from his seat. "Would it have been hidden in your checked luggage or your carry-on? Should I be imagining you under a pile of TSA agents at security, or them coming for you at the gate."

"You're not nearly as funny as you think you are."

"I guarantee this is a lot funnier than you think it is."

"Can you check my phone? See if we have reception?" She could make a good guess at which back roads to get them to Small Harbor, but she'd rather trust Siri. Assuming Siri hadn't decided this far off the grid wasn't worth her effort.

"If it's not your gun, whose gun is it?"

Lacey's fingers tightened on the steering wheel as she realized what she had inadvertently gotten herself into. Dang it. She should have chosen Louisa and left Victor in the wilderness.

"There's a tiny town nearby called Small Harbor. I have family there. I borrowed the handgun off them." Hopefully, he'd interpret uncle or cousin or something once removed from her words.

As long as he didn't get out of the car, it was still containable. Handing her competition her only weakness on a plate wasn't an option.

AT SOME POINT THEY HAD turned off the main road to Duluth and gone back roading in a way Victor was pretty sure wasn't covered under the rental car terms.

The green fields all looked identical, so Victor had no clue what Lacey was navigating by. The sun? The occasional signpost?

It has been at least half an hour since they had seen another vehicle or person. The landscape held a sense of desertion that made a man wonder how many bodies there were within a mile radius that would never be found.

What he did know was that as they got closer to their destination—at least he could only hope they were getting closer—the lines around Lacey's mouth and eyes tightened. Like a string being pulled taut.

Suddenly Lacey's phone lit up by his feet and started dinging as a traffic jam of messages had finally gotten a green light. They had reception, which meant they had to be close to civilization.

"You want me to get that?"

Lacey shook her head, curls bouncing. "No, it's fine."

The phone kept going. Dinging every other second for at least a minute. "You sure? Sounds like your boyfriend's been missing you."

His statement sounded like the ridiculous fishing expedition that it was. She didn't even deign to respond.

Indicating, she took a turn onto a real road. "We should be in there in about five minutes."

"So who am I going to meet?"

"What?"

"Well," he lifted a shoulder. "I thought that if you're taking me home to meet the family, it might be a good idea to let me know who they are. You know, so I can charm them with my British accent and all."

She didn't even look at him. Tough audience. "You are not going to meet anyone. You're going to stay in the car, and I'm going to run inside real quick."

They drove past a sign welcoming them to Small Harbor. Within a few minutes, they were in a neighborhood that if it had ever seen better days, they were a long way back.

Broken up sidewalks, abandoned cars in front yards, skinny children with big eyes peering off porches looking like they hadn't seen a bath in a week.

Lacey pulled into the driveway of a worn-down house with a broken fence, long grass, and grimy windows. A couple of large Amazon Prime boxes sat on the porch.

She killed the motor and stared at the front door for a few seconds.

"You okay?"

"Look." She couldn't hide the pleading in her voice or the way her fingers strangled the steering wheel. "I know you don't owe me anything. Especially when it's my fault we've been disqualified. But I would really appreciate it if you don't say anything about this to anyone."

Victor's spine prickled. Whatever was going on here, it did not feel good. "O'Connor, look at me."

She turned her head, but only the bare minimum.

"Are you okay? Is this place safe?" Despite four days in the wilderness together, he realized how little he knew about her. Anything could sit behind that front door.

"It's fine. I promise." Her body folded against the back of her seat, and she turned to face him. "The gun's my dad's and this is my parents' home. They're good people. It's just … complicated."

Her gaze broke from his, and she drew in a breath. Somehow he knew she had gifted him more about herself than anyone else in Langham had ever known. Victor steeled himself against the urge to cup her face in his hands and run his thumb over her lower lip. Instead, he settled for tucking one of her wayward curls behind her ear. His fingertips buzzing as they brushed her skin.

Her eyes widened, and he dropped his hand. "You're good people too, O'Connor. And you have nothing to be ashamed of. All families are complicated."

"I'll just be a minute." Leaning down, she popped the trunk and jumped out of the car like he had just made some kind of grand declaration.

After a minute or so of rummaging in her hiking pack there was a thump as the trunk closed and she walked past the driver's window carrying a lockbox and the holster. She jogged up the steps in her bare feet, paused, then knocked on the door.

A few seconds later, the door opened, and a tall man with a broad but saggy build that spoke of years of too much beer and not enough exercise filled the doorway. Even with Lacey about as far away from the glossy New Yorker he'd first met, Victor could not see a single similarity between them. Nothing to indicate they were blood relations, let alone father and daughter.

Lacey said a few words and handed over the gun and accessories. A couple more words. Then she stepped back as if to go. Not a single touch between them. Not the smallest gesture of affection.

The man said something, and Lacey shook her head. The man spoke again, giving a grizzled frown as he gestured toward the car.

This time as Lacey shook her head, her posture went ramrod straight. Another exchange and Lacey's shoulders bunched up toward her ears.

Victor's whole body coiled as if he was waiting for the starting pistol for a race.

The man stepped forward, and Victor was out of the car, his strides eating up the distance to the saggy porch before he even registered the sound of the car door slamming behind him. "Is everything okay?"

Lacey and her father had both turned toward the sound of the door. Lacey's father's hand was around her upper arm. It didn't look like it was a tight grip, but Victor's fingers still itched with the desire to slap them away.

"Who are you?" Lacey's father barked the words, and it was impossible to miss the way his eyes darted down to the box in his hands as if calculating how quickly he could get it open and a gun in his hands.

"It's fine, Dad. He's a colleague. We're traveling together." Victor couldn't read Lacey's flat expression and had no idea if he'd just made things worse or better.

But here he was. "Victor Carlisle. Mr. O'Connor. Sir." At least he hoped that was his name. Victor gave the man a nod from the bottom of the steps.

"Jim." Lacey's father shifted the gun box to one hand and stepped forward, hand outstretched. Victor took the steps in a bound and accepted the solid handshake. The man eyed up his scar with interest but didn't ask any questions.

"You hold any sway with my daughter, young man?"

He didn't even need to look at Lacey to be pretty certain

about the expression that would be on her face. "Your daughter is her own woman, sir. I'm just along for the ride." He wasn't getting in the middle of this. And whatever it was, he was Team Lacey all the way.

Especially with the unbroken expanse of rural Minnesota to hide a body fresh in his mind.

A hint of approval glinted in the man's eye. "Do you have siblings, Victor?"

"A brother, sir."

"Well, I was suggesting my daughter might want to stop in on her sister before she leaves town. Seeing as she rarely makes it this way."

"And, like I said, we have a flight we need to make tonight, and we're already cutting it close." Something tightened in Victor's chest at her casual use of *we*. Even though he knew it was nothing more than the most neutral use of a plural pronoun.

"And like I said, Betsy will be hurt if she hears you've been in town twice in a week and didn't stop by."

From the way Lacey bit her bottom lip and shifted on her feet it didn't take a genius to work out her relationship with Betsy was almost as complicated as his was with Peter.

Victor stayed silent.

"I'll think about it, okay. No promises. But for us to even have a chance, we need to go now."

"You're not even going to even say hi to your mother?"

"She's got two packages out here. You should take them to her." Lacey stepped back and shoved the packages into the doorway at her father's feet. "I'll get someone to come around and do a quote on painting the house."

"You don't have to do that. I said I'll get around to it." But the way her father diverted his gaze and leaned down to pick up the first package and move it into the house said everything.

Victor's gaze tracked over the man's shoulder and into the hallway that ran down the middle of the home. The sound of a television came from a nearby room. The door was half-open, held that way by another stack of packages.

"Bye, Dad. Tell Mom I said hi." Lacey stepped back, brushing against his side, the connection severed as quickly as it happened as she turned toward the steps. She was down them and walking toward the car before Victor had even caught his breath from their unexpected contact.

He nodded at Mr. O'Connor. Jim. "Goodbye, sir. It was nice to meet you."

Lacey's dad watched his daughter walk to the car. "Do you care for my daughter, young man?"

The unanticipated question knocked the breath out of him for a second. "She's an impressive woman, sir. And very highly regarded."

"She is. But between you and me, she's not as tough as she works so hard to make everyone believe. So if you could have her back, I'd mightily appreciate it." With that, the man picked up the second box and firmly closed the door.

CHAPTER FOURTEEN

I T TOOK EVERYTHING IN LACEY not to bang her head against the steering wheel and scream. The only thing stopping her was Victor loping down the broken weedy path back to the car. And he had already seen enough. Knew too much.

"You okay?" He asked the question before he was even fully in the car.

"I just ..." Lacey turned on the engine and put the car into reverse. "I just need to not be here." She accelerated out of the driveway and into the street, looking back at the front window, hoping to see some sign of her mother's attention. Any sign. Even a movement of the dingy curtain. Nothing.

Of course not.

Throwing the car into drive, she peeled down the street. Waited for some joke from Victor about how they'd be driving on the rims by the time they returned the car. Nothing.

His steady, silent presence sat in the passenger seat. At least he didn't offer any trite assurances or advice.

After a few seconds, she couldn't take it anymore. "Aren't you at least going to ask me about my sister?"

"Do you want me to ask you about your sister?" She glanced right, and his probing gaze pinned her against her headrest.

She couldn't answer. Did she? The answer, usually, would have been an automatic no. No, I don't want you to ask me anything about my family. It's none of your business. It has nothing to do with my job. I don't answer personal questions.

"Like I said to your dad, I'm just along for the ride. Wherever it might take me."

"We can't go and see Betsy. There's no way we'll make it out tonight." She didn't even know if flights had been booked. All they'd been told in Ely when they got handed the car keys was that they could pick up their original luggage at the hotel in Duluth, and the rental car had to be returned to the Avis airport counter.

"Do you want to see your sister?"

Lacey pulled into a parking lot and came to a stop in the nearest spot. Without even thinking about it she'd driven to the nearest Krogers. Her subconscious was clearly trying to tell her something.

"Can you pass me my phone? I need to check my email." If there was a flight itinerary out of Duluth tonight, that was the decision. She already had ground to make up from the disqualification. She wasn't risking losing more points in whatever this weird merger reenactment of *Game of Thrones* was keeping score on. Assuming she hadn't tanked her chances already.

Victor passed her the phone, and she tapped in the password she hadn't used for days. It felt foreign to her fingers, despite being used thousands of time before.

She tapped the mail icon, waiting a few seconds for it to connect and refresh. Scanned for anything that looked like a travel itinerary. Everything was color-coded exactly as she'd asked Janna while she was on the bus to Ely.

She scrolled back to the morning before, around the time they'd been disqualified. Nothing. Tapped into her travel subfolder, in case it had already been filed there. Still nothing.

It wasn't a big deal. She had a company credit card. Plus a gazillion points on every frequent flyer program going. "You got a company credit card?"

"I do, but the limit is minimal. They all got reduced to five hundred pounds after the whole bribery thing."

Lacey did an approximate conversion in her head. No chance that would be enough for a last-minute flight from Duluth to London unless his ticket was a super flexi fare. "No flights have been booked for me. So I assume nothing's been booked for you either."

"So what would you like to do?" Victor was the epitome of reasonableness. Not what she wanted.

"Can't you be an obnoxious jerk again? Like on the bus? Insist you need to get back to London asap because you're very important and have very important work to do and we can't stay in this podunk town a second longer?"

"I can be exactly that, if that's what you need me to be." She couldn't not look at him, at the seriousness in his gaze as he studied her face like it was a work of exquisite art.

He was giving her an out. Telling her he would say whatever she needed him to. The choice was all hers. If she needed him to be an arrogant jerk to give her a reason to be on a plane tonight, then all she had to do was say the word.

She closed her eyes for a second to get a break from the intensity of his gaze. What was even happening? How could she be in a car in a Kroger parking lot in Small Harbor with Victor Carlisle?

He'd stood on her parents' porch and not even flinched at the state of the house. Or her family. Or all the dysfunction that had been laid out like a welcome map.

She kept her eyes closed until she was sure that when she opened them, she wouldn't give in to the temptation to kiss him.

Because she knew exactly what kissing Victor Carlisle felt like. She remembered it too well. As if his lost memory of that evening had taken up residence in her body, making it doubly potent.

Finally, when she was ninety percent sure—because a hundred would mean sitting here all night—that she would be able to prevent her wayward thoughts from finding their way into her hands and lips, she opened her eyes.

He was still there. Just as close, his gaze just as clear and honest.

"I've never met my nephew. He's four." She put the confession into the air, needing to disrupt the energy between them. Before she said or did something that would change everything.

His mouth lifted on one side. "Well, then," he said, his gaze never breaking connection with hers as he reached over and tugged a piece of hair behind her ear. "I guess we should buy him a present."

THE SUGGESTION OF BUYING LACEY'S nephew—whose name he still didn't even know—seemed to have unleashed something in her.

Before he knew it, they were out of the car, and he'd been made captain of the shopping cart while she whizzed through the store filling it with so much food they'd needed to return to the front of the store for a second cart.

Many grocery bags and $250 later, they'd driven to a Walmart where she'd done exactly the same with kid's clothes and shoes and toys.

Using his Sherlock-like detective skills, the pile had told him that Lacey also had two nieces aged around twelve and six.

"You planning on leaving any clothes for the other kids in town?" Victor took a chance on a joke as Lacey dumped an armful of dresses into the cart.

Lacey stopped dead still, her thumbnail going into her mouth as she stared at the cart's contents. "You're totally right. What am

I doing? This is way too much." She reached back into the trolley, as if to take the contents out.

Victor reached out and curled his hand around her wrist. "You haven't seen them in years. Your nieces will love this. Don't overthink it, okay?" She looked up at him, eyes the most uncertain he had ever seen, and he battled the urge to fold her against his chest.

"It's just ..." she looked around the empty aisle as if to check no one else was eavesdropping. "Things aren't great with Betsy. I don't know how she's going to react to my showing up."

"I get it. It's the same with my brother."

"I know."

I know? Victor racked his brain to try and recall what he'd told her about Peter, but his thoughts were derailed by Lacey resting her head against his shoulder, her body whisper close to his. His heart reacted like it was in the middle of a rowing sprint.

"Okay." Before he could even respond, she stepped back, avoiding his gaze. "We should go. We need to be in Duluth tonight unless we want to get bedbugs at some fleabag motel here."

Ten minutes later, the gifts had been rung up by a wide-eyed cashier and were safely stashed in the back seat—the trunk being too stuffed to handle anything more—and they were back in the car, driving to another part of town. One as dilapidated as her parents'.

Lacey pulled in front of the house. No garage, so no drive-way. The front yard was neat and better kept than her parents. An abandoned swing set sat out front, one swing on its side, the chain a rusty trail in the grass.

She turned off the car and sat, her fingers opening and closing over the steering wheel.

"Will your father have told her we might be coming?" What

were they going to do if no one was home? They couldn't leave umpteen bags of groceries and clothes on the doorstep. They'd be gone before they'd reached the town limits. If only they could leave some food on every sagging porch.

"No." She attempted a smile but it landed flat. "Communication isn't a family strength." Pushing a hand through her hair, trying and failing to flatten the curls that had escaped her braid, she shoved open her door. "Let's grab the cold stuff first. And some of the clothes."

Victor got out of the car as she clicked the trunk open with the fob. "I'll get these. You grab some of the clothes." She'd probably carry the gallons of milk, bricks of cheese and bags of frozen processed food and dislocate a shoulder out of sheer stubbornness.

She paused as he reached past her and grabbed the handles, but didn't offer any objection. The second victory for the day. Miracles did happen.

Victor placed two heavy bags on the ground, grabbed two more, then closed the trunk on the rest. He waited for Lacey to close the back door and lock the car.

"Okay." She looked at the house with zero anticipation. "Let's get this over with."

"What if no one is home?"

"Someone will be home."

How did she know? Victor didn't even know what day it was. They'd all blurred together since he'd gotten on the flight from Heathrow and been thrown into an alternative universe. Was today Friday? Saturday?

He stepped back to let Lacey go ahead of him. No need to open the gate. That lay off to one side, the hinges cracked with rust. The bags pulled on his arms as he followed her up the path.

At the bottom of the porch steps, Lacey's shoulders went

back, and she strode up the steps and banged on the door like she'd slugged back a shot of Dutch courage.

Now they were closer to the house, she was right. The sound of voices and a muffled TV came from behind the front door. Running feet hitting hard floors came next, but the door didn't open.

Lacey looked over her shoulder at him, something indecipherable in her eyes then turned and banged again. This time the door dislodged from the frame and swung open as a woman lugging a wriggling child came walking down the hallway.

The woman's eyes widened, and she swore, almost dropping the boy. Then she lowered him to the carpet and stepped over him like a discarded toy. Her jeans were ragged, and not in the designer way. Her white T-shirt was splotched with stains.

"Surprise."

Victor had never heard Lacey sound so timid. Almost apologetic.

Lacey's sister covered the last couple of steps to the door, and Victor almost lost his grip on the bags. Betsy was another Lacey.

He couldn't tear his gaze away, even though he knew he was gawking. It was like he'd stepped into that 90s movie his mother had loved, the one where the woman either caught or missed the train and it changed everything.

This was Lacey if she'd stayed in Small Harbor and lived the life that would have been destined for her. If she'd never escaped.

Same wavy hair, same facial features, same build, almost identical height. But Betsy's features added a hardness to her, a wariness, that her younger sister didn't have, for all her take-no-prisoners cloak.

"What are you doing here?"

"Who is it, Mom?" The boy appeared, trying to squash past his mother for a better view of what was happening on the doorstep.

Betsy didn't even look down at she stepped half in front of him. "Go watch TV, Jake. I'll be there in a few minutes."

"But I'm hungry." The poor kid looked like he was short a few good meals.

This time she dropped down to his height and brushed his hair off his forehead. "I said go watch TV. I'll get you something in a minute."

The little boy slinked behind her and disappeared from view.

She crossed her arms. "What are you doing here?"

Whoa. And he'd thought his relationship with his brother was bad.

"We were in the area, and Dad mentioned that Mitch had lost his job. So I thought … I thought I'd drop by with a few things."

"He didn't lose his job. He was laid off. With severance. And he's looking for another." Betsy looked down and, for the first time, registered the bags in Lacey's hands. Then her line of sight drifted back, and she saw Victor at the bottom of the stairs.

"Who are you?"

"I'm Victor, ma'am. A colleague of Lacey's." For the first time in his life, Victor cringed at the sound of his own voice. His British accent decidedly out of place in the unfolding scene.

Betsy swore again. "So after years of nothing, you show up on our doorstep like the Fairy Godmother with your fancy British boyfriend. For what? So you could show him how far you've come? Who you've risen above?"

Victor ground his teeth together to stop himself from speaking. Anything he said could only make things worse.

"It hasn't been nothing. I send presents every birthday and Christmas. I email." From the set of Lacey's shoulders, Victor was guessing she did a lot more than send occasional gifts.

"Oh what, so you're here now because I don't reply to your emails? Well, in case you haven't noticed, some of us don't have flashy lives in New York." Betsy spat the words out like they were dirty. "Some of us are kind of busy just trying to get by."

"Look," Lacey's tone was even. "We don't have to come in. The girls don't need to know we were ever here. We can just leave all the stuff on the doorstep and leave. But we can't take it on the plane with us. So if you don't want it, say the word, and we'll find somewhere in town that does."

Betsy's gaze bounced between Lacey and all the bags, the battle between pride and need written clearly across her haggard face.

Victor didn't know what he would do if Betsy chose wrong. He knew, as clearly as he knew that Lacey was the strongest person he'd ever met, that if they went in the house and opened Betsy's cupboards there wouldn't be near enough to feed a family of five.

Grown-ups could make their own choices. But depriving children ... He wasn't sure he could stand by and let that happen. No matter what Lacey said. He had no dog in this fight. What were they going to do if he forced his way into the house and left the groceries on the floor? Have him arrested?

"Fine. But take it all around back."

"Thank you." Lacey said the words softly, then turned and tilted her head to Victor's right to show him which way to go.

Five minutes later, the bags had all been schlepped around to the back and left, by Betsy's instruction, outside the door. Even the grass felt haggard and weary under his bare feet.

"I'll send you photos of the kids. I will." Betsy looked at all the bags on her back porch then at her sister. Victor's stomach dropped like a rollercoaster as he read into the intonation. Lacey wasn't going to be allowed to see her nieces. She wasn't going to properly meet her nephew.

Lacey swallowed, then nodded. "Okay. Thanks."

"Betsy." The name was out of Victor's mouth before he even knew he'd spoken. Lacey's head jerked around, and she speared him with a *don't you dare* glare. Victor grabbed hold of the tail of his temper. "It was … um … very nice to meet you."

Betsy paused from where she had reached down to grab one of the grocery bags. "You're lying. But thanks for bothering." With that, she stood and shut the door.

Victor trudged back to the car, feeling more defeated than he had since the day he'd entered rehab. They were almost at the car when the front door flew open, and two blonde curly-haired girls in faded dresses and bare feet came flying down the stairs and up the path. "Auntie Lacey, Auntie Lacey!"

They slammed into Lacey so hard that Victor had to reach out and grab her to stop her from tumbling backwards. She didn't even seem to notice as she wrapped her arms around them and pressed kisses into their hair. "Hi, girls."

Jake stood up on the stairs, looking torn between curiosity and fear.

"Molly! Lucy! You get back in here right now." Betsy stood on the porch, her expression one of anger and something else.

Lacey pressed another kiss into both heads then tried to step back. "Listen to your mama, girls. I love you."

The girls didn't listen. If anything they just held onto Lacey more tightly and Victor watched her face crumble. "Girls, your mama's right." She could barely get the words out. "We have to go. I love you."

"Right now." Betsy's words sliced the air like a whip, and Victor suddenly recognized the expression on her face. Fear. Pure, unadulterated fear. Her hand gripped her son's wrist to ensure he didn't run to his aunt too.

Lacey looked at Victor as if for help, but he wasn't doing this. He wasn't physically removing children from the only hope they probably had of ever escaping this hole. Betsy could do it herself.

After a few more seconds, Lacey crouched down, murmured something to both of the girls, and their arms loosened.

Placing a hand on both their cheeks, she gave them each a final kiss and stepped back with all the energy of someone wearing cement boots. Tears streaked the girls' faces.

Lacey stepped back, then back again, her gaze only leaving the girls to give a wave to her nephew up on the porch.

Victor moved to her side. Her hand reached out and grabbed his, the weight of her body leaning into his arm like she needed scaffolding to remain standing. His fingers curled around hers, and he felt something between them.

"I don't even know if you can, but you're going to have to drive." She murmured the words as she pressed the keys into his palm.

Victor lifted his hand at the two heartbroken girls now clinging to each other on the cracked path. Then he turned, unlocked the car, and held Lacey's door open for her. He couldn't look at the terrible tableau for another second longer.

Lacey didn't speak for another hour but sat still, her gaze fixed on the road. The occasional blink and the rise and fall of her chest were the only things to show she wasn't chiseled out of stone.

"It's not what you think." She spoke the words so softly for a second Victor thought he might have imagined them. A glance toward him the only sign that he hadn't. "Betsy's even smarter than me. She was the school valedictorian. She had a full ride to Carleton. If you think she hates me for leaving, then you're right. But she hates herself even more for not taking her chance when she had it."

CHAPTER FIFTEEN

"LACEY! YOU'RE BACK." BECKETT HODGE'S baritone resounded in her ear from the other end of the phone.

"Indeed, I am." Lacey lodged her phone between her ear and her shoulder as she logged into her computer for the first time since the cocktail party.

Her gaze flicked toward the couch. Hard to believe only a week had passed since she'd found Victor half asleep on it. It felt like a whole other lifetime. *Focus, Lacey.* "How did the last signings go?"

Opening up her inbox, she watched her emails unfold down the screen. Most of them color-coded with Janna's flags. Red for urgent. Purple for follow-up. Blue for FYI.

Thank goodness for her industrious assistant. Lacey guessed that at least half the people returning from Meredith's little trip weren't going to have this level of organizational aptitude waiting for them.

And she would take advantage of whatever head start she could get.

"They were fine. I know you must be crazy busy just returning from your trip and all, but I was wondering ..." Beckett's voice trailed off.

Wondering what? She did not have time for people not getting to the point. Not today. She had two books launching in a couple of weeks.

Lacey forced herself to pull in a breath. Beckett was a good guy. And, compared to some of the athletes she'd worked with, very low maintenance. "Yes?"

"Do you prefer champagne or chocolate?" This time his voice didn't come from her phone. She looked up from her screen. The man himself stood in her doorway. Holding a magnum of champagne and a large box of Ghirardelli chocolates.

He flashed a grin at her. No doubt that grin had the receptionists downstairs falling over themselves to break protocol and give him access to the upper floors without notifying her.

Lacey preferred champagne, but she was tempted to say chocolates just to be contrary. "What's the occasion?" She placed her phone on her desk as she scrolled through her mental Rolodex. *The Accidental Olympian* had been a steady performer since it had released. It had debuted at number three on its *New York Times* Bestsellers list and stayed on there for a couple of months before dropping away. It hadn't made a resurgence in her absence. She'd checked all the bestseller lists while her hairdresser spent two hours depoofing her hair.

"I wanted to say thank you. For all the work you did on the book."

"I didn't exactly do it for free." She smiled at him to soften the words.

Beckett stepped into her office, then stepped back. "Sorry, I should have asked. Do you have something else you need to be doing right now?"

"I have a few minutes." She'd told Janna to keep her calendar clear for the morning so she could get on top of everything. Her estimation of Beckett went up a notch. Most clients, especially the men, would never have asked. They simply assumed she had nothing more important to do.

She gestured to the seat in front of her desk. "Come on in."

He placed the bottle and box on her desk, along with an envelope.

Lacey leaned back in her chair. The envelope was cream and clearly expensive. She'd seen a lot of them in her career. Funny how the first thing people thought she would like was a spa voucher. Not that she minded. She hadn't paid for a beauty treatment in about five years as a result. But it was predictable. Victor would never give her a spa voucher. She squashed the unwelcome thought flat.

"It's not a spa voucher."

Lacey looked up to see Beckett's dark eyes studying her. The question must have been written on her face because he shrugged. "I was here one day when some other client gave you one. From the look on your face, it looked like it was hardly a surprise."

"So, what is it?" Lacey picked up the envelope and tapped it against her desk. She couldn't help but be a bit intrigued.

"Why don't you open it and find out?" Beckett shifted in his chair, running his hand through his dark brown hair.

Lacey squinted at him as she slid her finger under the seal of the flap. Reaching inside, she pulled out two premium tickets to *The Book of Mormon*. For that night.

"You mentioned you'd never seen it."

If she had, it had only been in passing. She looked down at the tickets in her hand. They'd been purchased three months before.

Two tickets. For tonight. And Beckett was sitting right in front of her, his face crinkled in what looked like half apprehension, half hope.

Oh, man. This happened every now and then. Even though she made it clear that she did not date her clients. Ever.

Most of the time, if she did her job well, it was only a matter of weeks before any single male clients had more than enough admirers that any thoughts they'd had in her direction moved on.

But every now and then … "Beck," she kept her voice gentle. "You remember that I can't date my clients, right?"

Hopefully, he would say she'd misunderstood, that the ticket was for her to take a friend. Something that would allow him to salvage some pride.

He offered her a lopsided smile. "I'm not your client any more. My contract with Langham ended on Friday."

Oh.

"I'm sorry. You're right. It was a stupid idea." Beckett was on his feet, his ears tipped pink. "My mom, she always told me to go for the woman who knows what she wants and is her own success. I've admired your drive and determination ever since we first met."

Lacey's brain processed the words that weren't in that sentence. Beautiful. Hot. Sexy. When was the last time she'd been asked out by a guy that didn't involve some kind of allusion to what she looked like? "You're not my client any more." It was half statement, half question.

Beckett stilled. "I'm not."

She had never thought of him that way. She had trained herself to never think of any client that way. A couple of mistakes early in her career had drilled in the necessity of putting an iron wall between her and the men she worked with.

Beckett stood, waiting as Lacey sifted through her impressions of him. He'd only ever treated her with respect. She'd never had to pour him into a limo drunk after an event. Never had to try and clean up any kind of publicity mess because of his bad behavior. Everyone at his publishing house loved him.

It wasn't because he was putting on a front for her because he saw her "no dating clients" rule as some kind of challenge. Men like that had short attention spans. He would have moved on by now. Especially when his signings had had no shortage of ski bunnies suggesting he sign their cleavage rather than his book.

Beckett Hodge was, by all accounts, a good guy. And those were few and far between in her world.

Her mind flashed to a certain blond with a scar. To the second she had momentarily lost her self-control and leaned her head against his chest and found it felt just as solid and safe as she had imagined it would.

But solid and safe had been her dad once. Had been Mitch once. And look where that had gotten her mom and Betsy.

She looked down at the tickets in her hand. Then at the man standing in front of her, patiently waiting. She always had a cocktail dress in her office closet, just in case. She looked at the calendar on her screen. Janna had blocked out the evening with a cryptic note that she hadn't gotten around to asking her about. The man had gotten help from the inside. And she had always wanted to see *The Book of Mormon*. "Okay. Pick me up from here at six."

"Great, see you then." Beckett leaned against the doorway, the pink from his ears now spreading to his cheeks.

He left her doorway casually enough, but she could see the grin and fist pump as he walked past her window.

A date. With Beckett Hodge. Lacey tapped her pen against her lips as a smile threatened. She supposed there were worse things to do on a Tuesday night.

SINCE VICTOR COULDN'T GET INTO his computer until IT sorted out some update they'd accidentally set to run across the company twelve hours early, he had might as well do something with his time.

Well, something other than think about the woman with

crazy hair who had given him a tight smile and a brisk wave goodbye at JFK. She headed home, he to his connecting flight for London.

Victor dropped into the chair across the table from where Donald sat doctoring his coffee with four sugars.

"Welcome back." The man didn't even look up from stirring his concoction. He'd had a haircut since Victor had last seen him, his grey follicles now shorn back to a number-two cut.

"Thanks."

"You made it to a meeting yet?"

"Not yet."

At that, the man lifted his head and a bushy eyebrow.

"I know. I will." He'd only been back in the country for forty-eight hours, for goodness sake. And a third of that he'd spent sleeping. And when jet lag had him awake … well, there weren't many meetings going on at four in the morning. "I did fine. I'm still sober."

"Staying sober when you're in the wilderness with no access to alcohol is hardly a feat."

Victor bristled. "It's not like that was all there was. There were also minibars, booze on the planes, and a cocktail party."

Don took a sip of his coffee, regarding Victor over the brim. "I'm not trying to downplay the temptation you did face. It's just this is the danger zone. Take it from someone who knows."

"What do you mean?" He didn't know why he felt so defensive with the man who had been with him for every step of his sobriety since he first got out of rehab.

"How long have you been sober?"

"Three years, six months, two weeks." Give or take a couple of days.

"And you feel like you have it in the bag."

Victor couldn't deny it. It wasn't that alcohol didn't call to him anymore. But he felt confident in his ability to withstand the temptation. He'd been doing it for years. Saying no to drinks at every kind of event imaginable. Plotting his routes home to avoid liquor outlets when he'd had a hard day. Calling Don when the idea of a stiff drink started feeling a bit too alluring.

Don steepled his fingers. "I'm not criticizing you. It's human nature. You've gone this long. It's easy to think you've got a handle on it. So you go to a few less meetings, then stop going at all. You check in less frequently with your sponsor. All is well." Don shrugged. "Until it isn't. And it's never the things you see coming that take you out. It's the things you don't."

A waitress placed Victor's tea in front of him, and he nodded his thanks. Don had been sober ten years when he started as Victor's sponsor, so he was coming up on fourteen now. This time around. "What took you out?"

"Once it was losing my job. The second time it was just complacency. The second is by far the more dangerous."

Victor took a sip of his tea, the boiling liquid scorching his tongue.

"The job losses, the relationship breakups, the big things that knock you sideways. They're the easier ones to pick. You know you're going to want to bury your woes at the bottom of a bottle. But complacency?" Don shook his head. "That's the one that sneaks up on you. It's the one that whispers in your ear after three years, five years, ten years, that you've got this conquered now. That one drink can't hurt. That you can handle it. Just like that serpent in the Garden of Eden."

Well, he didn't have to worry about that for a while. His past was still too present, too raw, for him to be complacent about anything. He could find it in every skeptical glance from his brother. Every worried look from his mother. Every time his father slammed the fridge door because Victor was in the house, and his mother had got rid of all the beer.

"I'll get to a meeting this week. I promise."

Don nodded his acceptance. "You seeing anyone?"

Victor's hands tightened around his mug. He'd been more than clear about all of his character flaws when Don first became his sponsor. Wanted the man to know exactly what a failure he was signing up for. "No."

"Relationships aren't like alcohol, Victor. They're to be nurtured, not avoided."

"I know. That's why I'm doing my best to mend the ones I have." He had caused his family more grief and pain than anyone should ever have to go through. He would never be able to make that right, but he could do his best to never cause the same to anyone else ever again.

"Have you just not met anyone, or are you scared?"

"Scared of what?"

Don lifted a shoulder. "Just asking the question."

He wasn't scared. He was smart. Smart enough to know there were some things he would never be able to leave in the past. Some things that he couldn't trust himself with. Not ever.

Not to mention that the only woman who had caused him to have more than a second thought since rehab was untouchable. Untouchable and out of his league.

It was a strange thought. There hadn't been a girl—or woman—since he was sixteen that he hadn't known he couldn't charm if he wanted to. The combination of his looks, athleticism, and title had always been a potent combination.

But to Lacey O'Connor, he was an idiot lowlife lobbyist whose only redeeming feature was that he could carry a canoe. At least, that was what he kept trying to tell himself. Far safer to point his thoughts there than to the momentary settling of her head against his chest, an event that somehow etched itself into his memory like it was hours, not seconds.

"So, who is she?" Don tapped the side of his cup with his spoon with a pointed look.

Victor's phone buzzed, and he pulled it out of his pocket. Sean. "Sorry, I need to take this." His lifted his phone to his ear. "What's up?"

"Where are you? We just got an email saying they're releasing the new org structure in ten minutes."

"I'll be back in five." Shoving his phone back in his pocket, Victor took one last gulp of his tea. "Sorry, Don. I have to go."

His sponsor raised his mug at him. "I'll be at tomorrow night's meeting. You can tell me about her then."

IF THERE WAS AN AWARD for most torturous merger process of the century, then Meredith was a shoo-in for it. Lacey squinted at her phone screen as she tried to zoom in on the most relevant parts of the new structure.

At least the woman had now put a timeline on when the insanity would end. *From 1 August* was written across the top in bold font. Just over two months away, probably due to the complexity of merging two companies in different countries.

The buzz of the diner receded as she focused on a document designed to be consumed on a full-sized screen.

It was like a jigsaw puzzle. Some of the positions and names in the corporate support parts of the organization had been filled in. But further up the tree, only blank boxes appeared. No names or even position titles in the top four tiers. After a couple of minutes scrolling, she finally found Janna's name buried in a box called "USA admin support" with about five other assistants.

"Sorry, I'm late." Rachel slid into the booth opposite her. "Flight was delayed last night. I didn't get to the hotel until after one." Faint circles fanned under her eyes, and her hand rose to her lips to stifle a yawn. "Coffee." She looked over her shoulder and caught the eye of a nearby waitress, who hurried over to fill her cup.

"Can I get you ladies some breakfast?" The slender young woman pulled a pad out of her apron.

Neither of them needed to look at the menu. This had become their regular spot over the last six months whenever they were in New York at the same time.

Lacey placed her phone on the table. "An omelette with spinach and mushrooms, no toast, please."

"Pancakes, please. With extra bacon and syrup." Rachel slipped a hair tie off her wrist and twisted her sandy blonde hair into a messy bun on top of her head.

Lacey took a sip of her water so she couldn't change her order. Eggs were good. Eggs were protein. She liked eggs. Pancakes would go straight to her hips. Even if the outfit she was wearing was definitely looser than it had been before her little trip to the wilderness.

"So how's Lucas? Happy six-month anniversary, by the way."

Rachel's eyebrows lifted. "How on earth did you remember that?"

"Well, you guys were kind enough to get it together the same week your last book released." She also had a six-month reminder in her calendar for all the books she worked on so she could check on how their sales were going. "Don't tell me you forgot."

"Actually, I did. But Lucas didn't." A soft smile lit Rachel's face. Fair enough. It was her first serious relationship in a decade.

"You planning to make the move to Madison anytime soon?"

Rachel wrapped her hands around her mug. "No. I don't want to leave Anna, you know? And we're good. Long-distance isn't ideal, but it works for now." The other big reason sat unspoken. Her father. The damage the man had wrought on his daughter would keep Rachel's therapist occupied for years. But at least she was seeing one now.

"Anyone else back from Minnesota yet?"

Lacey didn't resist Rachel's change of topic. "I saw some of them yesterday. No one is any the wiser, though. Their stories were all the same. On Sunday afternoon, their guides told them it was over, and they all got extracted." No winners, no review, no debriefing, nothing. Just a bus back to the airport and a return flight home. "They put out a new org structure this morning, but it's only junior staff. No one who went to Minnesota is on it. Anyway, what brings you into town?"

Rachel took a tentative sip of her coffee, the diner having a record of setting its temperature somewhere near lava. "Waterstones wanted to talk to me about someone they're signing who's going to need a collaborative writer."

Lacey didn't ask for more details. Rachel was notoriously close-mouthed about her potential projects until they were in the bag. But it must be a big deal for them to fly her in.

Speaking of which ... "I saw Beckett the other day." Rachel had been the collaborative writer brought in on Beckett's book after the first writer bailed four weeks from deadline. She hadn't exactly gotten Lacey the publicist job, but Rachel putting in a good word with the bobsledder had certainly helped.

Rachel's cup paused halfway back to her mouth. "How is he? How's the book going."

"Good." Lacey coughed. She could just leave it there and move the conversation on. Beckett was a nice enough date, but it wasn't like they had a *thing*.

Rachel took a sip of her coffee. "And?"

Lacey took a breath. She didn't really do girl talk. But she had promised herself she would try harder with Rachel and Anna.

Push herself out of her comfort zone. "We went to the *Book of Mormon.*"

Rachel's hand jerked, and coffee sloshed over the rim of her mug. "Wait. What? You went on a *date* with Beckett Hodge?" Her cup landed on the table with a clatter, and she grabbed a napkin, rubbing it across her hand. "But you don't date your clients. That's Lacey's first commandment of book publicity."

"He's not my client any more. Not since Friday."

Rachel leaned forward, cogs turning behind her brown eyes. "Have you had a crush on Beckett this whole time and not said anything?"

"No!" The denial came out too loud, and the couple at the next table looked their way. "Not at all." She lowered her voice. "I don't think of my clients like that. But he showed up yesterday with tickets he'd bought months ago and said he wasn't my client any more. And, well." Lacey shrugged. "How was I supposed to say no to that?"

Rachel leaned back in the red booth, shoving a piece of wayward hair out of her face. "Beckett's a really good guy, Lace. Like a *really* good guy."

"I know." The guy hadn't even tried to kiss her last night, let alone invite himself in for "coffee." Leaving her feeling relieved and bemused … wondering if he would ask her out again. That was not a feeling she was at all used to.

"Look, all I'm trying to say is that he doesn't date casually. If he asked you out, that means something to him. And if you only said yes because you couldn't find a good reason to say no … well." Rachel's teeth tugged at her bottom lip. "Then obviously he's more into you than you are into him."

"I told you I don't think of my clients like that." Shame her powers weren't working as well on a future colleague. But she had three weeks until Emelia's wedding to get a grip on that. Maybe a couple more dates with Beckett would help.

"If you're attracted to someone you can't not think of them like that, even if you don't act on it. Are you seriously telling me that in all the time you worked with Beckett you didn't feel one shred of attraction for him and now that he's off your roster, boom, just like that it's suddenly magic?"

Lacey leaned back in her seat as her eggs landed in front of her. What was going on here? Beckett and Rachel had only worked together for a couple of months. Yeah, he was a good guy, but her friend was acting like he was her brother or something.

Across the table Rachel was chopping into her stack of pancakes with gusto.

"Have you and Lucas had a fight or something?" Rachel and Lucas had met through their jobs. Maybe Rachel was projecting. Just because she couldn't separate the personal from the professional didn't mean Lacey couldn't.

Rachel looked up from her carb massacre. "What? No."

"Then why are you jumping all over me about Beckett? I would've thought you'd be thrilled I'd gone on a date with a nice guy. It's not like I go through men like M&Ms. It's the first date I've been on this year."

Rachel sighed and put down her weapons. "You're right. I'm sorry. Beckett is a great guy, and you deserve a great guy."

"But?"

"Fine. Okay. I know it's totally stupid, but I may have," she mumbled something that Lacey couldn't decipher.

"May have what?"

Rachel looked a bit sheepish. "I may have thought if he was still single in a year that I'd introduce him to Anna."

"To Anna?" Lacey's tone pitched up, and the couple at the next table turned their heads in their direction again. She leaned over the table and shout whispered, "Cam hasn't even been dead a year! She still wears her wedding ring!" At least she had the last time Lacey saw her.

Rachel stabbed her fork into a piece of bacon. "I know. That's why I said in a year. *If* he was still single."

Lacey pushed her plate away, appetite gone. "Well, I guess that's that." She could hardly date Beckett now. Not now that she knew Rachel had mentally dibsed him for Anna. Beckett Hodge was the kind of man who had second chance at love written all over him.

He didn't live in New York, but he trained in Colorado at least half the year. He was already a better match for Anna than for her.

"What's what then?" Rachel spoke through a mouth of pancakes.

"Beckett. I'm hardly going to date him now, am I." Sure, their date hadn't set the world on fire, but she'd forgotten about the restructure for a few hours. Forgotten about Victor. And if he'd gone in for a kiss, she wouldn't have turned him down. Which was more than she could say for the last few dates she'd been on.

"No! No, no, no, no, no. You should totally go on another date with him. If you want to." Rachel's words tumbled out over themselves. "It was stupid. A crazy stupid thought. Let's be real. What are the chances he's going to be single in a year? And Anna will find a great guy with a click of her fingers, as soon as she decides she's ready. I order you to go on another date with him."

At that, Lacey's phone buzzed and started to shimmy across the table. Before she could reach for it, Rachel snatched it up and let out a whistle. "The man himself."

Lacey held her hand out. "Give it."

"Nah, ah." She tapped at Lacey's screen.

Since when did Rachel know her password?

"Lacey, thanks for a great evening. I'm back in New York next week. Dinner Thursday? Beck." She handed the phone back, and Lacey made a note to change her password. "There's totally going to be flowers waiting for you at the office."

"Flowers? What are you talking about?" But Lacey couldn't deny the warmth that spread through her chest at Rachel's words.

Rachel raised her eyebrows. "I'm just saying. Beckett Hodge is the kind of guy who sends flowers."

CHAPTER SIXTEEN

L ACEY KNEW SHE HAD ACHIEVED status in the publishing world the first time she had a designer asking if she could dress her for the annual Met Literary Gala.

This year, she'd had three. Three beautiful dresses. Three eager designers. It was usually her favorite event of the year. The gorgeous couture gown Janna had collected the day before should have soothed her pretzeled insides. Instead, she'd had to force herself into it, wishing she could trade places with her roommate, who was stretched across their couch in yoga pants with a bowl of popcorn.

To top it all off one of her biggest clients had been booked on *The Today Show* and the slot was when she was supposed to be in Oxford for Emelia's wedding.

"Lacey!" The head of marketing for Schnell & Cohen bore down on her, freshly Botoxed lips going in for the New York double kiss. "Mwah, mwah."

Then she stepped back, hands on Lacey's shoulders and looked her up and down. "You've lost weight. You look amazing. I'm so jealous. You have to tell me what your secret is." This from a woman who was skinnier than the average broomstick. Michelle's collarbones jutted out from the top of her dress like a pair of railway tracks. The only things Lacey had ever seen her consume were champagne and cigarettes.

Lacey smiled, the expression tight on her face. It wasn't like she didn't know that the last few weeks had seen five pounds disappear. She monitored her weight with the same amount of attention as she monitored the best sellers lists. "Just a fortunate side effect of a company bonding trip to the wilderness." Plus she'd struggled to eat a proper meal since she'd had to unwrap Molly and Lucy from her waist.

A plate of hors d'oeuvres passed by, the waitress not even pausing with the bacon-wrapped scallops. Had she looked at both of them and decided she wasn't going to get any takers? And she was right. Lacey never ate at events like this. Yet suddenly, for some reason, that peeved her right off.

"Excuse me. I'd like one, please." The young woman stopped and looked at her as if she was unsure if it was some kind of trick. Lacey reached out and took one of the oriental shaped spoons, popped the entree in her mouth, and the spoon back on the tray.

The combination of salty bacon and creamy scallop exploded in her mouth, and she had to wrap her fingers around her purse to stop herself from reaching for another one. "Thank you." She smiled at the young woman, who still looked deeply uncertain.

Michelle's expression showed a hint of triumph. Well, as much of one as her face could manage. In this twisted world, if another woman ate and you didn't, you were the victor.

Lacey looked around the crowded room, sizing up the contacts she needed to schmooze during the evening. She'd had a good week. Her newest book had debuted at number two on its list, but she was sorely aware that she needed every contact, every contract, every accolade she could get to try and bridge the gap being disqualified had created.

"Good evening, ladies." A smooth male voice interrupted her mental interlude, and Lacey brought her attention back to where Michelle was air-kissing someone with salt and pepper hair in a suit that fit so well it could only be custom made.

Then he turned to her and held out his hand. "I don't think we've met. Bradley O'Donnell."

She held out her hand, appreciating his firm shake. "Lacey O'Connor, Langham & Co." She knew exactly who he was. Bradley and his sister Natalie had built a home improvement empire from the ground up. Now they had an HGTV show, a chain of homeware stores, and they'd just launched a whole foods brand. Their first book two years before had gone straight to the top of the list.

"Oh, sorry." Michelle managed to snap herself out of her Bradley-induced adoration. "Lacey, we've just signed Bradley and Natalie for their next book. Part memoir, part home and living, part self-help."

Lacey felt her eyebrows rise. If they could hit all of those niches, Schnell & Cohen would be making bank. Though they needed to since Lacey had no doubt that the advance would be what Publishers' Weekly would term a "very, very nice deal."

"Brad, Lacey is the head of publicity at Langham & Co. She's one of the best with well over a hundred New York Times' best sellers in her portfolio." Michelle gave Lacey a significant look. "Brad and Natalie are going to be very involved in the formation of their marketing and publicity teams. Schnell & Cohen are putting our full weight behind this book."

In other words, Lacey had just been handed the opportunity to pitch for the biggest account of the year. Possibly the last five years, given the current state of the publishing industry.

"Congratulations." She tilted her head toward the golden boy. "I'd be very happy to talk to you about your project and what you're looking for whenever suits."

"We're both here now." Bradley swiped a couple of champagnes off a passing tray and handed one to her.

"Okay." Lacey took a sip of her champagne to give her a

moment to get her mental Rolodex in order. Brad and Natalie were a publishing dream. Small town background. Natalie had three Insta-perfect kids. Brad, as far as she knew, was single. Natalie led all the style and design work, and Brad was the quintessential handyman. Their easy sibling banter had set their show apart from its pilot. The demographics they reached were insane.

"I'll leave you two to chat." Michelle gracefully removed herself from the conversation. Her gap was filled by a waiter with another tray of food.

"Smoked salmon rillette?"

Suddenly, Lacey was hungry for the first time since Meredith had walked into the boardroom. "Yes, please." Lacey picked one up and popped it into her mouth. Oh, it was so good. *This* was what she'd been missing out on all these years?

"Thank you." Brad helped himself to one as well, and she looked up to see him studying her with a cryptic smile.

"What?" She was sure she had managed the bite-sized piece of food perfectly. No chance of there being a piece of creme marring her lipstick.

He leaned in, his voice dropping. "You ate something. Natalie hates these kinds of events because she says none of the women ever eat. The amount of food wastage drives her crazy."

"I'm pretty sure you'll find the minimum-wage catering staff out back, more than happy to take care of the food wastage." At least that was what had happened in the catering gigs she'd done back in college days. On a good night, after she'd eaten her fill, she'd been able to take Anna and Rachel home an abundance of rich people food.

"Well, that's doubly good news then. I can go home and tell Natalie that not only have I found a New York publicist who eats but also assuage her worries about where all the leftover food goes."

And with that, whether he intended it or not, Lacey knew exactly how the dynamic worked. Brad was in charge of the shortlisting, but Natalie would make the final decision. Her job tonight was to get the nod from Brad and make it to Natalie.

"So." Brad took a sip of his drink and Lacey catalogued the way he moved subtly closer to her as he did so. "Tell me about yourself." He held up a finger. "Something I won't read on your official website bio. Michelle will package up all of that stuff. Natalie and I are more interested in knowing the people we might be working with." Subtle emphasis on the *might*.

She had to hand it to him. Bradley O'Donnell might sell the small town schtick, but he was as smooth and polished as any big-city corporate exec.

She knew exactly how to play this. Even though she hated it. "I grew up in Minnesota, in a tiny town called Small Harbor." Let him imagine a Natalie-style Craftsman with a big wide open porch and iced tea with the neighbors. "You're looking at Lake County's junior target shooting champion of 2005."

"Impressive." He clinked his champagne glass to hers. "Are your family still there?"

"They are. My parents and older sister and her family. Two nieces and a nephew."

"Do you see them often?"

"I was just there last week." True. She didn't lie. Not even for big contracts.

"Do you miss it? Small town life?"

"I miss not seeing my nieces and nephew grow up." A pang traveled down her spine. Was her sister ever going to forgive her? Let her be part of the kids' lives beyond Christmas and birthday presents and the occasional photo?

"Maybe we could work Small Harbor, Minnesota, in our

book tour schedule." His hand landed on her arm and lingered there for a second.

"Maybe." She added a lilt to her voice, so it sounded receptive, but not quite flirtatious. Ninety percent of the people in her hometown lived within a stone's throw of the poverty line. An appearance from people like Brad and Natalie would be odder than a Presidential visit. The people of Small Harbor didn't buy thirty dollar glossy hardcover coffee table books for coffee tables they didn't own.

"Michelle is talking about a big nationwide book tour. Possibly a bus with our faces plastered along the sides of it. What do you think of that?"

"We'd want to take careful stock of all your obligations when deciding a release date. Especially the filming ones for your show. And Natalie's family obligations. A nationwide bus tour is a huge time commitment." Brad and Natalie might be two of the few people left with the crowd-pulling power to make it profitable.

"So, if you were our publicist, we'd spend quite a lot of time together in close quarters." His hand ran down her arm, and a seeing-eye dog couldn't have missed the way his gaze dropped to her lips, then lower.

She smothered a sigh. Dang it, Bradley O'Donnell was a creep. And she usually had an excellent radar for picking them. She kept her smile fixed firmly on her face. This was nothing she hadn't dealt with before. She'd dealt with far worse and managed to both put them in their place and land the pitch. "Unfortunately, my commitments to other authors would mean I wouldn't be able to travel on the bus with you. That would be one of my team. I'd meet you at strategic locations and events." A male member of her team. She made a mental note.

Something in Brad's gaze shifted, though his arm didn't. "This book is a big deal for us. It will be important to Natalie and me that the core members of our team are with us most of the time. They need to be just as committed to its success as we are."

Lacey stilled, her mind sifting through a range of possibilities and calculating her next move. She had to keep Brad on the line to get to Natalie. If she could get to Natalie, she had no doubt she could sell her team.

"Langham and Co's strength is in our publicity team. While I would be the lead, of course, a book this big with its extensive publicity needs will need at least three people on the team. And I promise you, I'm far more valuable to your efforts in the flight deck, not on the tour bus."

Something in his gaze glinted. "Natalie and I are very good at deciding where people are the most valuable to us. It's one of the reasons for our success."

Keep him on the line, Lacey. All you have to do is keep him on the line so you can get to Natalie. Land this account and Meredith will have to put you in the executive suite. But nothing came out of her mouth.

Brad gazed at her, a smile tilting his lips. "I've had a look at your portfolio of clients. You have some very impressive people there. Some of them are acquaintances of mine. They were highly complimentary regarding your services." His voice lingered on the last word, and this time there was no possible way of mistaking his meaning.

Lacey's hand gripped her glass. Either he was telling her a bald-faced lie, or one of her previous clients had fed him one. She hadn't made the mistake of getting involved with a client in over eight years.

Nothing was ever going to change if she kept playing the game. The thought hit her like a bolt of lightning. Enough. She was done. This whole time, she'd told herself that being at the top would mean she could make the company better for the women coming after her. But how could she make the company better for everyone else if she couldn't stand up for herself?

Brad might be all hot air. She could play the game to get to Natalie, hope to convince his sister that her way was the better way. But she wasn't putting any of her team on that bus with this creep, male or female. She wasn't doing it.

Lacey held his gaze as she shoved her champagne glass into his chest, leaving him no choice but to grab it or have it tip down his front. "I'm sorry, there appears to have been some kind of misunderstanding. I'm afraid Langham & Co won't be a good fit for this book, Mr. O'Donnell. Please let Michelle know we won't be pitching for it."

And she picked up her skirt and walked out.

CHAPTER SEVENTEEN

"HOW'S THE RESTRUCTURE GOING, VICTOR?" Peter asked as a tailor strode around him, making final nips and tucks to his tails.

"Fine." Victor pushed his feet along the plush carpet. Being slightly shorter than Peter had its advantages, including not having to have a suit custom-made.

All he'd had to do today was shrug into the rental Emelia had previously selected, proclaim it good enough, and the whole thing was done in a few minutes.

Peter had been standing on a pedestal thing for at least twenty minutes while the staff fussed about his change in measurements since the last fitting. Which was what you got when your client was a rower seven weeks out from the world championships.

It was borderline enjoyable watching his usually frenetic brother having to reign in his impatience. Even more so because the bespoke designer suit was a freebie in exchange for a mention in some exclusive magazine spread Peter and Emelia had sold the rights to.

"You confident you're going to be okay?"

Victor shrugged. "As confident as anyone can be. I brought in a new client last week, so that's something." A small family organic foods chain looking for some advances in food labelling laws, but it was better than nothing.

His phone buzzed on the couch beside him, *Mark* flashing on the screen. Finally. Victor had left him two messages since his return, trying to keep the iron hot even while Meredith's Machiavellian machinations moved at glacial speeds.

He grabbed up his phone as he stood. "Mark, hi." He walked a few steps away from Peter and his entourage. "Thanks for calling me back."

"Hey. Sorry, it's taken me a few days."

"No problem at all. I know you guys have a lot on."

"We do. In fact, things moved forward quite a lot while you were away."

"I'm happy to hear it. The team is ready to meet with the board and pitch whenever suits." The team being him and whoever he could happen to rope in. He knew he could impress them, if he could just get in the room, even without the job title they were looking for.

"I'm sorry, Vic. The exec have decided they can't wait around for Meredith to finish her restructure. They're going with McMillan."

The edges of his phone dug into his palm. "Oh. Um. Thanks for letting me know. I appreciate being considered."

"I'm sorry, buddy. Just bad timing."

"Of course. Well, you know where to find me if McMillan aren't up to it." Hopefully. With his one last hope at landing this major account gone, he was now going to have to be on the hunt for another. Right now, he was little more than an expendable junior lobbyist with a list of small-medium sized clients anyone could handle.

"There's one other thing." Mark's voice dropped, and Victor could almost see his friend looking over his shoulder to check no one else was listening.

"I'm listening." Victor glanced over his own shoulder to where Peter was standing. Good. Emelia had arrived and captured his brother's full attention. Peter's face transformed into something that resembled a Labrador puppy.

Probably not far off his own expression when Lacey had leaned against him. Minus the ginger. It was a good thing he didn't have her number. The number of times he had wanted to talk to her since he'd left Minnesota was irrational.

"We've got the go-ahead to do another limited set of human trials. Very limited."

"Really."

"You should get your mother's specialist to look into it. The Aditron trial. She might not qualify—the requirements are pretty stringent. But if they can submit an application in the next couple of weeks, she'll at least be considered."

Victor's grip on his phone tightened, the sting of losing on the account fading at the hope replacing it. "I will. Thank you."

"Don't thank me. Just don't mention me when you ask about it."

"Got it."

The line went dead, and Victor shoved his phone back into his pocket. Peter was sliding out of his pinned coat, the fitting finally over.

A drug trial. He might be able to finally do something good for his family. Bring something of value. He walked back toward the couch and scooped up his jacket. As soon as he got back to the office, he would get back to work. Come up with some plausible reason to explain why he might know about the new trial.

"Do you guys need anything more from me?"

Peter had looped his arm around Emelia's waist and pulled her in close, his lips brushing against the top of her head. A burst of jealousy hit Victor square in the chest, his desire to be back at a derelict Walmart in Small Harbor so strong he could feel the cracked linoleum and see the flickering fluorescent lights.

Emelia's eyebrows puckered together, her straight-lined mouth not exactly the picture of a joyous bride ten days before her wedding.

"Is everything okay?"

She sighed. "Sorry, it's not you. Just a blip. My cousin won't arrive until the day before the wedding. She's had some work stuff come up."

Victor searched his memory bank for any information about Emelia's cousin but came up blank. "Have I met her?"

Emelia cracked half a smile at his question. "Trust me, you'd remember if you had."

Victor wasn't entirely sure he wanted to know what that meant. Given the bits and pieces he'd heard about Emelia's dysfunctional family, it wasn't even worth hazarding a guess, so he changed the topic. "Do either of you know if Mum has a specialist appointment any time soon?"

Peter loosened his hold on his fiancé just long enough to pick up his jacket. "No idea. Em? You see her more than I do."

Emelia thought for a second. "Not that I know of. She hasn't mentioned one. Why?"

Victor paused. It was probably better that all of them were in on this, but if it turned out to be a dead-end then it would just be another way he'd disappointed everyone. "That call was a friend giving me a tip about a new drug trial he suggested we look into."

"Does your friend work for the company?" Peter regarded him with suspicion, as if Victor was suggesting they send their mother to visit the local witchdoctor.

His fiancée jabbed him in the ribs. "Peter, don't ask questions we don't need answers to." She turned to Victor. "I assume it's a properly approved and legal trial."

"It is. But it's limited. Her specialist would have to make an application for her in the next couple of weeks."

Emelia nodded. "Okay. I'll talk to her and make an appointment. Hopefully, we can get in before the wedding."

"Em, you have enough to do. Victor can do it."

"Don't be ridiculous, Peter. Why should Victor drive up from London to take your mother to the doctor when I'm right there? All the wedding stuff is pretty much sorted. It's just an appointment. Her specialist can look into it and work out if it might be good for her." She looked at Victor. "Assuming you can give me enough information for them to go on."

"I'll do some more research this afternoon and email you."

"Okay, done. I'll talk to her at church on Sunday."

Church. Victor should go this weekend. It had been a while since he'd graced the pews of his local parish. When he did attend, he was a distinct oddity among the pensioners and harried parents with small children. But that would require him to examine why he was feeling so cross with God, that the one woman he'd met who pulled him in like a fish on a lure was completely out of his reach.

Maybe a meeting would be better. No couples snuggling into each other during the sermon there. No small children running around with their father's hair and mother's eyes. Just people trying to make it through, one step at a time.

"Victor," Peter cleared his throat.

"Yes." He waited for some wedding errand that needed running or relative that needed collecting on his way to Oxford.

Peter shifted on his feet but looked him in the eye.

"Can you thank your friend for us? For letting us know?"

Victor just blinked at him. Granted, Peter wasn't thanking him for anything. But it was at least a grudging acknowledgement that Victor might have done something good.

Maybe miracles were still possible.

CHAPTER EIGHTEEN

THERE HAD BEEN FLOWERS WAITING for Lacey at the office
when she'd gotten in after her breakfast with Rachel, and
another bunch this morning. Big luscious pastel-pink peonies
with the distinct styling of one of New York's premier florists. If
she'd had any doubts about dinner, there were no doubts now.

They'd arranged to meet at her favorite Italian restaurant.
Beck had shown up all sportsman-style casual, dropped a kiss on
her cheek, complimented her dress, and pulled out her chair. It
was like a date from the fifties.

Menus perused and food and drinks ordered, Lacey leaned
back in her seat and let the background jazz wash over her. Beck
smiled at her over the flickering tea lights in the middle of their
table. It didn't twist up her insides like a pretzel, but it was nice.
"How—"

"Excuse me." A gorgeous barely-legal redhead poured into her
jumpsuit stood by their table. "Are you Beckett Hodge?"

Beck's eyes flickered to Lacey and then back to the girl. "I
am."

"I'm a huge fan. Would you mind …" Before she even finished her question, the girl had her phone out in front of her and
was leaning down, her fulsome breasts almost taking out the
single rose on the side of their table. Lacey suppressed an eye roll.

"I'm sorry." Beck put his hand up to block the shot. "I appreciate the compliment, but I'm on a date. And I'd like to focus on

her."

The girl froze, her face a caricature of disbelief. Lacey barely managed to keep her own jaw from unhinging. After a frozen second, the girl stood with a humph and flounced off.

Lacey took a sip of her water. "I'm pretty sure that has never happened to her before."

Beck reached for his own glass. "Yeah, well, I'm not a big fan of being someone's Instagram trophy. Especially when a second date with you is the only thing I've been thinking about since the first one." He gave her a wink, and she couldn't help but smile in response.

Beck was a gentleman. Beck was here. Beck sent flowers, and his hand hadn't so much as grazed her behind. Ever. Which was more than she could say for almost every other date she'd been on in the last decade. Most importantly of all, Beck wasn't an employee of either Langham or Wyndham.

She hadn't had any contact with Victor since he'd returned to London. Which was exactly as it should be. Although that wouldn't help her in a week when she'd have to face him in front of an altar as her cousin pledged herself to his brother.

Victor Carlisle in a suit had been irresistible once before. And that was when he'd been the worst version of himself.

"I heard Langham is being merged. What does that mean for you?" Beck took a piece of bread from the basket and broke it in half.

Lacey forced herself back to the man sitting across from her. "Not sure yet. Still waiting to see how the cards are going to fall."

She'd been working long hours on all her upcoming releases since the gala. A lot more than she was billing for. Between Minnesota and the Met debacle, she was pinning everything on the books she had releasing in the next few weeks doing better than expected.

The extra work had paid dividends, but it had also meant a

lot of groveling to her cousin as the week she'd planned to be in Oxford for the wedding had been reduced to a long weekend.

Emelia had been more understanding than Lacey had expected. Which made her feel even more guilty about the fact that she'd been half-relieved for a reason to cut her trip short. The less time she spent in the orbit of a certain charming Brit, the better.

"You have nothing to worry about. You're brilliant at what you do."

Focus, Lacey. Back to Beck. Back to the handsome, attentive, charming man seated mere inches away, not oceans. "Thanks." Even though the merger absorbed most of her thoughts, she felt no desire to talk about it with Beck. She wanted to talk to the man taking up way more real estate in her head than she'd ever given permission for.

She reached for her glass and took a long sip of prosecco to cover the battle going on in her head. She had been on plenty of dates where she had been planning her way to an early exit in the first five minutes. But she couldn't remember the last time she'd been on a date with one guy wishing an entirely different one was in his seat. *Get it together, Lacey.* "So what do you do when you're not training?"

Beck lifted one shoulder. "Honestly, I'm not that exciting. I do promo stuff for the team and my sponsors, help my mom out. I'm involved in a couple of heritage projects, mentor a few guys in my church's youth group ..."

He said something else, but Lacey's brain had stopped on youth group.

"You're religious?"

The words came out harsher than she'd expected, and Beckett stopped mid whatever else he was saying. He studied her carefully across the table. "Define what you mean by religious."

Lacey shrugged. "You know, go to church, keep the rules, pray." It wasn't that she had a thing against men who were religious per se. She'd even dated a few. Just as long as it wasn't the kind of religious that interfered with their lives. If they showed up at church for Easter and Christmas to make their parents happy, fine. Ditto with Hanukkah.

It was when things started getting personal that she drew the line. She'd learned her lesson long ago. She was never going to be good enough for those types.

Beckett swiped a piece of bread from the basket in front of him. "I would never describe myself as religious."

Phew. The discomfort started to lift.

"But I believe God is real and has a purpose for our lives."

Lacey shoved down the urge to fill her mouth with delicious, comforting focaccia. Of course, he did. She met a nice, charming, respectful guy, and he was proper religious. She sighed. She couldn't date Beckett. Not if he was a true believer. Not when he obviously didn't do casual dating. And not when—despite the flowers and the manners and the charm—she was sitting here wishing he was someone else.

"That's not the answer you wanted." Beckett dipped his knife into the butter and smeared it across his bread.

"I didn't say that." At least the whole religion thing provided an easy out. One that wasn't personal. One that had nothing to do with Victor.

"You didn't have to. Your face looked like I just told you I thought books were doomed."

Lacey sighed. "Look, I don't have anything against religion. All my best friends are religious." She paused as her words registered. All her best friends were religious. They'd fallen like silent dominoes. It felt like a conspiracy. "It's just not for me. And honestly, if it's something that's important to you, then you should date someone who it's important to as well."

"Do you mind if I ask why not?"

"Why not what?"

"Why isn't it for you?" He popped a large chunk of bread into his mouth.

Because I thought I had found somewhere to belong, and they discarded me like trash. Lacey shrugged and stabbed her fork into an olive to try and distract herself from the luscious basket of bread. Luckily she was good at telling the truth without telling the real truth. "I've done a couple of books for a couple of people who had big religious values platforms. Let's just say neither of them exactly made me want to buy what they were selling."

Beckett winced.

"Look, I'm not tarring you all with the same brush. I know not everyone is a hypocrite. I know there are plenty of religious types who are good, honest people doing their best to live what they believe. But I don't think that could ever be me. In fact," she waved her olive-loaded fork at him, "if it wasn't for the fact that my friend's husband just died, I'd set you up with her."

Beckett choked out a half-laugh around his mouthful. "Um, no thanks?"

Lacey studied him as if seeing him through new eyes. She should have picked it when he didn't go for a kiss goodnight after the musical. "Rachel was right. In a year or two, you could be perfect for Anna." She chewed down on the salty olive and swallowed. "What do you think the chances are you might be still available?"

"Sorry, available for what?" Poor Beck looked like he had conversational whiplash.

"A date with our friend Anna. Her husband just died. Well, not just. Not like last week. It was last year. But she's not going to be looking for a while. Actually, let me put a reminder so I don't forget when she is ready to re-enter the fray." Lacey picked up her phone, opened her calendar, typed a note to herself and set a recurring six-monthly appointment.

Anna would kill both her and Rachel if she had any idea this conversation was happening. Like proper dead. Which reminded her. She should update her will to include Anna and Libby.

"I'm sorry." Beckett was partly leaning across the table. "Did you just put an appointment in your calendar to contact me when your bereaved friend is looking for another husband?"

Lacey placed her phone back on the table. "Honestly, she's probably never going to be looking for another husband because Cam—that's her first husband—was the love of her life. Like the 'I wasn't sure how she would keep breathing when he died' kind of love. But you're great, and she's great, so who knows what could happen."

Beckett shook his head. "I have to be honest. This isn't how I saw this evening going."

"I'm just saying. You believe in God. She believes in God. She lives in Colorado. You train there, right? Maybe this is all part of his grand plan. Don't you guys say God works in mysterious ways?"

Beckett's eyes were so wide she almost wondered if he was going to abandon dinner and make a run for it. Luckily his path was blocked by the waiter arriving with their meals. And she was pretty sure she hadn't yet reached the crazy date level where a man would walk away from a bowl of freshly made carbonara.

Beckett tipped his head back and laughed. "Never have I taken a woman on a date only to have her ask me to take a rain check for a year on a date with a friend and convince me it might be God's will when she doesn't even believe in God and have me actually contemplating the idea."

Lacey grinned at him. "I guess now you know how I sell so many books."

Sigh. Beckett was off the table. So much for him being the one knocking Victor from the perch he'd somehow taken up in her head.

CHAPTER NINETEEN

A GAGGLE OF PAGE BOYS and flower girls. Could Lacey call them that? There were only four, but it felt like more. Many, many more.

"Katherine and Charlotte! Freeze!" Lacey bellowed as her two half-cousins eyed up a mud puddle in front of the church. Images of their white tulle skirts and ballet slippers covered in brown muck seared her mind.

She hobbled forward in her fitted dress and wrapped her fingers firmly around their wrists. "Where are your flower baskets, girls?"

They both looked up at her and shrugged, faces angelic. "Pwetty flowers." Charlotte lisped the words then wrinkled her brow. "Potty?"

This was not in Lacey's job description. She was only here alone with them because the photographer had insisted they go ahead while she took a few final photos of Emelia.

She looked around for their mother. Carolina's hat was a flying saucer-like construction that could probably be spotted from space, but she had chosen that moment to be conspicuously absent. Of course.

"Charlotte threw her flowers in the toilet," Katherine spoke with all the authority of the tattling older sibling. "I told her not to, but she did it anyway."

Charlotte nodded, her ringleted brunette curls bouncing.

"Pwetty flowers go floating."

Excellent. Fifty bucks of hand-picked rose petals down the drain.

"And then George pooped on them!" Katherine looked positively gleeful as she imparted that unnecessary detail.

Reason #243 why Lacey could never see herself with kids.

"Not on purpose." George bellowed from across the driveway. "You didn't tell me they were in there, and I told you I was busting!"

The seven-year-old had been wearing a permanently offended expression since he'd been levered into a cream shirt and a pair of grey silk breeches an hour earlier. Lacey didn't blame him. His oldest brother was supposed to be in the bridal party as well but—like any self-respecting ten-year-old—had flat out refused when he'd seen the getup he was expected to wear.

"Well, we can't do anything about Charlotte's flowers. But where are yours?" Lacey let go of Katherine's wrist to pick up the bottom of her own skirt before she put a heel through it. Another cream creation.

Lacey had thought Emelia was joking when her cousin said she was going to be wearing white. Even though, like millions of other Americans, she'd gotten up at some awful hour one morning in 2011 to admire Pippa Middleton's perfect cream-clad rear end holding Katherine's exquisite train at the front of Westminster Abbey.

Lacey had been counting on her cousin to have at least carried on the American tradition of the ugly bridesmaid dress. Instead, when she'd opened her designer-embossed dress bag, she'd thought she'd accidentally been given Emelia's dress.

"I left my flower basket in the car so it wouldn't get lost or damaged. Mommy says I'm the responsible one." Katherine enunciated each word with precision.

"Well, why don't we go and get it and see if we can find Charlotte's basket." Lacey glanced around. She could only see one boy clad in breeches. "George, where's William?" George shrugged.

Lacey spun in a circle, looking for the three-year-old with the long lashes and penchant for mischief. One long road that, thank goodness, she could see down a decent way. No small person.

One church graveyard. That appeared empty save for some bouquets wilting against headstones. She opened the back door of the Rolls-Royce and looked inside. Nothing except Katherine's petal-filled basket.

"George, watch Katherine and Charlotte." She slammed the car door and checked the other Rolls. Empty as well. Where on earth had Carolina gone? She was meant to stay here to help wrangle her progeny until Emelia arrived. Given Carolina had named not one, but all five of her children after various Windsors, the woman was no doubt in the church chatting up some minor nobility, her ridiculous hat obscuring the view of half the guests.

"Missing someone?" The British drawl behind her was amused. And oh so horribly familiar. She'd thought she'd have a few more minutes to brace herself before she saw him. At least an hour before she'd have to talk to him. "William here decided to take an extra practice walk down the aisle."

"Thanks." The word came out strangled. Maybe she could just stay facing the car. Pretend she had a stone in her shoe.

"I don't think we've met. I'm Victor, Peter's brother." He kept talking to the back of her head. Why? "You must be Emelia's cousin ..."

Good grief. Had he not opened the order of service? Her name was right there. In eleven-point Apple Chancery, silver. She knew this because the wedding planner had spent an hour of

Emelia's life forcing her thorough the pros and cons of Apple Chancery versus Lucida calligraphy. Then Emelia had spent an hour of Lacey's life reliving the torment so someone else suffered with her.

She turned, her heels crunching on the gravel. "Oh, we've met."

Victor gaped at her. At least that gave Lacey a second to steel herself against what Victor Carlisle suited up in tails did to her knees.

"Are you a pirate?" William asked from where he was perched on Victor's arm. God bless him. God bless the three other children now buzzing around them like bees.

"If you're Peter's brother, why don't you have red hair?" Katherine asked, with hands on hips and a critical gaze.

"Did you get that scar in a sword fight? That would be awesome!" That was George, wide-eyed and outright staring at Victor's cheek.

Victor dropped to a crouch on the ground, placing William down gently and giving the sprogs his full attention. "No, I'm not a pirate. I don't have red hair, because Peter has red hair like our dad and I have blonde hair like our mum. And it wasn't a sword fight, but it was close."

"Ouchy?" Charlotte ran her hand over Victor's jagged scar, rosebud lips puckered. "Charlie kiss it better?" Before Victor could say anything, the little girl leaned in and dropped a delicate kiss on Victor's cheek.

Good grief. Even the most cold-hearted person couldn't withstand that kind of frontal assault. If the wedding photographer could see the image he'd missed, he'd weep a thousand tears.

She pulled in a breath. *Get it together, Lacey. He's still your competitor. A titled heir who was born with the entire gold-plated cutlery set in his mouth.*

Except the words that had worked so well before Minnesota fell distinctly flat now.

"Thank you, Princess Charlie. That made it all better."

"Can I have your pwetty flower?" Charlotte reached out and fingered the cream rose pinned to his lapel. "Sure, Princess." He unpinned it in a flash and handed it over. Charlotte took the flower in her chubby fingers, looking at him like she was Rapunzel, and he was the knight rescuing her from the tower.

Victor rose to his feet, lifting an eyebrow at her as soon as he got to her face height.

"I'm warning you," Lacey murmured the words before he could say anything that would add to his terribly inconvenient charm. "She has a tendency to throw pwetty flowers into toilets."

He leaned in, his lips getting dangerously close to brushing her updo. "And here I was thinking the bonus was going to be the wedding planner losing her mind when she realizes one missing flower is ruining the military symmetry in the photos."

She couldn't stop the smile that stole across her lips even as she shuffled along the car to create some space. "I'm sure Meredith wouldn't consider this appropriate collegial distance, Mr. Carlisle."

"We're not colleagues quite yet, O'Connor. Besides ..." Victor stepped back and made no attempt to hide his gaze traveling down her body. "I think I'll take my chances. I'm pretty sure even you couldn't hide a gun in that dress."

SOMETHING IN VICTOR HAD RECOGNIZED Lacey as soon as he'd walked out of the church. The sweep of her neck, the tilt of her hip. But he'd shaken it off, convinced he had to be hallucinating. There was no way the woman who had wedged herself firmly under his skin in less than a week could be Emelia's cousin. He could not have missed a piece of information of that magnitude.

"You've kept your Pied Piper skills very quiet." Emelia leaned against the wall next to him, champagne glass in one hand, the train of her gown in the other.

Victor shifted a sleeping William in his arms. For reasons he couldn't fathom, the small boy had taken a shining to him. Small snores now emanated from the blond head resting on his shoulder.

"You never mentioned your cousin works at Langham & Co."

Emelia arched an eyebrow. "So?"

Victor shrugged trying to look nonchalant. "I thought you might have mentioned it, given our companies are merging."

"Huh." Emelia wasn't looking at him. Her gaze was across the floor, to where Lacey was being chatted up by one of Peter's teammates. Just one in a long list of men who had been desperate to make her acquaintance ever since she'd appeared at the end of the aisle. "Sorry. I must have missed that. Between all the wedding planning and her job, we haven't talked as much lately as we usually do. Lacey mentioned a merger, but I didn't know it was with Wyndham."

She looked at him then back across the dance floor. He could practically hear the cogs turning in her brain. "That merger team-building thing she was on last month. Were you on that too?"

"Yes."

"Victor." An edge of steel laced the two syllables.

He turned. "Yes?"

Emelia pinned him with a knowing gaze. "Lacey's my person."

"I know." Well, he hadn't known Lacey was Emelia's person, but he'd known her cousin was.

Emelia shook her head, loose curls bouncing. "I don't think

you do."

He waited. The small relaxed body draped across his body reminded him that right now, at least, one person in the world trusted him.

Emelia jutted out her jaw. "I don't want you chasing my cousin. She's not another conquest. She's the only friend I had some years. Of all the women in the world, I need you to stay away from her."

Her words slapped him in the chest. It didn't matter that he hadn't touched a drink in years. Hadn't been on a date in just as long. His past was a large ink blot on his character that nothing would ever be able to remove.

Even Emelia, for all she'd done to try and mend bridges between him and Peter, still saw him as the man he used to be. Or she suspected the old him was lurking in the background, destined to reappear sooner or later.

Victor tightened his hold on William. "Look, I may not know Lacey as well as you, but I know she will never be anyone's conquest. And if there was ever a woman worth chasing, it's her. But you don't need to worry. She's entirely focused on the promotion she deserves. I'm just one more person in the way."

Emelia's shoulders sagged with something that looked a whole lot like relief.

His sister-in-law would rather her cousin end up with any other man in the world than him. He steeled himself against the hurt coiling through his body.

A high-pitched laugh cut through the moment, and they both turned toward where Carolina was practically draping herself over Lord Busby. Her swaying posture suggested she'd had more of the wedding champagne than was wise.

Emelia's face blanched.

"I've got it." Her father certainly wasn't going to intervene.

He was at a nearby table, eyes closed, head tilted back, and mouth open. The age gap between him and his wife couldn't be more obvious.

"Thank you."

"Anytime." He could prove it. He could prove he wasn't the man they thought he still was. Could prove he wasn't one bad decision away from being who he used to be. *That he was worth Lacey.* The thought split through his brain like an ax through kindling, leaving him feeling like he'd just had a lobotomy.

"Carolina." He approached the woman cautiously. "William's fallen asleep. Do you want to take him up to bed?"

Carolina looked at him like he'd just suggested she strap William on a rocket and blast him to the moon.

"Lashey knows which rooms we're staying in. LASHEY!" She shrieked across to the other group, and Lord Busby took his chance to make a quick getaway. "Can you show Vance where our rooms are? I can't leave here. I'm hosteshing."

He was pretty sure his mother would disagree. Thankfully, she didn't appear to be in earshot.

Peter appeared at Carolina's other side. "Can you take him upstairs? I've got this."

Fine. She was now officially Peter's mother-in-law. Of the many things he'd envied Peter in his life, Emelia's stepmother wasn't one of them. Turning, Victor headed for the ballroom door.

"I can take him." Lacey's voice came from over his shoulder.

"It's okay. I've got it. I know what wing they'll be in."

"Then we had might as well take her up as well." Lacey nodded to a nearby table. He'd totally missed Charlotte sprawled across two chairs, half her small body hidden by a tablecloth. Also totally fast asleep.

"Besides, I could use a reason to escape." She tossed a damning look across the still-crowded ballroom. "There's enough silver spoons in this place to stir all the tea in Britain."

There was the chip on the shoulder he'd met on the bus. He needed to hold onto that Lacey, not the one he knew.

Bending down, Lacey gathered Charlotte into her arms and tucked her across her torso, shushing the girl when she stirred. You could practically hear the testosterone in the room surge as every single man imagined her as the mother of their children. "Lead the way."

He didn't need to be told twice. Leaving the ballroom, he made short work of heading up the main stairs and onto the second level. His mother had probably put Emelia's family in the Rose Wing with its three bedrooms, so he turned left.

Bypassing the master bedroom, he opened the next door and flicked on the light. Suitcases and children's clothes were strewn across the room. Whether this was the littles' room or the older kids, he figured one night in the wrong bed wouldn't hurt anyone, so he lay William on the closest one.

The little boy had long since discarded his shoes, socks, and waistcoat, so Victor pulled the cover over his still-suited body.

Lacey appeared through the doorway with a sleeping Charlotte, took her shoes off, and laid her on the other bed. Then she unraveled the tattered remains of her flowery headpiece from her hair then brushed a kiss on her forehead.

They both backed toward the doorway. Victor turned out the light, and darkness swamped the room. "Do you think we're okay leaving them here? What if they wake up?"

He tried to ignore the sensation of Lacey at his side, so close that she'd be resting against him with just one small shift.

She shrugged. "I figure we've gone beyond the call of duty as it is. We can leave the door ajar, so there's some light coming in if they wake up." She reached out and pulled the door, both of them moving back into the hallway. "Now, come on. We have a job to do."

"We do?"

"Yes." Lacey said the words decisively. "This has been a lovely classy wedding and all, but I wouldn't be doing my job if I didn't bring a little bit of America with me. Are you in or not?"

"Are you going to tell me what it is?"

"Nope." Lacey shook her head.

Victor paused, torn. His immediate instinct was to follow wherever Lacey led, just to spend more time with her. But his instincts hadn't served him particularly well in life, and Emelia's accusing eyes as she told him Lacey was *her person* were still fresh in his mind.

He shoved his hands in his pockets. He was already regretting it as he shook his head. "Look. I don't know what Emelia has told you about our family, but Peter and I ... well, we aren't exactly close. He would never forgive me if I did something that upset Emelia or put any kind of dampener on their wedding. So I'd better not. But I can get one of the ushers to help."

Gerrard would do. Gerrard was married and, from all appearances, besotted with his wife. He'd be the safest bet.

"I would never do something to upset Emelia. It's just a bit of fun. She'll be fine with it. I promise. C'mon." Lacey was already walking down the hall. If you could call her short teetering steps walking, given she was being hobbled by her dress. "You can decide whether you're in or out while I get changed." She looked sharply over her shoulder. "That was not an invitation."

"For what?"

She flushed, her cheeks turning pink. "Never mind."

"Except I do." There was an edge to his voice that stopped her as she placed her hand on a doorknob to what was presumably her suite. "What exactly did you think I might interpret that as an invitation to?"

"I don't know." Her voice was tight. "But I've learned over the years not to take any chances. You might be amazed at what some men read into the most innocuous comments." She shook her head. "Then again, maybe you wouldn't."

Then she opened the door and closed it in his face.

CHAPTER TWENTY

LACEY CLOSED THE DOOR AND leaned against it. Victor hadn't deserved that. He hadn't done anything to her. Hadn't made a pass. Hadn't uttered a single double entendre thinking he was hilarious. And she hadn't seen him give any woman so much as a flirtatious smile the entire day, even though there had been more than a few who had been looking for any bone he threw their way.

And now ... now she was trapped in her dress, in her bathroom, and he may or may not still be outside the door she'd just slammed in his face for no good reason.

Or, more accurately, a really good reason. Her acerbic attempts at self-defense hopefully covered up the fact that every time she found herself within a few feet of the man, she wanted to rest her head on his chest and feel his breath in her hair. Like a fish struggling to stay away from a well-set lure.

She should have stuck with Beckett. At least for a few more weeks. Just long enough to say *I'm dating someone* and have it be true. An imaginary shield to protect her from the unwelcome and distinctly unwise impulses Victor stirred in her.

She pulled her dress up so it bunched around her thighs and sunk onto the toilet seat lid.

Her head was killing her—thanks to the bobby pins the hairdresser had stabbed into her intricate updo—her feet were screaming at her, she was starving because she couldn't eat so much as an hors d'oeuvre in this dress, and she couldn't get out of this dress by herself.

She couldn't reach the zip, and the bodice was so fitted that her one attempt to get it over her head ended up with it wrapped around her ribcage like a satin python.

"C'mon, Lacey." She muttered the words as she levered herself back to her bare feet. The stilettos were abandoned by the tiled edge of the bathtub.

She turned her back to the bathroom mirror and looked over her shoulder, trying to maneuver her arm up to the zipper. Once ... twice ... her fingers came tantalizingly close to the zipper but never managing to grip it. Just like all the other times she'd tried.

She had to get out of this dress.

Victor would be gone. Victor would be gone, so she'd find Allie and get her to help. Leaving the bathroom, she limped through her suite and opened the door.

Blast it.

Victor was still outside, leaning against the opposite wall. Except he had obviously left at some point because his tie was loosened, a couple of the top buttons on his shirt were undone, and he held a plate of food in his hand.

"You didn't eat anything at dinner, and I thought you might be one of those women who get angry when you're hungry."

Her tummy growled at the torturous smell of the Beef Wellington entree.

His brow folded. "I thought you were going to get changed."

Lacey swallowed. "I was."

"And ..." Victor let the question tail off as he helped himself to a potato roasted in duck fat and popped it into his mouth. It took all of her willpower not to rip it out of his hand.

"I can't get out of my dress."

"Okay." Victor handed her the plate. Then he started heading back down the hallway.

"What are you doing?"

"I'm going to find Allie. I won't be long."

This man made no sense. She didn't like it. She had known exactly who he was before she met him. Again.

"Why can't you do it?" She couldn't believe she'd just said that. To Victor Carlisle. "It's literally an inch of zipper. Then I'll be able to reach it."

Victor turned but didn't stop. "I just saw her on the stairs. It'll only take a few seconds."

"Seriously. You're going to go and get Allie for the sake of an inch?"

At that, he did stop. His scar—which she hardly even registered any more—twitched as he fought whatever expression was trying to invade his face.

"I can't win, can I? Less than fifteen minutes ago, you thought I might interpret you needing to get changed as some kind of invitation for I don't even know what. Now I'm doing my best to avoid any kind of situation where you might feel uncomfortable, and I'm getting hassled for that too."

He was right. She hated that he was right.

"I'll be back in a second."

He disappeared down the hall. Lacey carried the plate into her suite, placing it on the low table in front of the love seat.

Victor Carlisle had either turned from a player into a gentleman in the last few years, or he was doing an amazing job at playing the part.

A groan rumbled from the back of her throat. She'd always been honest with herself. Brutally honest. So why was she trying to plant doubt when she knew exactly what the truth was?

Lacey paced the floor, her bare feet sinking into the plush

carpet. She didn't like it when people surprised her. Especially men.

Regardless, he was still her competition. She had to keep her eye on the prize. She scooped up her phone from her bedside table, scanned her email, and replied to a couple. If someone somewhere was auditing emails as part of this thing, doing work while on leave had to count in her favor.

A knock sounded, the door opening before she could even respond.

"I hear you have a wardrobe malfunction." Allie, Emelia's old roommate, closed the door behind her, all copper hair and curves encased in an emerald green cocktail dress. "I knew that dress was going to be trouble the first time Emelia showed it to me. Poor girl was naive enough to think maybe they could make a breastfeeding-friendly version." She let out a peal of laughter. "I told her that even if that was possible, not even a pair of cast iron-clad Spanx would get this post-pregnancy body levered into that dress."

Before Lacey could utter a word, Allie was behind her, and there was the blissful sound of the zipper traveling down her back, followed by the sensation of being able to breathe freely for the first time in twelve hours.

"Do you need anything else? Because if not, this is the first night Jackson and I have been out since Hadley was born, and I'm keen to make the most of my pass."

Lacey let the dress slip off her shoulder and puddle around her ankles, grabbed her blouse off the bed, and dropped it over her head. "I'm good, thanks." She pulled on a pair of jeans, only realizing as she did them up that she'd just stripped in front of someone she'd only met a few times. "Um, sorry for flashing you."

Allie looked a bit startled. "I didn't notice. It's amazing what having a rugby team's worth of people staring at your nether regions during childbirth desensitizes you to." She swept back toward the door and opened it, half closing it behind her before her head popped back around. "By the way, Victor is still standing out here, brooding like one of the angels guarding the Garden of Eden after the Fall. What should I tell him?"

Lacey didn't know the reference, but it wasn't hard to imagine Victor as a brooding guardian angel. Especially if there was one who had been in a sword fight. She looked at the food waiting for her on the table, and her stomach rumbled again. "You might as well tell him to come in."

His insistence on getting Allie was both disconcerting and reassuring.

"Oh, and can you make sure that Emelia and Peter don't try to leave for at least another twenty minutes?" She was way behind schedule. And, knowing Emelia, she had a color-coded spreadsheet dictating their departure down to the minute.

Allie gave her a wink. "Got it." Her head disappeared. "She says you can go in."

The door slowly pushed open, Victor's broad bulk filling the doorway. He leaned against the doorframe.

Lacey waved him in. "Come in. I'm just going to have some food. Thanks, by the way."

"I'll stay here, thanks."

"Fine." What was she going to do? Beg Victor Carlisle to come into her suite? Even if he was now being completely ridiculous. "I'm sorry if I offended you."

Something in his stance softened slightly. "You didn't offend me. I'm used to it."

Somehow that made it a hundred times worse. "I—" Whatever she was going to say was cut off by a shooting pain through her head that had her doubling over and pressing her fingers to her temples.

"Lacey?" He was across the room like the Flash. "What's wrong?"

"Sorry. It's fine. This hairdo has a lot of pins in it." She straightened up, but only made it halfway before another stab traveled across her temples. Her breath whistled through her teeth.

"Sit down." His voice rumbled as he pressed his hand against her elbow. "I'll take them out while you eat."

There were so many pins in her head, and the idea of his fingers in her hair while she ate felt entirely too intimate.

But the door was wide open. Anyone walking by would see right into the room. The love seat was exactly opposite the door. It may have just happened that way when he walked into the room, but something told her it was purposeful. And her head was throbbing. The thought of the pain being eased while she got to fill her angry stomach was pretty close to what heaven must be like.

"Or I can get Allie."

"No, it's fine." Lacey sunk down onto the carpet in front of the love seat and crossed her legs as she reached for a potato, cramming it into her mouth. Just this once. "Oh my gosh, this is sho good." She mumbled the words around the mouthful of crispy goodness.

And suddenly Victor Carlisle wasn't the competition any more.

But only for tonight.

VICTOR TRIED TO RETRACE THE steps that had taken him and Lacey from avoiding each other, to her sitting in front of him cramming food into her mouth while he de-pinned her hair. All in less than an hour.

He had pulled a dozen of the golden clips out, and her hairstyle hadn't moved. Not a single hair had dropped. The strands were stiff beneath his fingers, coated in so much product that if he lit a match, they'd probably both go up in flames.

Lacey's shoulder leaned against his knee, the food on her plate disappearing at a rapid rate.

Lacey's my person, Victor. He kept repeating the words in his head, under no illusions about what the response would be if Peter or Emelia happened to come looking for either of them.

Peter didn't even trust him with his mangy cat.

He pulled out another five pins. Finally, a curl dropped down and draped itself along the curve of Lacey's neck. His fingers followed the line, skimming her warm skin before he remembered himself and snatched them away.

Focus. This was strictly business. Platonic. They were multitasking. He was helping with her hair while she ate to save time. So they could get on with whatever it was that Lacey had up her sleeve.

Six more pins, and the bottom half of her coiffure unfolded, blonde hair spilling past her shoulders. He missed the wild hair from the last couple of days in Minnesota. This perfectly coiffed sheen felt like another piece of the wall Lacey used to keep people at a distance.

His fingers burrowed through her hair to try and find the last of the metal pieces of torture, and she groaned as they pressed into her scalp. Tension drained out of her posture as he pressed his fingers in circular motions around her temples.

Lacey titled her head back and looked up at him, a drop of gravy smeared just below her lower lip. "Why are you being so nice to me?"

"It's part of the best man's job description to be nice to the maid of honor." He tried to keep his tone light, even as she rolled her eyes at him.

"Not this nice. Not—" She clamped her mouth shut, but he didn't miss the way her eyes darted toward the bed.

"I am not trying to get you into bed!" His reaction thundered out of him, and they both flinched. "Sorry. I'm sorry." He said the words before she could say anything. "I just ..." He shoveled a hand through his hair. It wasn't like this was a one-time event. He would have to see Lacey again. The last thing he needed was to get offside with Emelia's cousin, the woman who would probably end up higher than him in the new organizational food chain.

He blew out a long breath. "Lacey, I don't know what Emelia has told you about me. Yes, we have a past, and I was a complete ass to her and Peter and almost ruined their chance at happiness. And clearly, she's told you I used to go through women like water. But I'm not that guy anymore, and I'm running out of ways to figure out how to prove it."

Lacey pressed her hands to the floor and stood up. He stayed still as a rock. Waiting for her to walk out. Or ask him to leave.

"Move over."

"What?"

She nodded toward the small couch. "You're in the middle. Shove over so I can sit down."

He moved across, and she settled in beside him, her knees pulled up toward her chest, bare feet with polished toenails poking out from the bottom of her jeans, toes pressed against the side of his legs.

She studied him for a second, then her gaze flickered over his shoulder for a few more before returning back to his.

"Yes, I've heard some stuff from Emelia, but there's something I need to tell you." She propped her elbow up on the back of the couch and leaned her head into her hand.

"What's that?" What else could there possibly be? If Emelia and Lacey were as close as they seemed, "some stuff" had to be the understatement of the decade.

"That part about you and women." She ran her hand through her hair, grimacing as it snagged. "The thing is … One of them was me."

One of them was me. The words thundered in Victor's ears. "What do you mean?" But exactly what she meant barreled into him as he said the words.

"We met in LA, about six years ago."

His body felt like both fire and ice. Lacey, *Lacey,* was somewhere in his missing memories. His brain whirred, trying to place her. But there was nothing. Until a minute ago, he would have sworn in a court of law that the first time they met was in her office in New York.

What had he done? The list of possibilities was as shameful as it was long. His body folded over itself, and he found himself with his elbows stabbing his knees, hands pressed against his forehead.

Was that why her gaze had darted to the bed? Not because she suspected the worst of him, but because she already knew the worst of him.

Had she woken up in the morning and discovered him gone? He'd been a pro at sneaking out in the pre-dawn hours like a ninja to avoid awkward scenes, the sleeping woman left behind blurring into all the others who had come before and would follow after.

"I'm sorry." The words were muffled by his hands. She probably wouldn't even be able to interpret what they were.

Step eight of AA required he make a list of all the people he had harmed and be willing to make amends. That was mighty hard to do when he knew the list was long but couldn't remember most of the people who should be on it.

And now one of those women was sitting right next to him. He searched his memory. Back to the moment they had met. Had he been in denial? Had there been a frisson of recognition he'd ignored?

He pulled his hands away from his face, pressed them to his knees, and forced himself to sit back up. "I'm so sorry." He couldn't even look at her. The shame of who he had been, of her experiencing who he had been, pressed down on his shoulders like the gravity of Earth had just doubled.

She shifted at her end of the couch. "You don't even know what you're sorry for, do you?"

"No." He turned his head, enough to see her out of the corner of his eye. "I have two years that are mostly missing from my life. I don't remember much of them, and what I do remember I am deeply ashamed of."

Silence fell as she studied him. Studied him as if weighing up the truthfulness of his statement and deciding if it was wanting.

He was going to have to ask. He was going to have to ask, knowing that the answer would probably change everything. "So, we slept together?" He braced himself for the answer, for a barrage of accusation and hurt.

Her expression changed from pensive to startled in an instant. "No!"

The rush of relief left him light-headed. "Then what happened?"

Lacey shrugged. "We met at a party in LA. I was the publicist for Ceecee Knox's biography. You hit on me. That's all."

There was something in her expression that said that wasn't quite all.

"What happened?"

Her legs curled further in toward her. "Nothing. We met, we talked, I went to the bathroom, and when I came back you had ... shall we say ... moved on."

It all rang true. He'd had the attention of a goldfish when it came to women. If he'd been drunk, or worse, high, he might not have even noticed that Lacey and whoever the next woman was were different people.

But there was something in the way her expression had shuttered that told him something was still missing in the story.

"And we kissed." They had. If he had just flirted with her, then she wouldn't have said one of the women was her. He would have been long forgotten. Just one among many.

The walls went up behind her eyes so quickly they had might as well be a physical obstacle. "Look." Her legs unfolded, and her feet landed on the floor. "We don't need to talk about this. It was years ago. Like you say. You've changed. It didn't mean anything. I just thought you should know. Since we're now cousins-in-law or whatever." She stood up without looking at him and moved away from the couch.

He got to his feet as she pulled a small and larger shopping bag out from the wardrobe. "I've got everything we need here. Here, you take one."

He'd kissed Lacey. *He'd kissed Lacey.* The knowledge shredded his brain. How could he have kissed Lacey and not remember even meeting her? "We should talk about this." He wasn't sure where the words came from. He wasn't the guy who wanted to talk about stuff. That was why getting through rehab and counseling and AA had been the hardest thing he'd ever done. They all required far too much talking and self-contemplation.

"I don't want to talk about it." She blinked against a sheen of tears. His heart thundered to his feet.

He didn't even know what he'd said six years ago. What he'd

done. But whatever it was, it hadn't meant nothing.

"I'm sorry." He said the words softly, like he would speak to an easily spooked horse. "I was a self-centered reckless idiot. I left a trail of human destruction in my path. I have no excuse. And you have no reason to accept my apology, but it's the only thing I have to give."

She turned away, refusing to look at him as she shoved her feet into a pair of flats. "We should get going. Peter and Emelia will be leaving soon, and we need to decorate their car."

And Lacey swept from the room like he hadn't even spoken.

LACEY'S FEET THUMPED AGAINST WOOD as she hurried down the back stairs, gripping the plastic bag like it was the President's nuclear football.

He didn't remember. Not even a little bit. As far as Victor was concerned, she'd never existed before last month.

She'd known that. Known it from the complete lack of even a flicker of recognition when they'd met. But she'd been foolish enough to hold on to a whiff of hope that maybe he'd remembered later and decided it was too awkward to bring up. That it was better to let past mistakes remain just that.

But the horror and disbelief that had just rolled off him were as real as it got. While she could still vividly recall the feel of his lips on hers, the weight of his hand pressed into the small of her back, he remembered nothing. Nothing.

She was just one blonde, exchanged for another in the five minutes it took to go to the bathroom and freshen her makeup.

The unwieldy bag left her unbalanced, but her stride was long and focused now that she was rid of the ridiculous shoes and constraining dress. All she had to do was decorate the car and hold it together to wave goodbye to Peter and Emelia. Then she could retreat to her suite.

Thank goodness she'd never told Emelia.

She could feel Victor's presence behind her. At least he hadn't spoken since she'd left the room. She couldn't believe she'd almost cried. It was just a kiss. Five years ago.

Which had meant nothing to him. Clearly. She'd known that from the instant she'd walked back to the bar and seen his head bent over another blonde, the same smile directed at the interloper that had been focused on her mere minutes before.

Which was part of the problem. She wasn't the type of woman who kissed random guys at parties for fun. And she'd never really understood why she'd kissed him. Just that there was something in the way he looked at her that had pulled her straight into his vortex.

A Google search the next morning had informed her he had that effect on pretty much every woman he met.

She hadn't cried that night. She hadn't cried over him ever. She certainly hadn't spent the last six years pining for the blond Brit with the rakish charm. She'd all but forgotten it had ever happened until Emelia's path crossed his.

"We can cut through the kitchen." Victor's voice rumbled from behind her. "This way." He gestured to a passage and took the lead. He obviously didn't know she'd visited here before with Emelia. She followed his broad back down the hall and into the large kitchen. Victor was already opening a door on the other side, his hand flicking a light switch on the wall. Outside, a light went on.

"There's some steps." He turned, not looking at her. "Let me take your bag."

She held the bag out without protest. Anything to get this over and done with as quickly as possible. She closed the door behind her, following Victor down the steps and onto the gravel driveway where a gleaming vintage Jaguar sat. The late spring air pooled around her.

The moonlight caught on Victor's scar as he placed the bags by the side of the car. She'd run her finger along its ridges that night. He'd been charming and funny and self-deprecating.

"We should get this done." She should change her flight as soon as she got back to her room. She was on an evening flight the next day, but maybe she could get an earlier one.

Brunch. Peter and Emelia were coming back for brunch with the family. She couldn't leave before that. She groaned under her breath as she opened one of the bags and pulled out the decorative tin cans.

They came with instructions on where to affix them and she squinted at the piece of paper, the light from the kitchen not giving her quite enough to read by.

"Here." Victor plucked them out of her hands. Before she could say anything, he was flat on his back in the gravel, head under the back of the car.

Lacey grabbed the shaving cream out of the bag, gave it a good shake, and scrawled *Just Married* along the back window complete with large hearts. Then she opened a bag of pink glitter and sprinkled it on the letters.

"Nice." Victor's voice rumbled behind her, and the last swoosh of a heart went sideways.

Lacey didn't even bother trying to fix it. "Thanks."

If this was a romcom, someone would say something flirtatious, and shaving cream fight would ensue. It would end with them making out against the car, because not even Hollywood was stupid enough to try and convince anyone that rolling around on small sharp stones was romantic.

But the air hanging between them was laden with all sorts of things, none of it light or flirtatious.

"What next?" Victor stepped away from her.

"We need to put these inside the car. Then we're done." Unlocking the car, Lacey picked up the larger bag from the ground and emptied sparkly silver balloons into the back seat. Finally, she cut the strings connecting them to the weight that had kept them grounded, and they bobbed along the grey ceiling.

Had Victor left? She glanced behind her to see him standing a few feet away, hands shoved in his pockets. With the moonlight on his ruffled blonde hair and scar, he looked like the brooding angel Allie had christened him.

Holding one recalcitrant balloon in, Lacey edged the door closed, removing her hand at the last second before closing it firmly.

He still didn't say anything.

Why on earth had she said something? Even if one—or both—of them didn't survive Meredith's cull, they were now related by marriage. It was inevitable that they'd run into each other. And now she would always be the woman he'd kissed once but didn't remember. "Look, I hope this isn't going to make brunch tomorrow weird."

Victor stiffened. "What brunch?"

"The one tomorrow morning. For family. Before Peter and Emelia go on their honeymoon." If you could call two nights a honeymoon. The joys of marrying an Olympian only weeks before the games.

Victor's eyes seemed to pierce the darkness. "I haven't been invited to a brunch." Maybe she was seeing things, but she was pretty sure his posture wilted as he said it.

Lacey closed her eyes for a second. That couldn't be true. Emelia was many complicated things, but rude wasn't one of them. She would never have excluded Victor deliberately. "Of course you have. Maybe everyone just thought someone else had told you about it. They only decided to do it this week."

"Maybe." He looked down at the ground, but the expression on the way there was anything but convinced.

Lacey took a couple of steps, his forlornness more than she could bear. "Look." She placed her hand on his arm. "I know your family dynamics are complicated, and I don't pretend to understand them, but I promise you're invited. Emelia would never not invite you to something like this. And Peter—well, I know you two have some big differences—but he wouldn't either."

Victor leaned against the trunk of the car. "Even if that's true, every time I'm around them I feel like I'm a reminder of all the worst things in their past. I wouldn't blame them if they didn't want me there tomorrow. They've been more than gracious having me here today."

She couldn't help but feel sorry for him. "You're family. Of all the people in the world, Emelia knows how important family is. Have you ever thought that they wouldn't be together if it wasn't for you? Who knows when she might have found the courage to tell Peter the truth? Yes, at the time, you did it to hurt them both, but it turned out for good. In some kind of bizarre way, this wedding is partly because of you."

Victor looked down at her. "Why are you being so nice to me?"

The question she'd asked him in her room. "What do you mean?"

He shifted and turned so he faced her more fully. The intensity of his expression stripped the air out of her lungs. "C'mon, Lace. Years ago, we met at a party I don't even remember. I hit on you, I kissed you, and I abandoned you for the next woman who caught my wandering eye. You have every right to think I'm the scum of the earth because that's exactly what I was. So why are you trying to help to mend the bridges I burned down with my family? What's it to you?" Even though they weren't touching, she could feel his body heat arching across the small gap.

The furrows in his brow were so deep they were like small trenches marching across his forehead. Her fingers pulsed with the desire to smooth them out. To tell him about her own broken bridges.

Lacey pushed herself off the car and took a step back, not trusting herself. "Emelia got her second chance. Maybe I think you deserve one too."

CHAPTER TWENTY-ONE

Anna: So, how was the wedding? You looked very Pippa in that gown. Right up to and including the internet going mad about your rear end.

Lacey: Please tell me you're joking.

Rachel: She's not joking. The good news is they haven't managed to identify you since it's paparazzi shots, and no one has leaked the names of the wedding party. Though they obviously know Victor, which just leaves you as the mysterious maid of honor.

Lacey: I can't be named! Meredith will never take me seriously if I'm plastered all over the tabloids because of my butt.

Anna: If I looked that good in that gown, I would give the photos to the tabloids myself. Sadly, thanks to Libby, there are some things that are never going to be what they once were.

Rachel: But you have the best boobs, so count your blessings.

Anna: True. Anyway, back to the wedding so I can live vicariously. Anything else interesting to report?

Lacey: Emelia's stepmother wore a hat so large a bird tried to land on it during the photos.

Anna: Any nice single men? Is the brother still

the villain in the story, or are the rumors of his path to redemption true?

Rachel: Ignore her. She's on a mission to set up every single woman she knows. I'm pretty sure she's eyeing up someone for you to meet when you're here next week. Thank goodness for Lucas.

Lacey: Is this some part of the grieving process I haven't heard about before?

Anna: My counsellor says setting up other people is a good distraction since my libido sadly didn't die with Cam.

Rachel: I can't wait to see what Facebook ads you're going to get from that sentence.

Lacey: I didn't think religious people were allowed to use that word. If you stop messaging, I'll know it's because you've just been struck down.

Rachel: You don't want to get her started on her God-created-sex lecture. Trust me.

Anna: What? It's true! I'm barely in my thirties. It's not like Cam died in his nineties and all we'd done was hold hands for the last two decades.

Lacey: Three decades. No one has sex after 65. It's a rule.

Anna: Since when?

Rachel: Lacey, please start talking about the wedding. I'm begging you.

Lacey: I think it's time we help Anna find a job. She clearly has too much time on her hands.

Anna: Way ahead of you on that one. Got my resume out all over the show. Strangely enough, there's not a whole lot of appeal in a single mom who hasn't worked for four years.

Lacey: You did some great projects before you had Libby. I'm sure it's only a matter of time.

Anna: My dad has offered to put in a word with some of his business contacts. I'm praying it doesn't come to that. Anyway, back to the wedding. Specifically, where we left off with the brother.

Lacey: Fine. Yes, it would appear that in the last few years Victor has made some progress toward becoming a decent human being.

Anna: Excellent. Everyone loves a good bad-boy redemption story.

Lacey: I would offer to introduce you, but I'm pretty sure he's not the churchgoing type. He's good with kids, so you can put that in his plus column.

Anna: No, thanks. I've had the great love of my life. I'm in the market for yours.

EMELIA GOT HER SECOND CHANCE. *Maybe I think you deserve one too.* It sounded easy in theory. Like handing out candy at a parade. But in his experience, second chances were harder to come by than Willy Wonka's golden tickets. Especially when the carnage left behind was broken relationships and shattered trust.

Victor eased out his legs in front of him as he scanned the tableau from behind his sunglasses. Somewhere around four, he'd decided to give the missing invite the benefit of the doubt and show up for brunch.

No one had even blinked at his presence, so it looked like Lacey was right. He was glad he'd taken the chance. There was something good for the soul about sitting in the sun, watching the tribe romp around while Carolina screeched at them from underneath yet another ridiculous hat.

Lacey was nowhere to be seen. Lacey, who he'd just realized during his sleepless night, had known who he was this whole time. Not just that he was a total cad. He could understand why she hadn't said anything about that. But she'd known he was Peter's brother, had known all about his family, and hadn't said a word. Not even when he talked about Anita.

It felt unfair like she'd had an advantage in a game he didn't even know he was playing. But there was also grudging admiration. He wouldn't have expected anything less from her than maximizing every possible advantage. Especially given the circumstances.

Closing his eyes, he let himself savor the warmth of the sun. It had been weeks since Minnesota. Meredith had to have something planned soon. And, unlike Lacey, he had no reason to be checking his emails over the weekend. No clients saw him as indispensable.

He opened his eyes as Peter dropped down into the empty seat beside him. "So, Emelia mentioned that Lacey works for the company Wyndham is merging with."

Victor's drink sloshed in his hand. Surely they'd had better things to do on their wedding night than talk about him and Lacey? He managed to keep the thought from exiting his mouth. For once. Instead, he took a long swig of his ginger beer while he formulated his response. No doubt Emelia had also told Peter about the rest of their conversation. "Has anyone ever told you your small talk needs work?"

Peter looked startled for a second, then gave a wry smile. "Emelia may have mentioned it a time or two."

"I guess it's an occupational hazard when you spend most of your time in a boat with a bunch of other men being yelled at."

Peter looked at him as if trying to find the barb beneath the words. "True." He stretched his legs out as well, quads and calves rippling with the results of hours of elite-level training.

Victor hadn't been prouder of anything in his life than the day his brother had made the Great Britain squad for the second time. Maybe he should tell him that one day. *Maybe he should tell him that now.* "I … um …" His words lodged in his throat. Peter didn't need his approval or endorsement. "When do you have to be back at training?"

Peter reached forward and poured himself his own glass of iced tea. "Tuesday. We'll have a proper honeymoon later in the year. Allie has Emelia sold on New Zealand."

"And you're not?"

Peter watched his bride as she spun Charlotte around in the grass. "I'll go wherever she wants. After putting up with me and my training schedule, it's the least I can do."

"By the way, do you know if Mum managed to see her specialist? About that drug trial?"

"Emelia went with her last week. She said she'd look into it. Hopefully, Mum will hear something in the next few days."

He'd have to remember to pray for a positive response … if only for his own selfish reasons of finally being associated by his family with something good.

His brother leaned forward, elbows on his knees, glass clasped. Victor knew the position. It was the one he usually took when he had something he needed to say and was preparing himself to say it.

"Just spit it out, little brother."

Peter looked over his shoulder. "You know Lacey means everything to Emelia, right?"

"I know. But if you're here to warn me off, you don't need to. Your wife has already done that. Not to mention that in case you haven't noticed, Lacey is about as fierce as they come." Victor tried to keep his voice level.

"I…" Peter ran his hand through his hair. "It's just you have this thing … this way with women. Whether you're trying or not, you just do. They can't seem to help themselves." The downward turn of Peter's mouth showed he was enjoying this conversation about as much as Victor was.

"Don't you think you should give Lacey more credit?" He could hardly blame his brother for his cynicism given he'd had a front-row view of the car wrecks that had been Victor's relationships … if you could even call them that. But Lacey was not most women. And she was certainly a whole league above the women in his old crowd.

"If something was to happen between the two of you. If Lacey was to get hurt…"

Victor knew what his brother was saying without him having to say it. Battle lines would be drawn. And he knew exactly what side the rest of his family would be on.

Victor leaked out a breath. Emelia obviously didn't know that something had already happened. That Lacey had already been hurt. If they ever found out, all his hard-fought gains would be for naught. It wouldn't matter that it had been years ago. That he had no memory of it.

"Lacey is focused on getting through this merger. Her promotion is what matters to her. Certainly not me." He wasn't under any illusions. Lacey's eye remained firmly on the prize. She wasn't going to do anything that might jeopardize her chances. Victor would put money on the fact that even if Meredith wasn't enforcing the no-fraternization rule, Lacey would have her own one. And given their newly revealed previous history, well, he'd have better odds of convincing Harry to return to royal duties than anything happening with Lacey.

"You both disappeared for a while last night." Peter's tone rained disapproval. Victor almost wished he'd done something to deserve it.

"To decorate your car. I haven't dated anyone since rehab, Peter. You know that."

"I know what I see here. But let's be honest. I don't know what you get up to in London."

Even though his brother's voice sounded more resigned than accusatory, the unfairness of the barb coiled within Victor. "Is that what you think? That I've been working my butt off for the last four years to try and prove myself to you and Mum and Dad while leading some kind of double life in London? I just can't catch a break."

He jerked to his feet before he could say anything else he might regret. The knowledge was steeping his veins that whatever he did, it was never going to be enough.

LACEY WALKED OUT ONTO THE back patio as Victor shoved his chair back and stalked away from his brother.

"Uh, oh. What did Peter say now?" The words were murmured from behind her, and Lacey turned to see Maggie holding a plate of cookies. The hand holding the plate trembled a little, one of the few signs of her multiple sclerosis. Though, according to Emelia, this was a good week.

"What makes you think Peter said something?"

"True. It could have been Victor. But it was probably Peter. He's not very good with change. Once he has people in a box, he prefers that they stay that way. Especially Victor. It's easier than trying to reconcile years of hurt."

"I see."

Emelia must have noticed Victor's abrupt departure as well,

because she was making her way across the grass toward her husband, Charlotte on her hip.

Lacey could no longer see Victor, who had disappeared around the side of the house. She steeled herself against the desire to go and find him.

She didn't have time to get involved in trying to smooth over whatever had gone wrong between Peter and Victor this time. She needed to go and pack. Her train to London was in less than two hours. This time tomorrow, she'd be home. And she needed to have her A game on for whatever Meredith had coming next. She couldn't afford to be distracted. Especially not by a man who knew nothing about having to fight just for survival.

Even if he wasn't who he used to be in his old life of partying, drugs, money, and women, he still had the luxury of unearned and undeserved privilege.

"He was watching you, you know."

"I'm sorry." Lacey turned back to Peter's mom.

"In the ceremony yesterday. Victor couldn't keep his eyes off you."

Lacey did her best to ignore the quake that traveled through her at the words. "He was probably surprised. Our companies are getting merged. It must be disconcerting when one of the people you're competing against for a job turns out to be your new sister-in-law's cousin."

Maggie just smiled as she held up the tremoring plate. "Do you mind taking him a couple of biscuits? They're his favorite, and this lot will probably demolish them by the time he's cooled down."

"I wouldn't know where to look for him."

The plate was pushed closer. "Well, there hasn't been the sound of a car flying up the driveway, so he can't have gone far. I'd go myself, but my legs are a bit tired."

What was she going to do? Say no to the request of a woman with a terminal degenerative illness? Lacey grabbed a couple of cookies and placed them on top of the paper she'd been intending to show Emelia. Added one for herself. She really needed to leave this place before Victor had her stress eating herself up a size. "I'll take a quick look, but I do need to finish packing."

"Thanks, dear." Maggie patted her hand as she moved past.

Cookies balanced on paper, Lacey walked around the side of the house. She'd do one round of the building's perimeter. That was all. The estate was huge, and if Maggie thought Lacey was going to go gallivanting through fields and lanes like she was an Austen heroine, she would be sorely disappointed.

"Lace!" Her cousin's voice came from behind her, and she turned. Emelia hurried down the pathway, sans Charlotte, the skirt of her summer dress flapping behind her.

Lacey stopped and waited for her to catch up. "You okay?" Between her last-minute arrival and the wedding, they hadn't had a proper conversation all weekend. Their plan to at least catch up while getting ready together scuttled by Carolina insisting on role-playing mother of the bride.

"Are you going to find Victor?" Emelia chewed her bottom lip. A sure sign she was anxious about something.

"Yeah, his mom asked me to take him some cookies." Lacey held the paper up as if offering proof.

"I think I may have contributed to what just happened. The whole storming off thing."

"Why?"

"We talked last night at the reception, and I kind of..." She trailed off.

Lacey tilted her head and waited.

Emelia rocked on her feet. "Fine. I may have warned him off you. Told him that you weren't just another conquest."

"Another conquest! Nice, Meels." She was going to give her cousin some kind of bridal brain pass for even thinking it, let alone saying it to Victor.

Emelia at least had the grace to look ashamed. "I know, but I saw him watching you, and it's just you're well, you and he, well, you know what he used to be like."

More than her cousin would ever know, but someone needed to stand up for the poor guy. "You don't need to protect me. I'm a grown woman. Trust me, I know what a womanizer after a conquest looks like, and it's not Victor. Not this version anyway."

Emelia shifted on the gravel path, not saying anything.

"He hasn't hit on me. Not once. Last night he wouldn't even unzip my dress so much as an inch so I could get myself out of it. He went and got Allie to do it. You didn't get held to ransom for your mistakes, Meels. You should at least grant Victor the same."

Someone called Emelia's name, and she looked over her shoulder. "I should get back. And you should go deliver your cookies."

It was her cousin's way of saying she was right without actually saying it. It would have to do for now.

Rounding the corner to the front of the house, Lacey looked along the sweep of the driveway down the treelined entrance. Maggie was right. The car she assumed to be Victor's still sat next to Peter and Emelia's. And there was no figure striding off into the distance. But that still left about a million acres of hiding places.

She cast her gaze along the large expanse of well-manicured grounds and sighed. Might as well admit to herself she was going to keep looking for as long as she could. The man came to Small Harbor and had her back while staring down her family's particular brand of dysfunction. He deserved the same from her.

After that, the debt would be settled, and he'd be nothing

more than a distant relative and occasional colleague.

But what if one of them wasn't in the new company? What if there was no no-fraternization rule in play?

Nope. Nope. Nope. Lacey shoveled half a still-warm cookie into her mouth to distract herself from the unwelcome thought. She almost moaned as the soft chocolate and crunchy sugar soothed her tangled emotions. When was the last time she'd eaten a cookie? It had to have been years. Her phone buzzed in her dress pocket, and she placed the cookies on top of the paper to free up a hand.

"Care to share?"

Lacey spun to find Victor behind her, seated on the front steps leading to the main door. The cement balustrade had concealed him from view. A coin sprung from his hand and spun into the air. He caught it then flicked it up again.

Her free hand grabbed the paper just in time to stop one of the cookies from sliding off. Thank goodness she hadn't been talking to herself. "Sure." She held out the newspaper with the two remaining cookies balanced on the top.

"Thanks." His enormous palm enveloped them. He winked at her, the move incongruous with his somber face. "You can let Mum know you've completed your mission."

That was what a smart woman would have done. Instead, she settled herself on the step next to him and watched the coin spinning in the air. Except it wasn't a coin. It was a bronze AA chip. "How many years?" She took another bite of her cookie. Contemplated swiping Victor's second one.

Victor palmed the chip and shoved it into his pocket. As if she'd caught him out somehow. "Three." He shoveled his first cookie into his mouth, swallowing it after one bite. "I called my sponsor, but it went to voice mail. Then I realized I'd be fine as long as I didn't get in the car. Mum hasn't kept liquor in the house since I went to rehab. I'm pretty sure Dad has a secret stash of whisky somewhere, but I'm not brave enough to mess with that even if I knew where it was."

"Do you want me to drive you to a meeting?" A ridiculous offer given that he could (a) drive himself and (b) she had a train to catch.

"No. But thanks."

The silence stretched for a few moments as they both chewed their cookies.

"What's this for?" He tapped the trashy tabloid she'd placed between them. The one that Rachel had somehow managed to get special delivered to the front door this morning.

She reached for it. "Nothing, it's—"

Too late. Victor picked up and flipped it open. A loud laugh left his mouth as soon as he saw the headline. WHAT A VIEW! splashed in fifty-six point font across the masthead.

"Peter Carlisle, the youngest son of the Viscount and Viscountess of Downley and Great Britain's hope for gold at the upcoming rowing world championships, married his fiancée, charity fundraiser Emelia Mason, in Oxford yesterday. The happy couple made a besotted pair, but all eyes were on a mysterious maid of honor who had clearly decided to give Pippa Middleton a run at breaking the internet."

Lacey didn't even lift her eyes, knowing that if she did, she would see hers and Pippa's rear ends side by side in their respective bridesmaid dresses.

"Excellent. I can even text in a vote for who did the dress best." Victor pulled his phone out of his pocket.

"Don't be ridiculous."

He swapped hands and held his phone out of her reach. "What do you mean? It'll be the best 25p I've ever spent. You should charge them a commission. Though then, of course, you'll have to tell them who you are." Victor winked at her as he tapped into his screen. Lacey leaned across him, grabbing at his arm, but there was the defiant whoosh as he sent his vote into the ether.

"I'll vote another twenty times if this is what it gets me." Victor grinned at her, and she realized in her attempt to get his stupid phone she had practically draped herself across his lap.

"I'm so glad you find it funny." Lacey wrenched herself back upright, taking extreme care not to have any of her touching any of him. The warmth emanating from his body, and the dimple that had formed on his cheek were more than enough. "I'm sure you wouldn't find it nearly so hilarious if you were the one on the front page of a tabloid, displayed like a piece of meat."

She should be used to it by now. No matter how hard she worked. How many times she proved herself. Eventually, she was always reduced to some leggy blonde with a nice behind.

"Been there. Done that. Got the T-shirt."

"What?"

Victor shrugged. "When I was in rehab, some paparazzi managed to breach security. There were photos of me exercising. Group therapy. My mum visiting. Not front page though. You win on that front."

"I'm sorry. That must have been awful."

Victor stilled. "I didn't know about it until I got out. I didn't care about me, but there were others from my group who were in the photos. They didn't do anything to deserve that. It became a breach of privacy case, but the damage was already done. Anyway ..." He lurched to his feet. "Thanks for the light relief. We should get back."

Lacey ignored him. Carolina would be looking for someone else to palm her progeny off onto, and she'd already done her duty yesterday. "What did Peter say that made you walk off like that?"

Victor scuffed the drive with his shoe. "It's not important. If anything, it's embarrassing. Somehow almost every conversation ends like we're twelve with one of us sulking."

His mother's words came back to her. "Sometimes, it's hard for people to accept that others have changed. Maybe it's just going to take time, and there's nothing you can do to hasten it."

"You're probably right. But it feels like no matter what I do, it's never enough, you know?"

That was exactly how she felt about her family. "One day, it will be. It has to be." She wasn't sure if she was saying it for him or her.

Victor looked down at her. "I hope you're not comparing yourself to me."

She didn't answer. Was she? At least Victor was doing his best to make amends. She had tried to make things right with her sister. But some things could never be undone.

Victor knelt down in front of her. "Look at me, O'Connor." She tried not to, but it was impossible when his face filled her entire vision. "You are the best woman I've ever met. Well, you and my mum. And I knew that before I knew you had met me at my absolute worst. I don't know your whole family situation, but I do know it is not on you."

The intensity of his charcoal eyes unnerved her, stealing the breath from her lungs like a brazen thief.

"You knew who I was the moment you saw me on your couch in New York. And, whether you meant it that way or not, you gave me the gift of not throwing my past back in my face. Do you ..." His voice caught, and he swallowed. "Nobody has done that for me before. Not ever."

Their gazes tangled, the air between them more charged than championship night at the Rose Bowl. Her traitorous body leaned in. Victor reached up and cupped her face with the palm of his hand, his thumb running across her bottom lip.

And she didn't care that he didn't remember her six years ago. Or that he was the competition. Or that anything with him could get her fired. Her promotion was probably dead in the water anyway. And the man kneeling in front of her was the best kiss she'd ever had. But first, there was one thing she needed to clear up. "Victor, I'm not that noble. I didn't not say anything for you. I did it for me."

Victor wound a lock of her hair around his finger like they had all the time in the world, his fingertip grazing her cheek with every rotation. "You said last night that you think I deserve a second chance. Is that true?"

She held his gaze. "It's even more true that it was last night."

Victor drew in a breath. "What if what I want is a second chance with you?"

"I—" Lacey's mind stalled. Giving in to the pull of attraction for a kiss was one thing. A kiss in the middle of the English countryside with no witnesses at that. But his question felt a whole lot bigger than just a kiss.

Then two phones buzzed in unison, causing them both to flinch. And buzzed again. Lacey's hand reached automatically into her pocket, breaking the moment. Her screen lit up with the subject of the incoming email New Org Roles: Tranche Two. Trust Meredith to send it on a Sunday.

"You got it?" She didn't know how she felt about the inter-ruption, so she chose to focus on pushing it from her mind and clicking on the email. Maybe it held the answer to his question.

"Yup." Victor moved to sit next to her on the step, his gaze on the screen.

The message had two attachments. She didn't bother to look at the email itself. It would just be weasel words Meredith's HR lawyers had forced her to include.

Lacey opened the first document, the same one she'd first seen at breakfast with Rachel but with more boxes filled in. She scrolled until she found names she recognized, her stomach settling as she saw some of the best people she worked with clustered in a new group called Publicity and PR. But not her. She scrolled and zoomed to double-check. Her name wasn't in any box.

That had to be good, surely. Based on Meredith's approach so far, if it was bad news, there would also have been an email telling her to collect her belongings from the office.

She studied the new org chart again. Assuming it was good news, then there were two options. The new Head of Publicity and PR for the US. Or, if she was shooting for the stars, their boss, the new VP of Publicity and PR who sat across the US and UK.

Beside her, Victor had stilled, his thumb frozen on his screen. "Are you there?"

He tilted his phone towards her and the words *Victor Carlisle – Senior Associate* leapt out at her from one of the squares like it was in font three sizes larger than anyone else. The role sat within a new group titled Government Relations. Disparate emotions clashed within her chest.

They weren't even in the same branch. They were no longer competing against each other. But he'd hoped for more. So much more.

"I'm sorry." Her buzz couldn't help but be dampened by his disappointment.

He managed to summon up part of a smile. "Hey, it's a promotion. I can hardly complain." He turned his phone over in his hands. "Let's be honest, Lace. If all the other people going for the upper-level roles are like you, I never really had a chance. And that's fair. I haven't done the time or got the experience."

It was true. Not that she was going to say so. But even if he'd got his job straight out of rehab, he'd been there a little over three years. At most.

He turned his gaze to her. "What about you?"

She shrugged. "Nowhere yet." She'd study the diagram in-depth on the train and work out who she was up against.

"In other words, a definite promotion." He nudged her knee with his.

She tried to temper her hopes. "Maybe. Or maybe not. I got evicted from the BWCA early, and I lost a chance at a huge book publicity contract recently. If Meredith has found out about that ..." She let the possible repercussion hang.

Victor studied her for a second. "I don't believe you."

"I'm sorry, what?"

"I don't believe you *lost* your chance. Or, if you did, it was your choice, not theirs."

Lacey blinked and tried to keep her surprise off her face. How did he know that? "Okay, that's true. But still."

Victor turned his body toward her, leaning on the step above. "But still, it must have been something pretty major for you not to pursue it. Not if you think getting it would have helped you get promoted."

"That's the thing. It wasn't. Well, it wasn't anything I hadn't handled before. I didn't want to play that game anymore." The words were out before she could filter them.

Something flickered in Victor's eyes, and she could tell he knew exactly what she hadn't said. "Do I need to fly to New York and put someone into a wall?" His fist clenched, and he looked like he meant it.

"No. He's not worth it. And if having to work with people like him is the cost of a promotion, then I don't want it." She shaded her eyes against the glare of the sun. She needed to get back to her room and pack. Get on a plane. Put some distance between the man next to her who made her wish they had more time. At least until this restructure played out a bit more.

"Okay, then." Victor stood and held out his hand. She took it, allowing him to pull her up off the step.

"Okay, then?"

He brushed a piece of hair away from her face. "Okay, then we need to get you on a plane back to New York. Lace, at the end of the day, even with the promotion, thousands of people could do my job. But this new company needs you at its highest levels. I think you're already a shoo-in, but you obviously don't, so you need to go and do whatever you need to do to make it so."

"Thank you." For most of her career, people had treated her job like a joke. Like it was the kind of thing a woman did when she wasn't smart enough to be a lawyer or a *real* professional. It took all of her willpower not to kiss him.

Instead, she wrapped her arms around his neck and tilted her body toward his. After a second, Victor moved forward, wrapping his arms around her and folding her into the safest harbor she'd ever known.

Her elevated position placed them at almost equal height. And, as she felt the thud of her own heartbeat, she could feel his as well. His cologne was cinnamon and spice. His breath wafted across her hair and down her neck, sending spirals of electricity down her body.

Lacey forced herself to pull away, avoiding his gaze. Knowing that if she allowed herself the luxury of surrender, she wouldn't be leaving any time soon.

Victor's question still hung in the air, but she couldn't answer it. He'd as much as said he was taking his promotion, and she couldn't walk away now. She had fought too hard, worked too much, to risk throwing it all away because a man who saw her like no one else ever had asked for a second chance at who knew what.

For the first time, she noticed that the corner of the eye closest to his scar was slightly longer than the other, the skin pulling toward where the stitching must have been. Her finger ran the length of the raised pink scar, from his upper cheekbone to his jawline, memorizing its puckered ridges.

Plastic surgery could work wonders these days. He could have had it fixed, or at least made less obvious. Why hadn't he?

"It's the only thing on Peter's list."

"I'm sorry."

Victor stepped back. "This scar is the only thing on Peter's side of the ledger. I stole the girls he fancied. Rubbed his sporting dreams in his face. Went after everything that was important to him. Kicked him whenever he was down. Basically made his life as awful as possible from the time he was born. I was a terrible brother to him for thirty years. The least I can do is keep the scar he gave me."

And people thought sisters were complicated.

CHAPTER TWENTY-TWO

I 'M NOT CUT OUT FOR this part of motherhood." Anna made the gloomy proclamation as she surveyed Libby's birthday cake. Or, more accurately, what was intended to be Libby's birthday cake.

Lacey looked up from the email she was typing and caught Rachel's eye across the kitchen table. Before either could attempt a soothing response, a chunk of pink frosted cake slid down onto the platter like a culinary landslide.

Even Lacey, who had never decorated a cake, knew you didn't try and ice one while it was still warm. But Anna had been too impatient. At least the frosting matched the rest of Anna's garishly pink painted kitchen.

"Libs will love it because you made it for her. That's what counts." Hopefully, Libby was too young to remember the custom-made professional cakes that had graced her birthdays when Cam was still alive. Surely she was.

Rachel held up her phone, the web browser open to a local cake shop and mouthed *backup?* in Lacey's direction. Lacey shrugged. She'd tried to offer to buy Libby's cake as part of her birthday present. Then Anna announced she was going to make one herself. No one knew anymore when they were supposed to let Anna go with it or insist on rescuing her, least of all Anna herself.

Anna swung around, catching Rachel before she had time to

holster her phone. Her hair, face, and grey T-shirt were streaked with frosting, and bright star-shaped sprinkles covered both her and the surrounding kitchen surfaces.

Anna sunk into the chair between them and buried her face in her hands.

Lacey leaned back and grabbed the tissues off the kitchen counter. Just in case.

For a few seconds, no one said anything, waiting to see where on the emotional continuum Rachel suggesting a Plan B cake might land.

"You okay?" Rachel asked, her tone tentative.

Anna peered through her fingers. "The unicorn one."

"What?"

"You should get her the unicorn one."

"Done!" Rachel's fingers flew over her phone, getting the order in before Anna could change her mind.

Lacey stood and grabbed a spoon off the counter, sliding it through the landslide and nibbling on a small piece of the still-warm chocolate mud cake. Then a bigger piece. She blamed Victor. "Well, the good news is, it's good. Which is more than we can say about the first one you ever made us."

Picking up the cake, she placed it in the center of the table while Rachel stood and grabbed bowls from the cupboard, then rummaged in the freezer. She emerged victorious with a pint of Chunky Monkey. She and Anna both scooped large servings of cake and ice cream into their bowls.

"Where's mine?"

Anna and Rachel both looked at her. "Your wath?" Rachel mumbled the question around a large mouthful.

"My bowl."

This time it was Anna and Rachel who exchanged a meaningful glance.

Rachel swallowed. "Restructure?" The question was directed at Anna, who thought about it for a second and shook her head.

"No. She's been through two before." She squinted at Lacey like she was a laboratory specimen. Then a smile crossed her frosted face, and she pushed the ice cream across the table toward her. "Okay, who is he?"

Lacey's spoon paused midair. "Who is who?"

Anna rolled her eyes. "The man."

Lacey tried to keep her face straight. "Who said anything about a man?"

Anna smirked. "Your spoon spoke for you."

Lacey squinted at her. "Did you perchance happen to be drinking while you were making this?" Her spoon still dangled over the ice cream. Putting it down would be too obvious, so she scooped a small amount into her mouth. Banana. Argh.

Anna squinted back. "Did you perchance happen to fall in love while I wasn't looking?"

Lacey swallowed and choked on a fudge chunk. After a few seconds of coughing, she managed to dislodge it.

"Give it up, Lace." Rachel dug back into her bowl. "We know you don't eat carbs or ice cream, and you don't even like bananas."

"I eat carbs." She was busted, so now all she could do was buy time while she figured out what to tell them. She'd had zero intention of telling them anything about Victor. Talking would make it a real thing, and it wasn't. And if every time she picked up her phone she wanted to call him and every time she closed her eyes she saw him looking at her like she was more known than she'd ever been … well, that would pass.

Anna rolled her eyes. "Brown rice and quinoa don't count."

Rachel pointed her spoon at her. "Stop stalling."

"Okay, fine. Just to be clear, I'm not in love with him."

"Who?" They both spoke in unison.

Lacey buried her head in her hands, in a move not dissimilar to Anna's a few minutes before. "Victor." She mumbled his name, but Anna had ears like a bat.

"Peter's brother? You're in love with Peter's brother?" Anna let out something that could only be likened to a teenage squeal.

Lacey looked up to see her friend making some odd twisty, claspy motion with her hands. "Not in love with."

"Okay, fine. You fancy. That's a great British term, right? Fancy. You fancy him."

"Does Emelia know?" That was Rachel. Her own dysfunctional family background meant she had an eagle eye for relationship tension.

Lacey sat up and put her shoulders back. "No, Emelia doesn't know, and she doesn't need to know, because nothing is going to happen."

"Why on earth not? I know that there's some unfortunate history, but that was years ago. She's married to his brother, for Pete's sake." Anna reached over and pulled the ice cream tub toward her.

"Maybe he's not interested."

Rachel snorted. "I've been on book tours with you. There wasn't a man with a pulse who wasn't interested."

That was a massive overreach, but whatever.

"Have you kissed him?"

Lacey would rather eat more banana ice cream than answer that question, but the option had been taken away from her. Anna cradled the carton against her chest like an infant.

"Nothing happened at the wedding."

Anna swallowed her spoonful of ice cream. "Clearly something happened at the wedding because you're sitting here eating cake and ice cream you don't even like."

Rachel studied her across the table. "You didn't answer the question. So you have kissed him?"

Gah to Rachel and her years of studying people and ghost-writing relationship books.

"You've kissed him?" Anna's eyes widened, her spoon in the ice cream tub.

"Whoa." This was getting way out of hand. "Okay, if you two give me the floor for like thirty seconds, I'll tell you, okay?" Might as well get it over in one hit, not this death by a thousand questions business. "Yes, I've kissed him, but it was six years ago. At a party. Nothing else happened, and he doesn't even remember." Anna's mouth opened, and Lacey held her finger up. "And yes, him being … well, him, and all the baggage with Peter and Emelia is less than ideal. But nothing can happen because he works for Wyndham and the no-fraternization rule is being strictly enforced."

Anna opened her mouth again but shut it when Lacey looked at her.

"No, I am not even considering quitting or freelancing or whatever. I have worked way too hard to get where I am at Langham, and I have a good shot at a promotion. If anyone is quitting, it's him."

That should be enough. Surely. She looked at her two friends.

Rachel's eyes were narrowed, and Lacey could pretty much watch her piece together the information she'd provided, identifying the gaps.

Anna had big eyes and the kind of soppy face she got in the closing declaratory scene in a chick flick. She was probably still stuck on Lacey's admission that they'd kissed.

"It was a great kiss, right? That's why you still remember it."

And bingo.

Lacey poked at a piece of cake with her spoon. "I think you

greatly overestimate the number of men I've kissed in the last six years." There was no way she was admitting it was the best kiss of her life. It was mortifying enough that it had happened.

"So," Rachel steepled her fingers in front of her then paused, obviously prioritizing her questions. "If it wasn't for the merger situation, then this would be a thing?"

"But there is a merger situation. Thinking about what could be if there wasn't is hardly constructive."

"Why him? It's not like you have any shortage of men asking you out, so what is it about him?" Anna conducted her questioning with the spoon jabbing the air.

Lacey bit her bottom lip. "It's hard to explain."

Anna gave her a pointed look. "Try. Try real hard. Because this is the best conversation I've had since Rachel and Lucas got together."

Nobody got to hold out on Anna. It was an unspoken rule. "Fine. He sees me. Like he gets the things I don't even say. He makes me feel safe. He asked me for a second chance, then almost took it back because he said me getting a promotion was more important." Plus, the fact that every time she was within fifty feet of the guy, it felt like every single piece of her DNA oriented itself toward him.

Across the table, Anna somehow managed another soppy grin around a spoonful of dessert.

Rachel just raised her eyebrows. She was the more skeptical one. The one who'd lived behind the scenes of her own life until she met Lucas.

"What do you think?" Lacey directed the question to Rachel. She knew what Anna thought. Anna thought she should jump on a plane to London and throw herself at Victor and let the chips fall as they may. Anna would buy the ticket herself if she wasn't broke.

"What I think isn't important. The question is, what do you want?"

"I want my promotion." She could make Langham a better company, a safer one. She knew it. In the long run, that was far more important than an almost definitely doomed to fail relationship. No matter how much her fickle emotions tried to convince her otherwise. Her own family was enough evidence of what happened when you let your heart rule over your head.

Rachel tilted her head. "You're allowed to want both. It doesn't have to be an either-or."

"Except I can't have both. And I've never believed in wasting time wishing for things you can't have."

VICTOR HADN'T WANTED A DRINK as much since he'd gotten sober as he had in the last week.

He'd done a meeting every day. Some days both morning and night. At least he was back into Don's good books. The nod of approval across the room meant more than he'd realized.

Hi, I'm Victor, and I'm an alcoholic. It's been almost four years since my last drink. That part was easy. But so far, he hadn't found the courage to say the next part.

Maybe tonight. Maybe tonight he'd find a way to say that he'd met a woman he wanted more than he'd ever wanted anything. But it was never going to happen because she was too good for him, and he could never be enough. And so, in the absence of any hope with her, he might need to pick up smoking to do something with his hands, hands that were desperate to wrap themselves around a squat whisky glass. A throat that was parched for the warm burn of strong liquor. A body that hungered for the buzz it brought.

Maybe tonight he'd sit in the drafty hall, and his desperate desire for a drink would fade in the face of the stories of the addicts who had it so much worse than him, who had lost so much more.

Maybe tonight, God would hear his prayers for clarity. Or at least his prayer to get through a day without thinking about the feel of Lacey's hair in his hands or the light touch of her finger as it traveled his scar.

Or maybe none of those things would happen. Maybe he'd just cling to sobriety the way a drowning man clings to a life preserver.

Victor blew out a breath as he scanned up and down the block. The church was in a less-than-salubrious area of London, so he loitered outside the entrance to the hall, keeping an eye out for trouble, nodding to the other regulars as they arrived. Some shuffled in with the smell of their last drink still on their breath, others furtively checked to make sure no one they knew was nearby. Women gripped their handbags, some with keys or pepper spray clutched in their hands.

He'd never been threatened. A combination of sheer size and the fact that when people looked at him, they didn't know if he'd been the victim of a knife fight ... or the instigator.

His phone buzzed, and once again, he wasn't fast enough to quash the momentary hope that Lacey would be the name on the screen.

Peter. They'd made a tentative truce before he'd left Oxford, Peter appearing just conciliatory enough to suggest that either Emelia or their mother had had a word while he was with Lacey.

He looked at the screen as it buzzed again. It wasn't that it didn't have time to take the call—the meeting didn't start for another ten minutes. But there was every chance that a conversation with Peter would heighten his desire to find the closest bar, not dampen it.

He sent his brother to voice mail and put his phone back in his pocket. It scrunched against the envelope it had been sharing space with. The envelope that had spent the last three years stashed at the back of his sock drawer.

Lacey and her insistence that he deserved a second chance had given him the courage to retrieve the last letter he'd written in rehab, the only letter he'd never sent. It was the hardest thing he'd ever written. Harder even than the letters he'd written to his parents and Peter.

Years later, the shame still pressed down on him when he'd retrieved it from its hiding place. Even though there was nothing written on the envelope to reveal its contents. Not even a name.

Now it was named, addressed, and stamped, and destined for the post box around the corner. He'd been trying to shake the conviction all week that it was time to send it. But it had only gotten stronger. He could only pray he was doing the right thing by finally dispatching it. And if he was wrong for sending it, if it would cause harm at the other end, he would pray it got lost in the mail and never reached its destination.

A second later, his phone buzzed again. Peter again. "Hi."

"Hi. I hope I didn't interrupt anything."

"No." Victor scuffed the tip of his shoe into the pavement. "Just heading into an AA meeting."

"Oh. Um, that's good. I didn't realize you still went to them."

"I'm an alcoholic, Peter. I'll probably go to them for the rest of my life."

"Right. Good. I mean, I'm glad if it helps you."

It was probably the nicest thing Peter had said to him in years. And he was probably deeply uncomfortable saying it, given they came from good British Army stock.

Peter cleared his throat. "Anyway, I wanted to let you know I went with Mum to the specialist today."

"I thought you were living in Caversham now." The last he'd heard, Peter would be in lockdown with the rest of the team during the week until they left. Luckily the Team GB rowing base was only forty-five minutes away from Oxford, so Emelia got to see her husband more often than some of the wives and partners.

"Late start this morning. Anyway, the specialist had looked into the trial of that drug you mentioned."

"Aditron."

"Yeah, and she thinks Mum could be a good candidate, so she's put in an application. She cautioned us not to bank on it, but she seemed to think Mum should have a decent chance at being selected."

Victor let out the breath he hadn't even realized he'd been holding. *Thank you, God.* "That's great news."

"It is, it's the most hopeful I've seen Mum in ages."

"Good. That's good. I'll give her a call after the meeting."

Peter cleared his throat. "So, um, the reason I asked her to let me call you was because there was something else I wanted to say."

"Oh?" Victor instinctively braced himself for whatever was coming.

"Yeah. Look, I know we've never got on. And I know I've been hard on you the last few years."

"You've been waiting for me to fail." Might as well say it. No point pretending otherwise.

Silence from the other end. Then, "That's fair."

No words. He'd never expected Peter to admit it.

"Anyway, I just wanted to say that I'm sorry. I'm going to try harder. To be less of a … well, you know."

It was such a large unexpected olive branch that Victor responded like he'd been whacked over the head with it. With more gaping silence. He cleared his throat, which seemed to have closed over. He might not have a chance with Lacey, but finally, finally, it looked like he had a real chance to rebuild things with his brother. "Thanks. I know I've caused our family a lot of harm in the past, so I appreciate it."

"Well, I don't want to keep you from your meeting. I'll talk to you later." And his brother hung up as abruptly as he'd offered something that looked a little like reconciliation.

And, for the first time since Sunday, Victor didn't feel the need for a drink.

CHAPTER TWENTY-THREE

"**I** PROMISE YOU, BECCA, THIS happens all the time. Not everyone is going to love your book. But as far as negative reviews go, this one is pretty good." Lacey lifted her gaze to the ceiling as, at the other end, one of her authors fretted over a less-than-stellar review she'd gotten.

She caught movement out of the corner of her eye. Janna stood on the other side of her office, making vigorous "end it" motions across her throat.

Lacey looked at the clock. Ten to eleven. She was scheduled to be on this call for another ten minutes, and she didn't have anything immediately after.

What? She mouthed the word as Becca started on another pity-party, something about her publisher not giving her enough support. No appreciation. Most of her fellow authors could only dream about their publisher forking out for an external publicist.

Get off. Now. Janna mouthed the words back, while still making slashing movements with her hand, her dark bob swishing. Whatever it was, it was important.

"I'm really sorry. Something urgent has just come up. Janna will be in touch to reschedule." She hung up before her client could even reply. This had better be good. "What is it? What's happened?"

The possibilities ran through her mind. Someone else had been fired? Meredith had heard about the gala, and Lacey was about to be fired?

The thought wasn't quite as unbearable as it had been a few weeks before. But if she had to leave, she wanted to be the one who made the decision. Not have it made for her. She could always quit before she got fired if it looked like it was heading that way.

"You've been summoned up to the fifty-first floor. Immediately."

"What? What's on the fifty-first floor?" Langham took up floors nineteen and twenty of their building. She didn't even know who the other tenants of the building were, apart from the large law firm that had naming rights and took up at least ten floors.

"Apparently, we have an office up there." Janna tilted her heard and raised her eyebrows with meaning.

"We have an office on the fifty-first floor?" Lacey was on her feet, pulling on her jacket as she struggled to process the words. "Who summoned me?"

"Guy's EA. She said your key card will work for the elevator, and once you're up there, you want …" Janna consulted a scrawl on her hand. "Suite 5101." Her PA looked at her with shiny eyes. "I think this is it, Lace. I think they're calling people in."

Surely it had to be good news, right? Surely she wouldn't be summoned like this to be told she hadn't made the grade. She grabbed her portfolio, checking to make sure it was a Langham & Co pen slipped into the side. She didn't need to check anything else. Her hair and makeup were always set to last until at least mid-afternoon, and she hadn't eaten anything yet today, so no need to check her teeth.

"Go!" Janna flapped her hands like she was sixty-seven, not twenty-seven.

Within a few minutes, Lacey was thirty floors up. The elevator doors opened with a swish, and she stepped out into plush gray carpet, the kind she could imagine babies sleeping on as an advertisement.

Muted classical music played. An expensive chaise lounge and a table with fresh fruit sat just across from the elevator bank as if the people who graced this floor were too special to even stay on their feet a couple of minutes as they waited for an elevator.

Apart from that, there was nothing. No one. Just a hallway, with an occasional indent for a door. Lacey took a stab and turned left. The first door she reached was labeled 5050. The next was 5101. She paused for a second, then knocked firmly on the paneled wood.

"Come in." Meredith. Lacey's spine prickled as she pushed open the door, making sure to close it firmly behind her before turning to the room.

A large suite faced her. A board table for about twelve was on her right. Floor-to-ceiling windows held a view of Central Park. In front of the windows, two leather lounge couches sat facing each other, separated by a glass coffee table with a large fruit bowl.

"Come, sit." Meredith gestured to the lounge chair across from her. "Coffee?" She was dressed in a royal purple pantsuit. It would have looked garish on anyone else, let alone someone with Meredith's flaming hair. But of course, on her, it looked chic and elegant. Lacey felt shabby in her designer shift dress.

The carpet swished beneath her as she made her way to the lounge suite and perched opposite Meredith. "No, thank you." There was already a tall glass of water on the coffee table in front of her, so Lacey picked it up and took a sip, just for something to do.

Meredith leaned back on her sofa, crossing one leg over the other, and studying her for a few seconds. Lacey let the awkward silence sit, determined she wasn't going to be the one to crack. She took a few moments to rehearse her pitch if this ended up being some kind of *gotcha* job interview.

"I have some people you need to meet," Meredith said in her usual brisk tone. Before Lacey had a chance to say anything, ask anything, Meredith looked over Lacey's shoulder and raised her voice. "You can come in now!"

There was a click. A door she hadn't noticed opened, and Bradley O'Donnell walked out, wearing jeans and a polo shirt, hands tucked in his pockets. Lacey pressed her lips firmly together as cuss words traveled across her brain.

"I believe the two of you have met." Meredith's gaze bounced between the two of them.

"We have." Lacey nodded at him. "Bradley." She didn't stand or offer her hand. She had zero regrets about what had happened at the gala. Her only regret was that she hadn't done it sooner.

"Lacey." Bradley didn't quite meet her eye as he dropped onto the couch next to Meredith. Huh.

"Well, we haven't met, I'm Natalie."

Lacey's head turned at the unexpected voice, and she stood as the curvy caramel-blonde approached. Natalie's floral wrap dress seemed to float behind her, pearl-pink toes peeking out from tan wedges. Her hair was cut in a bob, flipping just above her shoulder.

She held her hand out. "Lacey O'Connor."

"Lovely to meet you, Lacey. I'm a hugger." Before Lacey knew what was happening, Natalie Porter had wrapped her arms around her in a quick embrace. It was all over so fast that Lacey didn't have any time to react. Hugging her had to be like hugging a plank of wood, but Natalie showed no sign of anything unusual as she dropped to the couch. "So, elephant in the room. We owe you an apology. Well," Natalie rolled her eyes. "Bradley owes you one most of all. I about slapped him when I heard the audio. I'm surprised you didn't."

"I'm sorry?"

Natalie crossed her legs and leaned back into the couch. "My brother's not really a creeper. Though he did such a great job at behaving like one that I did wonder for a second."

"I set you up, Lacey," Meredith said the words with the same amount of emotion as she'd offered her coffee.

"I'm sorry. What?" The pieces were clicking into place, but not faster than her flustered mouth.

At that, Bradley finally looked at her. "What Meredith and my sister are trying to say, and failing miserably at I might add, is that I'm not a serial womanizer. I just pretended to be one at the gala."

"Well, you did a great job." Let him take that for either a compliment or aspersion. She wasn't even sure which way she meant it. "So, it was a setup?" Natalie's line about audio appeared again. "And you were wearing a wire."

"Yes to both." That was Meredith. "We can discuss the details later. Bradley and Natalie only have a few minutes before they have to go."

Next to Lacey, Natalie reached forward, took a banana out of the fruit bowl, and peeled it.

"Nat, you literally ate like two minutes ago."

She shrugged her shoulders at him. "So what? Potassium's good for the baby."

The baby? Lacey's gaze darted to Natalie's midsection. The flowing dress covered any hint of what must be beneath. But didn't she already have, like, three kids?

"You're right." At Bradley's words, Lacey shot her gaze to him. "This will be number four. Apparently, Nat and Ryan haven't discovered Netflix yet." Something arced between them as she held his amused gaze.

The moment was broken by Natalie throwing her banana peel at her brother, which he caught mid-air.

Meredith looked on, appearing, well, bored. But that could have just been her face in Botox rest mode.

"Anyway, we want you to do our book." Natalie pulled a face at Bradley. "That is if Bradley hasn't put you off us for good. Also …" She held her hand up as if in court taking an oath. "I would like to say I didn't know about the setup. Bradley just told me he would take care of shortlisting potential publicists."

"Because you had your head in a bucket most of that week."

Natalie looked toward the fruit bowl as if looking for another missile, but Bradley reached forward and removed it from her reach. "Anyway, we don't have a shortlist. Well, we do, but it's you. So, will you do it? Please?"

It was like being Alice in the looking glass. And Lacey felt distinctly uncomfortable about landing the publicity contract of the year simply because she'd turned down Bradley's advances. "There's plenty of excellent publicists in New York. Surely you want to at least meet a few more."

The siblings exchanged a glance, and Natalie pursed her lips. "It would seem that after your little exchange at the Met, my brother decided he would apply the same test to a few other publicists. And, it would be fair to say, none of them did as well as you."

Lacey cast her mind across the colleagues she remembered being there. At least a couple would have been all in at Bradley O'Donnell flirting with them, book deal or not. She felt an unexpected need to defend her brethren. "You know that him being good-looking, unmarried, and basically all the best things of the stereotypical All-American man is half of your success. I guarantee the majority of single heterosexual women who have watched your show have had more than G-rated thoughts about your brother."

Natalie's face crinkled. "Ew."

So said the woman pregnant with her fourth child.

Bradley shifted on the couch and cleared his throat. Interesting. Most men would have lapped up her description.

"Moving on, Nat and I would like you—and your team, of course—to do our book. If you're interested."

Lacey didn't know if she was interested or not. Not when she'd got the offer via some bizarre form of reverse honey trap. "I'll need to talk to Michelle and see what Schnell & Cohen are looking for. Then I'll take a look at what we've already got in the pipeline."

She assumed she would be in a position to do so. But this all had to be in her favor. Otherwise, she would have returned from the wedding to a box waiting for her at reception. And if she wasn't about to get handed what she deserved, well, Bradley and Natalie could be her first freelance clients.

Natalie pushed herself up off the couch. "We're off to meet with Michelle now, so she'll be calling you straight after that. Name your terms."

Spoken like someone who didn't need to worry about whether or not the book made money. Michelle's position at Schnell & Cohen, on the other hand, would be relying on this book achieving everything she'd promised the pub board when she convinced them to bid a low seven-figure advance.

Bradley also stood. "You've never said if you accept my apology."

"I don't seem to remember you apologizing. Unless you're counting your sister saying you owed me one."

"Touché." Bradley walked around, so he stood next to where she sat, forcing her to stand so she didn't have to crane her neck to look up at him. "Well, truth be told, I'm not actually sorry."

His green eyes had flecks of gold in them. The way they studied her without apology almost made her forget that Meredith and Natalie were mere feet away. Three months ago, he may have had her regretting her no-crossing-professional-boundaries-with-clients rule.

But he wasn't Victor. He wasn't the person who had skipped stones with her on a Minnesota lake. He wasn't the man who had known all she could handle was silence after her sister broke her heart again. He didn't make her want to close the space between them and see if her head fitted into the crook of his neck like she imagined it did.

She ignored his pointed comment. "It was lovely to meet you, Natalie."

"You too, Lacey. You're even better than I imagined."

"Let me show you out." Meredith's patience for niceties had clearly run out, as she ushered Bradley and Natalie out the door in less than ten seconds.

Meredith glanced at her watch as she strode back across the room, diverting past the large desk and picking up a black leather folio. Lacey sat back down on the couch.

"I'm assuming you've worked out why you're here." Meredith perched the glasses on her nose and unzipped the folio, manicured fingers flipping through the sheath of papers inside.

Time to put all her cards on the table. Go for what she had earned and deserved. "Head of Publicity and PR." That was the title in the empty box at the top of her group. The one that came with a seat on the US senior management team.

Meredith peered over her glasses at her. "No."

It took all of Lacey's strength to keep her posture rigid, her expression neutral. Her mind raced through the ways she could decline whatever more junior position she was about to be offered. She couldn't afford to burn the bridge, as tempting as it was to make some dramatic exit. If she freelanced, the new company could be a potential client one day.

"Talk to me about the tent in the canoe."

Lacey stiffened, even though she'd always known it would come back to haunt her in this very process. "There's not a lot to talk about. I got distracted securing it, I didn't check it properly. I have no excuse."

A flicker of a smile passed Meredith's lips. "You secured that tent just fine, Lacey."

"What?"

"Kelvin loosened it. Along with some gear in Jen and Richard's canoe. We knew there was a chance that one of you would come to grief in the rapids."

"But wh—" Before her mouth could form the words she knew the answer. "It was another test."

Meredith nodded. "The most important thing to me in this new company is the quality of the leadership. There were seven of you I had my eye on. You all faced two significant tests of your character under pressure. You passed both." Her painted lips twitched. "As well as bonus points for pest assassination."

The Chair removed a set of stapled papers, placed them on the table facing Lacey, and pushed them toward her. "So no, I don't want you to be a department head. I want you to be the new CEO."

CHAPTER TWENTY-FOUR

LACEY WAS IN OXFORD. HE was going to be seeing her in a few hours. Victor checked his phone again, the same way he had at every opportunity since the text had arrived, just to make sure it was true.

He'd even taken a screenshot of their messages and emailed them to himself, in case something happened to his phone. That was how truly pathetic he was.

If he hadn't already known he was a goner, his completely out of proportion exhilaration to her request had sealed it.

Her text had been entirely neutral. She was going to see Emelia and was hoping they could talk. He could come to Oxford, or she could meet him in London before she flew out.

He was the one overanalyzing every word. She might want to meet to say *thanks, but no thanks*. Except she could have achieved that with silence. Why initiate an unnecessary awkward conversation?

He knew what he had to do. It had been obvious since the wedding. He had to resign.

The decision rolled around in his mind as he zipped his overnight bag. Would Lacey see it as the open door that he did? It all made perfect sense to him.

They weren't technically colleagues yet, not until the first of August. So as long as he was out by then, he would never be an employee of the new company. They could start dating today, and she couldn't get in trouble.

But what if the no-fraternization policy was an excuse? What if there were other reasons, and she'd used the easiest one? What then? He'd already had one chance and had wrecked it. Quitting for a shot at love was one thing. Getting rejected and then having to find a new job was another.

But while he could admit he had used his powers badly in the past, he was good at reading women. And what had happened on his parents' front steps wasn't one-sided.

Peter wouldn't be thrilled. Emelia even less so. But all he could hope for was that he would at least be given the chance to prove he had changed. Even if they would be secretly hoping Lacey dumped his sorry butt before the summer was out.

Grabbing his bag, he lifted it off the bed and carried it to the front door, pausing to scoop his keys off the table. In a couple of hours, he would be in Oxford. Should he talk to Peter and Emelia before he talked to Lacey? It wouldn't change their minds ... but they might be a little less mad if he gave them some warning.

But Lacey was already in Oxford, so she might be doing that. At least with Emelia. Peter would be holed up with his team in Caversham.

The knock came as he reached for the doorknob.

He reached for his wallet as he pulled the door open, ready to donate to whatever charity someone had let in the building so he could be on his way.

"H—" The rest of the word choked in his throat as he saw the once-familiar blonde standing there.

"Hi." Sabine's face was inscrutable, hands shoved into the pocket of her oversized parka. Even that couldn't hide an athlete in top physical shape. She looked just like the last time he'd seen her, almost four years ago.

"How did you get my address?" It was an insipid question, needed to buy time. Because the other question, *what are you doing here?* wasn't one he wanted to know the answer to.

"It was on the envelope."

Of course, it was. He'd scrawled it at the last second. If the letter was undeliverable, he'd rather have it returned than spend eternity in the Royal Mail's lost letter limbo-land.

Down the hall, some neighbors waited for the lift. Not paying them any attention. That would probably change if she gave him the dressing down that he one hundred percent deserved.

He dropped his bag onto the wooden hall floor with a thump. "Do you want to come in?" He opened the door a bit wider.

"Not really. But I probably should." Her mouth was tight. As long as he had known her, Sabine had always had a laser focus on her goals. But a new toughness shimmered around her now, like invisible Kevlar.

Victor stepped back and opened the door wider, letting her pass him. "First door on the right." He followed Sabine into his small living area.

She paused, casting her gaze across the Ikea furniture and complete lack of any attempt to make his mark. He knew what she was probably expecting. His medal from winning the Boat Race. Some photos or news articles celebrating what many would regard as his only life achievement. A few token family photos.

Guilt twisted his gut. He hadn't spoken to Sabine in years. Hadn't had any contact at all. He'd been stupid enough to think that even if Sabine got his letter, she'd prefer to leave the status quo alone. He'd been giddy on hope, believing maybe he deserved another chance.

And now his greatest mistake was standing in front of him, about to destroy everything he had tried to build over the last three years. Every attempt to prove he was different. He could feel it.

Step 9: *"Make direct amends to such people wherever possible, except when to do so would injure them or others."*

He should never have sent the letter. Should have torn it up and burned it. Should have left Sabine alone. Should have known that contacting Sabine would injure her, just like he had a history of doing.

"Do you want a seat?" Victor gestured to his couch. "Some water?" He had hardly any food in the house, so he couldn't offer her a snack. Not that she would accept it. She was in a peak training regime. Every calorie counted. Every carb and protein gram logged.

His knees almost gave out. She would be based in Caversham. With Peter. He hadn't thought of that. She'd have seen his brother a lot. On the water. In the mess hall. The gym. Would probably see him almost every day between now and the end of the world champs. How could he have been so stupid as to send that letter now?

"No, thanks." She shook her head, her blonde ponytail bouncing against her shoulders.

Okay, then. Victor shoved his hands into the pockets, walked further into the room. "I'm sorry if sending the letter was the wrong thing to do."

Maybe he could salvage this. Maybe they could say whatever words needed to be said, and no one would have to know.

Peter would never forgive him. Never. This would wipe out the long list of grudges and misdeeds Peter had catalogued like a nuclear event.

"The wrong thing to do?" Sabine's voice was tight. "It's been years, Victor. What happened? Did you find it under your bed? Go, whoops! Forgot to post my Step Nine letter to my brother's ex-girlfriend. Drop it in a postbox and tally ho! Maybe she won't notice it's over three years late."

Victor stayed silent as her voice rose. She was both right and wrong. The truth was it had taken him months just to face writing the letter. He had written so many Step Nine letters in rehab he'd had to ask for extra paper. He couldn't deliver most of them because he didn't even have names to put to blurry hazy faces.

They had been easy to write.

Teammates that he'd let down. Harder.

His parents. Peter. Emelia. Even harder.

But Sabine? That had been impossible. Sleeping with his brother's ex-girlfriend had been the lowest of the low. It didn't matter that they'd already broken up. It didn't matter that she was the one who had made the first move. It didn't matter that they'd both had too much to drink. Standard for him, almost unheard of for her. None of it mattered.

"I'm sorry." They were feeble words that didn't come even close to the grievous wound he had caused. "I should have done it sooner."

Her hands were clenched at her sides. If she took a swing, he'd take it. Heck, he'd get on his knees to give her a good shot if that was what she wanted.

"When I heard you were in rehab, I thought one of these might be coming. Every day for months, I opened the mailbox half expecting one to be in there. It never was. But now, *now*, you decide it's a good time to show up with your words of apology."

Rehab. Everyone in his family thought that it was the fight— or more accurately brawl—that he'd had with Peter that had been the tipping point to him admitting he needed help.

The truth was, the morning he'd woken up next to Sabine had been the tipping point. The line he'd crossed that even he'd thought beneath him. So he'd provoked a fight with his brother. Wanted to feel Peter's fist in his face, desperate for his brother to give him the beating he deserved.

He hadn't counted on Emelia being there. Hadn't known she was part-ninja and could take him down before Peter had even started.

"Why now, Victor?" Sabine had his crumpled letter in her hands and was waving it in front of her. "For the love of all that is decent, why would you send this now?"

"I—" Victor couldn't find any words. Sabine was right. There was no excuse. No good reason. He should never have sent it. Never should have let Lacey get under his skin and make him think it was never too late to say sorry. Because clearly, it was.

"Oh my gosh." A brittle laugh. "I don't believe it."

"What?"

Sabine crumpled his letter in her fist. "You've met someone. I don't believe it. Victor Carlisle, Britain's biggest womanizer, has met someone. Is this what this is all about? You trying to prove you're good enough for her?"

"I'll never be good enough for her." The words fell out of his lips before they were even a thought.

"You've got that right." Sabine shoved his letter back in her pocket. "Well, thanks for this. It's been enlightening. You were obviously on your way somewhere, so don't let me keep you. I'll see myself out."

She brushed past him, but not before he saw the sheen in her eyes. She lifted her hand and swiped it across her face.

"Sabine."

She paused but didn't turn around.

"Why did you come?" The look of horror on her face that morning had mirrored how he felt—one of the other reasons he'd never made contact. But no part of this conversation explained why she'd showed up on his doorstep.

"Don't worry, Victor. I got what I came for. Just pretend I was never here. It's better that way. I promise. Good luck with whoever she is."

He followed her down the hallway, his stomach loosening a little. Sabine wasn't after revenge. She wasn't going to tell Peter. She wasn't going to wreck whatever infinitesimal chance he had with Lacey. He didn't know how she had gotten what she came for from their conversation, but he wasn't going to question it.

Thank you, God. Whatever bullet was coming his way, he appeared to have dodged it. Maybe it was a sign that he had finally paid enough.

Sabine's phone pinged, and she pulled it out of her pocket as Victor reached to open the door. Her screen lit up with the beginnings of a message. Sabine only glanced at it for a second before shoving it back into her pocket.

But a second was enough. Enough to see the photo on her home screen.

"Who's that?" His voice sounded distorted and far away like he was speaking the words underwater.

Sabine froze. "Who's who?" Her voice sounded calm enough, but there was a tremor threaded underneath.

"The photo on your phone. Who is that?" He didn't need an answer. He already knew. Already knew because he had seen enough photos of his own childhood to know what had stared back at him.

Sabine looked over her shoulder. "That's my niece. Now I should go. And you have someone to go and see." She offered the lie with a pointed look at his bag.

The offer hung there, the chance for them both to go back to their lives like the last ten minutes had never happened. Back to the future he had been so desperately hoping for.

Future possibilities in one hand, a grenade in the other.

He had a split-second to decide which one to grab. "Sabine, you don't have any siblings."

LACEY DROPPED HER CARRY-ON ONTO the stoop and knocked on Emelia's door. Her cousin's car was in the driveway, and there were lights on inside.

Can I take a week to think about it?

No one had been more surprised than her when the words came out of her mouth. When she'd walked out of her meeting with Meredith and told Janna she was taking a few days off and decimated her airmiles booking a flight to England for the next day.

At least the flight had given her plenty of time to look through the fat stack of paperwork that Meredith had given her. The offer she'd reread countless times still hadn't sunk in.

Her hair stuck against her neck in the warm summer air. One plane, two trains, and an Uber had more than left their mark. She needed a shower. First, she needed to talk to her cousin.

She knocked again. Then pulled out her phone. Maybe she should have texted her? But Emelia had sounded a bit down the last few days, with Peter away at training camp. She'd thought it would be a nice surprise if she just showed up.

It was nine. A couple of hours later than she'd planned due to her flight being late, meaning she'd missed her train connection. Surely Emelia couldn't be in bed already. She knocked again, then pulled up Emelia's number.

"Coming." The word came a few seconds before the door opened a few inches, held in place by its chain. "Lacey?" Her cousin's astonished eyes looked at her. "Hold on."

The door shut for a second, then a scrape as she unlatched the chain and threw it open. "Is everything okay? Are you okay? Come in, come in." Emelia dragged her in then closed the door behind them. From the lounge came the sound of a TV show. "What are you doing here?"

"I had a few days off, and you sounded like you could use some company while Peter's away."

"She could." His voice came from down the hall, where the man himself leaned against the doorway. The man who was supposed to be at training camp for at least another week.

She looked at her cousin, at her disheveled hair and pink cheeks.

"Good to see you, Lacey." Peter walked down the hall, the seams of his inside-out T-shirt about as subtle as ketchup on a linen tablecloth.

Awkward.

"Peter's teammate's wife went into labor early, so they got an overnight pass." Emelia's words fell out of her mouth. "He has to go back in the morning."

"Okay. I'll go grab a hotel for the night." But Victor was coming. Probably arriving soon. She'd told him to meet her here. Presumed she'd have had a chance to talk to Emelia before he arrived.

"No. Of course not! We have a guest room."

They did. But Peter and Emelia's house wasn't large, and she didn't fancy finding out how well it was soundproofed.

"Yeah, I think I'm going to leave you to your conjugal visit."

Peter didn't even offer a token protest.

Her phone buzzed and she looked at the screen. Victor. I'm outside.

Outside? Outside now?

She couldn't just walk out the door. She didn't have a car, and Emelia wouldn't let her wait outside even if she said she'd call a cab.

This was not how this was meant to go. She was supposed to be here two hours ago. Supposed to have had time to talk to her cousin. Supposed to have that out of the way before she talked to Victor. She didn't even know what to tell him. She'd just known she couldn't accept the job without addressing what had happened—or not happened—at the wedding.

Her heart thumped in her chest. "I ... um ..." She'd have to tell them. Tell them and wing it and see what happened. "Victor's outside."

"What?" Emelia couldn't have looked more surprised if she'd said Santa's sleigh had pulled up in the driveway.

Peter ran a hand through his hair. "Is there ... Are you ..."

"Give me a few minutes to talk to him, and I'll explain." Explain what? She had no idea what she was going to say to Victor. *So Meredith has offered me the CEO role, but I can't stop thinking about the kiss we didn't have.* What did she even want? A kiss before she was his boss and then she couldn't do it anymore? A declaration? Some grand gesture?

She wasn't used to not knowing what she wanted. She'd known what she'd wanted since she was fourteen and worked out that all that Small Harbor offered was poverty and misery.

Before either of them could say anything, she'd slipped out the door and closed it firmly behind her. She looked down the path that led to the front fence. Victor stood on the pavement, under a streetlight. Shoulders hunched, hands jammed in his pockets, head down. Something was wrong.

For the first time since they had met, there was no quick quip, no flirty smile. Just a whitewashed face and clouded brow.

It took her a couple of seconds to recognize the expression. Trapped. He looked like one of her clients when they'd been caught plagiarizing.

"What's happened?" No point beating around the bush.

"Same thing that always happens." He attempted half a smile, which made the despondency in his gaze even worse. "One step forward, ten steps back. Story of my life." He leaned against his car. Lacey joined him, ensuring she kept a few inches between their arms.

She stilled the words of assurance that leaped to her lips. Maybe he was exaggerating. But there was something in the slump, in the way he wouldn't look her in the eye, that said whatever had happened was about to derail everything.

"When I go in there …" Victor nodded toward the house, "It will probably be the last time in my life my brother speaks to me."

What have you done now? Lacey checked the blame her reaction carried before it took hold. The blame came from everything Emelia had told her about Victor from years before, not the man she knew.

So she waited as Victor ran his hand through his hair and studied his feet.

"I found out tonight that I have a daughter."

A child. Dismay rippled through Lacey, but not shock.

"You don't look surprised."

Lacey looked up at him. There was no nice way to say this. "You are?" What she really meant hung unspoken in the air. The guy had slept with a lot of women. If it was as many as she suspected, this was just the law of averages playing out.

"I was always—" Victor shoved his hand through his hair again. "God hates me. That's the only reason for this."

Lacey didn't say anything.

"Do you believe in God?"

Lacey tilted her head at the sudden change in topic. "I did once. Now I don't know." She shrugged. "I seem to be surrounded by people who do. But I think I'm too much of a control freak. I prefer to be in charge of my own destiny." It was better that way. Safer. She'd learned the hard way that it was best to only depend on herself. "But my friend Anna would be the first to say God doesn't hate you."

"Well, if God doesn't hate me, what are the odds that out of all the women I could have gotten pregnant, it's Peter's ex-girlfriend."

At that, Lacey's knees almost dropped her to the curb. "You have a baby with *Sabine*?" Oh, this was bad. This was so bad.

"You know Sabine?"

Lacey pressed her hands into the side of the car, trying to ground herself. "No, but Emelia mentioned her a couple of times when she and Peter were working out where they stood with each other." Something made all the more complicated by her cousin having a hidden identity, but that was a whole different story.

Lacey closed her eyes for a second. Peter and Victor's relationship was fraught at the best of times. When Peter found out that Victor had slept with his girlfriend ...

"Ex-girlfriend." Victor's sharp correction broke into her train of thought. "I'm the first to admit I was a terrible person, but I never crossed that line."

"So, when?"

If possible, Victor folded into himself even more. "After they'd broken up. After he met Emelia."

Somehow Lacey didn't think Peter would see much of a difference. Given their history, he would still view Victor sleeping with Sabine as the ultimate betrayal, whether it was after he'd met Emelia or not. "But that was years ago. How are you only finding this out now?"

Victor flinched. "I sent her a letter."

"Why?"

"Step Nine is to make amends. I had a letter I wrote while I was in rehab, but I never sent it. I was never brave enough. And it was such a huge mistake. For both of us. I thought I'd do more harm if I contacted her."

"So why send it now?"

Victor let out a bitter laugh. "I dared to believe it might be true. That I deserve a second chance. But I knew I had to ask Sabine's forgiveness first."

Because of her. He'd sent the letter because of her. Tried to make amends with Sabine because of what she'd said.

"So, she just showed up on your doorstep and told you that you have a child?"

Victor rubbed his face. "No, she didn't tell me. She wasn't going to tell me. I saw a photo on her phone screen. She looks so much like me when I was a kid. I couldn't pretend I hadn't seen it."

Lacey drew in a breath, pushing the selfish if-onlys out of her mind. If only he hadn't sent the letter. If only he'd left his place earlier. If only he hadn't seen the photo. "Then you have to tell Peter. Now. It will be worse if you keep it from him."

"Peter's at training camp."

"Not tonight. He got a pass to come home."

She didn't think it was possible, but Victor seemed to collapse into himself even more. "I just felt ... I was stupid enough to think maybe we were finally getting somewhere. That he was starting to believe I'd changed. This is going to destroy every-thing."

Lacey didn't say anything. Not when he was dead right. She wanted to lean into him and tell him this would all work itself out. Somehow. But she couldn't. Not given the complicated and volatile relationship between him and his brother. Not now that he had a child. Not now that her crazy half-baked plan, the one that had gotten her on the plane, was gone before Victor knew it had even existed.

VICTOR TROD THE PATH LEADING to Peter and Emelia's house like a man heading to the gallows. It was hard to imagine the dread twisting through his body would be any less if an actual executioner waited for him on the other side of the front door.

Lacey pushed the door open, shucking her shoes off in the entryway. Victor kept his own on as he closed the door behind him. He was ninety-nine percent certain he'd need to make a quick exit.

Lacey stilled for a second, her hand curling around his elbow. For a split-second, he let himself imagine it was out of desire instead of pity. "You'll get through this," she said with a sureness that eluded him.

He let himself study her folded brow, her intense gaze. At least he had one person on his team. Though that would probably change in an instant if she was forced to pick sides. And he wouldn't blame her.

Lacey tapped on the lounge room door. "You guys decent in there?" Without waiting for an answer or giving Victor another second to ready himself, she pushed it open.

Peter and Emelia were both on the couch, Emelia practically in Peter's lap, his arms wrapped possessively around her.

Newlyweds. A pang of envy shot through Victor so strong his skin singed. He had done so many things backwards and upside down.

Peter's gaze bounced between him and Lacey. "What's going on?" Suspicion laced his question.

Emelia sat straighter too. Her gaze also moved between her cousin and him, a wariness in her face. It was clear what they both thought. The irony was that until a few hours ago if things had gone his way for once, they would have been right.

Victor pressed his lips together to hold back the bitter laugh that threatened to burst out. If only he'd left his house five minutes earlier. The fork in the road of his life, all because he'd checked his emails.

Lacey stepped into the room, and Victor followed, his shoes feeling like they were cased in cement.

"Victor has something he needs to tell you, and I think you both should take a few moments to listen." She sat in one of the armchairs, folding one of her legs underneath her like a gazelle.

Victor took the other chair, barely touching the cushion, his whole body coiled for flight.

His brother leaned forward in his seat. Emelia's hand curled around Peter's elbow, in case she needed to stop her husband from taking a swing.

Sweat beaded on his forehead. Might as well just get it over and done with. There was no good way to land this. No words that would soften the blow. "I found out tonight that I have a daughter." His fingers folded into his palms, digging against the calloused skin. "I'm so sorry, Peter." He looked straight into his brother's wary green eyes. "It's with Sabine."

He heard Emelia's sharp intake of breath, saw her hand tighten around her husband's arm, but there was no reaction from his brother. Not so much as a flicker in his expression.

"I'm sorry." After a few seconds of weighted silence, Peter shook his head. "Do you mind repeating that?"

"I found out tonight I have a daughter. With Sabine." The words fell into the room a second time. Like a grenade on a cop show that looked like a dud before exploding into a cacophony of sound and light.

His brother was frozen. Not so much as a blink.

They all sat in suspended animation as the seconds stretched on.

"Peter?" Eventually, Emelia broke the silence.

"Get out." Peter's face was blank, like a cold slate of marble. "Get out of my house. We're done."

"Now's probably not the time to be making any hasty proclamations," Lacey said. "It's late. This is a big shock. Victor can leave and give you some space to process."

If he had to guess, she was using the soothing voice she pulled out on difficult clients.

"I don't need any space to process anything. I've been processing Victor's crap for years."

Victor had never seen Peter like this. When it came to him, his brother's temper tended to run as red as his hair. This cold, clipped, matter-of-fact person was new. Peter looked at Victor with no emotion, and it turned his stomach more than any punch or outburst ever could have done.

"We're done. I mean it."

The words shredded him. Of all the things he'd expected to hear, it had not been that. At the least, his brother's faith—the faith he'd always secretly coveted—would have kept a thread of hope in the frame.

Peter stood, and Victor braced himself for a fist in the face. But instead, his brother just walked around to the lounge door and held it open. "Get out of my house."

"Peter, please." Victor had never begged his brother for anything in his life, but he wasn't above starting now. "I'll go. But please, in a week, a month, whenever, just let me explain."

"Why? You've resented me from the moment I was born. You've never been a brother to me. Not ever. You've been a bully. The person who went after everything that was mine. You never cared who you hurt to get what you wanted. I know that you've tried to change. I know that the last three years have probably felt long to you, but have you ever thought about how long the previous twenty-seven felt to me?" Peter shook his head. "I can't even look at you."

Victor stood up and walked toward the door without a backward glance. Peter was right. Everyone would be better off if he wasn't around. He'd given his whole family nothing but grief for decades. He'd caused more pain and heartache than he could ever know. He had a daughter, *a daughter*, who didn't even know his name and was no doubt better off for it.

He pulled open the front door and let the night envelop him.

WELL, THAT WENT WORSE THAN Lacey had anticipated. And it had been a low bar.

She should have followed Victor out the door. But she'd been so shocked by Peter's vitriol that it had taken the sound of Victor's car peeling away to bring her back to her senses.

That had gotten her to her feet, demanding car keys from a stunned Emelia. She'd half expected to find Victor's car wrapped around the power pole somewhere as she'd navigated the narrow streets. Had almost had a heart attack when she'd turned a corner to find a series of flashing lights and emergency vehicles.

Her heart still hadn't slowed, even though neither of the two cars crumpled on the side of the road were his.

She didn't know Victor well enough to know where he would go. Didn't know Oxford well enough to have a clue what his favorite haunts were. If he had any favorite haunts.

So instead, she'd taken a stab at where an alcoholic would go after an enormous bust-up, searched Oxford pubs, and was slowly working her way through the list.

Thankfully, she'd remembered enough details about Victor's

car that she didn't need to go into pubs and try and elbow her way through Friday night crowds looking for him. A quick scan of the streets and car parks nearby was enough.

She'd been to five so far. But Oxford was a student town. The list of remaining possibilities was long.

Lacey's fingers tightened around the steering wheel as she contemplated saying a prayer. She'd always been contemptuous of people who turned to God in times of crisis like he was some kind of magic genie that showed up on a whim and disappeared again when the moment had passed.

She'd always figured that if you got yourself into the mess without any help or hindrance from the divine, then you should get yourself out of it too.

Siri informed her she was approaching the sixth pub, so she started scanning the streets for Victor's car. Nothing.

A sense of futility washed over her. He could be anywhere. She didn't owe him anything. His choices were nothing to do with her. She had her own dysfunctional family to worry about. There was no need to buy trouble by getting involved in his as well.

Her hands tightened on the steering wheel. Except she knew what it felt like to have every door slammed shut in your face.

There was no sign of Victor's car around pub number six. Was she really going to drive all night trying to find him?

She indicated and pulled over the side of the road. At home, she would have driven and talked without another thought. But back home they drove on the right side of the road. "Siri, call Victor." It went straight to Victor's voice mail. Just like the previous times she'd tried. She closed the call before it hit the beep. No need to add to the three voice messages and even more texts she'd already sent.

Lacey did the mental math in her head. Night in Oxford

meant afternoon in Colorado. "Siri, call Anna."

She took a few breaths as her connection bounced off satellites all over the globe, finally landing on her friend's phone. One ring, Two.

"Hey." Anna's voice flooded the car interior. "How's England?"

"Well, Victor slept with Peter's ex-girlfriend and found out today they have a daughter, and he just told Peter."

"Wait, what? Victor has a daughter with Peter's ex-girlfriend?"

"Yup. She's two or three. But Sabine—that's the ex—just told Victor about her today."

"And how did that go?"

"Massive bust-up. Victor left. And now I'm driving around all the pubs in Oxford trying to find him."

"How can I help?"

"I was hoping that you could maybe say a prayer. I figure I need all the help I can get."

"You know, Lace." Lacey could hear the smile in Anna's voice. "You could always say a prayer yourself."

A couple of cars drove past. Not Victor's. "Well, I could, but I figured you would have more weight. Being a regular caller and all that."

"Yours might get priority, seeing as he hasn't heard from you in a while."

Lacey was silent. It sounded so easy when Anna said it. But not even Anna knew what stood between her and God.

"Do you love him?"

"My feelings aren't what's important right now." Did she love him? What kind of question was that, when Victor might be drinking himself into a coma?

"Relax, Lace. I've already put in a prayer."

"How?"

"I'm a mom. Multitasking is my spiritual gift. Now, since I'm going to get the evil eye from Libby's teacher for being late, can you throw me a bone and tell me why this is so important that you phoned a friend to put in a word upstairs?"

"I ..." It was impossible to explain without risking divulging a piece of herself she had guarded closely for years. "I don't want him to fall off the wagon after all this time. On top of everything else." It sounded lame. Even to her own ears.

"Okay. I really have to go before I end up in Pre-K mom detention. Let me know what happens, okay?"

"Okay. Give Libs a kiss from me."

"Will do. And Lace?"

"Yeah."

"You should try giving it a shot. Prayer. What's the worst that can happen? Love you."

Anna was gone before Lacey could respond. What was the worst that could happen? God could answer, that's what.

Lacey knew how this went. If God answered, then she'd have to work out what to do with it. Just like Rachel. She'd thrown up a desperate prayer of last resort last year that had been answered. And now she was going to church and trying to work out what God wanted her to do with her life.

Lacey knew what she wanted to do with her life. She'd finally gotten the one thing she'd been fighting for for years. More than. She wasn't going to pray and risk God messing that up with other ideas.

Victor was a grown man. He didn't need her to rescue him. She'd try one more pub. If he wasn't there, she'd assume Anna's prayer hadn't landed. She'd give up, her conscience clear that at least she'd tried.

She checked the map, set it for the next pub on the list, and started driving again. Ten minutes later, pub number seven showed no sign of Victor's car.

This had been a fool's errand to start. Wherever Victor was, he didn't want to be found, and God didn't care if she found him either. So that was that.

At least this evening—while it might have created some kind of existential crisis for Victor—wasn't going to do the same for her.

Then her phone buzzed.

CHAPTER TWENTY-FIVE

VICTOR EYED THREE EMPTY SHOT glasses in front of him. One for each year of sobriety. And, as it so happened, one for every time Lacey had left a voice mail.

In his defense, he had (a) called his sponsor (who hadn't answered) and (b) turned down offers of company from more than a couple of women whose gaze he'd accidentally caught across the bar.

He might be drunk, but he wasn't stupid.

Scratch that. He wasn't even drunk. After three years of nothing stronger than apple juice, he'd expected to have a decent buzz on by now. That the look of undisguised loathing in his brother's eyes might have blurred at the edges. But the picture was as crystal clear as it had been when he was in the room with Peter.

But he had to be a little drunk. After all, he'd called the woman who'd just walked through the door and was scanning the room.

More than a few men eyed her up in return. Victor didn't have to be sober to see the exchanges across tables and attempts at casual glances over shoulders. Even in jeans and a shirt—granted, what looked like a very expensive designer shirt—Lacey was in a different league than the women in the bar in their tight dresses and well-displayed assets.

He knew the second she saw him because her eyes tightened at the edges. Some clown tried to intercept her, but she didn't even give him a second glance as she headed toward Victor's booth, pausing only to say a few words to one of the waitresses.

He had no chance with her. He'd known that the second he called Sabine out on her lie. His big romantic play was all in ashes. But even knowing their relationship was over before it had even begun, she was still the only person he wanted to talk to. To see.

"Was it worth it?" Lacey nodded at the empty shot glasses on the table. She looked irritated, like she'd somehow expected to find him nursing a glass of orange juice.

Just something else to add to the list of failures. He hadn't been man enough—strong enough—to absorb Peter's body blow. Instead, he'd driven here and proven he was exactly the person his brother knew he was.

He'd been arrogant enough to think he was beyond this. Don was right. He'd thought he'd had it in the bag. That he'd conquered his addiction.

Yet here he was. The three shots had wakened a raging thirst, and he'd known only an intervention would stop three shots from becoming a bottle.

That was why he'd called Lacey. Because even if he didn't have enough strength to get up and walk out the door, he had too much pride to drink himself into the ground in front of her.

She slid into the bench on the other side of the booth. "You couldn't have called five minutes earlier, could you?" She poured some water into a glass and took a gulp.

"Um ..." There wasn't really anything to say to that. He could have called five minutes earlier. That had been about ten minutes into the fifteen he'd spent trying to talk himself out of calling her before giving up.

"Now, Anna's going to say you calling me was an answer to prayer. And I really don't need that." A drink landed in front of

Lacey, and she took a sip while Victor tried to unravel what she was saying.

"And if I'd called five minutes earlier?"

"Then it would have been before I'd asked her to pray that I'd find you." She didn't quite end her sentence with a "duh," but it was implied.

Warmth spread through Victor's chest at her words, and it had nothing to do with the whisky filtering through his veins. "You were looking for me?"

"I was worried about you. I didn't want you wrapping your car around a tree or putting yourself on an express back to rehab just because your brother's a jerk."

Victor stared at Lacey, at her flashing eyes and fierce gaze. But, apparently, not because she was peeved at him. "I got his girlfriend pregnant. We have a daughter. I'd say he's allowed to be pretty mad."

"Nope."

"What do you mean, nope?" Had he entered an alternative universe? He looked at Lacey closely. "Have *you* been drinking?"

What other reason for this could there be? People didn't find fault with Peter. Peter was the golden child. Victor was the damaged one.

"Not until now." Lacey took another slurp of her drink. "Vodka, lime, and soda. And no, you can't have any."

"I don't want any." He'd like to say all thoughts of alcohol had fled from his mind the moment she had sat down, but they hadn't. But they had at least been pushed into the background. Hard for them not to be, when he needed all his focus to try and keep up with the firecracker across from him.

"You didn't get his girlfriend pregnant. You got his ex-girlfriend pregnant. Very different. Don't get me wrong. It's not exactly brother-of-the-year material. But there's worse behavior living in the White House. Possibly in Downing Street too. Though you lot go through Prime Ministers so quickly, I can't keep up."

Victor blinked, trying to work out how in the space of a breath they had gone from his philandering to politics.

Lacey seemed to see that he was struggling to join the dots. "My point is that Peter overreacted." She knocked back the last of her drink and thumped the empty glass onto the table.

"Yes, but that's just one thing on a long list of things that I've done to him. You know this."

Lacey was, after all, Emelia's cousin. Which meant she was well versed in the many many ways over the years Victor had stuck the knife into Peter. Sometimes deliberately, sometimes just through circumstance.

Lacey held up her finger. "Just a sec." She flagged down a passing waitress and ordered a Diet Coke.

"Right." Her pointer finger remained in the air. "Shall we cover the highlights? You gave Anita drugs the night she died, then lied about being there." Another finger. "You took up rowing after Peter got injured just to spite him." Next finger. "You tried to break him and Emelia up." Another. "He was the person you called to get you out of every scrape you landed in and helped cover it up with your parents." Thumb. "You have a daughter with his ex-girlfriend. Does that cover the major events?"

Yes and no. "I was a horrible brother. I was a bully, and I made his life miserable for years."

"Why?" A bowl of chips landed on the table between them. "Want some?" Lacey pushed the basket toward him. "You have to have some. I haven't eaten fries in years, and I need to be able to tell myself in the morning that I didn't eat them all."

Victor was getting whiplash from this conversation, but he

obediently took some of the hot potato batons.

"Why were you so awful to him?"

Victor shrugged. He hadn't known for most of his life what drove the instinctive need to get back at his brother. No one had ever tried to find out. His parents had put it down to a personality clash. Him, the loud attention-demanding son. Peter, the introverted quiet achiever. "It doesn't matter."

It had taken him months in rehab to unpack it. Even longer to accept that there was something more complicated behind the enmity between them than the narrative he had been told all his life.

Lacey bunched her hair behind her head, then let it go. It was wavier than it had been at the wedding. More like it had been when they left Minnesota. He liked it. "I'm not going to tell Emelia, if that's what you're worried about."

The thought hadn't even crossed his mind. "It's not that. I mean, I haven't talked about it with Peter." And never would. Not after tonight. "It's not a secret. It just feels so ..." He racked his brains for the right word. "Small." Especially considering the havoc it had wrecked across both their lives.

"You don't have to tell me if you don't want to." He watched as Lacey's eyes darted to the basket of hot chips, and her fingers tightened around her glass. "Or you could just give me the CliffsNotes version."

"The what?"

"The summary version. You know. Like mine is that I never rely on anyone because I grew up in poverty. My parents not being able to provide taught me I can never depend on anyone."

He knew that had cost her more than she would ever admit by the way she grabbed a handful of chips out of the basket and basically inhaled them.

He was no-turning-back in love with her. The knowledge

slammed into him like a comet. He was in love with her, and he could never tell her. He couldn't quit his job, because for all he knew, he was about to get hit with a claim for three years of child support. And he had a daughter whose name he didn't even know, and he hadn't met. And his life was a complete mess. Lacey deserved a world more than he could offer.

"What, you hadn't already guessed that?" Lacey raised her eyebrows as she lifted her Diet Coke up to her lips.

Things started slipping into place like a kaleidoscope. But he pushed them away. The only thing he could give her was to entrust her with the same thing she had entrusted him with.

"Peter was a prem baby. He was born at thirty weeks."

Lacey lowered her glass. "I didn't know that."

Victor offered up a ghost of a smile. "Well, you'd hardly guess, looking at him now."

"True."

"Dad was posted oversees when Peter was born. They didn't have a hospital with a neonatal unit where we lived, so Mum had to go to London. I stayed with my grandparents. For almost six months. Even after Peter came home, I still stayed with them for a few more months. I'm not sure why. But I hated him for it. He was a tiny, helpless sick baby, and I blamed him for taking Mum away from me. That's it. That's the terrible reason why I made my brother's life a misery for almost thirty years. Why I've poisoned pretty much everything I've ever been near."

"I'm sure that's not true."

"My parents almost split up over us. They were separated for a year after the poker incident. I stayed with Mum and Peter and Dad moved in with our grandparents. I think they were genuinely afraid one of us was going to end up dead."

"But they got back together?"

Lacey reached for the chips again. This time, she didn't even seem to notice she was doing it.

"Yes, but only after they scraped together enough money to send us to boarding school. Different schools, obviously. Somewhere around the same time, Mum started going to church more." Victor shrugged. "I don't know for sure, but I feel like that had something to do with it."

"You should tell Peter." Lacey said the words softly. "I'm not saying it will fix anything, but at least he'll know."

Victor shook his head. He'd thought it through many times and always came to the same conclusion. "It wouldn't be fair. It's been too long. There's too much water under the bridge. I'm thirty-two years old. I can't keep shafting all my poor decisions back to something that happened when I was three. There are plenty of kids who grew up with way worse." Like Lacey. Yet here she was, owning her life and, for some reason, trying to hand him a shovel to help him dig out of the pit that was his.

Lacey pursed her lips. The ones he'd kissed and still couldn't remember. Yet another thing on his eternally long list of regrets. "I'm not saying it will magically fix anything. But surely Peter deserves to have all the facts. Or do you want to be permanently estranged from him? Is that what you think you deserve?"

"It's not what I think I deserve. It's what I do deserve. Everything I do, I still cause him hurt. I've been trying for three years to try and make amends, and all I ever seem to do is make it worse." Victor ran his hand through his hair. "Maybe it's time to accept that some things are too much to forgive. Or that even if God forgives us, some people never will."

MAYBE IT'S JUST TIME TO accept that some things are too much to forgive. Or that even if God forgives us, some people never will. Victor's words looped around her head.

"Do you think God has forgiven you?" Lacey couldn't believe she was having this kind of conversation with Victor, of all people. But her body leaned forward against her own volition, waiting for the answer.

Anna would be quick to say God forgives everything but, apart from one indiscretion, Anna had lived a pretty much blameless life. And she'd lost her husband to a freak accident. Lacey figured she had to have a lifetime's worth of forgiveness on tap for that.

Victor rubbed his pointer finger down his nose then back up again, his gaze focused on a spot over her shoulder. After a few seconds, it switched back to her. "Yeah, I do. Honestly, Lace, if I didn't, I probably wouldn't still be here."

Memories that she had spent too long shoving down bubbled under the surface.

"Why?" Desperation tinged her voice. Desperation that she didn't want him to hear. Maybe he'd had enough to drink to not notice. But the way he stilled and laser-focused his gaze on her told her she was dreaming.

Victor muttered something under his breath.

"What was that?"

"Nothing. I was just thinking Peter or Emelia would be way better at explaining this than I am."

"I don't want Peter or Emelia to explain it to me. I want it from you." Like sanctimonious goody-two-shoes Peter had anything to offer her. Sorry, Emelia.

But maybe, *maybe*, if God had forgiven Victor, he could forgive her too. And if God could forgive her, maybe Betsy might find a way. One day.

Victor rubbed his hand through his hair. "Honestly, Lace. I'm three shots down, I haven't had this conversation with anyone ever, and I'm going to stuff this up. I know I am. And this sounds important to you. What about the friend you were talking about. Anna?"

"Either you believe God has forgiven you or you don't. And if you do, I want to know why. From you. Not Anna, not Peter, not Emelia. You, with your crappy decisions and your broken life." Lacey snapped the words, forgetting for a second that she was supposed to be here to stop Victor turning three shots into thirty. Not making him feel worse than he already did. A couple of heads turned at the nearest table, her very un-pub-like words cutting across the Friday night noise.

She didn't know where this was all coming from. Ever since she'd left Small Harbor, she'd been all about moving forward, never looking back for longer than it took to transfer the money needed to keep her parents afloat.

"Sorry." She pushed her half-finished drink away. "That was uncalled for, and it's none of my business. I apologize."

Victor's fingertip grazed across her right knuckle, and she felt it in the soles of her feet. "The truth is, it's really not that good a story. When I was in rehab, the only reading material I was allowed for the first couple of weeks was a spiritual text. So I chose the Bible." He quirked a half-smile at her. "Well, that was my second choice. First choice was the Book of Mormon. But it turns out that's nothing like the Broadway show. Anyway, once you've been to group counseling and one-on-one therapy and exercised and eaten and slept, there were still a few hours left in the day to fill up. So I read it."

"You read the whole Bible." She was impressed. That was one very long book with very small font.

"No. I tried, but I lost the will to go on at the part where a bunch of men begat a bunch of other men. Then the chaplain suggested I try the gospels. So I read those. A few times. Then the rest of the New Testament. After I'd done that, I was allowed more books, so I got Mum to bring in some to help me make more sense of it all. At the end, I decided that I believed it. And I figured I don't get to pick and choose. I don't get to believe Jesus was who he said he was but also believe my sin is too much for him to forgive. It's all or nothing."

Lacey sat, waiting for more. A lightning strike. A loud booming voice. A small quiet voice. Flip, she'd even take an unnatural sense of cosmic peace. But Victor had stopped talking, and it appeared that was the entirety of what he had to say.

Her hand found her drink, and she knocked back about half in a single gulp. "It's that easy?" She couldn't stop the serving of skepticism that her question carried.

"No." Victor's thumb ran across her knuckles again, making it almost impossible to concentrate on what he was saying. "It's that hard. It's the hardest thing I've ever done. Harder than rehab. Harder than knowing I bear some of the blame for Anita's death. Because it's not a one-time thing. It's not a magic moment. Every single day, I have to choose to believe he has forgiven me. Even though I still haven't worked out how to forgive myself."

"I don't think Betsy will ever forgive me. Which means I can't either." The words were out before she even knew they were hunting for air.

"For what?" Victor's hand enclosed hers.

For making the appointment to get rid of my niece. The words screamed in her head but lodged in her throat. She'd never said them before. Not to anyone. Not ever. She'd spent years telling herself it was in the past. That she'd done all she could to make it right.

Victor's fingers tangled with hers. "Lace." She forced her gaze from their entwined hands up to his stormy eyes. "You can't control what your sister does or doesn't do. You can only choose for you."

His lips were moving, but all she could think was how much she wanted him. She wanted him to get into her space and kiss her senseless and tell her they would take on their two messed-up dysfunctional, broken families together.

Before she could do something stupid, she was out of the booth and on her feet, her gaze steadily avoiding his. "It's getting late. We should go."

CHAPTER TWENTY-SIX

THE DRIVE BACK TO VICTOR'S parents' estate was shrouded in silence. Lacey focused on the unfamiliar roads, while Victor provided nothing beyond the occasional direction. He seemed to know not to push her to talk about the reason for her outburst at the pub.

"Will you be okay to pick your car up in the morning?" She'd insisted on driving Victor, even though he seemed as sober as they came. At least being with him meant not being alone with her thoughts.

"I'm sure I'll be able to get a lift with Mum or Dad at some point." Victor scrubbed his face with the palm of his hand, his jaw set in a grim line.

"Are you going to tell them about Sabine?"

"Dad will be asleep already, so I'll do it in the morning. You should stay." Victor changed the subject abruptly. "It's over an hour back to Oxford, and it's late. Why don't you stay and drive back in the morning?"

"I'll be fine." She didn't trust herself to stay. But she didn't trust herself to drive back alone with her thoughts either. They were both inadvisable for completely different reasons.

She was too aware of his every move. If they got in that house and he so much as touched her or looked at her like she really mattered ... Her traitorous lips tingled. Remembering what she had tried so hard to forget.

Victor let out a sigh.

"You okay?"

"Just trying to work out how I tell Mum and Dad they have a granddaughter I've never met. I can't even give them a name or a birth date."

His words slapped her like an unexpected snowball on winter's day. This wasn't the Victor of old who played his title and charm to maximum advantage. If they got in that house and Lacey threw herself at him, she'd no doubt be politely and kindly declined.

What was she even thinking? He was a colleague. Meredith had made it crystal clear when she'd made the job offer that she knew the no-fraternization rule was never going to hold for junior staff. But it was non-negotiable for management unless it came with a ring and an announcement in the New York Times.

"The entrance to the house is on the right in a few seconds."

Lacey slowed and indicated. She had no idea why, given they hadn't seen another vehicle in the last ten minutes. She made the turn into the long driveway. Now she had about a hundred meters to make up her mind. Stay or go. Stay or go.

She pulled into the gravel space in front of the house but didn't turn off the engine.

Victor turned slightly in his seat, tilting his body toward her. "Okay, I have a confession to make. The fact that it's late and it's a long drive back is only part of the reason I want you to stay."

Lacey turned her head and looked at him, breath stilling in her lungs at the way his grey eyes were focused only on her.

"I just ..." Victor's hands tightened in his lap. "I don't know why you're in my corner. I certainly know there's nothing I've done to deserve it. But the other reason I want you to stay is because if you're in the house tomorrow when I tell my parents about Sabine ... Well, being around you makes me braver than I actually am."

It was the nicest thing anyone had said to her in years. Even if it wasn't entirely true. "You don't give yourself enough credit. You've spent the last three years determined to show your family that you're different, knowing they expect you to fail. That takes more courage than anything I've ever done." Then her traitorous fingers turned the engine off.

Victor's eyes glittered at her words, and he swallowed before grabbing the handle and pushing this door open.

Lacey set the hand brake before opening her door. The gravel crunched under her shoes, and the cool night air cut through her blouse.

Victor had stopped about halfway to the house, his hands shoved in his pockets.

Lacey walked up beside him, careful not to get too close. Her hands might run up his arms and wind around his neck if she did.

"I need to tell you something." Victor's voice was rough as he turned to face her. The moon turning his face into a play of light and shadow.

There was more?

His hands ran down her arms, warming them down to the bone. "I haven't dated anyone since I got out of rehab. And I know what my reputation is, but I want you to know that I have never felt about anyone the way I feel about you. And it kills me that I can't remember the first time we met."

The first time we kissed. He didn't need to say the words for them to shimmer between them like a ghost.

At some point, his hands had stopped running up and down her arms, and their fingers were now twisted around each other. "Tonight, before Sabine came, I had this grand plan. I was going to come here and tell you I wanted a chance at whatever this is between us. And if you wanted it too, then I was going to resign. But I can't do that now. I have a daughter, and I have to do right by her. Which means I need my job."

Then as if he'd said too much, he turned and strode toward the stairs.

Lacey stood there for a second, trying to process his words. "Wait."

Victor turned, his foot on the first step, his eyes on her as she closed the ground between them, stopping on the second step.

"Did you just say you were going to quit your job? For me?"

"Yes."

"And if I'd said no, then what?"

Victor shrugged. "I probably would have quit anyway. There's only so much a man can stand." He gave her another half-smile. "Grovel to Dad to make me an estate worker. I'm pretty handy with a mower."

His breath wafted across her face, and it was everything she could do not to wrap her arms around his neck and press her lips to his.

A kiss wasn't *technically* a relationship ... except she knew with everything in her that one stolen kiss on his parent's front steps wouldn't be enough. Not with the man standing in front of her. Who she wanted, despite all his baggage and mess. Who had seen more of hers than anyone else, and still stood here looking at her like he'd found a pot of gold at the end of the rainbow.

Victor turned, pulling a key out of his pocket and using it to swing the front door open. His mother stood on the other side. Bathrobe clad, arms wrapped around her waist.

"Are you okay?" Worry etched across her face.

"I'm fine, Mum." He dropped a kiss to her cheek. "You shouldn't still be up. I told you I was going to be late."

"I know. But Emelia called. Said you and Peter had words."

The *again* hung unspoken in the air. "And that she hadn't been able to get hold of either of you since."

Lacey dug into her bag and pulled out her phone. Looked at the notifications of missed texts and calls from her cousin that must have come in since she'd found Victor at the bar. With a few taps, she sent a response, letting Emelia know they were fine and apologized for taking off with her car.

"We're fine. Are any of the spare rooms made up? It's late, and I'm trying to convince Lacey not to drive back until the morning."

"Of course, she shouldn't." His mum looked at her. "The same room you stayed in for the wedding is made up, Lacey. Make yourself at home."

Well, that was hard to do when her bag was back at her cousin's, and she didn't have so much as her toothbrush. She opened her mouth to decline, but a wave of fatigue suddenly hit. She'd be a danger to other people if she tried to drive back tonight. "Thank you."

"You two head up. I'll close up down here."

Victor and Lacey headed up the stairs. Behind them, the beeps of an alarm code sounded. At the top, Victor turned left, his easy gait heading straight for the guest room she'd stayed in before. Opening the door, he turned on the light, then stepped back so she could enter. Her gaze was immediately drawn to the love seat where she'd told him about their fleeting past.

Victor's throat cleared behind her. "I'm going to go. I'll see you in the morning."

Lacey turned, and their gazes tangled. She leaned into his space as if drawn by an invisible string, her head resting against his shoulder, her arms looping around his torso.

For a second, he stood as stiff and solid as one of the oak trees lining the drive, then his arms folded around her and settled her firmly against his chest.

Lacey closed her eyes and let the warmth of him travel down her entire body. Felt his battle for restraint as keenly as she felt her own.

After a couple of seconds, Victor let out a ragged sigh. "O'Connor," he murmured the word so that it drifted across her hair before reaching her ear. "I have to go. If I don't, then we're going to do something that will compromise you and that I won't be able to follow through on. Not now, anyway."

In response, Lacey tightened her hold. Could they not just ignore reality for one night? She had done everything right for years. Could she just not for once?

"Lacey, please."

At the bare desperation in his voice, Lacey loosened her hold, but only so she could look up.

"You have no idea what kind of promises I want to make you. But I can't. And you?" Victor reached up a hand and tucked a piece of hair behind Lacey's ear. "You have fought so hard for your promotion. Whatever it is. And you deserve it. Too many people have already lost things because of me. I can't take the chance you might get added to that list. I need the company because I need my job, but the company needs you to even have a chance at building something great out of its ashes."

Lacey blinked. He had turned her down. Because even in a reckless moment when she would have thrown it all away, he cared too much to let her.

No other man she knew would ever have done that. No, they would have murmured promises about being discreet and how no one would ever have to know.

She loosened her arms and took a deliberate step out of the danger zone. "No one has ever done that for me before."

"Done what?"

She chanced a look up. Struggled to try and put things into words under the intentness of his gaze. "Ever put my best interest ahead of what they wanted." Without even knowing they had been brewing, she felt a tear slide down her cheek. She wiped it away, but another one followed close behind. Then another.

Victor's hands reached up, cupping her jaw, thumbs capturing the tears and wiping them away. "Well then," he said, his eyes never leaving hers. "I guess it's well past time for that to start with me."

CHAPTER TWENTY-SEVEN

LACEY REACHED FOR HER PHONE before she'd even opened her eyes, its familiar buzzing pulling her from her sleep.

"Hello." Her voice came out as a croak.

"Morning." Anna came over loud and clear from Colorado. "Sorry if I woke you, but to be fair, I did send five texts you didn't answer."

"What time is it?" It had to be the middle of the night. Where was she? What time was it? She held her phone away from her ear and glanced at it. 8.37 a.m.? She hadn't slept that late in years. Yet her body felt weighted down to the mattress like she could sleep for decades. Not her mattress. Floral wallpaper. She closed her eyes as the last twenty-four hours rushed back.

"Time shtime. Did you find him?"

"Yes. He rang just after I talked to you."

"And?"

"And he was in a pub. He'd had a few shots but wasn't drunk."

"And?"

"And we talked. Then I drove him back to his parent's place."

"And?"

"And I slept in the guest room because it was too late to drive back to Peter and Emelia's."

"And?" Anna was as relentless as a bloodhound on the scent when she wanted something.

"And now I'm talking to you, and you still haven't told me what you're doing up in the middle of the night." Lacey didn't hold out much hope that her attempt at a diversion would work, but there was always a slim chance …

"Good try. Did you kiss? Did you talk about your feelings? Are you in love with him? You only need to answer one. Though, if you're a good friend, you'd answer all three."

"Fine. No, we did not kiss. We sort of talked about feelings. I don't know if I'm in love with him, but that's entirely irrelevant."

"Love is never irrelevant, but we're going to park that for now because I choose door number two. Feelings. What did you talk about?"

"Rachel would never make me do this."

"True. Because Rachel is as bad at talking about her feelings as you are."

Might as well get this over and done with. "He said he'd planned to quit his job. So we could have a chance. But that he can't anymore because he needs his job to support his daughter."

Anna was silent. After a few seconds, Lacey opened her eyes and checked her screen to make sure they were still connected. "Anna?"

"Sorry. I was wondering how on earth you don't kiss someone after they've said something like that."

This time it was Lacey who was silent.

"Oh, wow."

"What?" Lacey tugged the covers up to her neck.

"You would have kissed him, but he didn't kiss you. Why didn't he kiss you?"

It was like Anna had somehow hacked into CCTV footage of them from the evening before. "He said my job was too important. And that he didn't want to do anything that he couldn't follow through on." She rubbed her eyes. "I can't believe he said that when he doesn't even know." Oh, she hadn't meant to say that aloud.

"Doesn't know what?"

"You can't tell anyone. Like no one. Not even Rachel."

"Just tell me."

"Meredith offered me a big promotion. Like CEO big." It was the first time she'd said the words aloud. Lacey O'Connor. CEO.

Lacey held the phone away from her ear as a squeal reverberated from Colorado.

"So you pretty much threw yourself at him, and he turned you down. Because your job was too important, and he didn't even know about this."

She'd just told Anna she was going to be in charge of a large multinational company, and Anna had turned it straight back onto Victor. Fancy that. Lacey should be annoyed, but she was too busy trying not to remember the feeling of Victor's lips in her hair.

"So, not that I want to scare you off or anything, but you get that he loves you, right?"

Lacey managed a half-laugh around her increased heart rate. "Did you miss the part where we haven't even been on a date?"

"Lace, I know you haven't seen a whole lot of it, but this is what love looks like. Choosing the other person. Wanting the best thing for them. What he did last night? That's love."

The words hit Lacey so hard that she dropped her phone and had to scramble to find it among the blankets.

Anna couldn't be right. He couldn't love her. He barely knew her. She lifted the phone back to her ear.

"He can't love me." There was a tinge of desperation to her words. Attraction, she knew what to do with. Like, she knew what to do with. Flirting, she knew what to do with. But love?

The kind of love Anna was talking about? She had no idea what to do with that.

"Oh, honey, you don't get to have a choice. The choice is his, and he's chosen you."

There was a knock at the door, saving her from the conversation. Saving her from the feelings causing her heart to try and escape her ribs.

"Yes." It was an instinct answer. She should have said no. Or go away. Because there was only one person who could be on the other side, and she wasn't ready to see him with Anna's insistent words in her ears.

The door opened, and Victor stuck his head in. "Morning."

"Do you love me?"

DO YOU LOVE ME?

The words had flown out of Lacey's mouth from where she sat—in what Victor assumed was one of his mother's night-gowns—among a pile of sheets and blankets.

Her hair was disheveled, her eyes wide, and her phone was in her hand. Someone squawked from the other end.

"Nope, go back outside. Right now. We're going to pretend I never said that. Goodbye." Lacey untangled herself out from her bedding and strode across the bedroom like she intended to physically manhandle him out of the door. Good luck with that.

Do you love me? Heart thudding, Victor stepped into the room and closed the door behind him.

"Nope. Not acceptable. Uh uh. You're on the wrong side of the door." She was still holding her phone, which Victor plucked from her hand while she was busy jabbing him in the chest.

"Hello?"

"Hi, this is Anna." A very amused American accent came

from the other end.

"Hi, Anna. I'm Victor." Lacey was now grabbing for her phone, something his combined height and stature made reasonably easy to fend off. For now. She looked fierce enough to bite him. "I probably only have a few seconds. Is there anything you'd like to tell me before she knocks me out with a family heirloom to get her phone back?"

He was only half-joking, giving the way Lacey had spun around and was eyeing up the bedside lamp.

"She's not very good at feelings."

"Yup, got that."

"She's going to run away."

"That's a one hundred percent certainty." Lacey had grabbed her clothes and was stalking into the en suite, slamming the door shut behind her.

"But she's worth it."

"I know she is." He eyed up the bathroom door, knowing that any second it would be flung open, and she would be about two minutes away from peeling out of the driveway. Blocking her from the exit would be guaranteed to tip her over the edge. He moved so that he was clear of the path from the bathroom to the door. He loved her. And that meant he had to let her go. "But, I'm not."

"Last night, you showed Lacey more love than she's ever had from any man in her entire life. That makes you more than worth it. Tell her to call me." And American Anna was gone.

More love than she's ever had from any man her entire life. Anna's words twisted Victor's stomach. He had done so many things wrong in his life. He wasn't even sure he knew how to love someone. Not really. If that was true, what had the rest of the men in her life been like?

With a thud, the bathroom door flung opened. Lacey appeared, dressed, and hopping as she shoved her second shoe on her foot.

She looked between him and the door as if anticipating some kind of trick. "I have to go." She took a few steps. "Good luck with Peter and Sabine and everything. Your daughter. All of it. I hope it all works out."

He didn't move as she approached the door. Even though every muscle in him fought to sweep her up in his arms.

"Your phone." He held it out. She looked at his palm for a second then reached out for it.

"Thanks." She dropped it into her bag. Her gaze studiously avoiding his.

"The answer, by the way, is yes."

At that, her head jerked up, a deep wariness written behind her eyes. "No, it's not. You don't even know me."

Victor took a breath. He had to be careful. One wrong word and she'd be gone. "Lace, I may not know what your favorite food is, or whether you snore, or even your address. But people could date for years and know all the small things and not know what really matters. But I have seen enough, I know enough, to know I love you."

For a long moment, he thought he might have pushed too far. Her gaze darted back to the door, but her feet didn't move. He was all in now. No going back.

He gave her a couple of seconds, but she didn't say anything. "I'm not asking you to give me a chance. If you leave without another word, I'll understand. If you tell me the best I can hope for is distant colleagues, I'll accept it."

Lacey's gaze stayed firmly fixed on her toes that peeked out from her shoes. "Can you please look at me?" After a second, she raised her head. Her lips were pressed firmly against each other, her arms folded across her torso like a barrier.

"I know what I said last night. I know I can't do anything about it right now because I have too many other things that I need to try and fix. But I love you, and I'm in love with you. And I know I'm not worthy of you. But falling in love with you is the only worthwhile thing I've done in a long time."

"And what about me?" The words erupted from her, her eyes ablaze. There it was. Something real at last. Anything was better than the blank facade. Her fists were curled, and she was on her toes, right in his space. "What am I supposed to do with this? You can't choose me. You have to choose your job. You have to choose your daughter. I don't get to be a choice. Especially not when I'm going to be your boss. Why would you say you love me when you can't do anything about it?"

She made it sound like he had some grand plan when it was all he could do to keep his thoughts from scrambling every time he came within a few meters of her. "Because you asked me?"

Lacey grabbed fistfuls of his T-shirt, closing the little space that remained between them. "And then I unasked you, and you said it anyway!" She was so close he could see the tiny yellow flecks in her eyes, like comets against a summer sky.

Victor clenched his fists to stop his arms from wrapping around her. "I didn't think it would be news. Every time I'm near you, it feels like it's written across my face like a sign in Piccadilly Circus. And fair warning, if you don't get out of my space in the next second, I'm going to kiss you, and you can keep yelling at me after that."

Lacey blinked, but she didn't let go of his T-shirt, and she certainly didn't step back. Sod it. She couldn't say she wasn't warned. He leaned in and pressed his lips against hers, his arms wrapping around her back and lifting her off the ground.

For a split-second, her body was stiff against his. Then her hands splayed across his chest, and she folded into him, kissing him back with a fierceness that would have taken his breath away if he'd had any left to lose.

Something she'd said tugged at him. He pushed it away, focusing on the feel of Lacey in his arms as her hands traveled up his body and wrapped around his neck.

Victor walked backwards until he felt the back of the love seat against his calves. Then he loosened the kiss, pressing his forehead against hers. "O'Connor, if you want to kiss me like that, I'm going to need to sit down before I lose the ability to stand."

Lacey opened her eyes, glazed blue pools staring back at him. "I'm pretty sure you kissed me."

Victor sagged down onto the seat, tucking her close. "I'm pretty sure you were the one who took it thermonuclear ..." His hand weaved through her hair as he leaned in close. "Mine said, let's stop fighting. Yours said, let's take a drive to Gretna Green."

It was meant to be funny. It was meant to set up another kiss. But immediately, her eyes shuttered, and he knew he'd put his big mouth in something. But what? "It's a joke, Lace." He was the one who'd put himself out there. Who'd said he loved her, knowing it wasn't going to be coming back.

She shifted, pulling back from him. "Just so we're clear. Even if I wasn't going to be your boss, I'm not the marrying type."

Going to be your boss. Not the marrying type. The two statements slammed into him like an uppercut followed by a hook.

"My boss?" Victor repeated the words, but they made no more sense the second time. Unless Lacey was taking over an entirely different department, there was no way she could be his boss. The only place their two groups met in the new structure was at the CEO. *The CEO.* As soon as the thought struck, he knew it was true. It was a genius move and exactly the kind of thing Meredith would do. "You're going to be the new CEO."

Lacey leaned back a little further. "Yes. But I haven't accepted it yet."

"Why on earth not?" Meredith was all about meritocracy. The only reason she would offer Lacey the job was if she knew Lacey could do it, and she was the best candidate.

Lacey cast her gaze up to the ceiling and swallowed. "Because when she offered me the job, all I wanted to do was see you. Talk to you about it. I had this crazy idea that maybe ..." She trailed off, then shook her head. "Don't worry."

"Maybe what?"

"That you could find a job somewhere else so I could have the promotion and maybe a chance at whatever this is too."

Her statement covered him like a lead blanket. They'd been on exactly the same wavelength. He was going to offer to quit. She was going to ask him.

If he'd never sent that letter to Sabine, they would have had a completely different conversation last night. Today they could have been ... well, who knew. But not this.

But then he wouldn't know he had a daughter. A little girl with his nose and eyes, and Sabine's hair and smile.

The weight of having a birds' eye view of his life splitting down two paths, one where he hadn't sent the letter, one where he had, folded him over his knees.

Lacey shifted beside him. "I can't do this. I'm sorry. I have to go."

Victor didn't even look up as she walked across the room and out the door.

CHAPTER TWENTY-EIGHT

I'M GOING TO BE YOUR *boss.* The words had circled his head as Victor put himself through gut-busting rounds of press-ups, burpees, and pull-ups to stop himself from chasing after Lacey. The burn in his muscles and lungs almost distracted him from the revelation but did nothing to distract him from their kiss.

Lacey was going to be the CEO. Every time he opened the intranet, every major announcement, every organizational road would lead to her. She would be amazing. More than. She would be phenomenal. She would be a shooting star. He gave it six months before he couldn't walk past a newsstand that didn't have a glowing profile of her in some business publication.

She would be surrounded by the best minds, the smartest people, the highest flyers.

And what was he? A lobbyist with a daughter from a one-night stand that he hadn't even met. He wasn't enough for Lacey before, and he would never be enough for her now.

Pressing his face into his T-shirt, he scrubbed the cotton from his forehead to his chin. He didn't even waste time pretending he wasn't hiding. Hiding from the sound of Lacey driving away, hiding from his mother, whose slow-earned faith he was about to shatter. Hiding from once again being the person who let everyone down and broke their family.

Lacey was better off without him. His family was better off without him. His daughter could well be better off without him.

But at least with her, if Sabine let him, he had a chance to be something good. Even if it was only being a part-time father.

A knock came at his door, and he opened it. Probably his mum wondering why he hadn't been down for breakfast.

"Hey. Do you have a second?" His sister-in-law stood in the hallway, dark circles under her eyes, indicating she'd had about as much sleep as him.

Victor stepped back to let her in. "Sure."

Emelia looked down the hallway then half stepped into his room, just past the door frame. Like she wasn't supposed to be here. Which was probably true if Peter was even ten percent as mad as he'd been the night before. "Your mum called a family meeting."

"She what?" The last family meeting that had been called had been after the infamous poker event, when their parents told Peter and him they were separating so they didn't kill each other.

Emelia shrugged. "That's all I know. It's in ten minutes. I said I'd come tell you."

"Okay."

His sister-in-law looked at the ground for a second. "I called Sabine."

"You what?"

Emelia shifted on her feet, her fingers pulling at the hem of her T-shirt. "Lacey mentioned you don't know what your daughter's name is, and I had Sabine's number from when we worked on that fundraiser, so I called her. It didn't feel right that you didn't even know her name."

"And?"

"Her name is Peyton, and she just turned three."

"Peyton." Victor tested the name out, connecting it to the face he'd seen on Sabine's phone.

"Peyton Carlisle Montclair."

Victor blinked. Then blinked again. But that didn't do anything to stop the sudden moisture build-up in his eyes. "She has my name?"

Emelia's hands twisted over each other. "Sabine said she'd always intended to tell you. But you were in rehab. By the time you got out, she'd convinced herself it was better for everyone if you didn't know."

Victor scrubbed his hand over his head. "She announced her retirement from rowing while I was in rehab. I remember reading about it." Everything clicked into place. Sabine's retirement, the two-year break, followed by her return to rowing last year. She'd always been reserved about her private life. While some of her teammates supplemented their income with TV appearances and tell-all interviews to tabloids, Sabine never had. Leaving the GB squad meant her pregnancy and Peyton's birth got no media attention.

Emelia tapped her phone and held it out to him. "She sent me a photo for you to show your parents." His daughter, with hair in pigtails, grinned back at him. It was the photo on Sabine's home screen. "I'll send it to you."

Victor couldn't tear his eyes away from Emelia's phone. Peyton. His daughter. "Does Peter know you called her?"

Emelia shook her head. "No. He's still pretty mad. He's going to need some time."

"Well then, thanks. You didn't have to do that."

"Lacey also said in her message she's going home today." Emelia changed the subject.

Lacey. What a mess. "You don't need to worry. Nothing's going to happen there. Even without all of this, I'm not good enough for her." He didn't know what possessed him to say that. Maybe it was Emelia being kind to him when she had no reason to.

Emelia tilted her head as she tapped her phone, sending the photo off with a whoosh. His phone buzzed. "I used to feel that way about Peter. I believed I didn't deserve to be happy after what happened to Anita."

Victor dodged the unasked question. "Lacey has enough on her plate with her family. The last thing she needs is me, weighing her down with all my baggage."

Emelia's eyes widened. "What did she say about her family?"

"She didn't say much. That's just my own interpretation from when we were in Small Harbor."

"*You* went to Small Harbor?" Emelia looked at him like he'd announced he'd been selected for the next Mars Rover mission. "But Lacey would never take someone there."

He watched the cogs turning in Emelia's head and back-tracked some more. "She didn't have a choice. She needed to drop something back to her dad."

Emelia shook her head. "If she hadn't wanted you there, she would have found another way." She shook her head again as if trying to shake something loose in her brain. "Um, we should get downstairs for this meeting." She'd barely finished the sentence before she was out the door and down the hall.

Victor looked at his sweaty workout gear. The same T-shirt that had been captive in Lacey's hands only an hour before. It didn't feel possible that less than twenty-four hours ago, he'd been planning to quit, believing that maybe he had finally earned something good.

Victor headed downstairs to the kitchen, the designated space for family conversations. Although it might be the parlor if his mother really was scared they might start swinging. Then everyone could be seated a safe distance away from each other.

He trudged into the room. The rest of the family were already there. Peter and Emelia on one side of the rectangular table. His parents, on the other, leaving him the choice of seats at the end. He chose the one closest to the door.

Peter's jaw flexed, the only acknowledgment of his presence. Emelia's fingers wrapped around her husband's curled fist. Actual divine intervention. That was the only thing he could see ever salvaging his relationship with Peter. "Is this going to take long? I'm due back by lunchtime, and I'd prefer not to add a brassed-off coach to everything else."

His mother spread her hands on the wooden surface. "Peter dear, stop acting like a spoiled child. The world doesn't revolve around you."

Victor's jaw swung wide. He couldn't even remember the last time he'd heard his mother admonish her golden youngest.

Peter's eyebrows jerked up. "He hasn't told you."

"About whatever your latest falling-out is about? No. Are you going to do the honors?"

"Peter." Emelia's voice held a tone of warning.

Victor's stomach twisted like a fairground pretzel. If he didn't speak, his brother would probably explode. "He's entitled to be angry. I found out yesterday that I have a daughter. With Sabine." He directed the bombshell toward the tabletop.

Silence. Lingering awkward silence. He glanced up. His father was studying his cup of tea. His mother's hands shook as she shredded a napkin.

"How old is she?" Little white pieces of paper fluttered from his mother's fingers.

"She just turned three. Her name is Peyton." Victor's hands fumbled with his phone as he pulled up her picture. "Here." *Thank you, God, for Emelia and her mission of mercy.*

He handed the phone to his father. He took a quick look before handing it to his mother, who studied it like she was in the Louvre standing in front of the Mona Lisa. The side of her mouth lifted. "She's lovely."

"That's all he's going to get. *She's lovely.*" Peter's voice was so bitter it would have been cyanide in physical form. "Victor has a secret baby with my girlfriend, and that's all he gets? My whole life, all he's ever wanted is everything that's mine, and you two have never called him on it."

"That's not true." His mother was back to shredding the tissue. "Also, going by Peyton's age, it's ex-girlfriend. And given you're sitting here with your wife, you might want to dial down a bit on the righteous indignation."

Whoa.

His mother cast a glance his way. "You're not off the hook. Sleeping with your brother's ex-girlfriend was an asinine thing to do."

"I know." He tried to catch his brother's eye, but Peter's gaze was resolutely anywhere but on him. "That fight I picked with you before I went into rehab? That was because I hated myself for what I'd let happen with Sabine. I wanted you to beat me to a pulp. I would have let you if it wasn't for girl ninja here."

That managed to get a half-smile out of Emelia, and his brother at least looked his way.

Victor sucked in a breath. He only had one chance to say this right. "I'm sorry. More sorry than I can ever say. It never should have happened. I am so deeply ashamed that it did. And I'm sorry if it's hard for you, but I'm not going to abandon Peyton now I know she exists. I want to be part of her life if Sabine lets me."

His brother looked at him for a second, then gave the world's smallest nod. It wasn't forgiveness, but it was something.

"Okay, not that I'm trying to sideline this, but I need to talk to you both about something before I lose the nerve." His mother took a deep breath. "I've been seeing a counsellor again. Mostly about you two."

He'd put his mother into therapy. Again. There was a new low.

"She's helped me see that things are probably never going to be resolved between you if we don't tell you the truth about what happened when Peter was born."

"What are you talking about?" Peter tucked Emelia into his side, and Victor almost choked on envy. Had it only been this morning when he'd done something very similar with Lacey?

"She thinks the reason Victor saw you as his competition is because for six months after you were born, you had the only thing he wanted. Me."

Victor sat still. Not wanting to do anything to draw attention to himself. Not wanting anything to disrupt his mother's train of thought.

"What do you mean?" For the first time, Peter sounded unsure of his moral high ground.

His mother swallowed. "As you know, you were premature. You were in the hospital for three months. The first few weeks, we thought you might not make it. Your dad was deployed, and I had to be with you in London, so Victor stayed with your grandparents. Then—" she sucked in a shuddering breath and didn't continue.

His dad reached over and took his mum's hand and squeezed it. "Then, two weeks after you got home, your mum had a breakdown."

"She what?"

That was both of them.

His dad looked between his two sons. "She went for a walk with the two of you one afternoon to get some milk and didn't come back. The police found you all in a park six hours later, after a member of the public called. It was almost freezing. Peter was safe in his pram, but you were on a swing and hypothermic.

You had to be admitted to hospital." His dad took a long sip of his tea. This time, his hand was the one shaking. "Your mum was in a psychiatric facility for almost three months. Peter, you went with her because you were so young, but Victor ..." Whatever came next seemed to lodge in his throat.

Victor what? His shoulders tensed, sensing that whatever was coming wasn't something he'd heard before.

His mother looked at him with glassy eyes. "I'm so sorry. Your grandparents did their best, but they weren't equipped for the long-term care of a three-year-old. Your dad was in special ops. He couldn't come home. So you bounced between your grandparents and other extended family. A week here, a week there. Most of them strangers to you."

Victor dug into his memory bank. Tried to summon up anything from that time. But all he had was vague impressions of being lost and alone, the occasional blurry image of one of his grandparents. Nothing of anyone else. "I don't remember any of that."

"Your father finished his mission only a few weeks before I was well enough to come home. By then, you were a different kid." She shoved a hand through her grey hair. "The first thing you said to me when I was released from hospital was 'Baby take mummy away.'" She barely managed to choke the words out as tears dripped down her cheeks.

The words settled over the group.

"Why didn't you ever tell us? It's been thirty years." Peter's hand grasped Emelia's in an iron grip.

"I was scared. People didn't talk about mental illness back then. Not like they do now. And I didn't know if it might make it worse. I talked to your doctor when Victor was five, and he reassured me that he'd grow out of it. That three was too young to be permanently affected. Turns out what did he know." She gave a bitter laugh.

Victor tried to absorb what he was being told. "I have no memory of anyone else. But I've known since rehab that part of the problem between us was me blaming Peter for taking you away when he was born."

"Why didn't you tell me?" Peter actually turned his face fully toward him.

Apart from his brother acting like he was the prosecutor in a courtroom trial? "What was I going to do? Say 'oh, by the way, all that expensive rehab that almost bankrupted Mum and Dad made me realize our rift is all your fault for being born premature.' How ridiculous does that sound? That something that happened when I was three shaped our whole lives." He'd never thought about how much rehab cost while he was there. Foolishly assumed it was covered by the NHS. He still felt sick when he thought about the loans his parents had raised against the estate to pay for it.

His mother leaned into his father, wrapping her hands around his arm. "Except it's not. My counsellor showed me the brain science. The first three years of a child's life are critical to healthy brain development. Yours was disrupted by trauma and grief. It doesn't have to make sense. Peter was the enemy. Your brain translated what happened as that everyone who loved you would abandon you. Your dad left you for the army. I left you for Peter. You got passed around like a parcel between strangers. So your instinct now is to push everyone away because you believe they'll leave you. Especially the ones who somehow find a way under your armor and get too close."

His mother was talking about Lacey. But that wasn't what he was doing. He was letting Lacey go because he loved her. Because she needed him in her life as much as she needed a ball and chain around her ankle. Because he needed to accept the consequences of his foolish, selfish actions. "I have a daughter, Mum. I have responsibilities to Peyton. To Sabine. I have to do what's right for them." Peter flinched, but the trench-sized furrows in his brow were more troubled than angry.

"I'm not saying you don't. I'm just saying that maybe you can find a way to make room for both."

CHAPTER TWENTY-NINE

LACEY PACED. TWELVE STEPS FROM one side of her condo's living space to the other. Then back. Her kimono-style robe flapped behind her like a cape. The tie had come undone many laps ago. Now it lay on the polished floor like a satin snake.

I'm not a choice. I'm your boss. Betsy will never forgive me. Start with me. Being around you makes me braver than I actually am.

Her fingers itched to twist the cap on the cold bottle of Sav in her fridge. To pour a large glass, then a second. But she knew the same confusion would still be there, at the bottom of the bottle. Except she'd be a lot more liable to do something stupid with all her big feelings.

Like, call Victor.

So instead she picked up her phone. Again. Checked her emails. Again. If sheer force of will could summon a PR emergency, she'd be dealing with the biggest book world scandal since Romance Writers of America turned itself into an organizational dumpster fire. But alas. No new emails had appeared in the last three minutes, let alone one that required an immediate crisis intervention that could justify her returning to work early.

Early. She'd gone into the office with her offer paperwork all signed and witnessed by her lawyer, only for Meredith to take them and tell her she wasn't allowed back for another three days. That had never happened. Almost every vacation she could recall for the last five years had been cut short.

Something thumped outside her door, followed by a scraping sound in the lock. What? According to the note taped to her bedroom door, Grace wasn't supposed to be back for another two days. Her hectic international flight schedule was one of the many things that made her an ideal roommate.

The door handle turned, and Lacey tried to rearrange her face into something vaguely welcoming. At least she hadn't been crying, so she didn't have any bloodshot eyes to explain.

"Aha, it still works! Though you should talk to your co-op about changing the door code more than once a decade. Just to be safe." Anna dragged a medium-sized suitcase into the room and let the door swing shut behind her.

Lacey blinked. Her expectations of the appearance of Grace's navy and white pilot uniform was a distinct mismatch with the reality of Anna in a green tunic dress, tendrils of sweaty brown hair plastered to the side of her face.

Just Anna.

"Where's Libby?"

"She's having a girls' weekend with Rachel." Anna pushed her sunglasses to the top of her head. "Couldn't get me into the Uber fast enough when she heard. I'm parched. Have you got some water?" Anna was at the fridge and opening the door before she'd even finished the question, pulling out a bottle and unscrewing it in one smooth twist. She gulped some back then held the bottle against one cheek. "Ah, that's better. Nice robe, by the way. I'm starving. Can we have sushi for dinner? Or have you already eaten? I'm starved."

Lacey squinted at her. Anna was in New York. By herself. "What are you doing here?"

"Well," Anna stuck her head in the fridge, rummaged around, and emerged with a Diet Coke. "Given that I have spent the last nine months processing all the big feelings, it would seem I have developed quite the radar for them. So I'm here to help you with yours. Unless you have a therapist I don't know about. Also, you didn't call me back, and Emelia said you'd come home early. So here I am."

She cracked open the soda can. "And, in case you hadn't noticed, not only have I lost my favorite form of exercise, but I've also made an art of eating my emotions. So you're going to need to stock this place with something a whole lot better than cottage cheese and petrified celery." She opened a cupboard and stood on her tiptoes to peer inside. "Do you seriously not even have a chocolate stash? Oreos? Anything?" Her tunic lifted up to reveal a behind that was indeed more voluptuous than Lacey remembered.

"Tell me what you need, and I'll get it delivered." Anna's grocery list was definitely a safe zone. "Or we could go out for dinner. There's a great sushi place just a few blocks away that's open til midnight."

Anna closed the cupboard door, defeated. "Or we could get delivery and sit on your couch and talk about you. It is your turn, after all. And I would like to hear more about the man you love but haven't kissed yet. Well, yet again. Unless you have now. In which case, I would like to hear about that."

Just to give herself something to do Lacey picked up the belt to her robe and tied it around her waist. "I have spent, at most, a week with Victor. You can't love someone you don't even know."

Anna kicked off her flats, leaving them where they landed before carrying her soda can to the couch. "You have a problem, Sherlock. You see, I spoke to Victor. Admittedly, it was for all of two minutes. But just from that, I could tell he knows you better than any other man has in the thirteen years I've known you."

"That's ..." Lacey's denial trailed off as Anna's words registered. She'd constructed a wall when she left Small Harbor.

Hadn't let any man close since.

That was one of the reasons why the night she'd kissed Victor was so out of character. She wasn't a woman who went around kissing random men at parties. No matter how attractive and charming they were.

Anna settled in on her couch, the very picture of a woman who wasn't going anywhere without getting what she came for. "I've been meaning to ask. Does Emelia know about the first kiss?"

"No. I mean," Lacey pivoted. It was easier to talk, get the words out, if she wasn't looking at Anna for all of it. "I was going to tell her, but then the whole Sabine thing blew up. And there's obviously no point now."

Anna let out a low whistle. "I would've loved to be a fly on the wall for that. Especially when Emelia moved to England and fell in love with Peter, of all people."

"What are the odds." Lacey huffed out a breath. She turned to find Anna smiling at her. A big Cheshire cat smile. "What?"

"Well, really, what are the odds?"

"You know what I mean."

Anna held up a finger. "You meet Victor at a party six years ago and have a *moment*, as you call it. Then Emelia moves to England and falls in love with his brother." Second finger. "Victor *happens* to work for the company you're getting merged with." Fingers three and four. "Then he *happens* to end up on the same team as you in Minnesota and then..." Her thumb came out. "You *happen* to get evicted together, and he *happens* to take a little side trip with you to meet your family. Who, I would like to note for the record, I haven't even met."

Anna wriggled her fingers around like she was at cheer camp. "I'm no mathematician, but I'd say those odds are beyond any rational explanation."

Lacey knew exactly what Anna was getting at, and ordinarily, she wouldn't take the bait. But nothing about this whole thing was ordinary. "So what? You think *God* just made this all happen? That's he's got some grand plan in all this?" The question shot out of her like it was a cuss word.

Anna paused, studied her. Took a considered sip of her drink. "It doesn't matter what I think. What matters is why the idea that it's possible bothers you so much."

Lacey threw her hands in the air. "Because he has a daughter. Because we work for the same company. Because I'm going to be his boss. Because there is a massive rift in his family and Emelia's on the other side of it." But even as the excuses tumbled from her mouth, the real reasons simmered under the surface like lava. Because what she felt for Victor scared her. Because God couldn't care about her. Not after everything. He certainly shouldn't have forgiven her.

It's all or nothing. Victor's words reverberated from the pub. She knew he was right. Knew Anna was right. The chain of events was so unlikely that design made as much sense as accident. That didn't mean she had to like it.

"What's the real reason?" Anna asked softly from her perch. "Because we both know that even if Victor didn't have a daughter, if you didn't work for the same company, and if his family was just peachy, you would have another excuse. And that wouldn't be the real reason, either."

Lacey shoved her hands through her hair. Her wavy hair, because somewhere in the last few weeks she had stopped having tolerance for buying into her own sleek chemically altered brand. She was going to be CEO. Choosing her own hair was a self-designated perk.

"Lace?" Anna prodded. Anna didn't use to prod. Before Cam died, Anna would have asked the question and backed away when she didn't answer. But widow Anna had apparently decided that other peoples' personal real estate came with her new territory.

"What?" Lacey didn't know what to do with her hands. They twisted her hair around and around. Her eye twitched. Her left foot traced a semi-circle across the hard floor. On repeat. Like all the words that she had forced down inside for years were physically fighting against her skin to try and escape.

"Why won't you let Victor love you?" Anna's gaze refused to look away from her. Her brown eyes laced with steel.

"I ..." The words choked her.

Anna sat, waiting. Her best friend, the woman who had lost everything in the last year. Who was flat broke but had somehow found the money to get on a plane because she knew Lacey needed someone. Even when she hadn't even admitted it to herself.

That person sitting on her couch, deserved the truth.

Because I don't know how.

Because I don't deserve it.

Because giving up control always means losing.

The day Betsy changed her mind and decided to marry Mitchell, Lacey had made a solemn vow that she would never be like her sister. Never give enough of herself to anyone that she could never get it back. People might think they loved her, but she'd always curated the parts of herself that she'd let them see. Only let them love the parts of her that she chose to share. Charming Lacey. Smart Lacey. Driven Lacey. Loyal Lacey. Superficial Lacey. Even with Emelia, who knew her better than anyone else, she'd put up a façade a lot of the time.

Until Victor.

Lacey pushed the thought away as she wrapped her arms around her waist. Her fingers curled into the slippery material. "Because all love has ever done for the women in my family is trap them."

Anna's eyes widened a little. Other than that, her expression didn't change.

"My grandfather abandoned my grandmother, left her with four kids. She became an alcoholic and drank herself into an early grave. My mum worked two jobs my whole childhood, and my dad lost the little money we had on bad investments. She gave up, and now she spends her life on the home shopping network. Betsy got pregnant and let herself be charmed into marrying her dropkick high school boyfriend. I'm the only one who got out. I'm the one who's keeping them all afloat. And I promised myself a long time ago that I will never *never* let myself get trapped by a man." The words fell out of her, one on top of another, like a sudden snowstorm.

Anna tilted her head. "So, that's why you always date down."

"What do you mean?"

"All those bland doctor, lawyer, banker types, with their trust funds and nice pedigrees. It was obvious you were never going to fall in love with any of them. That was the whole point, wasn't it?"

Lacey tried to think back on the men Anna was referring to, but they all blurred together into a generic mass. "I guess. Maybe. Being trapped isn't just about poverty. I've met plenty of wealthy women ensnared by manipulative and controlling spouses."

"What about Cam? What about Lucas? Do you think they're traps Rachel and I should have avoided?"

Cam and Lucas were the exception to the rule. Even Peter, with all his flaws, was the best thing that had ever happened to Emelia. Lacey shook her head. "They're different, Anna. But they're not the rule. You know that."

"Okay, so what has Victor done to make you feel trapped?"

Nothing. Victor had done nothing. The feelings tightening

her chest were all about what she felt for him and the fear that if she gave in to it, she would never recover.

"Letting yourself love someone won't break you, Lace. It might feel like it will. Trust someone who knows. But maybe that crack you're feeling in your heart isn't a sign of weakness. Maybe it's a sign it's finally ready to really let someone in."

"I don't know how." Except she did know how. In the same way someone stumbles across something they'd thought was lost but had really been there all along. Because it wasn't a crack that she felt in her heart. It was like Victor had somehow split it wide open. Then she said something she had never admitted to anyone. "I'm scared."

Anna smiled, "It's okay to be scared. It means that this matters. God will never force anything on you. But you're the only one who can choose. Faith or fear. What's it going to be?"

CHAPTER THIRTY

THE HOUSE LOOKED NO DIFFERENT than it had a couple of months ago. Lacey was the one who was different. She'd felt Victor's presence as she drove, had seen him in the aisles as she bought groceries. She kept turning around, half expecting him to be behind her.

But he wasn't. And she couldn't move forward—whatever that meant—without going backward.

The front door opened, and her sister leaned against the door frame, shielding her eyes with her hand. Her hair was pulled up in a messy bun, white T-shirt and cutoffs revealing tanned summer limbs. "You need some help?"

"Sure." Lacey popped the trunk of her red rental car and grabbed four bags, the plastic handles digging into her fingers. When she looked up, Betsy was halfway down the path. "They didn't have any of the yogurt brand you said, so I got a different one. Still strawberry, though. I hope that's okay."

This time she'd emailed ahead. Asked her sister if she could visit, asked what they needed, what the kids liked. Said she was sorry for surprising her with the last visit. Hoped it would be enough to start this visit off right. Accepted she had little control over whether it did or not.

"I'm sure it'll be fine." Betsy hefted the last three bags out of the trunk. "Thanks."

Thanks. Lacey savored the word as she headed up the path

and onto the porch.

"Just take them through to the kitchen." Betsy nodded down the hallway toward the back of the house.

The house was silent. Lacey took the opportunity to peak into rooms as she walked down the hall. The girls shared a bedroom. Pink comforters on twin beds parallel to each other. A smaller room held a single bed, with cars scattered on the floor. A yellow car sat at the bottom of a ramp like it had been left mid-play. Lacey swallowed back the question as she dropped the grocery bags on the kitchen floor and shook out her hands.

Betsy placed her bags on the counter. "The kids are out with Mitchell. They'll be back in a couple of hours."

Whether or not she got to see them hung in the air. She took a breath. Pushed back on the urge to press her sister for some kind of invitation. "How's his job hunt going?"

Betsy shrugged as she reached down to grab some milk. "It's hard. There's not a lot around. But he's doing his best. Put applications in everywhere that has something going."

"I hope he finds something soon." She could buy this house. On her CEO package, she could probably buy every house on the street. She'd offered before she'd bought her parents' house, but her sister hadn't even replied to the email.

Betsy opened the fridge and dropped the milk containers into the door. "How about you? How's Victor?"

Hearing his name so unexpectedly had her taking a step back. Like even those six letters could throw her off balance. She tried to cover up her response by reaching into the nearest bag and grabbing boxes of cereal. "I assume he's fine."

Her sister left the fridge door open and walked back to the counter for the next addition. "What do you mean, you assume he's fine?"

Lacey shrugged. "We're not a thing."

"Wait. What? Betsy froze mid-reach into her bag. "You're not a thing with the hot Brit who's head over heels in love with you? The only guy you've ever brought here? The one who would literally walk over molten lava for you?"

Lacey couldn't answer. Just trying to swallow past the boulder in her throat felt impossible. "It's complicated, Bets. We work for the same company. We're not allowed to date. He has a daughter. I live here. He's in London." All the excuses were as empty as the cupboard she shoved the cereal boxes into.

"But you love him, and he sure as anything loves you."

"You can't know that. We were here for literally five minutes."

Betsy was silent as she loaded cheese and yogurt into the fridge, then closed the door. "I know that we haven't been close for a long time but before that, we were as close as sisters could be. So I do know that."

"How?"

Betsy studied her for a second, arms folded. "You don't lean into anyone, Lacey. But you leaned into him."

Even as she said it, Lacey could feel Victor holding her up as they stood at the end of the path, watching her nieces go back to their mom. His steady, unwavering presence had grounded her. If it hadn't been for that, she probably would have been on the pavement.

"Maybe I'm not cut out for love."

Her sister shook her head. "You can't believe that. You love fiercer than anyone I've ever known. We haven't lived in the same place for years. I don't know any of your friends. But I still know that."

Was it true? She didn't even feel like she knew anymore. She thought she loved Anna and Libby and Rachel. But did she really? "But look at us. You've never forgiven me for what happened." She managed to get the words out even as a wave of longing hit her. She'd always told herself that Betsy had made her choices, and she had made hers. But it had been years since she'd let herself think about how much she missed her big sister. What they had once had.

Betsy turned her back, crumbling the paper bag in her hands and then tossing it in the trash. "It's not that I haven't forgiven you, Lacey. But yes, it's hard to forget you wanted me to abort Molly."

Well, that was one interpretation of history. "I didn't want you to abort Molly. I wanted you to do whatever you chose. I was supporting you. You were the one who brought it up, who said it was what you wanted. I never pressured you into anything. I just made the appointment. I always told you I would stand beside you, no matter what." But she'd never tried to talk her out of it either. Because they were dirt poor in a town that had no way out once you had a kid.

Betsy moved onto the next bag, stacking up boxes of Goldfish crackers in her arms. "Which is easy to say when the person is going to do what you think they should. But the look on your face when I told you I'd changed my mind, that I was going to marry Mitchell and have the baby? You acted like I'd betrayed you."

Lacey folded her arms and pressed them into her stomach. "Because I wanted you to have a great life. Because I wanted more for you than—" Lacey bit off the end of her sentence before she could finish it.

"This." Her sister did it for her, her body sagging against the peeling kitchen cupboards. "You wanted more for me than this. You wanted more for me than being stuck here in no-hopeville with three kids and a husband you think is a total loser."

"I've never said that."

"Good grief, Lace. Your entire speech at our wedding was about how Mitchell didn't deserve me and how out of his league I was."

"I was eighteen." Also, it was true. If it wasn't for Mitchell, Betsy would have gotten out of Small Harbor. Just like Lacey had.

"You couldn't get out of here fast enough, and I don't blame you. But you never come back. It's like you think even stepping foot in this town is going to taint you or somehow ensnare you in its net. You've never been ensnared by anything. If anything, it's the opposite. You're the one who leaves and never looks back."

"What are you talking about?"

"How many guys have you dated in the last few years?"

Lacey shrugged. "I don't keep count. But to be fair, most of them never made it past a few dates. Only a few were exclusive."

"Because they didn't ask, or because you had one foot out the door the whole time?"

Lacey didn't say anything. The truth was she was always the one who ended things. But none of them had ever made her want to stay.

Until Victor.

She closed her eyes. Tried to bat away the memory of Victor's arms around her and his lips on hers. How even in the silence, his love for her was louder than anything she'd ever known.

Betsy crumbled the next bag, the paper crunching between her hands. "Why do you think I don't want you showing up here out of the blue like the Fairy Godmother? Because you break the kids' hearts when you disappear again. They never know if or when you're going to come back. If you want a relationship with my kids, you have to show up. Not once every few years. Often. Summer. Christmas. Thanksgiving. You have to be here for some of it. Otherwise, you're never going to be anything more than the mysterious aunt who sent gifts and threw money at their college fund."

"What if I came to visit more often. Like …" She tried to conjure up something but had no idea what she could promise with the demands of the new job. "Twice a year?"

"That depends. Can you be nice to their dad?"

Lacey couldn't even remember the last time she had even seen Mitchell. It had to have been just after Annie was born. But she wasn't mean to him. He was just there. Like the thrift store furniture.

Betsy sighed. "Mitch is a good man, Lace. He doesn't drink, he treats me well, he loves our kids. And trust me, he is so aware of what I gave up for him. Then you show up, looking at me like I'm a hostage who needs rescuing. Every time you're here, you make my husband feel like an utter failure. He's told me that I should leave him. That we should get a divorce because he knows you would give the kids and me a much better life than he can."

Mitchell had said that? Mitchell hadn't trapped her sister in a life of poverty and drudgery? Mitchell had offered Betsy a way out? Lacey gaped at her sister. The gap between what she thought she knew and what Betsy was saying so big it was like she'd started speaking another language.

Betsy walked over so that she stood right in front of Lacey. Her own eyes staring back at her. "I need you to understand that I don't need rescuing, Lace. I could leave tomorrow. Do you think I don't know that all it would take would be a phone call to you, and we'd have everything that we need? But I'm not going to. Because I love him. And I love our family. Do I wish I could have both? Do I wish I could have them and have what you have? Of course, I do. But I can't. And so I choose this. I choose them."

Lacey held her ground, even as her mind scrambled for a foothold. "B—"

Betsy held her hand up. "I'm not trapped, little sis. So if you've pushed Victor away because you're scared of losing control, because you're afraid of giving up a piece of yourself that you'll never get back, then I have nothing to say to you except that's what love is. And I'm telling you, I don't think you're ever going to get any better than that man I saw propping you up."

Lacey opened her mouth, but Betsy was still talking in a don't even try to stop me until I've said my piece kind of way. "Now if what you're after is a half-in, half-out kind of relationship, one where you don't let anyone get too close so there's less collateral damage if someone wants to leave then that's up to you. If you don't want to be with the person who holds you up, and sees all of you, and meets your sweary angry sister and doesn't take so much as a step back? Then I feel sorry for you. Because I will take our rundown town, my unemployed husband, and cutting coupons over your empty New York life any day."

CHAPTER THIRTY-ONE

VICTOR HADN'T BEEN THIS NERVOUS ever. He wiped his hands on his trousers as he sat on one of the seats bordering the Kensington Gardens playground, the wooden planks pressing into the back of his legs.

He checked his phone again. Diana Memorial Playground. Yes, that was definitely what it said, and it was definitely where he was. He'd been here an hour early. Forced himself to take a walk through the enormous grounds, so he didn't look like some creepy single guy watching a children's playground.

Sabine was now officially six minutes late. Not late at all by London standards. The fact she was coming at all when she and Peyton were flying out with the GB rowing squad the next morning was borderline miraculous.

Around him, kids and caregivers made the most of the warm July day swarming the pirate ship structure and splashing in the nearby water feature. It was an excellent opportunity to observe supervision techniques. Some parents let small toddlers roam freely, keeping an eye out from a distance, while others hovered over much older kids.

Not that he'd ever given it any thought, but he'd always assumed he'd be a free-range parent. But as he observed a red-headed toddler coming to near-calamity with a swing, he wasn't sure he had the nerves for it.

"Sorry we're late. Bus took forever." Sabine had somehow

snuck up on him. He turned around, his attention skimming right over her petite frame to the small blonde person at the end of her hand. Blonde hair stuck out the side of her head in two bunches, and her fingers were curled around a bucket and spade. She had zero interest in him. Her hand tugged at Sabine's, seeking release.

"I wanna dig."

"Hat first." Sabine let go of Peyton's hand and reached into the bag hanging from her arm, fishing out a floral sun hat and plonking it on top of a head that now sported a petulant brow.

"Not have it." Chubby fingers reached up as if to yank it off.

"You know the rules, Peyton. No hat, no playing."

The little girl thought for a second, then her hand dropped. "I go play now." She was already running off.

"Do you want to follow her?"

Sabine shaded her eyes with her hand as she watched Peyton traverse across the grass and onto the sand by the pirate ship. "No, she won't go far. Once she's found a spot of sand, she'll entertain herself for a while. We're good as long as I have her in my line of sight."

"Okay."

Silence took up residence between them. Sabine seemed to be in no hurry to move it on.

"Thanks for agreeing to come." After the family meeting, it had taken him a few days to work up the courage to call Sabine. A call that had gone directly to voice mail and resulted in a long rambling message. Followed by some of the most torturous days of his life. Missing Lacey. Wondering if he had given up something great only for Sabine to have much-deserved second thoughts and decide to shut him out of Peyton's life.

"I'm not doing this for you." Sabine's rules for him to see Peyton in person had come with a locked-down set of specifications. The most important was that she would not be telling Peyton who he was, and he wasn't to either.

He would have agreed to anything. All that mattered was doing the right thing by Peyton. And Sabine. It didn't matter what he wanted or what it would cost. And Sabine needed to know that he was willing to step up in every and any way. "Um ... so ... would you like to get married?"

Something between a laugh and a strangled yell came out of Sabine. It was so loud that the closest person turned to look at her. "What?"

"I just ..." Victor shoved his hands in his pockets. "I know it sounds crazy, but I've done a lot of things wrong in my life, Sabine. I want to do the right thing by you. Both of you."

Sabine put her hands on her hips. "And you think this is the right thing? Marrying a woman you don't love because you both made a mistake one night and now you have a daughter?"

"I don't know." Most people would think he was bonkers, but the weird traditional part had risen up in him the last few weeks. Maybe this was what he was supposed to do. Marry the mother of his child. Sacrifice anything and everything to give them the best life he could.

Though Sabine seemed to have managed perfectly well without him.

His gaze stayed on Peyton, who, as Sabine had said, was totally entranced with pouring sand into her bucket and tipping it out.

"You know, I promised myself something after Peter." Sabine put some sunglasses on, then dropped her bag onto the seat behind them. "I promised myself that no matter what my feelings were, I would never settle for a man who loved someone else. It's not like we even have anything to try and salvage. We just made one terrible mistake. Even if that mistake did result in the best thing in my life."

She was right, and they both knew it.

"Are you seeing someone?" He'd checked for rings before he'd broached marriage but realized their absence didn't mean anything. Not when she would have been shedding every spare ounce to get ready for the world champs.

"Not at the moment."

What did that mean? She had been? She might be soon? Victor quashed the questions. It wasn't any of his business.

Silence sat between them for a few seconds. They both faced forward. At least Peyton provided an excellent excuse to not look at each other during this excruciating conversation.

"Please tell me you didn't break up with your woman because you felt some bizarre kind of duty to marry me."

"Not exactly." Actually, the idea of marrying Sabine had shown up as he'd tried to work out what God wanted him to do. But he was hardly going to tell Sabine that when she'd turned him down.

"What does that mean?"

"We work in the same company. Or will soon—there's about to be a merger. There's a no-fraternization rule. I was planning to quit, but obviously, this changes everything."

"How so?"

"For a start, I owe you three years of child support. And I need to keep my job to meet my ongoing obligations."

Sabine scuffed the grass with the tip of her shoe. "I didn't tell you about Peyton because I'm after money."

"That's good. Apart from a few quid in my savings account, there's not a lot I can offer you. At the current rate, I'll be paying the trust back for rehab until I'm sixty." People looked at the estate and assumed his family was loaded, when the truth was the house was a financial sinkhole. And that was before months in rehab had been added.

"You've done some stupid stuff in your life, I grant you, but at least you did most of those while you were drunk. This whole doing it stone-cold sober is a new thing."

"Lacey's not just anyone. She's going to be the CEO, Sabine."

"So?"

"So she deserves someone a whole lot better than me." It hurt him just to say that, even though he knew it was true. He missed her with a fierceness that didn't seem possible, given how little time they'd actually spent together.

"Did she say that?"

"Not exactly. But look at me. I'm a third-rate lobbyist at best, with a daughter I only just found out about, and I need to be here. I know you said no to the marrying thing, but I want to be part of Peyton's life in any way you'll let me."

"You will be. I just need to figure it out. Now's just obviously not the best time."

She seemed to be sincere, but Victor couldn't help reflect that if he hadn't sent the letter, he might never have known he had a daughter. "Am I on her birth certificate?"

Silence.

"Sabine?"

Sabine lifted her glasses and rubbed her eyes. "Yes, you are. I didn't tell you about her because I wanted to see if rehab had stuck. And then, honestly, there was always an excuse to delay it. We've built a life that works. Selfishly, I wanted to keep it like that."

Victor watched Peyton as she played in the sand. She'd been joined by a little boy who was using his hands to help fill her bucket.

"Do you love her?"

"Peyton?"

"Lacey."

At her name, Victor's throat tightened. "Yeah. But Peyton's my priority. And whatever I need to do to prove that to you, I will do it."

Sabine pushed her sunglasses onto her hair, shielding her eyes as she watched her daughter. "I'm not going to withhold Peyton from you if you're with someone. You're not who you were. The fact that you were willing to show up today and propose because you had some well-meaning, but bonkers, idea that it was the right thing to do proves you're not the same person. But it's not the right thing to do. I deserve to be with someone who will love me with their whole heart. And so do you." Sabine turned and looked at him properly for the first time. "Go fight for Lacey, Victor. I promise Peyton and I aren't going anywhere."

CHAPTER THIRTY-TWO

"**H**I." LACEY LEANED AGAINST HIS door frame like it was something she did all the time. Over her shoulder, Victor caught a glimpse of Sean's gaping mouth.

His eyes drank her in, the sight of her better than a bottle of Gatorade at the end of a long run. Her hair fell curly and loose, more structured than it had been in the wilderness, but so much more free than the glossy pulled-back do.

He'd known she'd let the curls stay. They'd been prominent in the large photo the Financial Post had printed as part of the profile they published the week before after it had been announced she was taking over as CEO.

Beside him, his printer whirred and clicked as it spat out the document he'd just finalized.

"Hey." He managed to croak the word out.

"Do you have a minute?" She stepped in and closed the door behind her. Not that it would shield them from much, given the recently installed window that ran the length of his office—one of Lacey's first moves when her appointment was announced. No one in the company would ever again be able to hide bad behavior behind a closed office door.

"Of course."

Lacey glanced toward the window, a small smile on her lips as at least three people ducked their heads and pretended to focus on their screens. No doubt, the company's instant messenger network was running even hotter than it had the day the restructure was announced.

Pressing his hands on his desktop, Victor forced himself to his feet, half-surprised when his knees held. "We can leave the fishbowl if you'd like. Go somewhere else."

Apart from his desk, the only other furniture was a bookshelf, a cheap industrial-looking sofa, and two uncomfortable chairs.

Lacey took a couple of steps into the space as he came around his desk. "This is fine. I won't be long. I have a meeting."

"Oh, okay." Why was she here? Surely it couldn't be to check that he wasn't going to say anything about the two of them. She could have done that by text. Not by making them the talking point of the entire building. And surely she knew he would never betray her. He'd never do a single thing that would risk undermining her.

He leaned against the front of his desk, his hand knocking over one of the framed photographs. It clattered on the surface, and he reached down to prop it back up.

"Is that her?"

Victor looked down and realized he'd knocked over the photo of Peyton.

"Yes. Her name is Peyton."

Lacey reached out and looked at the photo for a second before standing it back up. "She's lovely."

A beam of pride spread across his chest. He couldn't take any credit for the little girl he'd only seen once, but he was already counting down the weeks until their next agreed visit.

Lacey's fingers drummed against his desktop. "Have you met her?"

"Just once. She and Sabine are overseas for the rowing world champs at the moment."

"How is Sabine?"

He didn't want any more secrets. No even small ones. Not even ones that didn't even matter. Not when he and Peter were the product of his parents keeping secrets for thirty years. "I asked her to marry me."

Lacey visibly flinched and stepped back. "Oh. Well," she forced a smile on her face. "Congratulations."

Victor stepped forward. Stopping when their bodies were close, but not touching, barely keeping hold of the desire to touch her. "Lace, she said no."

Her brow furrowed. "Is she with someone else?"

"No. But she's not interested in a man who's crazy in love with someone else. I stupidly thought that asking her to marry me was a way to make things right. To do the right thing for her and Peyton. But, as she pointed out, she deserves to be with someone who can love her with his whole heart. And that person isn't me. Because my heart is yours. And it would appear I'm not going to be getting it back anytime soon."

Lacey drew in a deep breath. "I—"

Victor held up a finger. "Can you hold that thought for just one second, please. Stay there."

He grabbed a pen off his desk, paper off his printer, and scrawled his signature on the bottom of the page. "I wasn't sure who this should go to, but now that you're here, I figure you can make sure it gets to the right place."

Lacey looked down at the letter in her hand. "You're resigning?" Her face gave nothing away. Still, he knew it was the right decision.

"I think technically, as of two seconds ago, I've resigned."

"Do you have another job?"

"No. But I'll find one." He'd applied for twelve in the last two weeks. He figured if he applied for enough jobs, he'd have to get one, just through the rules of statistical probability.

"What about Peyton? What about doing the right thing by her?"

"I'm going to do the right thing by her. I'm going to get another job. I'm going to support her and her mum. I'm going to be in her life. But that job doesn't need to be here. And quite frankly, turns out being in love with the CEO is really not ideal, so it's better for the company if I find something somewhere else."

Lacey closed her eyes for a second. It was everything he could do not to run his hands up her arms and tangle them in her hair. But he couldn't. Because only a few meters away, an entire office full of people watched them. Even though he'd resigned, anything between them would create gossip she didn't deserve.

"I thought I could do this, Lace. I thought I could stay here and be your biggest advocate and help you build a great company, but I can't. There is too much going on. With Peyton and Sabine, with Peter and me. To do right by that, by them, to do my part in fixing all of this, I also can't be here, trying to get over the only woman I've ever loved who also happens to be my boss's boss's boss. There's only so much therapy a guy can afford."

LACEY COULD SEE VICTOR'S RESTRAINT as clearly as if a stunt plane had written in the air between them. She glanced toward the window. At least four people had given up any pretense of working and were staring at them with naked speculation.

The Lacey of three months ago would leave now, before she did any more damage to her reputation. Though it was already too late. It had been too late as soon as she'd walked into his office and inadvertently turned it into a stage. So she might as well put them all out of their misery. Including her. But most of all him. The man she loved.

She held up a finger, mimicking Victor's action of a couple of minutes ago. "Can you give me one second?"

She walked to the door and opened it, looking for the blonde guy who had shown her to Victor's office. "Sean?"

He scuttled forward. "Yes, ma'am. Ms. O'Connor, ma'am."

"Can I borrow a pen, please?"

He immediately pulled one out of his breast pocket.

Leaning against the wall, she scribbled a sentence on Victor's letter then handed it to Sean. "Can you send this to Jen Shiloh in HR, please? Immediately." Tomorrow, this would be way below Jen's pay grade. But right now, Jen was the only person Lacey knew in HR. She could consider it a promotion present.

He didn't even look at it, half bowing as he backed away. "Yes, ma'am. Right away. Thank you, ma'am."

If she hadn't already been planning to spend half her time in the London office, she certainly would be now. Closing the door behind her, she turned back to Victor.

He leaned against his desk, his hands in his pockets, gaze studying her like a paleontologist who had just found an undiscovered species of dinosaur.

"So." She strode across the small office, reaching him in five steps.

"So." Victor didn't so much as twitch from his position.

"I went and saw my sister."

If he was surprised by the sudden change in topic he didn't show it. "How is she?"

"Good. We had a good talk."

"I'm glad." He still didn't move. If anything, he leaned a little further back.

She should have written speech notes. She'd never considered her words might fail her. "The thing is, my whole life, I've been afraid of being trapped by a man. That was all I saw. Loving someone made you weak. Loving someone took away your choices, required you to give up everything. My grandfather did it to my grandmother, then my dad with my mom, and Mitchell had with Betsy."

She drew in a breath, smoothing her damp palms on her pants. "At least, that was what I thought. But I was wrong. Betsy isn't trapped by Mitchell. She chooses him and their life. The only thing keeping her there is her. Because it's what she wants. Because he's who she wants a life with."

Victor didn't say anything, just watched her intently.

"But the thing is, even if it was true, even if loving someone did mean giving everything up … You're not Mitchell. You're not my dad. You're not my grandfather. You have never tried to trap me. All you have ever done is love me enough to let me go."

Victor's hands curled around the lip of his desk. He wasn't going to make the first move. Not here. Not with everyone watching.

So she stepped into his space until the toes of her shoes covered his. When she lifted her head, the warmth of his breath mingled with hers. "Anna says this couldn't have happened by chance. She says God is in all of this."

Victor's lips curled. "She's a smart woman, that Anna."

"I don't know what you said to her on the phone, but she's your biggest fan." Lacey could hear Anna's voice ringing in her head. *God will never force anything on you. You're the only one who can choose. Faith or fear. What's it going to be?*

Reaching out, she grabbed Victor's hands, twisting her fingers between his. Then tilted her head up.

Untangling one of his hands from hers, he lifted it up and ran his fingers down her face, his thumb against her bottom lip, and then tipped his head so his forehead touched hers. His other hand palmed the small of her back, pulling her flush against him.

There was nothing to be afraid of here.

Her hands traveled up the front of his shirt and wrapped around the back of his neck. "I don't want you to get over me." The declaration whispered through her lips. "Because I'm never going to get over you."

"I'll say this," Victor murmured his words against her mouth. "You sure do know how to make a guy sweat."

"Sorry." Not that sorry. Not now. Not when she'd done what she needed to do to be here. Knowing with everything in her, this was the right thing.

He pressed his lips against hers, and she clung on to the deepening kiss until they were interrupted by cheers and whistles.

Lacey turned her head to look at the whole floor on their feet. "Stupid window. Whose terrible idea was that?"

Victor leaned back slightly and kissed the tip of her nose. "The new CEO. I hear she's a spectacular kisser."

Then, because he was a smart man, he kissed her again before she could hit him. By the time they both came up for air, they were both gasping. Victor trailed his hands down her side, then back up again.

Lacey ran her hands up his face, her pointer finger tracing the scar like it had always wanted to. "I love you." Now that she was here, she wasn't sure how she had ever thought she would be okay without him.

Victor stilled as if he couldn't quite believe she'd said the words.

Lacey leaned into him, wrapping her arms around his waist. "I fell in love with you that night on the beach."

Victor funneled his hands through her hair and pressed the kind of kiss to her lips that had her missing it before it was even over. "I've loved you since you tore shreds off me on that bus."

She couldn't stop smiling.

"And, we have," Victor looked at his watch. "Eight hours until you're officially my boss, and this won't be allowed while I work out my notice. We should go on a date."

Lacey grinned up at him. "I'm paying out your notice. I've already told Jen to send me the bill."

Acknowledgements

This book. Wow. It feels like an absolute miracle being able to sit here and type these words. I started writing *Start With Me* in mid-2018. Now here I am in 2020, writing the acknowledgements in the middle of a global pandemic. And it feels like an entire lifetime in between the first words and these final ones.

As many of you know, I stopped writing in March 2019 after we lost a dear friend suddenly and my sister was diagnosed with cancer. I truly did not think I would ever write another book.

Our family will never forget the people who walked-and are still walking-through the hardest of hard with us. The people who showed up physically and virtually in the months where putting one foot in front of another felt impossible. The meals, the co-parenting our kids, the baking, the messages, the books, the prayers, the passing of tissues and shoulders for tears, the love and care we received will never be forgotten. I'm not even going to try and name you all because I know I will forget many. Thank you from the bottom of our hearts.

Josh, it has been a year plus some of all kinds of hard. Thank you for still choosing me and showing up every day. I love you.

Team Bonnevie, Team Collins, Team Isaac, Team Athea, Team Beard, Team Benson, Team Conway, Team Williams, Team Holmes, the SisterChucks, the Boulcott Bistro Brigade, there will never be the words to describe what you mean to us.

Eternal gratitude to my sister who read the first messy dis-jointed 30,000 words in July 2019 and told me that I had to finish it because it was the best thing she had read in months (almost undoubtedly not true but it was what I needed to hear to start writing again!) and who has always been my first and last reader when I'm writing a new book.

Laurie Tomlinson who months later read the world's ugliest 2/3 of a first draft and sat with me on a couch in Nashville for hours when I was so sick and jet-lagged I could barely think and helped me find my way out of some enormous plot holes and believed in Victor and Lacey's story until I did too.

Jaime Jo Wright for reading early chapters and helping me with guns which I know absolutely nothing about. Any firearm mistakes are hers (no, not really, they're her husband's ☺).

Iola Goulton and Kristin Avila, editors extraordinaire whose combined powers made this book so much better than I ever could have managed on my own, and Evelyne Labelle from Carpe Librum Book Design for the gorgeous cover.

Finally, but most importantly, Jesus. We would never have chosen this season and we've only made it so far because of you. Thank you for grace upon grace upon grace over the last 18 months. For sustaining us, providing for us in every possible way, and going before, behind, and beside us every day.

About the Author

Kara Isaac is the RITA® Award-winning author of contemporary romances filled with humor and hope. When she's not chasing three adorable but spirited little people, she spends her time writing horribly bad first drafts and wishing you could get Double Stuf Oreos in New Zealand. She loves to connect with readers at www.karaisaac.com, on Facebook at Kara Isaac – Author, Twitter @KaraIsaac and on Instagram @karaisaac.author

Made in the USA
Las Vegas, NV
21 November 2020